The Bone Fire

Also by S D Sykes

The Butcher Bird
Plague Land
City of Masks

The Bone Fire

S D Sykes

HODDER &
STOUGHTON

First published in Great Britain in 2019 by Hodder & Stoughton
An Hachette UK company

1

A CIP catalogue record for this title is available from the British Library

Hardback ISBN 978 1 473 67999 3
eBook ISBN 978 1 473 68001 2

Typeset in Perpetua Std by Hewer Text UK Ltd, Edinburgh
Printed and bound in Great Britain by Clays Ltd, Elcograf S.p.A.

Hodder & Stoughton policy is to use papers that are natural, renewable
and recyclable products and made from wood grown in sustainable forests.
The logging and manufacturing processes are expected to conform
to the environmental regulations of the country of origin.

Hodder & Stoughton Ltd
Carmelite House
50 Victoria Embankment
London EC4Y 0DZ

www.hodder.co.uk

'Cito, longe, tarde'
'Fly quickly, go far, return slowly'

The counsel of Hippocrates, at the first news of plague

For Mum

December 1361

To the finder of this letter,

If you are reading this, then I am dead. Taken by plague. If your nose does not lead you directly to my body, then look in the chamber beyond the curtain — for this is where I shall go to die. I would ask you to bury me, as this will give comfort to my family, but I shall not condemn you for taking the other option. These are wretched, savage times, and I know why the fires blaze and the bones burn.

If you have the heart to place my body in the soil, then wrap me in my cloak and bury me alongside the other graves in the ground behind this cottage. Elsewhere the soil is hard and icy, and will not yield to the spade.

If you are well yourself, then I beg you to take this letter to Castle Eden, as my wife must know my fate. She will not thank you for this news, but she will reward you for your service. You may look upon my decaying, corrupted body and see a poor man who has died in this lonely place, but you should know this. My name was once Oswald de Lacy, Lord of the Somershill estate.

Chapter One

Our party left Somershill in the November of 1361, as soon as we heard that plague had crossed the river Darent. There were five of us – myself, my wife, son, and mother, and just a single servant, my valet, a boy named Sandro. I chose the plainest cart and the sturdiest pony from my stables, and we left with enough food and drink for the whole winter, or so we hoped. I expected every last grain of barley and every last cup of wine to be consumed before we returned to Somershill in the spring – for we were retreating from the world. Heading to a place that was far away and difficult to reach. Somewhere that plague could not find us.

We made good speed on our first day. The roads were dry and empty as we headed south, and we found rooms easily enough at an inn near Battle Abbey. But our luck ran out on the following day as we reached the coast at Tenterden. It was here that the weather turned against us. A spiteful wind had arisen in the English Channel, and then gathered malice as it crossed the vast salt marsh between us and the open sea. We were heading for an island within this marsh – a stretch of land that rises from the waters like the long back of a sleeping sea monster. The Isle of Eden cannot be reached at low tide with a cart, as the muds are too treacherous to cross with a heavy vehicle. At high tide, there is only one way to traverse the short channel of sea – aboard a wide-bottomed ferry. But the ferryman would not consider setting off that day. The waves were too high, and the wind was too strong. And so we were forced to stay another night, at another inn, waiting for some respite from the storm.

It was little better the next morning. The wind still blew in from the sea in icy, piercing bursts, and the waves still assailed the coast in long, diagonal lines – but we could not afford to wait any longer. Knowing that plague was chasing our tails, I offered the ferryman more than twice the usual fee to make the crossing. He agreed to this, but warned me that the passage would be rough – and he had not lied. The ferry rocked and creaked in the swell, as the storm grew in intensity. Above us the sky was invaded by black clouds, surging towards land like the fists of an angry god. As the rain fell in long and heavy strikes, I felt sick, cold and wet, and so I kept my eyes ahead, trying to think about where we were going and not what we had left behind.

The Isle of Eden is only six miles long by three miles wide, with few inhabitants other than a collection of tenant farmers. The sweetest apples grow here. The fattest walnuts and the ripest grapes, as the soil is usually warmed by the sea and sheltered by a succession of folding valleys. On my previous visits, the island had always lived up to its name – a true Garden of Eden. And yet, today, the island ahead of us was shrouded by an ominous, swollen gathering of clouds – so low and dark that this scene could be mistaken for the entrance to Hell.

We eventually reached the far shore, surviving the rains and the winds of the crossing, before we came to a ramp covered by waves. At first our pony refused to pull the cart from the ferry, shying away from the water and then attempting to rear. It was only when the ferryman threatened the whip that the pony finally agreed to move off, allowing us to follow the cart through the water to reach the shingle beach at the other end of the ramp. Our feet had barely touched the shores of Eden, before the ferryman turned his craft back towards the mainland. Seeing his boat retreat into the distance, I felt panicked for a moment, and nearly called out for him to return. But I bit my tongue, took a deep breath and forced a smile onto my face. We had to go on. We could not turn back.

Once we had settled the pony, I looked out for Godfrey, as he had promised to meet us here – but the shore was deserted, with not even a watchman from the nearby village to greet us and demand to know our business. I decided not to wait for my friend. This was the final stretch of our journey and we needed to reach his castle before darkness fell. And so we set off, taking the only road that crosses Eden – a track that bears south, following the spine of the island through a patchwork of field and forest.

The pony reared again as we headed up the first steep hill and then refused to move. It was scared by the change in the weather as much as anything. The rains had stopped now, but something worse was brewing – a sea-fog that was cold, white and heavy with vapour. For a moment I was tempted to abandon the cart and come back for it the next day – but our load was too valuable to leave about on a deserted track. It would be a rich prize for any thief. In the end I followed the ferryman's example and reluctantly threatened the pony with the whip, finding that it still responded to the threat of pain.

As we pressed forward in the thickening gloom, Mother struggled to keep up whenever she was required to get out of the cart and walk. I took her arm and helped her up the steeper inclines, but she complained bitterly at each step. 'I don't know why we had to come here, Oswald,' she hissed, as she stumbled into a rut and nearly fell.

I caught hold of her before she landed in the mud. 'Yes you do, Mother,' I said, once she was steady on her feet again. 'We couldn't stay in Somershill.'

'So we've run away from the Plague,' she huffed, 'only to die in this cold. This is not how I wanted my life to end.'

'Keep going,' I urged her, ignoring the comment about her nearness to death. It was a common refrain of late, now that she was over seventy years of age. 'It's not far to Castle Eden,' I said. 'We should be there within the hour.'

'Eden,' she puffed disparagingly. 'Your father wouldn't have run away to a stranger's castle. I can tell you that much.'

'There's no shame in fleeing plague,' I said. 'And the owner of this castle is not a stranger. Godfrey is an old family friend. You've met him many times.'

'But I didn't say that I liked him, did I?'

'Then you should have gone to Versey,' I said. 'To stay with Clemence.'

She looked at me witheringly. 'You know I can't abide your sister.'

'Then you will have to make the best of this choice. Now come on,' I said, pointing ahead at the two blurred shapes in the fog. 'We mustn't let Filomena and Hugh out of our sights.'

I took Mother's arm and we caught up with my wife and son, finding that Filomena was shivering and Hugh was sucking his thumb. I think he would have been crying, had he possessed the energy. When he saw me appear at his side, he pulled his hand from Filomena's grasp and held up his arms to me, begging to be lifted.

'How much further is it?' Filomena asked, as I picked Hugh up and let him burrow his head into the fur of my hood.

'We're nearly there,' I said confidently, though, in truth, I was beginning to fear that we were lost. The track was now descending into another valley, where the fog lay at its thickest. If this lack of visibility were not bad enough, I soon became aware of shapes in the mist about us. Shadowy forms that followed our progress at a distance, but never came into focus. Fog will bend any benign shape into a monster, and any ordinary sound into a threat. I guessed that they were sheep, since the island was home to many herds, but their tramping hooves soon became the stalking footsteps of wraiths. Their low bleats were ghostlike calls.

I was not the only member of the party to be bothered by our sinister followers. The pony was misbehaving again, now stubbornly refusing to walk through this shrouded glade. Even the threat of the whip no longer held any fear for the creature, no matter how menacingly I waved the leathers in front of its eyes. In the end my valet Sandro produced an apple from his pouch, which finally persuaded the pony to move off again. We then trudged along behind the cart, like a party of mourners following a coffin to the graveyard.

At that moment, I couldn't remember feeling more miserable. My feet were squelching inside my boots. The cold air was causing Hugh to cough and Mother was groaning loudly at every step. Only Filomena kept going without complaint – but her silent forbearance was perhaps the hardest torment to bear. Guilt welled inside me as I watched her small frame bent forward like an old woman's. This was not the life I had imagined for my wife, when I brought her here from Venice. I turned my eyes back to the path, for I could not surrender to these thoughts.

'I think we should stop for a while,' said Filomena, once we had climbed out of the low hollow onto some higher ground, moving quickly past the gallows, where the body of a man hung limply from the gibbet. 'When the fog lifts, we can see where we're going.' This was an appealing idea, but I feared that if we stopped now, we might never start again. Night would fall soon, and then the air that was currently cold would turn into a freezing miasma.

'We must carry on,' I said.

'But Hugh is exhausted,' she argued. 'And your mother cannot keep up.'

'Don't worry about me,' said Mother, suddenly looming through the mists like an effigy above a tomb. 'There's nothing wrong with my legs. I'm as fit as a young woman.' As she said this, she leant against the side of the cart and her knees nearly buckled beneath her.

Filomena looked at me sharply and took a deep breath, and I wondered if an argument would follow – but instead, my wife pulled me to one side and whispered, 'Are you certain that you know where we're going, Oswald?'

'Yes,' I said. 'There's only one road across this island, and we're definitely on it.'

She regarded me for a moment – unsure whether to argue, before she set off again, her head lowered once more against the elements. We followed behind her, making slow progress along this track until something caught my attention in the distance. It was a light, glimmering thinly through the gloom.

'Can you see that?' I asked Filomena, as I pointed ahead. 'I think Godfrey has lit a beacon for us.'

This was a welcome thought, so we pressed on, gathering speed with each step. Even the stubborn pony seemed excited by the promise of an end to this journey. But, as we neared the flames, we realised that this was no beacon. Instead it was a fire, devouring the wooden carcass of a small cottage.

We left Hugh with Mother and Sandro at the cart, and then Filomena and I cautiously approached the fire, stepping forward until the heat prevented us from getting any nearer. We stopped to stare into the flames, like two children gazing at the spectacle of the midsummer bone fire. I was so transfixed by the sight, that it took me a while to notice the figure watching us from the other side of the burning cottage. He wore rough clothes and his face was hidden by a rag wrapped about his mouth and nose. When I called out to him, he lifted a bucket from the ground and then quickly retreated into the fog.

'Who was that?' Filomena asked me.

'I don't know,' I said.

'And what is that smell?' She sniffed at the air. 'It smells like . . .' She paused for a moment and clasped my arm. 'Like the oil that fishermen use in Venice. To paint the boats.'

I had smelt it too. A sharp and choking scent. 'I think it's birch bark oil,' I said, now realising what had been inside the mysterious man's bucket. 'It was probably used to start the fire.'

Filomena nodded, but continued to sniff at the air. 'But there's another smell, Oswald,' she said. 'Something I don't recognise.'

I did recognise it. In fact, I knew this perfume of old. It was pungent and sickening. A scent that clings to the nostrils for moments, but to the memory forever. 'Come on, Filomena,' I said. 'Let's get out of here.'

'Why? What's the matter?'

I tried to pull her away from the fire, but she resisted me. 'No, Oswald. Tell me what it is.'

'I don't know,' I said.

'Yes you do,' she replied. We had been married for over two years now, and she knew when I was lying. 'I won't leave here until you tell me the truth.'

I looked at the determined expression on her face and surrendered. 'There are bodies in the fire,' I said. 'That's what you can smell.'

'What?' she said, wrinkling her nose in disgust. 'I don't believe you.'

'Look closer, Filomena,' I said, pointing into the heart of the flames, where the wooden struts of the cottage were now collapsing onto the remains of three people. Two were adults, but one was a child, perhaps not much older than Hugh. Their corpses were scorched and blackened, but they were still identifiable as human.

'Mother Maria!' She looked away and crossed herself. 'Why would anybody do this? Only heathens burn their dead.'

'I think they died of plague,' I said with a sigh.

She stepped back. 'But you said plague was behind us, Oswald. That's why we came to this island.'

'Please, Filomena. Let's argue about this later.' I took her arm again. Now, more than ever, we needed to reach our safe haven.

She didn't need any further encouragement to leave. We hurried back to the cart, and refused to answer any of Sandro and Mother's questions, as we concentrated on persuading the pony to move off again. But, just as the pony agreed to budge, we heard the sound of approaching hooves through the fog. I took out my sword instinctively, and asked Sandro to do the same.

'Who's there?' I called out, fearing it was the masked man from the fire again. He circled us on his horse, a tall palfrey, its flanks covered with a richly decorated caparison. This was not the roughly dressed peasant I'd seen before. This was a nobleman – robed in the livery of his estate. When he lifted back the hood of his cloak, I recognised his face straight away – though his hair was unkempt and his red beard had grown as long as a hermit's.

'Godfrey,' I said, dropping the sword to my side. 'Thank goodness.'

'What are you doing here, Oswald?' he said, his face knotted into an angry grimace. 'This is a plague house.'

'You knew about this?' I said.

'Yes. I gave orders for this cottage to be burnt down.'

'But the dead were inside, Godfrey,' I said. Mother gasped at my words, and I could see Sandro crossing himself out of the corner of my eye.

'No. That's not true,' said Godfrey.

'I saw them myself,' I said. 'Within the flames.'

He balled the fist of his left hand. 'The dead were to be buried first,' he growled. 'Those were my explicit instructions.'

'Well, they weren't honoured.'

Godfrey rubbed a hand across his face. For a moment he looked so much older than his thirty-two years. He then quickly tugged at his reins and turned the horse away from us. 'Come on,' he shouted. 'We need to get back to Castle Eden. It's not safe here.'

We trailed Godfrey's horse through the fog for a mile or so in complete silence, following a track that was constantly rising.

Not even Mother had the energy to complain. Eventually we came to a headland. It was here that the fog lifted and we were finally able to look up at our destination. A castle perched on a lonely cliff, standing out against a cold, white sky with gloomy defiance. Beyond this castle there was nothing but marsh, grey and flat as it seeped out into infinity.

It felt as if we had reached the very edge of the world.

Chapter Two

By 1361 we had not seen plague for a number of years – or perhaps we had just decided to forget about it, as a person ignores a sore foot when they are determined to dance. Now we were being punished for this slight however, for plague had reawoken to take another bite at the English.

When I first heard the rumours coming out from London, I decided to stay within the walls of my home in Somershill. It is a large fortified manor in the middle of my rural estate in Kent – somewhere that I could keep my family safe from contagion. Or so I hoped. But then, as the weeks went by, and new tales trickled out from the city, I began to change my mind. They were alarming stories, accounts of a changed disease. This time plague was killing the young in many more numbers than the old. Some were even calling it the Children's Pestilence, as if this outbreak deserved a name of its own.

My son Hugh was only four years old, and soon I began to worry for his life. He was my only child, born to my first wife – my beloved Mary. She had died during his birth, and subsequently I had rejected Hugh – blaming him for Mary's death, as if he had somehow been complicit in this deed. This stupidity had ended when I met Filomena in Venice, for she had helped me to shake away this destructive and selfish delusion, urging me to become a proper father to my motherless son. After this very poor beginning, I had come to love Hugh with all my heart, and now I would do anything to save his life.

And so, when we heard reports of plague within ten miles of Somershill, I knew that it was time to leave. But where were we to go? We could hardly retreat to the other de Lacy house, in the city of London, as this was at the very heart of the contagion. And then I remembered that my friend Godfrey, lord of the Eden estate to the south of Somershill, had once offered us refuge in his remote castle, should the Plague ever reach Kent. I had laughed privately when he made this invitation, never thinking that I might need to accept – but now I found myself writing to Godfrey, advising my friend that we would be arriving at his home by the middle of November. He wrote back immediately, with a list of foods we should bring and the advice that we should hurry to get there before he closed off his castle from the outside world. Once he had lowered the portcullis of Castle Eden against the Plague, he would not raise it again. Not for anybody.

Filomena and my mother had objected strongly to my choice of sanctuary at first, though neither of them had denied the need to flee Somershill. They didn't care for Godfrey, nor like the sound of his lonely castle on the Isle of Eden, but they had no other suggestions. I convinced them both that Godfrey was better company than he first seemed, and though his home was isolated, it would afford very good protection from plague. I didn't confess to them that I also found Godfrey a little difficult, and had my own misgivings about spending a whole winter in his company.

Our friendship had started in London two years previously, when we had been drawn to one another at a feast to celebrate Pentecost. I suppose we each recognised something in the other: a shyness in large groups, and a sense of being different, outsiders even. Godfrey had been interesting company on that evening, as we had spoken about astronomy and philosophy, even sharing some amusement at the pomposity and self-importance of our host. After this introduction, I had invited him to stay at

Somershill on his return trip to the south coast, and this had become a regular arrangement thereafter. Whenever Godfrey was travelling to London, he stayed at Somershill for at least one night in order to break up his journey.

It was on these visits that I had discovered another side to my friend's character. As well as being a congenial and educated man, Godfrey could also be suspicious, if not occasionally irrational. His religious convictions were becoming strong. Too strong. At times I feared that they were warping his sanity. He believed, with utter conviction, that the world was coming to an end – a belief that was only confirmed when rumours of the Plague surfaced. To his mind, plague was a punishment from God upon humanity, and most especially upon the church. It was a retribution for all the many corruptions and sins of the clergy.

He had become so obsessed with the notion that we were approaching the Day of Judgment, that many people had taken to avoiding his company. The fact that I still invited Godfrey to stay at my home and didn't rudely contradict his views had led him to believe that I shared his fears. This was, perhaps, the only reason that he had extended an invitation to my family to join him at his remote hideaway. And so, in some ways it had turned out to be a friendship worth cultivating.

And yet . . .

And yet, as our cart trundled through the archway of Castle Eden on that first evening, I wondered if I had made the right decision after all? Godfrey's welcome could hardly have been described as warm, and this castle was as bleak as the White Tower. I looked up at the high walls of the inner keep, and couldn't help but shiver. This would be our home for the next few months – a quad of cobblestones, surrounded by a high curtain wall with a tower at each corner. There was nothing more. No outer keep or enclosed gardens. Just stone walls and sky.

Our pony had been released into the forest after our arrival, since the castle could not accommodate any more horses. As I watched the creature jauntily trot away into the distance, surprised to be given its freedom, I suddenly had the urge to run through the gate and join its escape. But then the portcullis was lowered for the last time behind us – its heavy chains clanking loudly as they turned on the wheel. It was too late to leave now. For better or worse, this was where we would remain for the whole winter, or until the Plague had cared to burn itself out.

Godfrey strode over to our party, as Sandro, Mother and Filomena huddled about me like penned sheep. 'You need to get dry, Oswald,' he said. 'Go to your rooms, and we'll move your cart to the stables.' He then turned to look over his shoulder. 'Now, where is my steward?' he said. 'I told Mistress Cross to be here when you arrived.'

'Your steward is a woman?' I asked, unable to hide my surprise, since such roles were always the preserve of a man.

He nodded awkwardly. 'Yes,' he said. 'You'll find that all the servants are women here. I've dismissed the men.'

'Why?' I asked.

'Because they eat too much, Oswald. And we have limited stores of food.' He looked around again for his steward. 'Where is she?' he said, now putting his hands to his mouth and bellowing her name about the inner ward. 'Mistress Cross. You are required here. Please come immediately!' This call went out three times before a woman eventually responded, bustling around the corner and then striding towards us as if we were a herd of pigs who had invaded her vegetable garden.

Alice Cross was as wide as she was tall, with a face of weathered freckles and large hands that wouldn't have looked out of place on a wrestler. I ventured a smile, but was greeted by a look of indignation that bordered on hostility.

'Come with me,' she barked, demanding that we follow her to a door at the foot of one of the towers. She stopped here to count us, as if we might have doubled in number since beginning our short journey, and then, with a great puff of dissatisfaction, she opened this door onto a dark, winding stairwell that led up to the only rooms in this part of the castle.

As we trailed her skirts up the steps, we soon learnt that Alice Cross was justly named. She was cross that we had arrived so late in the day. She was cross at having to ascend these steep stairs on our behalf. She was cross that the door to our chamber was stiff, and she was most especially cross that Godfrey had allocated us the two best rooms in the castle. These interconnecting chambers, she haughtily informed us, were usually reserved for the King – kept perpetually ready for an unannounced arrival. By this point, despite my exhaustion, I could no longer tolerate the woman's manner, so I pointed out that the King had never chosen to stay at Castle Eden to my knowledge, preferring Pevensey or even Sandwich to this remote fortress.

My observation only elicited another puff of disgust, before she then continued to issue us with a litany of rules, turning to address Filomena and my mother in particular. Perhaps she thought that the women would make better enforcers than the men, but she was wasting her time in this instance. I could tell that Filomena was struggling to understand the woman's strong Kentish accent, and Mother wasn't listening. The long journey, followed by the steep ascent of the staircase, had exhausted her, and she was resting on the nearest stool with her eyes closed.

The fact that Mother was sleeping did not deter Mistress Cross from continuing, however. Amongst her many instructions – far too many to possibly be remembered – we learnt the times for supper; where we should leave the dirty chamber pots and why we should not, under any circumstances, touch the precious glass in the windows of this room. At the end of this recitation she looked us over with a final disgruntled sigh and then left the room with a flourish of resentment. As the door closed, Filomena muttered something in Venetian under her breath.

'What's the matter?' I asked, as if this wasn't obvious.

She looked away. 'I don't like this place, Oswald.'

'It's just different to Somershill,' I said, trying my best to sound cheerful. 'That's all. You'll get used to it.'

I expected her to argue with me, but instead she took my hands in her own. 'Please, Oswald,' she said softly. 'Let's go back to Somershill. It's not too late.'

'I'm sorry, Filomena,' I said, taken aback by this appeal. 'It is too late. You know that. You saw those bones burning in the fire. We're surrounded by plague. It's not safe to leave this castle.'

'But I don't feel safe here. This place is . . .' She dropped my hands from hers and then crossed her arms. 'This castle is so cold,' she said. 'And there are bad spirits here. You must have felt the eyes upon us as we came in? Nobody is pleased to see us.'

I had, indeed, seen faces at the windows above the inner ward, as we followed Alice Cross across the cobblestones – but I had read their peeping as nothing more sinister than the usual nosiness. 'The other guests are just interested in us,' I said. 'I'm sure everybody will be very friendly. There's really nothing to be worried about.'

'No, no, Oswald. Filomena is right,' piped up Mother, from the other side of the room. 'I've felt it too. There is a malignance here. A pervasion of evil.'

'I thought you were asleep,' I said, as Mother padded towards us with a slow and disturbing determination.

'I shall be wearing this at all times,' she said, pulling a large gold pendant from beneath her tunic. 'It contains a fragment from the vestments of Saint Thomas a Becket. This bloodied cloth can protect us from anything.'

Filomena inspected Mother's pendant with disdain and then felt within her embroidered tunic, pulling out her own coral rosary. 'And I will ask the Virgin for protection,' she said haughtily. 'Mother Maria is more powerful than any saint.'

They displayed these trophies to one another, like two children arguing over the longest stick, or the brightest stone.

'Please remember,' I said. 'You mustn't go about the castle with such jewellery on show.'

'Why not?' they said, turning to me in unison.

'You know Godfrey's opinion of relics and rosaries.'

'Well, he's not here now,' said Filomena. 'And anyway, my rosary is not jewellery. These beads are holy.'

Mother folded her arms. 'And so is my pendant, Oswald. It is a verified relic. Blessed by the Bishop of Bath himself.'

'I'm just asking you not to flaunt them,' I said. The two women exchanged a glance at this. 'This is Godfrey's castle,' I continued. 'So we must respect his wishes.' I paused. 'We were lucky to be invited.'

'Well, I don't feel lucky,' said Filomena, turning away from me.

'And neither do I,' said Mother, mimicking Filomena's stance. 'This place is cold and miserable. And your wife is right. There is evil here.'

'There is no safer place than this,' I said, now concerned that the two of them were uniting against me for once. 'In the months to come, you'll be pleased to be in this castle. When plague is sweeping through the villages and towns of Kent, you'll have a fire, a bed and enough food for many months. You'll be alive, while others are dying.'

Mother shrugged at this, unimpressed by my impassioned speech. 'You think this is a sanctuary, Oswald,' she said. 'But I cannot agree.'

'It *is* a sanctuary,' I insisted. 'Plague will not breach these walls.'

She headed for a nearby chair and then let herself slip down into the seat, releasing a long sigh of pleasure as she took the weight from her feet. 'That doesn't matter, Oswald,' she said, as she closed her eyes again. 'There is death here already.'

'That's not true,' I said, vexed by this foolish talk. How could my mother possibly have sensed the presence of death and evil?

We had only just arrived. I threw off my cloak and changed into dry clothes, before we ate a supper of bread and hard cheese, and then crawled, with complete exhaustion, between the icy sheets of our beds.

But I did not sleep well that night. Instead, I fell into a fitful doze – my dreams invaded by the shadow of plague. I was an eighteen-year-old boy again, escaping from the monastery with an old monk – a priest named Brother Peter. I was lying on a dirty bed within a dirty hovel – somewhere that I had never been before. I didn't know why or how I'd got there. I only knew that my body was drenched with the sweats of a fever, and that there were large, throbbing lumps in my armpits, neck and groin.

When I looked down at these buboes, I could see that each one of them was swollen to near bursting point with blackened blood. Pain gripped my body, but soon fear swamped even this emotion, as a figure loomed over me in the darkness, wielding a knife. It was Brother Peter. He wanted to help me, and yet I did not want his help. As he laid the cold metal blade against the lump in my armpit, I screamed for him to stop. I didn't care when he told me this was my only chance. I didn't care when he insisted that he must lance this bubo and release the corruption within. He was trying to save my life, and yet I struggled against him. Even though I was so close to death, I feared the pain of his barbaric surgery more than I desired his cure.

I woke as Brother Peter made that first incision, poking the tip of the knife into my skin. I sat up straight in a cold panic and for a few moments, I couldn't remember where I was, until I recognised the room at Castle Eden. Hugh had crawled into the bed between Filomena and me, and was softly breathing. There was nothing to fear.

I kissed my son on the head and then fell back against the bolster, resting for a moment as I let my hand run over the bumpy scar in my left armpit. My breathing slowed and my eyes closed. I was alive.

Chapter Three

I was awoken the next morning by the sensation of something passing across my face. I instinctively jumped out of bed, ready to defend myself, when I realised that my assailant was nothing more dangerous than a large crow, strutting along the ledge outside our window as it cast a beady eye inside the room. We regarded one another for a moment, before the crow tapped its curved, silvery beak at the window, as if it expected to be let in. I clapped my hands and tried to shoo it away, but the crow ignored me and continued to tap at the glass, until I banged on the inner side of the window myself. It then flapped its wings in some indignation before gliding down into the inner ward, where it landed on the shoulder of an elderly man dressed in the black habit of a Benedictine monk. When I saw that a number of people were standing with him – huddled in a group at one end of this courtyard to catch the thin shards of winter sun – I realised that we must have overslept.

I woke Filomena and Hugh, and then opened the connecting door to the other room in our apartment, where my mother had spent the night. My valet Sandro was curled up on a straw mattress in the corner, and only stirred when I tapped him on the shoulder. He jumped to his feet immediately, embarrassed that I had been required to wake him.

'I'm sorry, Master Oswald,' he said, rubbing his face and then pushing the curls from his eyes.

'Don't worry, Sandro,' I said. 'We're all tired after yesterday. But it's time to help my mother from bed.'

'There's no need for that,' came Mother's voice from the other side of the room. 'I can still stand up on my own, you know.'

I gestured silently to Sandro, nodding for him to go over to her bedside anyway. 'Very well, Mother,' I said. 'But please take care. The bedstead is high.'

She opened an eyelid and I was suddenly reminded of the slowworms that I used to catch in the monastery garden when I was a boy. A grey linen nightcap clung tightly to her scalp. Her face was pale and notched with lines, as if she were coated in a membrane of silvery scales. 'Please send Filomena in to dress me,' she said. 'I won't have that Venetian boy doing it.'

'Very well,' I said, knowing the reaction that this command would provoke from my wife.

'Don't look at me like that Oswald,' said Mother. 'You were the one who wouldn't let me bring a lady's maid.'

'Those were Godfrey's instructions,' I replied. 'We had to keep our party to the minimum. Remember? More servants means more mouths to feed.'

'And yet you felt able to bring your valet?'

'I couldn't leave Sandro in Somershill,' I said. 'He's part of our family.'

We were dressed and about to leave the apartment, when Godfrey knocked at the door and strode in with exaggerated cheerfulness. I could tell immediately that he felt guilty about the poor quality of his welcome to us the previous day, for he was stepping quickly from foot to foot, his small frame restless with nervous energy. 'Good morning to the de Lacys,' he chirped. 'How pleasant it is to see you all.'

'Is it a good morning?' snapped Mother as she waved towards the window. 'Looks as if there's another storm out there to me.'

Godfrey smiled. 'Well, we are surrounded by sea, my Lady,' he said. 'So we cannot complain at being subject to the elements.'

'Never mind being surrounded by sea,' she huffed, obviously needled by Godfrey's condescending tone. 'I feel like a siren, perched on a crag.' She then wrapped her arms across her chest and gave a shiver.

There was a short, embarrassed silence as Godfrey struggled to think of an answer to this, but at least Mother had succeeded in suffocating his false jollity.

He gave a bow to my family and then took me to one side. 'I'm sorry about yesterday, Oswald,' he admitted. 'I should have met you by the ferry.' He began to dither. 'But, you see, I was late setting off from the castle and then the weather turned against me.' He wiped his face and took a deep breath. 'And of course, there was the incident at the cottage.' He dropped his voice to a whisper. 'I gave specific instructions that the family should be buried before the place was set on fire. You must believe me about that. I would never sanction such a sin as burning the dead.'

'Did you know the people who died there?' I asked.

'Yes,' he said. 'They were tenants of mine. A good, God-fearing family.' He paused. 'When this plague has abated, I will return to the cottage and bury their bones myself. And the guilty man will be punished, I can assure you of that. Next time he will follow my instructions precisely.' He forced a smile and then stepped back to direct his next comments to the others. 'So,' he said with a clap of his hands. 'Did you all sleep well?'

'Yes, thank you,' I replied on their behalf. 'We were exhausted after our long journey.'

'And you are all well in yourselves?' he asked. 'No sign of coughs or fevers?' He tried to make this sound like an offhand question, but I knew its true purpose.

'No, Godfrey,' I said. 'We are all well. Otherwise we wouldn't have come here.'

He gave a short, embarrassed cough. 'Of course, Oswald. It was a foolish question. I know that you, of all people, would not take risks with other people's lives.' Then, in a bid to change the subject, he patted Sandro on the head. 'I see that your trusty valet has accompanied you here?'

'Of course,' I said. 'But don't worry, Godfrey. Sandro eats no more than a woman.'

Godfrey tried to laugh at this. 'Well, that's good to hear,' he said, before foolishly attempting to repeat the gesture. As his palm neared my valet's head, Sandro made a sudden bow that left Godfrey's hand waving clumsily in the air.

I couldn't help but smile at this, for I knew what had motivated Sandro's quick move. My valet was now fourteen years of age – or so we believed. We couldn't be sure of this, since he wasn't sure of it himself. Whatever his age, Sandro was old enough to be growing a thin covering of hair on his top lip, and yet he did not reach my shoulder in height. Unfortunately this lack of stature meant that Sandro was often mistaken for a child. A pat on the head was a regular indignity, along with a pull to his ear or a pinch to one of his cherubic cheeks. I had even seen people stroking the crop of glossy black curls that fell in ringlets about his face, even though this boldness clearly made Sandro uncomfortable.

My valet was something of a curiosity. A Venetian novelty. When asked about his history – which frequently happened – I said that I had recruited the boy at a palazzo in Venice, where he had impressed me with his skills at serving our hosts. The truth couldn't have been more different. I had discovered Sandro three years previously, living on the streets of Venice as a ragged and starving child. Our paths had crossed when I was searching for a murderer. He had helped me, as much as I had subsequently helped him. But that is another story, for another time.

After the awkwardness of the failed pat to the head, Godfrey turned his attentions to Filomena and Hugh. 'And here is your son and beautiful wife,' he said flamboyantly. 'Come all the way to see me from Somershill.' Godfrey approached Hugh and unwisely attempted to lift the boy, which only caused my small son to cling to Filomena's legs with a squeal of fear. 'He has grown again,' observed Godfrey, pretending not to be embarrassed by Hugh's reaction. 'And it's only three months since I last saw him.'

It was supposed to be a light-hearted comment, but my wife did not register the comedy in it. In fact, she seemed determined to be affronted by Godfrey's observation. 'I may not be Hugh's true mother,' she said, 'but I always make sure that he eats properly.' She then let her hands rest for a moment upon her coral rosary.

Godfrey's eyes darted away, as if they had been stung. 'Talking of food,' he said quickly, turning back to me. 'Thank you for bringing all of the provisions I requested, Oswald. I've inspected your cart already, and it seems that you followed my instructions precisely.' He grunted a laugh. 'Which is more that I can say for some of the other guests. They don't seem able to read.'

'Your list was very helpful,' I said, remembering the exhaustive directives that I had received from Godfrey.

'Thank you, Oswald,' he said, stepping towards the door, now keen to leave. 'Perhaps you and your valet would assist in moving the sacks and barrels into the storeroom now?' He rubbed his hands together and smiled with genuine pleasure at last. 'And then I want to show you something. I think you'll be very impressed.'

Sandro and I followed Godfrey through the inner ward, passing the handful of fellow guests who were still loitering in the meagre sunshine. I wanted to introduce myself, but Godfrey urged me on.

'You can meet them later,' he said with a wave of his hand. 'There's no rush. We will have months together.'

From the inner ward, he led us down some steps into a dark, musty-smelling passageway that branched out into the network of cellars beneath the castle. Godfrey pushed at one of the many doors along this passageway and then we entered a large vaulted chamber, thinly illuminated by an unexpected shaft in the ceiling, near to the far wall. The room itself was cold, but smelt fresher and drier than the passageway outside. As my eyes became accustomed to the poor light, I saw that this chamber was stuffed with food – from the barrels on the floor, to the many hessian sacks on the shelves. Smoked hams hung from hooks on the ceiling, like a colony of bats roosting in the eaves.

Godfrey strode across the room and then stood proudly beneath the shaft of light. 'I had this ventilation tunnel built recently,' he said. 'It is my own design.' He waved us over. 'Come and see, Oswald. It funnels fresh air into these storerooms from outside of the castle walls.'

'Outside of the walls?' I said in surprise, as Sandro and I peered up the shaft. It was a very thin tunnel, only the width of a dinner plate, leading up towards the daylight at a sloped angle.

'Of course,' said Godfrey. 'I didn't want to draw the stale miasmas of the inner ward into these rooms. Our food is stored in here, and it needs fresh air.' He dropped his head and strode purposefully back towards the door. 'But let me show you something else,' he said proudly. 'I've replaced this door and frame with new timber.' Sandro and I wandered over to inspect this carpentry, without, I have to say, a great deal of enthusiasm. Godfrey didn't notice this lack of interest, however, since he carried on in the same, ebullient manner. 'Once these doors are locked, then nobody will be able to kick them in.' He paused for effect. 'Not even with a battering ram. If the castle is stormed, then the raiders will never get their hands on our food.'

'Are you expecting an invasion?' I asked, exchanging a sly smile with Sandro.

This time Godfrey noticed our disdain and turned on me sharply. 'This is no laughing matter, Oswald,' he said. 'I'm prepared for plague.' I went to apologise but he continued. 'Who can tell what will happen in the months to come?' he said. 'Who can tell what desperate souls will do, when they run out of food? The people on this island will only have their own measly stores to rely upon. Whereas we have this. A cellar full of provisions. Enough to feed us all for many months.'

'It's very impressive,' I said, suitably chastised for my moment of mockery.

He fixed me with a glare, seemingly still annoyed at my lack of sincerity. 'We are at the End of Days, Oswald. The Son of Man prepares to send out his angels from Heaven. Soon they will gather the sinners from His kingdom and throw them all into a flaming furnace.'

Sandro cast his eyes to the floor, but I kept my friend's gaze. I had heard Godfrey quote these verses from the Gospel of Matthew before, and I was in no mood to hear them now. 'I think it's time to unload our food,' I said quickly, walking back into the passageway and gesturing for my valet to join me. 'Come on, Sandro. Hurry up.'

We spent the next hour heaving sacks of grain and dried peas, barrels of wine, whole cheeses, smoked hams and sausages from the cart and then placing them onto the shelves according to Godfrey's precise instructions. Godfrey supervised our work without making any efforts to lift the food and drink himself. Instead he worked at a table, making a list of each contribution and recording the shelf on which it was stored. I wondered if this meant we would only be allowed to eat the food that we had brought ourselves, but Godfrey assured me that his lists only existed so that he could plan out our meals for the next few months.

When we'd finally unloaded the cart, I sent Sandro back to our rooms to see if Filomena needed his help, while Godfrey promised to take me on a tour of the castle, ending with the unveiling of his surprise. We began the tour in his library — a room high up in one of the towers that faced the sea. Godfrey had enlarged an existing arrow slit in the exterior wall of the room, to form a great window onto this view. I lingered here for many minutes, staring out at the low mist that lay upon the marsh like a feather quilt. It was liberating to look into the far distance again, since all of the other windows in the castle looked down upon the small inner ward, which only intensified the feeling of enclosure. I fancied that I could make out Rye to the west and Dover to the east, but this was just my imagination. The light of the marsh plays tricks on the eye.

Godfrey soon dragged me away from this view, keen to show me the next of his improvements. These were the ancient murder holes that he had reopened in the ceiling of the gatehouse — a set of circular mouths above the entrance tunnel, from which we could pour boiling water onto the heads of those raiders he imagined were intent upon storming the castle and stealing our food. This time, however, I didn't laugh at the idea. Instead, I praised Godfrey for his foresight — not wanting to prompt another lecture about the End of Days.

After this, we inspected the well in the inner ward, looking down the deep shaft to a tiny silver circle of water, far below us. The well had been abandoned for many years, having become polluted with all sorts of debris, meaning that the servants had preferred to collect water from an outside stream. But now we had a source of clean water within the castle walls themselves. I congratulated Godfrey with genuine respect this time, for he had been lowered down the well himself in order to clear out the muck. It couldn't have been a pleasant job, but he had not shirked from it.

And then, at last, we came to Godfrey's surprise. We retraced our steps along a passageway in the cellar, to a door that appeared to be locked at first, until Godfrey threw it open to reveal a room illuminated by a bank of lanterns. I stepped inside to look, in wonderment, at what lay before me. It was a large iron frame – as tall and as wide as a man, and filled with an array of wheels, cogs and pulleys. I recognised this immediately as the mechanism of an astronomical clock – a rare device in England, not usually seen outside the abbeys or royal palaces.

I stepped nearer, wanting to touch the clock, when a man appeared from the shadows and warned me off. Beside him was a girl of maybe ten or eleven years of age, dressed in the clothes of a noblewoman. She did not acknowledge our presence, but continued to stare at a wheel that was rotating at speed within the frame.

When Godfrey noticed the girl, he flinched. 'Why is Lady Emma in here?' he asked the man.

'She likes to watch the clock, my Lord,' he replied. 'She's not doing any harm. She never bothers us.'

'I don't think her father would be very pleased about this,' said Godfrey. 'She's supposed to stay in their room.' Godfrey approached the girl, leant down and suggested, in a quiet and gentle voice, that she should leave. The girl didn't look up at Godfrey while he spoke, or make any effort to reply. Instead, she simply obeyed his request and glided out of the room like a small and silent swan.

Once the girl had left us, Godfrey then introduced the man who had appeared from the shadows as Pieter de Groot – a master clock builder from the town of Delft in the Low Countries. De Groot was a squat and muscular man, with arms as thick as ham hocks and a bulbous nose that was split at its tip, like the crack of an arse. Whilst Godfrey was making his introductions, a thin youth of maybe eighteen or nineteen years slunk out of an adjoining room. When he saw our faces, he reddened, and then quickly disappeared again. Godfrey made no attempt to even acknowledge this slender boy, let alone introduce him.

Godfrey ran his hands over the large cog that I had been warned away from. 'Isn't this the most wonderful invention, Oswald?' he said, not sensing de Groot's obvious twitchiness. Once Godfrey had released his hands from the clock, de Groot took a rag to the cog and wiped the area that Godfrey had just touched. Godfrey seemed oblivious to the slight and continued to speak. 'This clock will hang from the wall above the dais in the Great Hall,' he said. 'Though none of these wheels and cogs will be on show. We will only see this.' He then walked over to an object that was hidden by a sheet – pulling it back to reveal a large circular dial, painted with golden stars against a dark blue background. Godfrey's actions caused de Groot to inhale sharply, but once again, Godfrey didn't appear to notice his clockmaker's obvious annoyance.

'Look at these numerals, Oswald,' said Godfrey, pointing to the symbols painted about the edge of the dial. 'They represent the hour of the day. From one to twelve on this side, and then again on the other.' He was becoming excited. His breathing rapid. 'And this,' he said, pointing to a thin rod capped by an emblem of the sun. 'This hand will rotate around the clock face throughout the day, showing the correct hour. And this,' he said, running his hand over a small disc at the centre of the clock. 'This is the most remarkable part of all. This shows the age of the moon, from one to thirty days.' He sighed in pleasure. 'Have you ever seen such a thing?'

'There's the clock at St Albans abbey,' I said unwisely, before quickly adding, 'Though I have not seen it myself.'

Godfrey bristled, but de Groot nodded at my words. 'I have heard of that clock, my Lord,' he said. 'It was built by Richard of Wallingford. A very fine piece, I'm told. But this will be as fine,' he said, tapping the same cog that Godfrey had previously touched.

'If not finer,' said Godfrey. 'This will be the most accurate clock that Master de Groot has ever built.'

De Groot huffed, 'If I ever have the funds to finish it,' he said acidly. 'And who knows when that will be?'

The comment hung in the air, before Godfrey hastily directed me to the door. 'Let's leave Master de Groot to his work, Oswald,' he said, ushering me out of the room. 'He's a very busy man.'

Once we were back in the passageway and the door was firmly closed behind us, Godfrey whispered to me, 'You mustn't take any notice of his gruff manner, Oswald. I'm afraid that de Groot can be rather rude. But he really was the finest clockmaker I could find.'

'Who was the girl?'

'That was Lady Emma,' he answered. 'You'll meet her father, Lord Hesket, later. She's rather strange, but you'll get used to her.'

'Who was the other man in the room?' I asked. 'The thin boy.'

Godfrey frowned. 'Oh him?' he said dismissively. 'That's de Groot's nephew, Hans. Apparently the boy is an apprentice. Though I'm not sure that he has any relevant skills.' He paused to sigh. 'Not in clock-making anyway.'

I was about to ask more, when we were taken by surprise as a large, wiry-haired dog suddenly sped around the corner of the passage with its nose pressed to the floor. Godfrey tried to catch hold of the creature by the collar as it passed us, but it was in no mood to be caught.

'Is that your dog?' I asked.

'No,' said Godfrey, running after the creature as it sped towards a door at the end of the passageway. 'It belongs to Sir Robert of Lyndham,' he said, pulling it away from the door. 'The knight I've engaged to protect the castle. You'll meet him later as well.'

'Perhaps you should release it?' I suggested, as the dog was now barking with frantic excitement.

'No,' said Godfrey, making another attempt to subdue the creature. 'This dog must learn some manners.' But his attempt at discipline was to no avail. The dog soon escaped from Godfrey's clasp and threw itself at the door, scratching madly at the wood.

'I think there's something inside,' I said. 'Why don't we let it go in?'

I went to lift the latch, but Godfrey put his hand on mine. 'Please, Oswald. I don't want you to go inside this room.'

'Why not?'

'Because—'

It was too late. The dog had pushed the door open, and was now racing into the darkness, making a succession of high-pitched squeals as it bound about the room in a frenzy. I followed without further discussion, finding myself in a dingy and stale-smelling cellar – a room without the benefit of Godfrey's ingenious ventilation shaft. As my eyes became accustomed to the light, I could see shapes in the dark. Long, thin boxes resting against the walls like a circle of silent watchmen. The dog darted between these boxes with its nose to the floor, until it flushed out a tiny grey mouse. As the mouse and the dog shot past us and disappeared back into the passageway, I turned to Godfrey, hardly knowing what to say.

'I warned you not to come in here,' he said. 'I knew it would upset you.'

'Is there a coffin for each of us?' I asked. He nodded in response. 'Even Hugh?'

'Yes.' When I gave a short groan, he added, 'I had to prepare them, Oswald. You must understand that.'

'Did you?'

'Yes. If we are to die, then we must be buried correctly. Our bodies laid to face the East, so that we may rise at dawn on the Day of Judgment. To see the coming of Christ.' He hesitated. 'You remember what happened to the dead at the last plague, Oswald. You remember the horror of the pits.'

He was right. I did remember the plague pits of 1349. But then again, who could forget them? My own father and two older brothers were buried in such a hole, somewhere in the town of Rochester. Their deaths had been a tragedy and yet this turn of fate had changed my own life for the better. In 1349 I was only the third de Lacy son. A spare. The boy who had been sent to the monastery as an oblate at the age of seven – destined to become a Benedictine monk for the rest of his life. Instead, I had become Lord Somershill. I was a husband, with a wife and a son.

Like so many others after the last plague, I had a pit to thank for this outcome. The accident of my brothers' deaths had become my own chance at life.

Chapter Four

That evening we gathered in the Great Hall for a feast, organised by Godfrey to mark our arrival at Castle Eden. I use the word 'feast' loosely, for it was difficult to overindulge on a stew of boiled fowl and onions, accompanied by the roughest barley bread. Nevertheless, I knew better than to complain about the quality of the food. At least we were eating, and there were many months ahead when the hams and the cheeses would be more appreciated.

The supper provided the opportunity for Godfrey to formally introduce us to the other guests – though he did not make a particularly good job of this. He seemed distracted as he quickly pointed at the row of fellow diners along the table, reeling off their names, as I made a concerted effort to remember each one of them.

Sitting next to us at the table were the Heskets, a family of three who had travelled here from their palace in London. Lord Hesket was a man of around fifty years in age, with a bushy beard that hid the majority of his face, and a pair of dark eyes that stared without reserve. His beautiful wife, Lady Isobel, was young, but gave the impression of being jaded with life, despite her youth. As she yawned with boredom and picked at her nails, I noted that her mouth was already set in a downward slant and that there were already frown lines across her forehead. If she did not take care, then her beautiful face would be set forever in a scowl.

Mother was acquainted with the Hesket family, and felt compelled to share her knowledge of them with me, leaning over to whisper in my ear. 'Of course, that woman is not Hesket's first wife,' she said, looking across at Lady Isobel.

'I guessed that,' I replied discreetly.

'His first wife died of the King's Evil,' she said. 'Her neck swelled up to the size of a tree trunk. But would Hesket take her to visit the King? No, he would not. Even though everybody knows that the Royal Touch will cure the affliction.'

'I'm not sure that's true,' I said.

'But it is, Oswald,' she said indignantly. 'Last year King Edward cured many sufferers. It's a well known fact.'

I decided not to argue. 'Well, it's a shame that the poor woman died of such a cruel disease.'

'Yes, it is. And she was such a sweet thing,' she sighed. 'Unlike this one. Just look at her. Lady Isobel, indeed.' She gave a huff. 'She might be blessed with the beauty of Aphrodite, but she hasn't got a scrap of kindness in her soul. See how she ignores Hesket's daughter.' She heaved another, regretful sigh. 'I know the girl is a halfwit but she doesn't deserve such a cold fish as her stepmother.'

It was probable that Lord Hesket heard this last comment, for he turned sharply to regard us with a look of consternation on his face. If Mother saw censure in his stare, then she did not acknowledge it. Instead, she simply raised her goblet and nodded her head to him. 'Good evening to you, Lord Hesket,' she said. 'How lovely it is to see you and your family again.'

When Hesket had returned his eyes to his meal, I took the opportunity to watch his daughter, Lady Emma, for a while. The girl was as silent now as she had been earlier, when I'd first encountered her in the clockmakers' workroom. In fact, she had not said a single word during supper. Even so, I thought that

Mother's verdict was too cruel. Lady Emma might be a silent and detached child, but I had the sense that she understood what was going on around her. She simply chose not to engage with anybody, not even her own father.

When I realised that my interest was making Emma uncomfortable, I turned to look at the other guests. The first face to my left was the craggy profile of Godfrey's uncle – the elderly Benedictine monk whom I'd seen earlier in the inner ward. Known as Old Simon, he was a crooked, blue-skinned man, whose toothless gums were causing his jaw to subside into his face. Alice Cross was the only person who would serve him, since his crow – the same creature that had tapped at our window earlier – pecked viciously at the other maids when they tried to clear his plate. As Old Simon fed the bird with pieces of meat, he explained to Filomena that he had found her as an abandoned nestling, named her Corvina and then taught her to speak. My wife smiled politely at this story, clearly not believing a word of it, until Corvina suddenly squawked *Ave Maria* and *In nomine Patris* in her ear. Old Simon rewarded the crow for this performance with yet more tidbits that should have been saved for human consumption.

Further along the table, and keeping his distance from the monk and his crow, sat Robert of Lyndham – the knight whom Godfrey had mentioned earlier. I did not know whether Lyndham's role as the protector of this castle was a paid position or not. Certainly, the man was being treated with the privileges of the other guests, and was sitting amongst the noble families on the dais. He cut a memorable, even intimidating figure, though he was dressed in a simple tunic. He was tall and broad-shouldered, with a booming laugh and a face so disarmingly handsome that it was difficult not to stare at him. Lyndham might have been conceited because of this gift, but he seemed pleasant and self-effacing, though his conversation seemed to stray little further than the hunting abilities of his deerhound – the dog that

I had met earlier, as it chased a mouse between Godfrey's store of coffins.

There was one empty place at the table, to the left of Robert of Lyndham's, laid for Godfrey's younger brother – a man named Edwin of Eden, who was said to be too unwell to join us. At the mention of his name, Mother once again leant in to speak to me in a whisper, giving me her opinion of this excuse.

'Of course, Edwin of Eden is not ill, Oswald. The man has been drinking all afternoon,' she said. 'Everybody knows what a drunken, indolent fool he is.' She put a hand to her chest and smothered a belch. 'Remember what he was like when he came to stay with us at Somershill? He was so drunk he couldn't even mount a horse.' I did remember Edwin's last stay, and not fondly. He had been accompanying Godfrey on a trip to London, and the two of them had planned to stay for a single night with us, before they crossed the North Downs and headed for London Bridge at Southwark. The one-night stay had become three, since Edwin had availed himself of our cellars in the middle of the night, and was subsequently too unwell to travel until he had sobered up. I remembered that he vomited all over one of our best quilts, and then spoke so offensively to Filomena that we had been forced to lock him into his bedchamber. Godfrey had apologised profusely for Edwin's behaviour of course, but I was so infuriated that I had asked him never to bring his brother to Somershill again.

Mother must have read my mind. 'If Edwin of Eden is not drunk, then he'll be in the kitchens,' she said. 'Pestering one of those poor scullions. The man's as randy as a ram.'

Lord Hesket leant forwards at this point. 'Would you keep your voice down, please, my Lady.' He gestured towards his daughter. 'There is a child seated near you.'

Mother gave a perfunctory smile, before she inclined her head towards mine again. 'I don't know why he worries,' she whispered. 'That poor girl can't understand a thing. Her brain is addled, Oswald. Addled.'

Hesket's shoulders rose with indignation, for he had most certainly heard this last comment.

'Please, Mother,' I said. 'Keep your voice down.'

Beyond Edwin's empty place was a second table, still on the dais, but separate from our own. Such is the hierarchy of chairs and tables in a Great Hall. Pieter de Groot and his thin nephew Hans were seated at this table, slurping their stew as if it might be their last meal. The pair were not guests of Godfrey's, but neither were they his servants – hence their location on the dais, and not at the servants' table at the other end of the hall, beyond the central fire.

I now had the opportunity to study Hans properly. Whereas his uncle was thickset and robust, this boy was slight-framed, with a shock of sandy-coloured hair that sprouted from the top of his head like a tussock of sedge. I couldn't help but stare at him for a while. In this poor light, his ashen skin and pale blue eyes gave him the ghoulish, sinister appearance of a moving corpse. The only part of his face that appeared living was a pair of fleshy, crimson lips.

My attentions were drawn back to my own table when Alice Cross and the three maids served us with the last course of the meal – the slimmest slice of hard cheese and a thimble of spiced hypocras. After we had consumed these delicacies within a blink of an eye, Godfrey stood up to make a short speech in our honour.

'I would like to welcome Lord Somershill and his family to Castle Eden,' he said, raising his goblet in the air. 'Now that the de Lacys have arrived, it seems that we are almost full.'

'Almost full?' said Lord Hesket. 'What do you mean by that, Eden? I hope you're not planning to let anybody else in?'

Godfrey was taken aback by Hesket's reaction, though he dared not reply in the same tone. This might have been Godfrey's castle, but Lord Hesket was the richest and most influential man within these walls. 'I only meant that this castle could still hold more people, if required,' said Godfrey, trying to steady his voice.

'Required by whom?' asked Hesket, his fulsome beard failing to hide a look of disdain. 'You said that we'd lowered the port-cullis for the last time yesterday. When the de Lacys arrived. Did you lie to us?'

'No, no, of course not,' Godfrey gibbered. 'I think you've misunderstood me. I just thought you should know that we could accommodate more people in an emergency.'

Hesket leant forward to fix Godfrey with a stare, resting his chin upon his hand. 'There is no emergency that would require you to open this castle to new guests, Eden, do you understand?'

'But—'

Hesket thumped the table. 'We only came to this godforsaken place because you promised to lock the gates.' I noticed this disparaging comment about Godfrey's castle raised a rare smile from his wife. 'Now you keep them locked, do you understand? Nobody out and nobody in.'

We all turned our eyes to Godfrey and I wondered, for a moment, what he would say. I must admit that I had found my friend's initial comment and subsequent vacillation equally trou-bling. Now that we were surrounded by plague, the lives of my wife, son and mother would be at risk from any newcomers to this castle – no matter how great the emergency might be. Hesket's words might have seemed callous, but I could not object to them – for I felt the same.

Godfrey bowed his head. 'I apologise, Lord Hesket. I didn't mean to alarm you.'

Hesket folded his arms. 'Well, you did.'

'That was certainly not my intention,' replied Godfrey. 'I can assure you that I'm as committed to spending a winter here, in complete isolation, as the rest of you.'

Hesket puffed his lips. 'Well, Eden. You're certainly commit-ted to spending,' he muttered. 'That much is true.'

Godfrey appeared deflated after this exchange and made his excuses – saying that he needed to attend to some matters in his library. I might have made my own excuses at this point, as Mother was tired, Filomena was still uncomfortable at sitting next to a talking crow, and Hugh was beginning to whine. The sooner we returned to our apartment, the better, so that I could light a fire and we could warm ourselves up after supper in this freezing hall. I was about to stand up and announce our departure when forced to take my seat again, for the evening's entertainment had begun early and now there was no chance for a quick exit.

It transpired that Godfrey, with his love of planning, had gone to the lengths of employing a man to entertain the guests at the castle in the long months to come. He might have been better advised to have engaged a minstrel, rather than this jester – for The Fool, as this man introduced himself, appeared almost immediately to be lacking in any talent for comedy.

He began his act by clumsily cartwheeling across the hall and then jumping onto the dais in front of me. It was clear that I had been singled out as a new victim, much to the relief of the other guests about the table. He then pulled a peacock feather from his belt, waved the feather about in the air above my head and then tickled my face with its tip. I made a pretence of laughing at this, in the hope that I might spark some amusement among my fellow guests, but as I looked along the table I saw a row of bewildered faces looking back at me. The only mirth came from a dark corner, where Sandro held a hand over his mouth as his shoulders shook with laughter. For some reason, my valet seemed to find The Fool's act hilarious.

Having tickled me with the feather, The Fool then waved it about in the air, before poking it down his braies, with the suggestion that this action was causing him some pain. When nobody laughed at his writhing, he then struck upon the idea of pretending instead that the feather was giving him pleasure.

Now, as he rubbed the feather up and down, he pulled twisted, contorted faces of ecstasy.

My mother, who had fallen asleep at the end of the meal, suddenly stirred from her torpor. 'What's that man doing, Oswald?' she said loudly as she squinted through the gloom. 'Is he playing with himself?'

There was a moment of silence, before the knight, Robert of Lyndham, gave a great guffaw of laughter. His amusement at Mother's comment prompted others to start giggling. At first it was just a titter, even a chuckle, but soon there was genuine hilarity along the table. Even Lord Hesket, who had previously been staring at The Fool with a most disapproving expression, managed to summon a smile.

If only the evening had ended on this note – but it didn't.

Mistaking our response as some sort of appreciation for his act, The Fool felt encouraged, even emboldened to continue. He jumped down from the dais and then retrieved his citole from his sack of tricks. Returning immediately with the instrument, he proceeded to stroll up and down the platform, performing a song that he claimed to have written that very afternoon.

> 'These castle walls are cold, 'tis true,
> They freeze with winter ice and snow,
> But a man can always warm his pole,
> Inside a tight and furry hole.'

At this last line The Fool returned his attentions to his braies, dropping one hand inside the folds of cloth and pretending to grasp his cock. He looked about for another laugh, but our amusement had turned to stunned silence. Unfortunately this cool reception did not discourage him from continuing. In fact, he seemed encouraged by the flinty reception to his song, for the second verse was even worse than the first.

'I know I'm not the only man,
Who longs for comfort from the cold,
I've heard the creeping feet at night,
Looking for a new delight.
If ever there was consolation,
To this frozen isolation,
It is found, in every guise,
Between a woman's warming thighs.'

The Fool had barely strummed the last note before Lady Emma let out an ear-piercing wail that rebounded about the room like the shrieks of a vixen. It was a shock to hear the child make any sort of noise, given her dogged silence all evening, but it now appeared that she was in possession of a fine pair of lungs. As she screamed, Lord Hesket grasped Emma to his chest and held onto her with a determination that spoke of experience. She rocked and repeatedly tried to kick her father, as Hesket's wife Lady Isobel quietly withdrew into the shadows with a look of jaundiced annoyance on her face. She was not about to offer her husband any help. The Fool's response to Emma's screaming was to drop his citole and then back away, nearly falling from the dais, as Robert of Lyndham launched a loaf of bread at his head.

'Get off,' shouted Lyndham. 'No one thinks you're funny.'

I approached the girl myself, wondering if she might be suffering from an attack of the Falling Sickness, but I could see immediately that this was a different malady. Emma was conscious, and at intervals she even paused to take a breath before she resumed her screaming. Hesket waved me away when I offered my assistance, holding onto his daughter until she kicked him so hard in the shins that he was forced to release her. Following this, she threw herself onto the floor and continued to convulse in a rage, banging her fists and then her head against the rushes of the floor.

We all stood about helplessly, until Sandro crept forward and gently took one of the girl's hands. At first she resisted his interference, but Sandro answered each rebuff by repeatedly grasping her hand, and then staring fixedly into her wild, frenzied eyes. Once the girl finally met his gaze, she suddenly focused. It was as if my valet had cleaned a pane of misted glass, and now she could see through. She blinked and then looked about, almost surprised to see our faces peering down at her. She took a final gasp, and scrambled to her feet – running to her father and burying her face in the folds of his long cloak.

Lord Hesket nodded a guarded thank-you to Sandro and then led his sobbing, exhausted daughter from the room. His wife trailed after him, managing to puff out a regretful sigh as her long skirts swept through the door. The rest of us soon followed, for there was no reason to stay in the Great Hall any longer that evening. The food had been bad. The conversation not much better, and the entertainment had been terrible.

We returned to our chambers, and as Mother and Filomena prepared for bed I tried to warm our freezing apartment by lighting a fire. As I cursed the damp wood, Filomena took me by the hand.

'Hugh has gone to sleep in your mother's bed,' she said softly. 'We are alone for once.' She kissed me on the cheek. 'Now come and spend some time with me, Oswald. I'll warm you up.'

I didn't need to be persuaded. But just as I had abandoned the fire and was beginning to undress, there was a knock at the door.

Filomena put her finger to her lips. 'Don't answer that,' she whispered. 'Come to bed.'

I stood perfectly still and waited – hoping that the knock would not come again. There was silence for a few moments, and it seemed that my visitor had given up, when the knocking returned. This time it was forceful and demanding, and I knew that this person would not go away.

'I'd better see who it is,' I said with a groan.

Filomena folded her arms. 'Why?'

'It might be important.'

I opened the door to find Alice Cross looking back at me from the darkness. Her lantern was casting a beam of light upon her cheeks, highlighting the abundance of freckles that had joined together to form ragged blotches of pigment. 'So you are in there, my Lord,' was her greeting.

'What do you want?' I said tersely. 'We're going to bed.'

She looked over my shoulder at Filomena, and then pulled a knowing, if slightly disgusted face. 'Lord Eden requests that you come to his library. He needs to speak to you immediately.'

'What about?'

'I've no idea,' she said.

'Can't it wait until the morning?'

'I only know that it's important,' she said. 'My master doesn't like to be kept waiting.'

Filomena stepped up to my shoulder and gave a curt and irritated cough to remind me of her presence, and suddenly I found myself caught between the wills of two women – unsure which one to obey. But this was Godfrey's castle, and we would be his guests for the next three months at least. I had no choice but to answer his summons.

Had I already undressed, then I would have stayed in bed and ignored Alice Cross. But such is our path through this life. Important turns balance and rock upon the frailest of pivots. By answering the door, I changed many things. Not least the ending of this story.

Chapter Five

A silvery moon illuminated the inner ward as I made my way to Godfrey's library. There was a sharpness and clarity to the light, so different to the leaden haze of rain and fog on the previous day – but then again the air was much colder, stabbing my face with its tiny, frozen daggers.

I hurried across the cobblestones, clasping my cloak about me as I headed towards the tower where Godfrey's library was located, opening the door to the stairwell, to find Lord Hesket coming in the opposite direction. He stormed past me, nearly knocking me aside, but offered no apology, nor even an acknowledgment. Instead he sped off across the inner ward with his cloak flaring behind him like a sail. He must have come from Godfrey's library, since there were no other rooms in this tower.

I proceeded to climb the stairs cautiously after this encounter, wary of meeting any other angry guests, but my path was clear. When I reached the second floor, I knocked at the door and entered to find Godfrey hunched over a book at his table. He gave an embarrassed smile when he saw my face and then quickly directed me towards the fire, where two stools were positioned next to the hearth. I sat down on one of these seats and drew my hood about my face, for the room was still bitterly cold, despite this fire. My breath was misting into the air like steam from a kettle.

Godfrey stowed something away in the chest next to his table and then poured two goblets of wine. 'Thank you for coming up to see me,' he said, offering one of the goblets to me.

'I saw Lord Hesket on the stairs,' I remarked, after I'd taken a long sip of the wine. It was Sweet Malmsey – spiced and warming. 'He seemed very angry.'

Godfrey took a seat on the stool beside me, and I noticed that his eyes were as red as his beard. 'Hesket has such a temper,' he replied. 'Sometimes it is difficult to reason with him.'

'What was he angry about?' When Godfrey tried to shrug away my question, I added, 'Was it The Fool's song? I suppose you've heard that it upset his daughter?'

Godfrey hesitated. 'Yes, Hesket told me about that,' he said wearily. 'Was it very crude?'

I smiled in an effort to make light of the subject, as Godfrey seemed so despondent. 'It was just The Fool's attempt to set a fabliau to music,' I said. 'Something about a man creeping about at night in search of a woman's bed.'

Godfrey groaned. 'Written about my brother Edwin, no doubt,' he said, before taking a long glug of the Malmsey. 'Perhaps I shouldn't have hired him.' He stared into the empty goblet. 'But then again, Robert of Lyndham did recommend this man to me. Apparently The Fool has worked for some of the most noble families in London.' He heaved a sigh. 'Mind you, Sir Robert didn't mention anything about vulgar songs.'

'Most jesters sing such songs these days,' I said. 'It's a fashion from France.'

'Do they?' said Godfrey with a shrug. 'I'm not very informed on such matters, I'm afraid.' He stood up to fill his goblet again from the jug. 'Still,' he said. 'At least The Fool brought along his own food. A rather generous amount, as it happens.' He looked up at me hopefully. 'And I'm told he can juggle.'

'Then we must make sure that he sticks to juggling, and discourage him from composing any more songs,' I said. 'Particularly ones about your brother.'

Godfrey raised his goblet to this. 'Agreed.'

'So,' I said purposefully, mindful of the warm bed that I'd left behind. 'What is it that you wanted to speak to me about Godfrey? I am rather tired.'

Godfrey returned to his seat and then prodded at the fire with a long iron poker. 'I was wondering what you thought about this plague, Oswald?' he said, without turning to look at me. 'I'd like to know your thoughts on its meaning.'

'Could this not have waited until the morning?' I said, unable to hide my irritation at this being the reason for my summons.

'I'm sure that you've given it some thought,' he replied calmly, refusing to acknowledge my reaction. 'You're an intelligent man.'

'I only know that it came from the East, over ten years ago,' I said with a sigh. 'And that it's never truly gone away.'

'And its meaning?'

'It has no meaning, Godfrey,' I snapped. 'It's a disease, like Leprosy or the King's Evil. It attacks the good and the bad with equal measure.'

He turned to gaze at my face. 'I'm not so sure,' he said, his eyes now gleaming in the firelight. 'I think that there's more to this infection than chance.'

'Plague is an unthinking monster. It has no will or skills of discrimination,' I said. 'Other than to find human life and destroy it.'

Godfrey sat forward at these words. 'Exactly, Oswald. But how does plague decide which human life to destroy? That's what interests me.'

'It just assaults the first person in its path,' I said. 'You know this yourself, Godfrey. It's why you've set up this fortress.'

'But—'

'You know that the only way to keep safe from the Plague is to keep out of its reach.'

Godfrey lifted his goblet from the floor, took another gulp of his wine and then wiped his lips. 'I understand your point,

Oswald,' he conceded. 'And it's true that I have gathered together a band of my friends and members of my own family to this castle. But we are still at God's mercy. The Plague will still kill those who deserve to die.'

'I don't agree, Godfrey. This disease has nothing to do with the punishment of sins. If you think—'

He held up his hand to silence me. 'Please, Oswald. Let me provide you with some evidence for my argument. I want you to consider where plague was most devastating at its last onslaught.'

I knew exactly where his line of reasoning was heading, for I had heard his opinions on this subject enough times before. 'It hit the monasteries the hardest,' I said wearily.

'Exactly. You grew up in a monastery, Oswald. You saw what happened for yourself at the last plague.'

'Yes. But the mortality was only so high because the monks lived in such close proximity to one another,' I replied. 'As soon as one brother caught the illness, then the others had no chance of escape.'

Godfrey shook his head. 'No, no. There has to be meaning to this, Oswald. Many abbeys lost nearly all of their monks.' The excitement in his eyes was turning into a feverish agitation. 'God was punishing the church, don't you see? He took the lives of so many priests and monks because of their many sins.' I drew back, as he was now spitting. 'Our Lord sees what is happening to our church. The cult of pilgrimage and the selling of relics and indulgences.' He balled his hand into a fist and waved it in the air. 'There is no mention of such trinkets and baubles in the bible.'

'That's true,' I replied calmly. 'But these trinkets, as you call them, are important to many people. They take comfort in buying an indulgence or visiting a shrine. I don't see the harm in it.'

'That's because they've been tricked,' he spat. 'By the church itself.' He leant forward and fixed me with fierce, impassioned eyes. 'Don't you see, Oswald? This is why God is so angry. The last plague was designed to warn the abbots and archbishops to reform. To put aside their worldly desires and ambitions, and look to the bible for the truth.'

'Yes. But——'

'I know that I'm right about this, Oswald,' he said. 'The church should have heeded this warning. But they did not. If anything, the deceivers and Pharisees have become emboldened since then. Now they are using another plague to turn God's house into a tawdry market. A place where they can prey on those poor souls who fear for their lives. Selling them worthless pieces of paper to offer protection against the Pestilence.' He grasped my arm. 'You know that I'm right, Oswald. We are at the End of Days. Soon His angels will come forth from Heaven and throw the wicked priests into the flaming furnace!'

I folded my hands on my lap, as there was no point in arguing further, but unfortunately Godfrey was not deterred by this. 'I have something that I want you to read,' he said, jumping to his feet and striding across to a bookshelf on the other side of the room, before returning with a small and well-worn manuscript. He pressed this booklet into my hands.

'What is it?' I asked, not recognising the title, *The Last Days of the Church*. It sounded like one of Godfrey's more turgid reads.

'It's written by John Wyclif,' he said. 'Read this, and I think you'll be equally moved.' Godfrey and I had discussed the author many times before. Wyclif was the Master of Balliol College in Oxford, where he had become the focus of a growing movement to reform the church. He was known as the 'Gospel Doctor' in some circles, due to his many sermons on the importance of reading the bible – a stance to which the church itself was generally unsympathetic. In fact, I knew of many clergymen who had never read a single verse of the bible in their whole lives, preferring the works of the theological philosophers such as Thomas Aquinas, Scotus and Peter Lombard, to the actual scriptures. Wyclif's teachings were seen as troublesome at best, and

heretical at worst, and it was only thanks to his friendship with
the Archbishop of Canterbury, that he remained tolerated at all.

'I'll certainly see what Wyclif has to say,' I answered, taking
the book from Godfrey.

'I know that you will appreciate Wyclif's words. I know that
we think alike.'

I looked into Godfrey's eyes and wondered if now was the
time to tell him the truth – that we would never think alike? We
had spent many hours together discussing religion, but Godfrey
had never really listened to my opinions. He was so consumed
with his own beliefs that he had always misconstrued my detach-
ment from God as a shared dissatisfaction with the church. But
then, how does a person openly admit to doubt in an age of faith?
How could I tell him that I had lost my belief in God, as a young
boy in a monastery, and that since those days, I had never recovered it.

'I'll give this back to you in a few days,' I said.

'There's no hurry,' he replied. 'I've read it many times. Now
it's time for me to act upon Wyclif's words.'

'Act? What do you mean?' I said nervously, remembering that
Godfrey had a history of acting on his conscience. I recalled the
occasion when he had threatened to kick over a stall selling
pilgrim's badges in Canterbury cathedral – just as Christ chased
the money changers from the temple of Jerusalem. I had talked
Godfrey out of this proposal on that occasion, but I doubted I
would win a similar argument again. If anything Godfrey had
become more zealous in recent months. His self-imposed seclusion from society had only served to fuel his radicalism.

Godfrey went to answer, but then appeared to change his
mind. 'Forgive me, Oswald,' he said. 'I didn't mean to alarm
you. It's just a turn of phrase, that's all. I only meant that I intend
to live my life according to Wyclif's principles.'

I wasn't sure whether to believe him or not, but equally I
didn't have the will to explore this conversation any further. He

had ruined a rare moment of privacy with my wife, so that he could lecture me on the meaning of the Plague, before presenting me with a manuscript that I didn't want to read. At that moment, I felt only resentment towards the man. 'Well, thank you for the book,' I said, rising to my feet. 'I'll say good night now.'

Godfrey jumped up from his seat. 'Don't go yet, Oswald,' he said. 'Please. There's another reason I wanted to speak to you.'

'Oh yes?' I groaned.

'Please. Sit down,' said Godfrey, looking at me with some censure. 'This is important.' He perched back on his own stool and ran his hands over his face. 'I need to tell you something.'

'What is it?'

He hesitated. 'I'm leaving the castle tomorrow.' Before I could ask another question, he quickly added, 'I will only be gone for a few hours. You must not worry.'

I thought back to Godfrey's mysterious remarks that night at the supper table, and couldn't help but repeat Hesket's warning. 'I thought we had all agreed to stay locked within the castle, Godfrey. So why are you putting yourself at risk by leaving?'

He hesitated again. 'I have no choice,' he said. 'I have to reach two people on the island. I have to bring them back here.'

'Who are they?'

Godfrey hesitated. 'You'll know soon enough,' he said.

'But what if you return with the Plague?' I said. 'Or what if these two other people are suffering from the affliction?'

'They don't have the Plague,' he said.

'But how can we be sure of that?'

'You'll just have to take my word for it,' he said adamantly. 'Just as I accepted your word this morning. When I asked you to be honest about the health of your own family.'

'But how will the others feel about this?' I argued. 'Especially Lord Hesket. You heard his thoughts on new guests at supper tonight.'

'This is my castle. They will all have to put up with it.'

'But they'll object as soon as you raise the portcullis,' I said. 'They might even try to stop you leaving.'

'Don't worry about that,' he said. 'I'll slip in and out of the castle without anybody noticing.'

'But Godfrey—'

He stood up sharply, his patience obviously stretched. 'Please, Oswald. Stop questioning me. I asked you here because I need your help. If you're refusing me, then you can leave.'

I looked up at him, wondering for a moment if I did want to help him. 'I'm sorry, Godfrey,' I said at length. 'What is it that you want me to do?'

He walked back towards his wooden chest and retrieved two folded squares of parchment from within. 'I need you to look after these two letters for me,' he said. 'You must deliver them, in the event that I don't return tomorrow.' He smiled briefly. 'After the Plague has abated, of course. I wouldn't expect you to deliver them until the spring.'

'Who are they for?'

He passed me the first letter. 'Take this one to the Archbishop of Canterbury. But only if it's still Simon Islip,' he added. 'I don't trust anybody else at Canterbury.'

'Very well.'

He passed me the second square of folded parchment. 'And this other letter must go to Father John Cubit, at Merton College in Oxford.'

'Ah, him,' I said with a huff.

Godfrey regarded me with surprise. 'Don't you like John?'

I'd met Cubit in London about a year ago, when the man had ruined a pleasant evening by haranguing the company on the subject of piety. 'I found him a little serious,' I told Godfrey, 'that's all.'

'But John is a dear friend of mine. You must get to know him better, Oswald. He thinks as we do.'

'And if Cubit hasn't survived?' I said quickly, not wanting to be drawn on the subject of our supposedly shared convictions.

'That will not happen,' said Godfrey with a firm shake of his head. 'John is the most devout of men. He openly speaks against the corruption of the church. Of all the people on the earth, God will not punish him.'

I stood up again to leave, but Godfrey put his hand on my shoulder. 'There's something else I should mention before you go,' he said, now with nervous hesitation in his voice. 'You must keep these letters secret, Oswald. Don't tell anybody else that you have them.'

'Why's that?'

He dropped his voice to a whisper, even though we were alone in a turret that was far away from anybody else in the castle. 'I suspect that somebody opens my correspondence,' he said. 'I've found the seals tampered with.'

'Do you know who it is?'

'I have an idea. But I won't trouble you with it now, as it's probably nothing worse than idle prying.' He paused. 'But keep these letters secret anyway, Oswald. I want them to reach their destinations without being opened.'

I bowed my head to him. 'Good night, Godfrey,' I said. 'And take care tomorrow. Wherever it is that you're going.'

'Good night to you, Oswald,' he said. 'And thank you. My dear, trusted friend.'

I opened and shut the heavy door without looking back, before heading down the steps at speed, holding a lantern in one hand and Godfrey's two letters in the other. Luckily I had succeeded in leaving the library without Wyclif's manuscript, and Godfrey did not chase after me with his gift.

As I reached the bottom of the stairs and emerged into the intense cold of the night, I met another person, creeping along the periphery of the inner ward, with his hand leaning against the wall. At first I was startled by this small, skulking figure, but when I lifted my lantern, I discovered that it was only Godfrey's younger brother, Edwin of Eden. He was dazed by my light and lifted his hands to cover his eyes.

'Ah, de Lacy,' he said, wiping a hand across his greasy face. 'Have you been summoned to the library of my dear brother as well, then?' He lifted a wobbling arm into the air and then pointed at the two letters I was holding. 'I see that Godfrey's given you some lists?' He screwed up his eyes and then released them, as he attempted to focus on my face. It was obvious that he was extremely drunk. 'Godfrey loves lists, you know.' He laughed. 'It makes him feel important.'

'These documents are my own,' I said quickly, remembering the promise I had made, only moments before, to keep these letters secret.

Edwin tapped his nose mockingly. 'Ah yes. Whatever you say, de Lacy. Whatever you say.' He then swayed forward and grabbed my arm to steady himself. 'Godfrey will have chores for me, you know,' he said, breathing beery fumes up into my face. 'Did he tell you what they were?'

'No, he didn't.'

He grasped me more tightly. 'He probably wants me to muck out the stables, or sweep out the hall.' He then belched – onions and beer. 'That's what he thinks of me, de Lacy. His own brother. I won't be surprised if I'm told to empty the chamber pots next.'

'Good night to you, Edwin,' I said.

'Where are you going, de Lacy?' he said. 'Come back.'

'Good night,' I repeated.

I walked away, but he called out to me. 'May it be a good night for you,' he shouted. 'In the arms of that mouth-watering little Venetian of yours.'

I stopped dead and then stalked back to him, pointing a finger into his face. 'Don't speak that way about Filomena.'

He laughed. 'I was paying you a compliment, de Lacy. Your wife is a thing of beauty.' He prodded my chest and repeated the words with a lascivious lick of his lips. 'A thing of beauty.'

I grasped hold of his finger and pushed him away. 'Stay away from my wife, do you hear me?'

He only laughed at this threat, before he fell against the wall again. His eyes were now closed as he slipped down onto the cobblestones, and suddenly I had the urge to kick him. I walked away quickly, heading for the stairs to our apartment, before I gave in to this impulse. But I could not escape Edwin of Eden quite so easily. As I climbed the steep staircase towards our door, I could hear his wild, drunken laughter echoing about the inner ward. It was a strange, unnerving sound – shrill and repetitive, like the jeering yaffle of a woodpecker.

I closed the door on him – pleased to finally be returning to Filomena and our warm bed. I threw off my cloak and then crawled between the sheets beside my wife, forgetting all about Godfrey and his unpleasant younger brother, until I realised there was somebody else in the bed with us. It was Hugh – his small body curled up like a cat in the space between us. I couldn't help but laugh at this final defeat, at the end of this trying day. My son had impeccable timing. It was no wonder that Filomena and I were yet to conceive a child.

Chapter Six

I woke early the next morning to find that Filomena and Hugh were still sleeping. Weak shafts of daylight were creeping through the draughty window, and the air was thick with silence – that wonderful stillness that only exists in the hour before a castle fully awakens. I turned to gaze at Filomena for a while. She looked so beautiful when she was asleep, her olive skin dark against the pale sheets. I then listened to her breathing – gloriously content in my moment of peace.

It was then that I remembered my conversation with Godfrey from the night before, and my contentment evaporated. Had my friend already left the castle on his secretive mission? If so, he must have been very quiet, since I hadn't yet heard the clanking chains of the portcullis being raised. The more I thought about it, the more convinced I became that Godfrey was still within these walls – though this was not a soothing conclusion. Godfrey never gave up on an idea easily, so he must have decided to leave later in the morning, which hardly seemed like a good idea. If he had been planning to slip out of the castle without being noticed, as had been his assertion to me the night before, then surely it would have been wiser to leave before the others were awake?

I rose from bed without disturbing Hugh and Filomena, left our apartment and then went to look for Alice Cross, finding her at the other end of the inner ward, where she was limply throwing down handfuls of grain for the chickens.

'Have you seen your master this morning?' I asked her.

She looked up from her reverie, almost shocked to see my face. 'No, my Lord,' she said. 'I haven't.'

'Is he out of bed yet?'

She gave a shrug. 'I expect so. My master likes to be up at first light.'

I paused for a moment. 'I wondered,' I said, trying to sound nonchalant. 'Was the portcullis raised overnight?'

She furrowed her brow, clearly baffled by my question. 'No, my Lord. Of course not.'

'Are you sure about that?'

'Why would anybody want to raise the portcullis?' she said with a huff, before returning her attention to the chickens. 'Everybody knows that there's plague out there.'

Godfrey's promise to slip in and out of the castle came to mind once more. 'Is there another way out of here?' I asked, once again trying to sound as if this were the most normal of questions.

'What do you mean, my Lord?' she said, now screwing up her eyes and looking at me as if I were mad.

'I don't know,' I said. 'Is there a tunnel somewhere? Or maybe a secret doorway?'

'No, my Lord,' she said firmly. 'There's nothing like that. Why do you ask?'

'It doesn't matter,' I said. 'It was just an idea.'

I wandered back to our apartment feeling bad-tempered – not only because of this conversation, but also in anticipation of the bitter argument that was sure to transpire later that morning, when Godfrey tried to leave the castle in front of the other guests – particularly Lord Hesket. Godfrey would expect me to take his side in such a confrontation, and this was not a prospect that I relished.

I helped Filomena to dress my mother and Hugh, before we made our way outside for our morning exercise. With so little outdoor space within the confines of the castle, we needed to make the most of this stingy square of cobblestones. Gathered alongside Lord and Lady Hesket, Robert of Lyndham and Old Simon, we squeezed together at one end of the inner ward, vying for the few shards of low sun that made it over the high walls at this time of year. Suddenly I felt like a chicken, enclosed in a coop, constricted, even suffocated – overwhelmed again by an urge to escape. I took a few deep breaths and let the feeling pass, distracting myself by making conversation with the others. When I discovered, after making a few gentle enquiries, that nobody else here had seen Godfrey that morning, I decided it was time to search for him again.

I started in the obvious place, climbing the stairs to Godfrey's library, wondering, with each step, why he was leaving his departure so late in the morning. When my knocks went unanswered, I tried the door, and found to my surprise, that it was unlocked. As the heavy door slid open inward, I then expected to find Godfrey at his work, since this room was only left unlocked when Godfrey was inside, but instead the place was completely empty. A little mystified by this, I then made my way to his bedchamber, knocked and entered to find that this room was empty as well.

By now I was becoming concerned rather than puzzled by my friend's disappearance, so I searched out Alice Cross once again. This time I found her in the kitchen, where she was pummelling a boulder of dough with her strong, capable arms. Behind her, the firewood was already blazing inside the blackened dome of the bread oven. I was surprised to see another person in the kitchen. It was Lady Emma, standing beside the bread oven and staring at the flames with fascination. Her cheeks reddened by the heat.

'I haven't been able to find Lord Eden yet,' I told our steward. 'I've looked in his library and bedchamber, but he's nowhere to be seen.' Alice Cross went to answer, but I carried on. 'He can't have left the castle, because the portcullis hasn't been raised. So, unless you know of some other way out?' I paused, waiting to see how she would answer this.

She lifted her hand from the dough and wiped some of the floury residue across her face. 'No, my Lord,' she said wearily. 'I told you that before. I've lived here all of my life. If there were any secret tunnels in this castle, then I would know about them.'

'Then you need to come with me and look for him.'

'But I'm baking, my Lord,' she said, before she waved her arm disparagingly towards Emma. 'And looking after this child.'

'Never mind that. We need to find Lord Eden.'

'But I can't leave Lady Emma in here alone,' she protested. 'The foolish girl tries to pick up the embers in the bread oven. I have to watch her like a hawk.'

'Then I'll take her back to her father,' I said. 'But please, Mistress Cross. We need to hurry up.'

I sent our truculent steward to the cellars, whilst I led Lady Emma back to the inner ward to join her father and stepmother, before then climbing the stairs to the parapet walk at the top of the curtain wall. I had the idea that Godfrey might have decided to spend the morning admiring the view from these elevated paths, but the walkways were empty.

For a moment, I stopped to look out across the marsh myself. The grey clouds were low and ominous, painting a gauzy murk across the far horizon. Rather than lift my spirits, this sight only served to increase the sense of dread that was settling in my stomach. I turned my back and went to descend the steps again, when I met Alice Cross coming up in the other direction. Her face was bright red as she struggled to breathe.

'Lord Somershill,' she panted. 'You must come quickly.'

'What's the matter?' I said.

'Lord Eden's been found.'

'Where?'

Alice Cross leant against the wall to catch her breath. 'The poor master is dead,' she said. 'The clockmakers found him in their wooden chest.'

'What?'

'The master is dead, my Lord,' she repeated, now struggling to speak between each gasp. 'I've seen him with my own two eyes. His body's been left in a box. In one of the cellars.'

I tried to ask more, but Alice Cross had fallen to her knees, overcome with shock. I left her for a few short moments until her colour returned, and then helped her to stand up and take me to Godfrey – though she would not accompany me into the cellar itself, claiming that she could not bear to look at her master's dead body again.

I entered the dark room alone, finding de Groot and his nephew Hans standing in one corner, holding their lantern over an ornately carved chest. This was the long box that the clockmakers had used to bring all the parts for their astronomical clock from Delft, and yet now it held the corpse of a man. Even from the door, I could see that it was Godfrey inside the chest. His reddish-brown hair was poking over the sides like the curling tips of dried bracken.

I walked across the room and pushed past the two Dutchmen to look inside the chest, but I'm ashamed to say that the oddest thought came to mind when I first saw Godfrey's body. I found myself wondering if this was some sort of joke, orchestrated by The Fool. That Godfrey was only pretending to be dead, in order to play a stupid trick on me. I prodded him sharply, but Godfrey did not wake up and laugh. Instead he remained perfectly, profoundly still, and my notion that this had been a joke soon dissipated. My friend was dead. Murdered – for his sunken face was smothered with blood. For a moment I turned my eyes away, for I could not bear to look at him. It was only hours since we'd been discussing the Plague and its causes – and yet now Godfrey was lying in front of me, as an immobile, inanimate corpse. No more capable of debate than the wooden slats that surrounded him.

I wiped my face and tried to ignore my churning stomach. 'Who found the body?' I asked, turning to de Groot.

'It was Hans,' he told me. 'The poor boy came into this room to pack away some tools into our chest. He opened the lid of the box and found this.' The clockmaker waved a hand over Godfrey's dead body and then shook his head. 'Poor Hans,' he sighed.

I turned to 'poor' Hans. 'Is this true?' I asked. The young Dutchman didn't answer. Instead he stared back at me with a blank, inscrutable expression on his face. 'You don't speak English, do you?' I said, realising that I was yet to hold a conversation with this boy.

'Of course my nephew speaks English,' said de Groot. 'He's been properly educated.'

'Then why doesn't he answer my question?' I said.

'Because he's distressed, my Lord. The poor boy has never seen a dead body before. It's very upsetting for him.'

I looked at Hans, who was now peering back into the chest with such prurient interest, that it seemed to me that he was fascinated, rather than upset by Godfrey's corpse. When he poked his spidery fingers into Godfrey's bloodied hair and then lifted them to his nose, I grasped hold of his tunic and pulled him away.

'Stop doing that,' I told him.

Hans looked at me for a moment – his expression still blank, until a smirk curled across his crimson lips.

'Just get out of here,' I said. When he hesitated, I shouted. 'Get out! Come on. Both of you.'

I steered the pair towards the door, though they were reluctant to leave – especially de Groot, who argued that he should be allowed to remove Godfrey from his valuable chest as soon as possible, before the foul fluids of his death started to stain the casing. I closed the door on de Groot's noisy protests and then contemplated leaving myself. This was a tempting idea, but on the other hand, I wanted to take a proper look at Godfrey's body before this cellar became full of onlookers and grievers. I wanted to understand what had happened to him.

And so, with some hesitancy, I returned to the wooden chest in the corner, feeling a tear form in the corner of my eye as I looked down at my friend's bloodied face. Godfrey had been a man with energy, hopes and ambitions – all of which had been snuffed out by this act of violence. And for what reason? Why would anybody have wanted to kill a man such as Godfrey? It didn't make sense.

I wiped away the tear and looked again, now realising that his body had not been dumped randomly into this chest. Quite the opposite. In fact, it seemed to me that Godfrey's corpse had been arranged into a pose, with his cloak wrapped about his body, as if the murderer had tucked him into bed. The result was a grotesque tableau. A dead man put to sleep inside a wooden box. Godfrey was not a large man, but nevertheless this improvised bed could not accommodate his slight frame. His legs were bent at the knees and his head was squashed up against one end of the box, so that his chin was resting on his chest. It looked as if he might open his eyes at any moment and start reading an imaginary book that was resting against his knees.

I took another deep breath, and then leant in more closely, wanting to look at the wound on Godfrey's temple. It was a wide but shallow gash, surrounded by swollen and bruised skin, and was probably the cause of his death. But just to be certain, I quickly ran my hand beneath the cloth of his tunic, to find out whether I could feel any other obvious injuries. I found nothing but cold, hard flesh that was unyielding to the touch – suggesting to me that Godfrey had been dead a few hours already.

As the first stale eddies of his death reached my nose, I was suddenly reminded of my childhood in the monastery, where it had been my duty to prepare the dead of our brotherhood for burial. I had washed, dressed and then laid out their bodies in a coffin, so I had a familiarity with the dead – an understanding of how the body changes in those first few hours after life is extinguished. I had never felt saddened by this work, because most of these dead men had been elderly monks, with whom I'd had little contact. But I was sad about Godfrey. And guilty. I had been rude to my friend at our last meeting – angry and churlish about being summoned to his library. I had deliberately left behind the book that he'd tried to lend me, and I'd only agreed to take his letters on sufferance. We had been more than acquaintances, but at that moment, I felt that my own part in our friendship had fallen short.

I was covering Godfrey's face with his cloak when the first of the visitors arrived. It was Godfrey's younger brother, Edwin of Eden, who sprinted into the room dressed in a dirty nightshirt, even though it was nearly noon. He smelt as badly of beer and onions as he had done the previous night, when we had bumped into one another in the darkness of the inner ward.

'I've only just heard,' he said breathlessly, running his hands through his greasy hair. 'Where's Godfrey?'

'In the chest,' I said, pointing to the box.

He gulped. 'Are you sure?'

'Would you like to see him?' I asked.

Edwin held up his short arms in alarm. 'Good God, no thank you, de Lacy. I can't stand the sight of dead bodies.'

'Godfrey was murdered,' I said. 'Did they tell you?'

'Yes,' he said, suddenly leaning one hand against the wall, as if he were about to faint. His head dropped and a bead of spittle fell from his lips. I thought he was about to vomit, until he stood upright again and took a deep breath. 'Why would anybody want to kill my brother?' he asked. 'I know Godfrey could be an annoying bastard, but this . . .' He nodded his head towards the clockmakers' chest. 'Why would they put his body in there?'

I went to answer, when he fell against the wall again, now holding both hands to his mouth, as his cheeks puffed in and out like a pair of bag bellows. It was only moments before he noisily heaved the contents of his stomach onto the floor. As I had suspected, it seemed he had been consuming beer and onions.

When Edwin had nothing left to bring up, I put my hand on his shoulder. 'Come on,' I said, trying my best to sound sympathetic. 'You need to clean yourself up and speak to everybody.'

'Me?' he said with some surprise. 'Why?'

'Because they'll expect to hear from you, Edwin. You're Lord Eden now. The head of this castle.' His jaw dropped for a moment, and I had the impression that this sudden rise in status had not yet occurred to him. He then ran his thumb and forefinger around the edge of his mouth, removing the last traces of vomit from his lips.

'By the saints,' he said slowly. 'You're right, de Lacy.' But this realisation didn't appear to please him. Instead he lunged forward and grasped my arm. 'Oh God,' he groaned. 'I don't know what to do.'

I took his hand and gently removed it from my sleeve. 'You need to gather the guests together,' I told him. 'Tell them what's happened to Godfrey, and then reassure them that you're searching for his killer.'

I had hoped that this advice might help, but Edwin only lost more colour. 'Searching for Godfrey's killer?' he said. 'But how on earth am I supposed to do that? I'm not the constable or the sheriff.'

'But you've got to do something,' I said, finding that my sympathy was beginning to wane. 'Your brother was murdered, Edwin. Inside his own castle.'

He looked back at me with fearful, pathetic eyes, and suddenly I felt sorry for him again, for I knew the weight of expectation that lands upon a man when he unexpectedly becomes a lord. Eleven years previously I had also been required to solve a

murder on my estate almost immediately after inheriting my
new title, so it occurred to me to offer my help to Edwin. It was
clear that he was floundering, and after all, I did have experience
in looking for murderers, on many occasions.

And yet . . .

And yet, I also knew the risks of such an undertaking, for I had
nearly lost my life during my last investigation in Venice. This
time it was not my fight, it was Edwin's – or so I reasoned at that
moment. But then I changed my mind again, as I looked at his
pale, trembling face. I could not trust this shambling man to find
Godfrey's killer – not least because we needed to act quickly.
The murderer was among us. A person who might be planning
to strike again, for all we knew. And then, another thought
occurred to me. This time it was one of guilt and regret, as I
realised the true extent of my mistake in coming to this place.
My plan to keep my family safe had produced the very opposite
result. I had locked them away from the Plague, only to lock
them inside this castle with a killer.

I cleared my throat and stirred myself to say the next words.
'Why don't you let me help you with this investigation, Edwin.'

He looked at me askance, his upper lip arched. 'You?'

'Yes. I've found killers before,' I said. 'I have the experience
you'll need.'

He continued to regard me with puzzlement, until a smile
slowly replaced the look of consternation. 'Oh yes,' he said, the
colour coming back to his cheeks. 'I remember now. Godfrey
told me about this. You were some sort of hero in Venice, weren't
you?'

'I wouldn't put it that way.'

'Oh, don't be modest, de Lacy,' he said. 'You found a murderer
and uncovered a ring of spies. Sounds fairly heroic to me.' He
licked his lips. 'In fact, I heard that the doge was so pleased with
you, that the lovely Filomena was your reward.'

'No,' I said sharply. 'That is not how I met my wife.'

'All right, all right,' he said, backing away and holding up his hands in surrender. 'I'm sorry. I didn't mean to offend you, de Lacy.' He bowed his head and resumed his cringing, pathetic pose. 'Did you mean it about helping me?' he said. 'Was it a genuine offer?' I nodded in response, prompting him to slap me on the back, as if we'd just agreed to ride to London together. 'Good man,' he said. 'I'll go and speak to the others now. I'll tell them that you're looking for the murderer.'

'No, Edwin,' I said. 'Tell them that I'm assisting you. That's all.'

He waved his hand at me, as he stumbled out of the cellar. 'Of course, de Lacy,' he muttered. 'Whatever you say.'

Chapter Seven

I returned to our apartment to face Filomena and my mother, knowing that they would be desperate to hear more news of the murder. They pretended to be warming themselves by the fire when I opened the door, but it was obvious they had been lying in wait.

'Is it true?' asked Filomena, even before I had untied the clasp of my cloak. 'Has Godfrey been killed?'

'Yes,' I said. 'I'm afraid it is.'

She crossed herself. 'And is it also true that his body was left in the clockmakers' chest?'

I nodded. 'Yes.'

'Poor man,' said Filomena, as she flopped down upon the bed, giving Mother the opportunity to launch into a well-prepared speech.

'I told you there was death in this place, didn't I, Oswald?' she said, wagging a bony finger at me. 'I said it was a bad decision to come here. We should return to Somershill immediately. Before somebody else is killed.'

'We can't leave, Mother,' I said. 'You know that. We're surrounded by plague.'

'I'll take my chances, thank you very much,' she blustered.

'Well, that's up to you,' I answered. 'But you'll be going home on your own, as the rest of us are staying here.'

Filomena looked up again. 'But perhaps your mother is right, Oswald,' she said. 'I don't want to stay here either. There's a murderer in this castle.'

Mother gave a surprised smile that soon turned into a gloat. It was not often that my wife agreed with anything she had to say.

'Please don't worry,' I told them both, hoping to sound confident. 'There's no reason to think that anybody else is in danger. Especially as we're going to start looking for the murderer straight away.'

Filomena stiffened. 'What do you mean by that?' she snapped.

I hesitated. 'I've offered to help Edwin with the investigation,' I said.

'Why?'

'You know why, Filomena,' I replied. 'Edwin is a fool. I couldn't trust him to find a killer on his own.'

'Let Edwin take care of this himself. It is his castle.'

'I can't do that,' I answered. 'It's too dangerous.'

She gave a huff. 'I see,' she said. 'So you *do* think this person will kill again.'

'I'm not saying that,' I protested, as Mother interrupted our argument.

'Goodness me,' she exclaimed, pointing down into the inner ward. 'Come and look at this, Oswald. Edwin of Eden is addressing a crowd from a stool.'

I joined Mother at the window, peering down to see Edwin below, surrounded by the other guests. He cut a strange figure, as he had thrown a very long cloak over his nightshirt. It was a garment that covered his feet and created the illusion that Edwin was floating above the cobblestones. I wondered if this cloak had belonged to Godfrey, because it certainly hadn't been made for Edwin's frame. Godfrey may have been short in stature, but Edwin was barely taller than Sandro. I couldn't hear what our new lord was saying from our window, but I could see that he was being harangued by Lord Hesket, Old Simon and the knight, Robert of Lyndham. The three men were launching questions and hardly giving him the opportunity to answer.

'Just look at that fool,' said Mother. 'Waving his arms about on that stool. Who does he think he is?'

'He's Lord Eden now,' I replied.

She gasped. 'Goodness me, Oswald,' she said. 'I hadn't thought of that.' She continued to peer down. 'Well, I wonder what he's saying to them all?'

'Why don't you go and listen?' I suggested. 'Sandro can help you down the stairs.'

'No, no,' she said. 'I'd rather stay here with you and Filomena.'

'Very well then,' I said, knowing better than to insist. 'Edwin isn't telling them anything that you haven't heard from me.'

We continued to watch for a while longer as Old Simon staggered towards a door, with the aid of Alice Cross. Behind him, the argument continued to rage between Hesket and Edwin, culminating in Hesket attempting to push our new lord from his makeshift podium on the stool. The excitement was now of the highest quality and far too good for Mother to miss.

'I think I will go down after all,' she said blithely. 'A dash of fresh air might do me some good.'

'Do you think you should?' I asked, a little mischievously. 'It does look very boisterous down there.'

'A woman of my age must take her daily exercise, Oswald. I will not be talked out of it.' She looked over her shoulder. 'Now where is that small Venetian?' she said. 'Sandro, Sandro.' She called out his name until my valet ran into the room, trailed by Hugh, who was beating the floor with a long stick – blissfully ignorant of the drama that was unfolding about us.

When Mother, Sandro and Hugh had departed for the inner ward, I went immediately to my strongbox, with the intention of retrieving the two letters that Godfrey had given me the previous night.

Filomena watched me with suspicious eyes. 'What are you doing, Oswald?' she asked, as I turned the key in the lock, and then delved into the coffer that contained all of our most valuable possessions.

I lifted the two letters aloft. 'Godfrey gave me these last night,' I said. 'For safekeeping.'

Filomena paused for a moment, and I could see that she had not fully forgiven me for our last disagreement, but curiosity got the better of her in the end. 'Why was that?' she asked me.

It was my turn to hesitate. My wife was no delicate flower, apt to wilt at the first chill – but was it a good idea to involve her in this investigation? 'Come and sit with me,' I said, once I had made my decision. 'Then I'll explain.'

She didn't move. 'Do those letters have something to do with Godfrey's murder?' she asked.

'I don't know,' I replied honestly. 'They could have.'

I had piqued her interest at least. 'Why did Godfrey give them to you?' she asked, as she slowly walked across the room to join me by the fire.

'He wanted me to deliver these letters in the event of his death,' I said.

She sat down and then drew her stool close to mine. 'The event of his death?' she repeated, wrinkling her nose. 'Did he think his life was in danger, then?'

'Yes,' I said. 'Though the death he feared was from the Plague, not murder.' I hesitated again. 'Even so. These letters might tell us something. So we need to read them.'

She laid a hand on my arm. 'Are you sure about that, Oswald?' she said. 'Remember, if you open those letters, then you are caught in this tangle. You cannot escape.'

'It's too late,' I said. 'I'm already trapped, whether I like it or not.'

'Why's that?'

'Because Godfrey told me a secret last night,' I said.

'Oh yes?'

'He told me that he was planning to leave the castle today and bring two people back with him.'

'Who?'

'He wouldn't say,' I replied.

She withdrew her hand from my arm and laid it gently over the other in her lap. 'You're right, Oswald,' she said solemnly, 'we should read them now.'

I broke the seal on the first letter, unfolded the parchment and then read the contents aloud. The first one was addressed to the priest, John Cubit, in Oxford.

'My dearest John. I have asked Lord Somershill to deliver this letter to you in the circumstances of my death. You must know that I have never swerved from our path. To the end, I have laboured tirelessly upon our shared vision, knowing this to be the way of righteousness. I have taken the greatest pains to hide our work from prying eyes, but you will know where to find it. May God go with you. Your true friend, Godfrey, Lord Eden.'

Filomena frowned. 'Shared vision?' she said. 'What does that mean, Oswald?'

'I don't know,' I said.

'And who is this John Cubit?' she asked, pointing to his name on the letter. She was learning to read English and liked to show me that she was making progress.'

'He's a priest,' I said. 'A radical.' She pulled another face in response, and I knew that this word had confused her. 'Cubit wants the church to change,' I said. 'There is a group of such men in Oxford. Led by a man named John Wyclif.'

'Was Godfrey part of this group?' she asked.

'Yes, I think he was,' I said. 'At least, he tried to foist a book by Wyclif onto me last night.'

'What was it about?'

'I don't know,' I admitted. 'I deliberately left it behind.' When she arched an eyebrow, I added, 'I didn't want to read this book, Filomena. I'm not interested in Wyclif's dangerous beliefs.'

'Dangerous?'

'Wyclif's not popular with the church,' I said. 'But he's able to speak his mind because he's protected by a powerful friend.'

'Who's that?'

'It's the Archbishop of Canterbury, Simon Islip,' I said. 'They were once fellow students at Oxford. But Islip's protection cannot last forever. As soon as Islip is dead, the church will decide that Wyclif is a heretic.' I paused. 'And we all know what happens to heretics in the end.'

She crossed herself. 'This work that Godfrey has hidden from prying eyes?' She dropped her voice to a whisper. 'Do you think it's heresy?'

'Probably,' I said.

She paused. 'But we don't know where it's hidden?'

'That's right.'

'And we don't know what it is.' Filomena drummed her fingers upon her knees for a moment. 'We should open the second letter, Oswald. It might tell us more.'

'Yes,' I said. 'Especially as this one is addressed to Islip.'

I tore at the seal and unfolded the second square of parchment, and then began to quickly scan the words. 'Godfrey begins with best wishes to the archbishop's household,' I told her. 'And then . . .' I let my finger run along the words. 'God's bones, listen to this.'

'What is it?' she said.

I read the letter aloud.

'I am writing to request your assistance. Calling upon our history of friendship and common interest. I know you to be a man of the greatest honour. A person whom I can trust without fail.'

I paused for a moment, almost unable to speak the words of the next sentence.

'What is it?' said Filomena urgently. 'Please, Oswald. Read the letter to me.'

I turned my eyes back to the words.

'I wish to inform you that I have married a local woman in the past year, but have yet to announce this union to my family. Her name is Abigail Franklin, and though she is not born of nobility, she is a God-fearing woman from a good family. I have decided to keep my marriage a secret from my own family thus far, but please do not doubt that Abigail is my true wife. We were married by the priest John Cubit, according to God's law.'

Filomena stood up. 'Did you know about this marriage, Oswald?' she asked.

I shook my head. 'No. Of course not. Or I would have told you about it before. But listen. There's more.

'In the month of August in this year of 1361, my wife gave birth to our first son, a boy named Simon. I beg of you to acknowledge Simon as the rightful heir to Eden, as my younger brother Edwin will oppose Simon's claim to the estate. I ask you, as my friend and previous bene-factor, to both recognise and protect Simon's position. At my death, it is my son, and not my brother, who becomes the true lord of this estate.'

I folded the letter again and paused for a moment. 'This makes sense now, Filomena,' I said. 'The two people Godfrey intended to bring back to the castle must have been his own wife and son. No wonder he was behaving so secretively.'

'Are you sure that nobody else knew about them?' she said.

'You mean Edwin?'

She nodded. 'Yes. I do mean Edwin. Didn't you tell me that he was also called to Godfrey's library last night? Perhaps Godfrey told Edwin the truth, before he brought two new members of the family into the castle? It might have made Edwin very angry.'

'Are you suggesting that Edwin killed Godfrey?' I said.

She paused. 'Well, it's possible, isn't it?'

'Yes. It is,' I said, standing up and reaching for my cloak. 'I'll go and speak to him now.' I poked Godfrey's letter to Simon Islip under my belt, and then patted it. 'I'll ask him what he knows about this.'

I put on my cloak and reached the door, when she called after me. 'Be careful, Oswald,' she said. 'I don't like that man.'

I found Edwin lying on his bed, with the long cloak now draped across his head. He didn't stir when I entered the room, so I nudged him gently at first and then with more urgency. 'Edwin,' I said. 'Wake up. I need to speak to you.'

He groaned and turned away from me. 'Go away, de Lacy,' he said. 'I did as you asked. I spoke to the household, and was pushed over for my troubles.'

I pulled the cloak back, exposing his face to daylight. 'I said, get up. I need to speak to you.'

'What's the matter with you?' he squealed as he jumped up from the bed to avoid a shaft of light. 'I told you to leave me alone. So off you go!' When I didn't move, he added, 'You have to do what I say now, de Lacy. I own this castle. I'm Lord Eden.'

I ignored this remark and pressed on with my questions. 'Did you know that Godfrey was planning to leave the castle today?' I said.

Edwin squinted at me. 'What?'

'Is that why Godfrey called you to his library last night?'

Edwin continued to stare, his mouth hung open like a fish gulping for air. 'Uh?'

'For goodness' sake, Edwin,' I said, 'just listen to me. Did Godfrey tell you that he was planning to leave the castle today? Yes or no.'

'No.'

'So why did Godfrey want to see you last night?'

Edwin let out a long groan. 'Oh God, I don't know,' he said, pushing the hair out of his eyes. 'It was just the usual stuff,' he said. 'Stop getting drunk. Leave the maids alone.'

'He didn't tell you that he was married and had a child?'

Edwin drew back. 'Godfrey was married with a child?' he repeated. 'Says who?'

I pulled the letter from my belt. 'It's in here,' I said. 'Written by Godfrey himself.'

He let his mouth hang open again, before he shook his head and rubbed his eyes. 'Where did you find that?' he said.

'Godfrey gave it to me last night. For safekeeping.'

'Let me see it,' he said, trying to snatch the square of parchment from my grasp. I pulled the letter away quickly, until he held out his hand politely. 'Look, de Lacy,' he said. 'You can't say that you have a letter like that and then not show me. If I can't read it, then I won't believe you.'

I hesitated, because he was right. Edwin needed to see this letter, if only to acknowledge its existence. I passed the folded square of parchment to him with some reluctance, but made sure to stay close in case he made an attempt to destroy it. After all, its contents were hardly in his interests.

Edwin ran his fingers along the writing, mumbling the words aloud as if he were a child learning to read. He went through this same process three times in a row before he flung the letter back to me in disgust.

'So you knew nothing about this woman and child?' I asked him.

Edwin sank down upon the side of his bed. 'What is this, de Lacy? An interrogation?'

'I just need you to be honest with me,' I said.

'I am being honest with you,' he protested. 'I knew nothing about this Abigail Franklin and her child. Or Godfrey's plan to leave the castle.' He ran his fingers through his hair, forming valleys across his scalp. 'I'd like you to leave now, please,' he said. 'My brother has been murdered and I'm grieving.'

I ignored this instruction and made my way to a table on the other side of the room, where I filled two cups from a jug of Malmsey wine. 'This news about Godfrey's son must be a shock for you,' I said, returning to Edwin's side, and passing him one of the cups.

'I'll get over it,' he replied, as he took the wine from me. 'Now, as I keep saying, I'd like you to leave.'

I sidled up to him instead — even though he smelt very stale at this close proximity.

'You have to obey me,' he said. 'This is my castle.'

'Do I?' I replied. 'You see, now we know that Godfrey has a son, it turns out that you're not Lord Eden after all.'

He bristled. 'Not necessarily,' he said.

I tapped the letter that was once again tucked beneath my belt. 'Well, that's what this says, Edwin. And Godfrey gave it to me himself, so we know it's genuine.'

Edwin stood up to get away from me. 'Well, let's see if this boy survives the Plague, shall we? Then we can argue about who is the rightful Lord Eden.' He stalked over to the door and opened it. 'Now please leave.'

'Aren't you concerned about Godfrey's wife and son?' I said.

'No,' he answered, letting go of the door for a moment. 'Why should I be?'

'Because this child is your nephew, after all. And the rightful Lord Eden. He's somewhere on the island, at risk from the Plague. Don't you think that you should bring this boy and his mother to the castle? It's what Godfrey was planning to do.'

'No. Of course I don't, de Lacy,' he said. 'I'm not going out there.' He then paused, allowing time for a smile to cross his face. 'But if you're volunteering to leave the castle to find this woman and her son, then I wouldn't stand in your way. In fact, you would have my blessing for such a selfless and noble act.'

We stared at each other for a while, both knowing that I would not make such an offer – not for the sake of a woman and child I'd never met. I might have looked down my nose at Edwin of Eden, but we were not so very different at heart. We were both ruthless and self-centred, when it came to the people that we loved most. The difference was that my love was for my family, whereas he only cared for himself. But did this quality make Edwin a murderer, as Filomena had suggested? I didn't think so. I had investigated other murders and learnt to trust my instincts. My instincts told me that Edwin was too stupid to be guilty.

'What are you going to do with that letter?' he asked, before looking away, unable to meet my gaze when he made the next suggestion. 'Perhaps I should have it, for safekeeping?'

'I don't think so,' I said, almost wanting to laugh out loud at this preposterous idea.

'Are you going to tell everybody what it says, then?' he asked me.

I hesitated. 'No, Edwin,' I replied. 'I'll let you do that yourself.' I paused. 'But please do not doubt me. If you have not said anything about Godfrey's son by the time we are ready to leave in the spring, then I will tell them all myself.'

We raised the portcullis for a short period the next morning, in order that a party of men from within the castle could dig a shallow grave for Godfrey in the graveyard of the family chapel – the small, stone building that lay just beyond the gate of the castle. We had no option but to bury Godfrey's body outside, since we could not dig up the cobblestones of the inner ward and lay him to rest within the walls. Leaving the castle was a risk we had to take, so we acted quickly to make sure that we kept our time outside to a minimum.

The gravediggers were myself, Pieter de Groot, his nephew Hans and the knight Robert of Lyndham. Sandro joined us to watch out for any strangers as we worked, but we felt safe enough. The castle sat on top of a steep bank of land at the southern tip of the Isle of Eden, and was surrounded by the marsh on three sides. To the other side there were open fields, with the nearest woodland being about three hundred yards away. It was unlikely that anybody could approach us without being seen. Our real enemy that morning was the harsh wind, battering us as we dug at the hard, icy soil. Consequently the pit was a shallow hole for this unexpected burial. The true gravediggers would have to return in the spring, as this temporary grave would not suffice as a permanent resting place.

Once we'd lowered Godfrey's coffin into this hole, the other guests and servants from the castle briefly joined us for the most rapid service of committal that I'd ever attended. As Old Simon sprinkled holy water onto Godfrey's coffin, I wrapped my cloak about my shoulders and then looked around the grave at my fellow mourners, studying their faces, one by one. Each wore a respectful, if frozen, expression. Some were even shedding a tear, but there was deceit here as well as grief. One of these people was a killer – a person with the self-composure to watch their victim being buried, without displaying even the slightest tremble of guilt.

Chapter Eight

I had planned to begin our search for the killer as soon as Godfrey was buried, but Edwin was in no fit state to join me. He had drunk so much wine in honour of his dead brother, that he had been forced to retire to his bedchamber with a head-ache. I thought about waiting for him to sober up, but decided to proceed anyway, knowing that Edwin was unlikely to be of any real assistance to me – whether drunk or sober. In fact, he was more likely to be a hindrance, so I asked Sandro to help instead, knowing that my valet had many skills that would be useful in this investigation. We began by returning to the obvious place – the cellar where Godfrey's body had been discovered.

The room was as dark and empty as before, apart from de Groot's chest, which smelt strangely of wood tar. I think the clockmaker had already scrubbed out the inner casing of the chest, such had been his alarm at the foul residues from Godfrey's dead body.

'Do you know why Lord Eden came here, Master Oswald?' asked Sandro as he surveyed the room. 'It seems odd to me.'

'I agree,' I said. 'This was not one of Godfrey's storerooms.'

'Perhaps Lord Eden was interested in the parts for his clock?' suggested Sandro, pointing at de Groot's wooden chest.

'The chest was practically empty,' I said. 'The clock is nearly finished.' I paused. 'There has to be some other reason why Godfrey came to this cellar in the middle of the night.'

Sandro nodded at this, before dropping to his knees in order to feel about on the flagstones, letting his fingers skim the surface, before lifting them to his nose.

'What are you doing?' I asked.

'If Lord Eden was killed in this room, Master Oswald, then there should be some blood on this floor,' he said. 'But I can't smell any.'

A thought struck me. 'What if Godfrey wasn't killed here?' I said. 'What if the killer only chose this place to hide his body?'

'Why here?'

'I'm not sure,' I said. 'But there's something that's been bothering me, Sandro.'

'Oh yes?' he said, as he got back to his feet.

I continued. 'When I first saw Godfrey's body in de Groot's chest, it seemed to me that the killer had arranged him into a pose. Almost as if Godfrey was being mocked.'

Sandro seemed puzzled by my theory. 'I see,' he said, not seeing at all.

'Never mind,' I said. 'It was just an impression I had.'

He hesitated, not sure how to answer. 'So, Master Oswald. If Lord Eden wasn't killed here, then where was it?' he said at length. 'In his bedchamber perhaps?'

'No,' I said. 'Godfrey was dressed in his day clothes and not his nightshirt, when I found him. They were the same clothes that he'd been wearing when I saw him the previous evening.' I thought for a moment. 'We need to search Godfrey's library.'

'Do you have the key?' Sandro asked me.

'No,' I said. 'But Alice Cross will have it.'

We found our steward in the kitchen, sitting on a stool and plucking the feathers from a large, white goose. She held the bird's webbed feet in one hand, letting its long neck dangle between her knees as she pulled the down from its breast.

'I would like the key to Lord Eden's library,' I said.

She looked at me blankly, before blowing a feather from her lips. 'I haven't got that key, my Lord.'

'I thought that you kept all the keys for this castle.'

'All except that one,' she said. 'There was only one key to his library and Lord Eden made sure to keep it on a chain about his neck.'

'You didn't find it on his body when you prepared him for burial?' I asked.

'No, my Lord.'

'So, his library is still unlocked, then?'

She turned her attention back to the goose, now scraping a knife over its loose skin to remove the last of the stubborn feathers. 'Well, I can't lock a room, can I, my Lord?' she said sourly. 'If I don't have the key.'

Sandro followed me up the steps to Godfrey's library, but hung back as I pushed at the heavy door. It opened with a creak, and then released a sigh of air into the passageway, as if the chamber beyond was pleased to welcome us at last. I took a deep breath and then stepped over the threshold, finding that Godfrey's library was colder than ever. The shutters were closed and the air inside smelt damp and salty, as if the mists of the marsh were already reclaiming this room as their own. I let my eyes adjust to the gloomy light and then looked about, seeing nothing but an ordered library – much as it had looked on the night that Godfrey had summoned me for our last ever meeting.

Sandro stepped cautiously into the room behind me, as if the murderer might still be hiding behind a chair. 'What would you like me to do, Master Oswald?' he asked tentatively.

'Just look around,' I suggested. 'To see if anything seems unusual to you.'

Sandro looked at me for a moment, dissatisfied with the vagueness of my instruction, before he wandered off – pacing aimlessly about the library and running his hands along Godfrey's furniture and books. 'I can't see anything, Master Oswald,' he soon declared. 'I think we should search Lord Eden's bedchamber instead.'

I was tempted to agree, and yet there was something amiss in this library – I knew it. I couldn't say why exactly, but my suspicions were tickled, if not exactly raised. If anything, this chamber appeared too ordered, as if somebody were trying to throw me from the scent.

I pulled back the shutters of the window that gave onto the inner ward, hoping to literally shed some light onto this room, but something caught my eye below. It was Lyndham's deerhound, tied to a post by a long leash as it sprawled out across the cobblestones, looking thoroughly despondent with life. This gave me an idea.

I turned to Sandro. 'I'd like you to fetch Sir Robert's dog,' I said. 'It's tied up in the inner ward.'

My valet looked back at me with a puzzled expression. 'Why's that, Master Oswald?'

'Just bring the dog here, Sandro,' I said. 'I'll explain later.'

The boy puffed out his lips but did as I requested, soon returning with the dog, which had lost its despondency and now pulled my valet into the room with great excitement. As soon as it saw my face, it tried to leap up at me as if I were its long-lost master, before it knocked over a stool with its powerful tail. I grabbed the dog's leash before it caused any damage and finally brought the spirited hound to a firm halt. The dog submitted with some reluctance, its tongue hanging out in a pant as it sat in front of me, waiting to be rewarded for its obedience. I had nothing to give it, but luckily Sandro was able to produce a crust of bread from his pouch. Once the dog was more settled, I led the creature about the room on its leash, waiting for it to drop its famous nose to the floor.

'What are you doing, Master Oswald?' asked Sandro, now even more baffled by my behaviour.

'I think somebody has recently cleaned this room,' I said. 'But this dog will be able to smell if there was any blood here.'

Sandro raised his eyebrows. 'Very good idea,' he said dubiously. 'I hope it works.'

At first the dog was too excited to concentrate and continued to blunder about, causing Sandro to bite his lip in an attempt not to laugh at me. I must admit that I nearly gave up on this plan, as it had begun to seem like a fool's errand, but then the dog picked up a scent. After its initial unruly exuberance, it was focused on its task – snuffling about the floor with determination, before heading towards Godfrey's desk and then licking ferociously at one of the table legs. I passed the leash to Sandro and then dropped to my knees to look beneath the table, and there, sure enough, on the underside of the table lip were smears of blood. The murderer had missed these small pieces of evidence in their rush to clean up after the crime.

'Come and look at this,' I said, beckoning for Sandro to join me.

The boy knelt down to study the blood. 'It's fresh,' he said, wiping it from the surface and lifting his fingers to his nose. 'From the hands, I would say.'

'I agree,' I said. 'Godfrey must have grabbed the table with bloodied fingers.'

With our attention taken up by this discovery, the dog took the opportunity to jump up at the table, resting its two paws on the table top as it desperately tried to stretch its neck towards the mazer that sat next to Godfrey's bible. Sandro jumped back to his feet and tried to pull the dog away, but it was now so anxious to reach this large feasting cup that my suspicions were raised.

Once Sandro had distracted the dog with another piece of food, I picked up the mazer to inspect it more closely. It was turned from burred maple and decorated with a stand and rim of embossed silver, and had been presented to Godfrey when he was in Oxford. I studied the silver decoration, and could see an inscription in the boss – some warning or other about the dangers of drinking too much wine. But there, in the depressions of the lettering, I could also see the traces of blood.

'I think this cup was used to kill Godfrey,' I said, passing the mazer to Sandro, and pointing to the inscription. 'The killer hasn't been able to clean the blood from these tiny crevices.'

Sandro held the mazer to the light to look at it properly. 'It's a beautiful thing, Master Oswald. And very heavy.' He then ran his finger around its hard edge. 'This would hurt a person's head, I think. But enough to kill a man?'

'Yes, I think so. If it was used with force,' I said, before adding, 'The wound on Godfrey's head was wide and shallow, so he was attacked with something blunt and heavy.' I pointed to the mazer. 'It must have been this.'

Sandro placed the feasting cup back upon the table and then pushed his hair from his eyes. 'A strange way to kill another person, I think, Master Oswald. I would choose a dagger or an axe.'

'Yes, I agree. But it tells us something, doesn't it?'

The boy nodded in response. 'The murderer didn't come here to kill.' Sandro ran his finger about the rim on the mazer for a moment, before he pulled it away, as if his skin had been burnt. 'Was it an argument that turned into a fight?' he asked.

'Possibly,' I said. 'Though I don't think that Godfrey had time to fight back. He was killed by a single blow to his temple.'

Sandro nodded again. 'You think that the murderer took Lord Eden by surprise?' he said.

'Yes, I do.'

We might have discussed this further, but the dog was now straining at its leash again, its claws scratching urgently at the floor as it tried to reach the door of the library. Sandro pulled it back, until I told my valet to relax his grip a little, as the creature was clearly following the scent again. We followed the dog out through the door, and then down the steps where it stopped to lick at an invisible spot, before it careered off again at speed. Within moments we were at the bottom of the stairwell and bursting out into the inner ward, nearly knocking Old Simon and Alice Cross from their feet as we did so, since they must have been standing just the other side of this door.

'By the heavens,' exclaimed the monk. 'Where are you going in such a rush, Lord Somershill?'

'I'll tell you later,' I said, as the dog dragged us across the cobblestones, towards the door that led down into the cellars. The creature was moving faster than ever now, panting with enthusiasm as it pressed its long nose to the flagstones, leading us directly to the cellar where Pieter de Groot's wooden chest still rested against the wall. It was here that the dog began to bark with excitement, scratching and licking at the chest, as if it still contained the body of a dead man.

Sandro rewarded the dog with its final treat, and then we looked at one another without speaking. This dog's illustrious nose had identified the location of Godfrey's murder and the weapon that had been used to kill him. If we had been in any doubt about the link between the blood in Godfrey's library and the body in this cellar, then the dog had put our minds to rest, by leading us straight from one room to the other. I now felt that I could make a very good guess about what had happened to Godfrey on that night.

He had been attacked by surprise in his library, before his corpse had been lifted down to this cellar and then laid out in its strange arrangement in de Groot's chest. But why had the killer gone to these lengths? Why had they not just left Godfrey's body in his library? It wasn't as if a corpse could be concealed forever in this wooden chest. The crime was bound to be detected sooner or later.

It was another question on top of all the others, and though I was pleased with the dog's work, it had done nothing to sniff out an answer to the real question at the heart of this mystery. Why had somebody chosen to kill Godfrey? What had they hoped to gain?

Chapter Nine

We made our way back to the inner ward and released Lyndham's dog, only to hear Filomena knocking at the window of our apartment – gesturing down to me that she required Sandro to return. I sent the boy to her and then wandered over to the well – peering over the edge of the deep shaft to see nothing but soft blackness, as the sky was too overcast to make its usual silver reflection in the circle of water far below. When I looked up, I realised that the child, Lady Emma, was standing on the other side of the well, watching me intently with apprehensive, almost fearful eyes. Her lips were pinched together and her light blue eyes were glistening, as if she had just been crying. In one of her hands she held a small, wooden wheel – its edges cut with teeth, so that it resembled one of the cogs from Godfrey's astronomical clock.

I smiled at her. 'What's that you have there, Emma?' I asked, pointing at the wheel. 'Did Master de Groot make it for you?'

She continued to stare, and I wondered if she had understood me, until she nodded cautiously in response.

'Are you interested in clocks?' I said.

She nodded again.

'Your cog looks very realistic,' I said. 'Can I see it?' I held out my hand to her, but this was my mistake, for it only caused the girl to back away, as if I'd threatened to rob her. When I repeated the gesture, in an attempt to show her that I meant no harm, she reacted with even more dismay, turning on her heels and scampering off. Unfortunately the suddenness of this dash caused Lyndham's dog to give chase, as if she were an escaping rabbit. Soon she was pinned against the wall, cringing from the large hound as it tried to lick her face. In my experience, there is nothing more guaranteed to provoke a dog's unwanted interest than cowering from their attentions, so I called for her to relax whilst I pulled the creature away.

'I'm so sorry,' I told her, fearing that this episode might provoke a tantrum, not least because she had started to make a low moaning sound in her throat. But once I had removed the dog, Lady Emma fled from the inner ward, bolting at speed towards the nearest door.

I watched her disappearing feet, and suddenly I was reminded of another member of her family, tearing through this courtyard at speed. It had been her father, Lord Hesket, on the night of Godfrey's murder, when he had nearly knocked me over in his retreat from my friend's library. This memory prompted me to consider how little I knew about Godfrey's last hours. What had he been doing before his death, and who else had visited him?

With this in mind, I went to look for Alice Cross again, finding her halfway up the stairwell of the great chamber block – the part of the castle in which the other guests were accommodated. Our steward was sweeping the stone steps with a hazel brush, disturbing more dust than she was clearing away. She turned to me with an unfriendly stare, especially when she saw that I was being trailed by Lyndham's deerhound.

'That damned dog,' she said, as we both approached. 'It walks mud all over this castle. If you ask me, we should have thrown the stupid thing out with the horses.'

'That would have upset Sir Robert, don't you think?' I said. 'I'm told this dog is worth a lot of money.'

She scowled at my answer and stepped aside. 'Did you want to get past, my Lord?' she asked me, forcing a smile.

'No,' I said. 'It's you that I wanted to speak to, Mistress Cross.'

'Me?' she said, climbing up one tread on the staircase. 'How can I help you, then?'

'I was wondering,' I said, trying not to sneeze, thanks to all the dust that was still floating about in the air. 'Who else did Lord Eden ask you to summon to his library on the night he was murdered?'

'Just yourself, my Lord, and then Edwin of Eden.'

'What about Lord Hesket?' I said. 'I saw him leaving as I arrived.'

She shrugged at this. 'Lord Hesket must have gone to see my master of his own accord,' she told me. 'I wasn't asked to fetch him.'

'So there were no other visitors to Godfrey's library that night?'

'No, my Lord,' she said. 'Not to my knowledge.'

'Well, thank you, Mistress Cross,' I said, smiling sweetly in response. 'That's very helpful.' I made a show of turning to leave, even though I had no intention of doing so. 'I wonder,' I said, suddenly lifting a finger in the air, as if this thought had just occurred to me. 'Where were you that night?'

She bristled. 'What do you mean?'

I smiled again, noting that my friendliness seemed to disturb her. 'The night that Lord Eden was murdered. I was wondering what you did after attending to his orders?'

She gave a huff. 'Well. First I went to the kitchen, to make sure that the fires were out,' she said. 'Then I went to the Great Hall and locked the other servants in.'

'You locked them in?' I said, with some surprise. 'Why was that?'

Her expression changed from indignation to embarrassment. 'It was Lord Eden's idea.' She cleared her throat. 'We were having some problems, you see. With Edwin of Eden and the younger girls. My master thought it was better to keep temptation out of his way at night.'

'So your three maids and the cook were locked inside the Great Hall until sunrise.'

'Yes,' she snapped. 'That's right.'

'But not you.' I smiled again – my courtesy continuing to unnerve her. 'So where do you sleep, Mistress Cross?'

'I have a room to myself in this chamber block,' she said proudly. 'As befits the steward of this castle.'

'Indeed,' I said, about to ask more, when Edwin clattered around the corner, descending the circular stairwell at speed. He stopped dead when he saw my face. 'Ah, good,' he said. 'I was looking for you, de Lacy.'

'Oh yes?' I said. 'Are you feeling better now?'

'Yes, thank you,' he answered, before casting an awkward glance at Alice Cross. 'I need to speak to you in private,' he said, taking my arm. 'Come with me.'

We had ascended one revolution of the winding staircase with the dog in tow, before Edwin summoned the nerve to shout down to our steward. 'Please bring up more Malmsey wine to my room immediately, Mistress Cross. My jug is nearly empty.' He then set off at speed, climbing two steps at a time so that he didn't have to wait to hear her answer.

Edwin's bedchamber smelt no better than it had the last time I'd come in here – but even so, Edwin wouldn't allow Lyndham's dog into the room, claiming that it was a repulsive-smelling creature. I didn't like to tell him that his bedchamber already smelt worse than a kennel after the dogs have been hunting in the rain, but I followed his instructions and closed the door on the whimpering hound – before quickly taking up a position beside the window, where I could catch the threads of fresh air that crept through the gap in the ill-fitting frame. Had I been able

to open this window somehow, then I would have done so immediately, in order to get some fresh air into this room – but the
panes were set into their leads, like the windows of a church.

While Edwin busied himself in pouring two cups of wine for
us, I took a moment to look down into the inner ward, seeing
that it was filling up with guests again. Old Simon was playing
with his tame crow – waving his arms like a fool and tottering
about in a small circle while the bird flapped its enormous wings
in time with its master's movements. I noticed that Lady Emma
had returned, this time accompanied by her stepmother and her
father. Old Simon was trying to entertain the girl with his
dancing bird, but Lady Emma was no more enamoured with his
crow than she had been with Lyndham's dog, as she was once
again pinned against the wall in terror. Nearby I could see Lady
Isobel, watching this whole spectacle with an expression of
wearied boredom etched across her face, whereas Lord Hesket
was walking his fine palfrey about the cobblestones. Unlike the
rest of us, Hesket had been allowed to keep his horse in the castle
and not abandon the creature to the nearby forests.

I turned away from the window as Edwin passed me a cup of
wine. 'Why did you want to speak to me?' I asked.

'I wondered if you've discovered anything yet?' he answered.
'I'm very anxious to find Godfrey's killer, you know.'

I considered telling him about the library and the mazer, but
decided against it. 'Nothing as yet,' I said instead. 'Have you
thought of anything that might help?'

He smiled somewhat triumphantly at this. 'Yes,' he said.
'Actually that's why I wanted to speak to you. I remembered
something that could be very important.'

'Oh yes?'

'Yes,' he said, 'that's right.' He then cleared his throat. 'I overheard Godfrey having an argument with Pieter de Groot. It was
about four days ago. In de Groot's workroom.' He paused. 'They
didn't know I could hear them.'

'So where were you, then?' I asked.

He hesitated, biting his lip. 'I was having a sleep in the cellars.' I went to say something about this, but he didn't give me the chance. 'Don't look at me like that, de Lacy. I was hiding from my brother. I've told you what it was like for me in this castle. Godfrey was always after me to do one of his boring chores. This time it was something to do with counting out sacks of grain. Can you believe that?' He finished his wine in one guzzle. 'I didn't always do what Godfrey told me to,' he said, 'so I had a sleep instead.'

'What was their argument about?' I asked.

'It was about that clock that de Groot has been building,' he said. 'Have you seen it? All moons, stars, and tiny wheels.' He poked a finger into his ear and then pulled it out to examine the tip. 'Can't see the point of it myself. You wake up when it's light and go to bed when it's dark. Who needs a clock to tell you that?'

'Was Godfrey unhappy with his clock, then?' I asked, steering the conversation back to the overheard argument.

Edwin paused. 'Well, I think that's what it was about. Though I couldn't hear every word.'

'But Godfrey and de Groot were definitely arguing?'

'Oh yes,' he said with conviction. 'They were trying not to raise their voices, but it was not a friendly conversation, I can tell you that for nothing. In fact, Godfrey was so angry that I heard him use the Lord's name in vain.' He said these last words in the mocking tone of a young scholar trying to impress his friends. Nevertheless, there was something revelatory in this disclosure. Godfrey was very strict about blaspheming. He had even chastised my mother once for saying 'Dear God' under her breath as she stubbed her toe. If de Groot had caused Godfrey to use a profanity, then he must have made my friend very angry indeed.

I passed Edwin the cup of wine. 'Thank you,' I said. 'I'll go and speak to de Groot now.'

'Shall I come?' he asked.

'No,' I said quickly, trying to conjure up an excuse. 'It might be better if I questioned him alone. De Groot will speak more freely if there is just one of us.'

Edwin nodded reluctantly at this, but then darted forward as I reached the door, placing his hand onto the latch and preventing me from leaving. 'You see, the thing is, de Lacy,' he whispered. 'I think de Groot might be our killer.'

'Why's that?' I said.

'Think about it. First there's this argument that I overheard. Then Godfrey's body is found in de Groot's chest. It's got to mean something, hasn't it?'

'Let's see what de Groot has to say first, shall we?' I said, reaching again for the latch.

'But you must admit that it's very suspicious?' said Edwin, finally releasing his hand from the door. 'You must agree with that.'

I pushed past. 'Just let me speak to him, Edwin. Before we start making accusations.'

I found Pieter de Groot in the Great Hall, sitting beside the fire with his apprentice Hans, as the boy messed about with a stick in the flames. The only other person in this large chamber was Alice Cross, who was now flaying the floor of the dais with her hazel broom. Hans gave me a sideways look as I joined them at the fire, before continuing to prod about in the ashes with the stick – smashing the burning embers into tiny sparks of fire. When I asked Hans to leave so that I could speak to his uncle alone, the boy stood up with some irritation and then kicked at the reeds on the floor, causing some of them to fly into the fire pit and momentarily set alight. De Groot stamped out the flames, then censured the youth in their own guttural language, after which Hans slinked away, looking back at me with a brooding, resentful look upon his face.

De Groot shook his head at this episode, as if Hans were an impossible child. 'My nephew is very bored here,' he said. 'He misses his friends in Delft. This castle is a prison.'

'We should be thankful for this prison,' I observed, taking the stool that Hans had vacated. 'It will save our lives.'

De Groot shrugged at this, and then returned his bottom to the other stool. 'Or end it, Lord Somershill.' He hesitated. 'There's a murderer here,' he whispered. 'Somebody in this castle killed Lord Eden.'

'Yes, I know,' I said. 'That's why I wanted to talk to you.'

'Me?' He drew in his chin, causing his thick neck to bulge. 'I don't know anything about it.'

I sat up straight. De Groot was a hefty, muscular man, but I had the advantage of height. 'Why did you recently have an argument with Lord Eden?' I said.

'What argument?'

'It was four days ago in your workroom. You were overheard, de Groot, so please don't deny it.'

My warning annoyed him, but he had the sense to hesitate before answering, forcing his face into a smile. 'Oh, that,' he said, with a flippant wave of his hand. 'That wasn't an argument.' He then attempted a short chuckle, as if recalling an amusing memory. 'I would call it more of a discussion.'

'A discussion about what?' I asked.

De Groot spread out his legs. 'If you must know, Lord Eden was concerned about his clock.'

'Why was that?' I asked.

'It doesn't matter,' he said. 'The issue was quickly resolved.'

'I'd still like to know,' I said.

He rubbed his hands over his thick thighs. 'Please don't suggest that there was hostility between us. It is not true.' He then rose to his feet. 'Now I must go and find Hans.'

'Sit down again,' I said. 'We haven't finished.'

'But—'

'I said, sit down!'

My raised voice caused Alice Cross to momentarily cease her battering of the floor, and look up sharply. But when her eyes met mine, she looked away.

Pieter de Groot reluctantly took his seat again. 'If you must know,' he said, 'Lord Eden didn't have enough money to pay the last part of my fee.'

'So you were angry with him?'

He regarded me for a moment. 'Oh, I see what's happening here,' he said, with a slow and deliberate nod of his head. 'I see what you're trying to suggest.' He then wagged his finger at me, and only just stopped short of prodding its tip into my chest. 'You want to blame this murder on a Dutchman. Pieter de Groot from Delft. Oh yes. Why not? He must be guilty.'

I pushed his finger away. 'You were heard arguing with Lord Eden, and then his dead body was discovered in your chest. Can you blame me for being suspicious?'

His cheeks were now as red as a rasher of bacon, and sweat was beading in the indentation at the end of his nose. 'I had nothing to do with Lord Eden's murder,' he hissed. 'Even though he tricked me. Telling me that he could finish paying for the clock.'

'Are you saying that Lord Eden lied to you?'

'Yes,' he spat. 'That's exactly what I'm saying.'

This deceitfulness didn't sound at all like Godfrey, and I felt the sudden compulsion to defend my friend. 'You must be mistaken, de Groot. Lord Eden would never have commissioned a clock that he couldn't pay for.'

'He thought that he would have the money,' said de Groot. 'But then something changed.'

'What do you mean?' I asked.

De Groot hesitated, suddenly uncomfortable with himself for making the last disclosure.

'I said, what do you mean?'

'I didn't know this at first,' he said with a sigh. 'You must believe me about that. Lord Eden didn't mention his problem with money until our discussion four days ago. This argument that you tell me was overheard.'

'What was the problem?' I asked.

He heaved another sigh. 'Lord Eden was borrowing the money to pay for my clock. Everything was arranged, but then his bene- factor changed his mind. The money was suddenly no longer on offer.'

'Do you know why?'

'No.'

'Do you know who the benefactor was?'

De Groot hesitated again, now poking his tongue about his cheek before deciding to answer. 'It was Lord Hesket,' he said at length.

I rose to my feet. 'Thank you.'

He regarded me sourly. 'So, I'm not under suspicion?'

'Not at the moment,' I said, dusting the charred reeds from my boots. 'But don't go anywhere, de Groot.'

'How can I go anywhere?' he exclaimed, banging his hands down on his muscular thighs. 'I'm locked inside here. I told you before. This castle is a prison.'

I looked at his enraged, choleric face – his cheeks now streaked with purple veins. 'Don't get so angry, de Groot,' I said. 'It was just a joke.'

Chapter Ten

Iknocked at the door to Lord Hesket's apartment, to be admitted by the man himself. I then stepped inside a room that was as warm and dark as a birthing chamber. The lack of light and the profusion of red cloth about me only increased this sense of confinement, as if I had entered the abdominal cavity of a giant creature. It seemed that Hesket had secured the best accommodation in this castle, despite this not being the apartment that was supposedly intended for the King. With its lower ceilings and smaller windows, this chamber was far more congenial for a winter of isolation than our own rooms – especially given the thick Persian carpets and richly coloured tapestries that covered the floor and walls. For a moment, I looked about and felt as if I were back in Venice, in one of the many opulent chambers that I had visited in my time there.

Lord Hesket gestured for me to sit beside the fire, where his wife Lady Isobel was currently seated. When she realised that she was required to move, she made an attempt to hide her irritation by gifting me a smile, but I noted that her mouth only curled at the corners, while her eyes remained steadfastly cold. Her displeasure at my appearance was only increased when Hesket then asked her to take Lady Emma for a walk about the inner ward, claiming that his daughter would benefit from some fresh air. Lady Isobel produced another sour smile in response to this, arguing that she had only just returned from the last excursion, but Hesket insisted that she leave us anyway. At this instruction Lady Isobel grasped Emma roughly by her hand and pulled her towards the door. The girl protested, but luckily this objection did not escalate into a tantrum. She looked plaintively at her father, before he softly blew her a kiss and then waved her away.

Once we were alone, Hesket walked over to a side table and offered to pour me a goblet of Madeira. 'I will have to serve this myself, I'm afraid,' he said wearily. 'I don't know about you, Lord Somershill, but I'm sorely in need of a servant.'

'Godfrey didn't allow you to bring a maid?' I asked.

'Of course he did,' answered Hesket. 'But unfortunately the woman died on the way here.'

I sat upright. 'She died?'

Hesket passed me the wine. 'It was not plague, Somershill,' he said. 'Don't be concerned. She fell into a river.'

'I'm sorry to hear that.'

'Yes,' he said ruefully. 'It was a shame. Especially as she was the only person whom Emma would speak to.'

'So Lady Emma can speak?'

'Of course she can speak,' he snapped. 'My daughter is not a dullard. She's just very selective about talking.' He took a gulp of his wine and then banged down the goblet on the table beside him. 'I'm afraid to say that she has never chosen to speak to me.'

I knew better than to ask more. 'How did your servant come to fall into a river?' I asked instead.

Hesket leant forward to fix me with one of his unnerving stares. 'You are an inquisitive fellow, aren't you, Lord Somershill? Are you investigating the death of my servant now, as well as Eden's unfortunate murder?'

'No, no. Of course not,' I said defensively. 'It was just a question. Nothing more.'

He continued to stare at me, but I met his gaze. 'If you must know, I didn't see what happened,' he said, eventually blinking and looking away. 'One moment we were crossing a footbridge. The next moment the woman had slipped into the water. Lyndham and that jester fellow tried to save her, of course. But the river was swollen.'

'Lyndham and The Fool were with you?' I said, surprised to learn this.

'Yes. Of course they were,' he said. 'I would never have journeyed here from London without a guard. A rich man does not ride about England without a knight.'

I reflected briefly on my own decision to travel to Castle Eden alone, with only Sandro to assist me in fighting off any outlaws and thieves – but luckily the shabbiness of our cart, and the stoutness of our pony, had deterred any interest in our wealth. 'It must have been difficult for Lady Emma?' I said. 'It's distressing for a child to witness the death of another person. Especially as she was close to this woman.'

Hesket regarded me with a sharp eye. 'My daughter has borne it well enough, Lord Somershill. And, of course, she has my wife to comfort her.'

I thought of the woman who had just steered Emma from the room with all the tenderness of a man herding cattle to market, and couldn't think of a suitable answer to this.

Hesket slapped his knees, so thankfully the topic was closed anyway. 'I presume you're here to ask me questions about the death of Lord Eden?' he said. 'And not that of my daughter's maid?'

'Yes,' I said. 'That's right.'

He wiped the end of his nose. 'I must say that I find it strange that Edwin of Eden has started this investigation already. In my opinion it might have waited until spring.'

'I think we need to catch the killer before then, don't you?' I answered.

Hesket snorted with his usual disdain. 'Why's that, then, Somershill? Are you afraid that this person will kill again?'

'Who can say?'

'I see,' he said, 'so you are afraid.' He paused for an instant and then leant towards me, resting his hands on his thighs to give the slant of his upper body more stability. 'But what about justice for Godfrey?' he said. 'Do you care about that as well?'

'Of course I do,' I said defensively. 'Godfrey was my friend. But equally, I make no apologies for also wanting to protect my family. I'm certainly not content to leave them at the mercy of an unknown killer for the whole winter.'

'So you think you can find him?'

'Of course I do.'

Hesket gave another disdainful huff. 'Yes, well, I have heard of your reputation, Lord Somershill. And not only from your mother's boasting. Your exploits in seeking out murderers are talked of in London.' He hesitated. 'But tell me this,' he said. 'I've always wondered, what makes you so interested in this pursuit?' He fixed me again with one of his intense stares. 'Is it because you like prying into other people's lives?'

'I wouldn't call it prying,' I said. 'I call it seeking answers.'

This didn't satisfy him. 'Yes. But why do it, Lord Somershill? That is my question. Why pay so much attention to the dead?'

I froze for a moment, unable to think of an answer. Why had I spent so much time hunting murderers in the last eleven years? There had to be an answer to this – and yet I could see no particular pattern to my investigations. To begin with, I had been acting from a sense of duty, as those early murders had taken place on my own estate. It had been my role, as Lord Somershill, to find and punish the killer. My involvement in my last investigation had been different again. I had been seeking payment for the finding of a killer, in order to settle a mounting gambling debt to an angry and terrifying creditor. On the surface there was no thread running between these investigations. And yet . . .

And yet, I had driven each of these investigations to its end. In each case I had found the true murderer, sometimes at great risk to my own life, and consequently I had made certain that this person was punished for their crimes. There had to be more to my involvement than duty or self-interest. But, if there was a common motive, I could not see it.

Hesket's question had made me uncomfortable, so I muttered some platitude about seeking fairness, before I quickly diverted his attention by asking some questions of my own. 'I understand that you promised to loan some money to Godfrey,' I said. 'To pay for his astronomical clock.'

Hesket sat back sharply, as I had clearly taken him by surprise. 'Goodness me, Lord Somershill. You have been poking around, haven't you? What fast work.'

'Is it true?'

'Yes.'

'But then you changed your mind and withdrew the offer?'

He cleared his throat. 'Yes. It was Godfrey's fault. He had reneged on a promise to me.'

'What was the promise?'

He hesitated. 'I'm really not sure that this is relevant, Somershill.'

'It could be,' I answered.

He heaved a long and regretful sigh. 'Look. If you must know, I lent Godfrey a good deal of money to make this castle more suitable for our stay this winter.'

'Suitable?'

He looked at me with consternation. 'You're not telling me that you like this frozen garrison?'

'It's what I expected from an old castle.'

'Well, it's not what I expected,' he said. 'And it's certainly not what I paid for.'

'What do you mean?' I said.

'It's very simple, Lord Somershill,' he answered. 'I requested that Godfrey create a solar for our daytime use. It's what my daughter and wife are accustomed to in London. The Great Hall here is very old-fashioned and draughty, so we are forced to sit in our bedchamber all day. It was a blessing that I sent a cart of our own belongings ahead in the late summer, or we would be living in all the comforts of an anchorite's cell.'

'These are your own carpets and tapestries?' I asked.

'Of course they are,' he replied. 'Do they look like something that Godfrey would have bought? No, they don't,' he said, quickly continuing before I could reply. 'Godfrey was addicted to living like a Cistercian monk. All wooden floors and bare walls.' He took another long gulp of the wine. 'It was quite a shock when I arrived here, I can tell you. When I discovered what Godfrey had really used my money for. Instead of creating some private rooms for our use, he'd knocked a great window in the wall of his own library and added some sort of ventilation shaft in the cellars. Why on earth should I care about that? And then . . . and then, as if the window and the shaft were not bad enough, he'd spent a fortune on that ridiculous astronomical clock. An utter waste of my money, if ever I saw one.' He paused to catch his breath. 'So, when Godfrey asked me for yet more money to complete the clock, I refused to lend him another penny. And can you blame me?'

'So you were angry with Godfrey?' I asked.

'I certainly told him my opinion of his deceit.'

'You looked very angry to me on the night of his murder. If you remember, you nearly knocked me over as you left his library.'

'The man had infuriated me,' he said.

'About the loan?'

He paused. 'Yes. Of course it was about the loan. The man had made promises to me, Lord Somershill. Promises that he had flagrantly broken.' He paused, banging his finger against the stem of his goblet. 'Promises that his dim-witted brother is also refusing to honour. But——' He shook his head and then smoothed over the hair of his beard. 'None of this has anything to do with

Godfrey's murder.' He stood up. 'So, I thank you for your interest in my private family matters, Lord Somershill, but there is
nothing I can tell you.' When I didn't move, he waved his hands
at me, as if trying to shift a stubborn dog from the hearth. 'Come
on. Off you go. I've told you everything that you need to know.'

Night had fallen by the time that I left Hesket's apartment. The
inner ward was completely bathed in darkness, so that I could
barely see the walls about me. For a moment I stood still and
enjoyed the illusion of being in a much wider space, until a
lantern was lit in one of the rooms above, creating a disembod-
ied square of light in the air. I walked across the cobblestones,
heading for the door to our apartment, when I bumped into
Lady Isobel.

'Have you finished speaking to my husband, my Lord?' she
asked.

'Yes,' I replied. 'I apologise that you had to leave us.'

'It's no matter,' she said politely. 'It does Emma good to be
outside.'

'And where is Lady Emma now?' I asked, expecting to see the
child by her side.

'Oh, don't worry about Emma,' she said. 'She's run off to find
Master de Groot.' She paused. 'The girl is obsessed with that
clock.'

I bowed my head and then moved off quickly, as the air was
nipping at my face with frozen claws. When I opened the door to
our own apartment I discovered Filomena and Sandro, huddled
together about the hearth. These two Venetians already found
English winters difficult, but now they were drooping like
frosted buds. Filomena had even pulled up her hood, as her teeth
chattered – though this might have been an affectation for my
benefit. When Hugh ran into the room and crawled up onto her
lap, she forgot about shivering, kissed the boy's head and then let
him burrow into her cloak.

'Why don't you light the fire?' I asked, taking off my gloves and placing them next to the lantern.

'I tried to light it, Master Oswald,' said Sandro. 'But the wood is too damp.'

Filomena interjected. 'These logs make a bad smell when they burn, Oswald. The smoke affects your mother's lungs.' She coated this observation with the wearied tone she preserved uniquely for any mention of my mother.

'Talking of Mother, where is she?' I said, looking about the room, expecting to see her busying about in a corner, or snooping out of the window.

Filomena pulled her hood further over her head, so that I could barely see her face. 'She's visiting the cook. She doesn't like the food.'

'Mother went down the stairs alone?' I asked.

'I tried to assist Lady Somershill,' protested Sandro, 'but she refused my help. I offered three times.'

My valet was clearly keen to absolve himself from any blame in this matter – afraid that I would chastise him for disobeying my orders. Recently Mother had fallen down the stairs at Somershill with the regularity of a drunkard outside a brothel – so I had asked her repeatedly not to descend any stairs without the assistance of a servant. Unlike a floppy-bodied drinker, she had hurt herself badly at each fall – causing a succession of garish, painful bruises.

'It's true,' said Filomena, defending Sandro. 'Your mother would not listen to us.' She paused, before adding, 'as usual.' There it was again. That special tone in her voice.

I drew up a stool and sat down next to them, feeling the urge to replace my gloves. However, this would have been an obvious admission that the room was as freezing as Filomena claimed, so I folded my arms instead, tucking my fingers into the folds of my velvet tunic and trying to disguise my own chilliness.

Filomena sidled up to me. 'Listen, Oswald. There's something I want to tell you.'

'What was it?'

Filomena glanced at Sandro, and a look passed between them, making me realise that they had already discussed this topic. She wriggled on her seat, moving Hugh's head before speaking. 'I saw something while you were out,' she said. 'I think it's important.'

'Oh yes?'

'I was looking out of the window, and I saw Edwin creeping across the inner ward. He seemed suspicious, so I ran down to follow him.'

'Where was he going?'

'He went into the stables,' she said, 'where he met with that Dutch boy, Hans.' She anticipated my next question. 'It was not a chance meeting, Oswald. They were talking in whispers.'

'And they didn't see you?'

'No.'

'Are you sure about that?'

She shook her head. 'Of course I'm sure. I'm good at being invisible. But listen to me. They whispered for a while, and then Edwin passed the boy a large bag of coins. A whole purse.' She raised her eyebrows. 'You must find that suspicious?'

This did sound odd. 'Do you know what the money was for?' I asked.

'No,' she said. 'I tried to listen, but they were talking so quietly. It was as if they were plotting something.'

'Plotting what?'

She hesitated. 'I couldn't hear, Oswald. But if you ask me, Edwin is definitely the killer you seek.' I tried to answer, but she carried on. 'Of course, I don't think that he did it himself. He had a . . . a helper.'

'You mean an accomplice?'

She scowled at being corrected. 'Yes. Whatever it is that you say in English.'

'And you think that Hans is Edwin's accomplice?'

Filomena repositioned Hugh again, so that she could turn to look me in the face, causing my son to grumble in some displeasure. 'Yes, I do,' she said confidently. 'That's why Edwin gave a purse of coins to Hans in secret. To pay the Dutch boy for killing Godfrey.'

'That's quite an accusation,' I said.

'Yes, but I know that I'm right.'

'Why don't I ask Edwin about the coins first?' I said, now giving in to the cold, and returning my gloves to my frozen hands.

My wife screwed up her nose at this suggestion. 'You don't believe me, do you, Oswald?' she said.

'Of course I do, Filomena. It's only that I'm cautious about making such a leap, before I've even questioned Edwin or Hans about these coins.'

'Then go and speak to them now,' she urged me. 'Hurry up. It could be important.'

Our conversation was cut short as Alice Cross rang out the supper bell across the inner ward. 'Let's eat first,' I said, thankful for this excuse to delay my next session of cross-questioning. 'I'll speak to Edwin after supper.'

Filomena turned her back on me. 'Don't be fooled by that man, Oswald. Edwin is pleased to be the new Lord Eden. He's not sorry that his brother is dead.'

Chapter Eleven

We filed into the Great Hall, as The Fool plucked out a jovial tune on his citole, clearly forgetting that we had buried the lord of this castle that same morning. A fire roared in the centre of the room, but it was difficult to heat this voluminous hall in the winter, so the place was still as icy as a minster. The food didn't promise to warm our spirits either, even though there was actually some meat floating about in the pottage that evening. It seemed my mother, on her expedition to the kitchen, had prevailed upon the cook to add some smoked ham to the usual mix of peas, turnips and minced onions.

Godfrey would not have approved of this luxury, of course, even on the day of his burial, but I was pleased to find some ham in my pottage. Unfortunately Mother had also persuaded the cook to add two other ingredients – vinegar and powdered cloves. I could almost hear her words to the cook. *It will balance their humours on this trying day. A hot and sharp tonic for their damp and cold dispositions.*

Hugh didn't care for the pottage, which was entirely predictable, given that my son was notoriously picky, preferring only the blandest of dishes. His appetite for the sweetest foods never waned, however. The spiced plums, the apples baked with honey and nuts, and the custards made with precious sugar and currants. Not that such delicacies were on offer that night, so Hugh was faced with eating the strangely spiced pottage or going to bed hungry. Luckily it was a choice that he seemed resigned to making. Filomena let him sit on her lap as she spooned the pottage into his mouth, though he still grimaced after each serving, as if she were trying to poison him.

Mother tapped me on the shoulder. 'The boy is four years old, Oswald. He should be sitting up at the table like a young man.'

'At least he's eating something,' I said.

'Your wife is too soft with him.'

'That's because Filomena knows that kindness works better with Hugh,' I said pointedly, recalling some of the painful episodes at Somershill, when my mother and her lady's maid had attempted to push spoonfuls of boiled trout into Hugh's mouth, only to receive a shower of regurgitated fish for their troubles. I'm pleased to say that my son had inherited his birth mother's temper, and would not meekly give in to the barbarous antics of his grandmother and her fearsome assistant.

'I know why Filomena fusses over him, of course,' said Mother with a knowing smile. 'It's very obvious why she treats him like a baby.'

'Please be quiet, Mother,' I said. 'Or she'll hear you.' But, thankfully, my wife wasn't paying us any attention. Instead, she was distracted from listening to our conversation by singing to Hugh, tickling his chin each time he agreed to eat more.

'Filomena wants her own child, Oswald,' whispered Mother. 'You must see that? Especially after her own daughter died.'

I continued to eat. 'We're in no rush, thank you, Mother,' I said equably. 'And please don't let Filomena hear you talking about her daughter. It upsets her.'

Mother shrugged her shoulders. 'We've all lost children, Oswald,' she said. 'It's the way of things. And at least you don't have to bring up a daughter that isn't your own.'

'Please, Mother,' I said. 'I've had enough.'

She was not deterred, however. 'I worry about your line,' she said.

'I have a successor. Hugh is sitting two yards from you.'

'Ah yes,' she said, tapping my arm with a bony finger. 'But one son is never enough. Look at me. I had eight children.'

'No, you didn't. You had nine.'

She waved this comment away, as if I were being pedantic. 'The point is that only you and your sister are still alive, so you cannot assume that Hugh will reach maturity. He could die at any point.'

'Thank you for that thought, Mother,' I said.

Mercifully this conversation could not continue as Edwin had risen to his feet and was now clapping his hands to gain the attention of the whole table. I was pleased to see that he looked cleaner than usual. His hair was brushed and he had taken the time to trim his beard, though I was surprised at his choice of clothing. His cloak was a richly embroidered garment, edged with squirrel fur and fastened with a silver clasp. I recognised it immediately, for it had belonged to Godfrey – though I must say that Godfrey had only chosen to wear this fine cloak on feast days, or when visiting the archbishop. I suddenly pictured Edwin searching through his brother's wardrobe and picking out the most expensive garments, even though most of these cloaks, surcoats and tunics would be too large for him. And then an image stuck in my mind – of a carrion crow picking over the bones of a dead rabbit. Filomena must have read my thoughts. She looked at the cloak and then she looked at me with a pointed expression. *Edwin is not sorry that his brother is dead.*

Edwin clapped again for silence. 'Dear friends,' he said, holding out his arms and looking along the table. 'I wanted to say some words to you all on this tragic day.' He followed this opening flourish with a long pause, during which I found myself wondering if he had forgotten what he planned to say next. Hugh filled this silence with a grizzle and a complaint about a piece of fat that was caught in his teeth. It was this interruption that spurred Edwin back into action.

'This morning we buried my brother,' he said. 'And I am distraught with grief.' As he ostentatiously wiped a tear from his cheek, Filomena again caught my eye.

Edwin continued, making sure to look in my direction, and now I wondered if he was about to make an announcement about Godfrey's son. But I should have known that this was far too noble an act for such a man. Edwin only wanted to talk about himself. 'Now that I have become Lord Eden,' he said, still staring at me, 'I feel it's important to reassure you all that it is my intention to honour Godfrey's plan.' He cleared his throat and then paused for dramatic effect. 'And so,' he announced, 'I extend my welcome to you all. Please. Be my guests here at Castle Eden until the danger of plague has passed.'

Lord Hesket answered with a loud harrumph. 'We're not going anywhere,' he said, as he chewed upon a hunk of bread. 'Your cellars are full of our food.'

The candlelight caught the twitch in Edwin's eye. 'Of course,' he said, with a nod. 'I only meant to pledge my own commitment to Godfrey's plan.'

Hesket snorted. 'That's very good of you,' he said scornfully. 'Though I'd like to see you try to throw us out.'

Edwin flushed, trying to smooth over this humiliation by lifting his mug of ale from the table and holding it aloft. 'I raise a toast,' he said. 'To Godfrey's death and to our long lives.'

We raised our own mugs without enthusiasm, for this was hardly a fitting toast. If Edwin's unfortunate words did not leave enough of a bitter taste in the mouth, then the ale succeeded in doing so. The cook had added honey, cinnamon and galingale to disguise the sourness of the brew, but it was still barely palatable.

When I realised that Edwin intended to carry on speaking, I quickly rose to my feet. 'If you don't mind, Edwin,' I said, making a point of not calling him Lord Eden, 'I would like to take this opportunity to say a few words to the household myself.'

Edwin was surprised, if not a little annoyed, at my interruption, but had the good grace to bow his head to me. 'Please, de Lacy,' he said, sitting down with a thud. 'Carry on.'

I looked at my fellow guests along our table, before calling to the servants at the other end of the hall. 'Come forward and join us, please,' I said. 'I would like to speak to everybody.' My request was met with silence, since the servants of this castle were not used to being summoned to the dais. They only padded past the central fire, once Alice Cross had rounded them up like a determined sheepdog. I noticed that Hans crept into the hall at this point, skulking through the shadows and joining his uncle at their own table, at which point he received a stern reprimand from de Groot for his late arrival.

Once everybody was gathered in front of me, I began. 'As you all know, Godfrey, Lord Eden, was murdered yesterday.' My words were met with nods and sighs from everyone except Lord Hesket, who continued to chew loudly upon his bread, as his sleeve dipped in and out of his bowl of pottage. His wife, Lady Isobel, subtly lifted the sleeve from the bowl and laid it back on the table without Hesket even turning his head. She looked embarrassed by her husband's poor manners, especially when his clumsiness caused the three maids to nudge one another surreptitiously and smile.

'Godfrey was a good friend to me,' I continued. 'And I am shocked by the manner of his death.'

'He was a good friend to us all,' said Robert of Lyndham, once again causing the maids to nudge one another, though this time it was the knight's deep voice and handsome face that caused the giggling.

I continued, once Alice Cross had silenced the girls with a fierce stare. 'I believe that Edwin of Eden has already informed you of this,' I said, 'but I wanted you to hear it from my own lips.

In the coming days, I will be looking for Godfrey's murderer. It is my intention to find this person as soon as possible.'

'That's right,' said Edwin, jumping to his feet again. 'I appointed Lord Somershill to this task myself. It was my idea.' He then waved his hands about awkwardly, seemingly lost for words. 'So, just do what he asks,' he said, before returning his bottom to his seat with another thud.

I thanked Edwin for this contribution and was about to continue, when Old Simon's crow Corvina swooped down from the roof truss above us with a great flapping, before she landed clumsily upon the monk's shoulders. The elderly monk was perhaps the only person in the hall not to be alarmed by this, since the crow had misjudged the angle of her descent, and had only just missed my mother's head. As Mother shrieked, the monk turned to me and spoke sharply. 'Please, carry on, Lord Somershill,' he said. 'Corvina is just a crow. She won't hurt anybody.'

Following her master's words, Corvina scrutinised me for a moment with one of her beady eyes, before flaring her wings and commencing to noisily preen her plumage – her curved beak flicking industriously through her feathers.

I looked away and continued. 'I want you all to think back to the night that Godfrey was murdered,' I said.

The bird squawked. '*Ave Maria.*'

This caused some giggles, particularly from the three maids again, but I raised my voice and carried on. 'For example, did you hear or see something unusual that night? Is there anything that has made you suspicious in the last couple of days?'

The bird chirped again. '*In nomine Patris. In nomine Patris.*'

I spoke louder. 'Or perhaps you have some other information that you'd like to tell me? In confidentiality, of course.'

'*Ave Maria. In nomine Patris.*'

By now I had lost my line of thought, which caused more muted laughter – and not just from the three maids this time.

It was Lord Hesket who brought this farce to an end. He thumped on the table, and shouted out in his gruffest voice. 'Will somebody silence that damned bird? It's like eating supper in the royal menagerie.'

Old Simon stiffened at his words. 'Corvina is only rejoicing in her faith, my Lord. She's not hurting anybody.'

'It's a bird,' replied Hesket. 'It's not capable of faith.'

The old monk stuttered. 'I . . . I don't think that's—'

'*Ave Maria*,' squawked Corvina. '*In nomine Patris.*'

Hesket thumped the table again. 'By God. This is insufferable.' At which point, a stone hurtled past my nose before hitting the bird soundly in her chest. This missile caused Corvina to flap her wings and retreat back to the roof beams with a grating squawk.

'Who did that?' said Old Simon, struggling to his feet in outrage. 'Was it you?' he said, pointing at Hans, who was the obvious culprit. For his part, the young Dutchman made no efforts to hide his guilt. In fact, he was smiling and looked rather proud of himself.

The monk waved a fist at the boy. 'How dare you attack Corvina? She is one of God's creatures.'

'Please sit down, Father,' I said. 'I have some more to say.'

Old Simon squinted at me. 'But that brute just threw a stone at my crow, Lord Somershill. The boy should be reprimanded at the very least.'

'He should be congratulated,' said Hesket. 'The stupid thing is quiet at last.'

Old Simon folded his arms. 'It was an act of cruelty. If a man would hurt a bird so freely, then I ask this. What else would he do?'

It was Pieter de Groot's turn to jump to his feet, pointing his finger at the old man. 'Be careful what you're saying, priest,' he shouted. 'You're not blaming a Dutchman for this murder, just because Hans threw a stone at your bird. Any one of these people could be the killer.' When this assertion was met with shouts, he continued. 'Yes, that's right. Somebody in this hall is guilty.'

'Please sit down, de Groot,' I said. 'I want to continue.'

There was no point carrying on, however, as the hall had descended into noisy uproar – the guests and servants airing their fears and suspicions about Godfrey's murder in a cacophony of accusations and denials. The loudest voice belonged to Pieter de Groot as he continued to defend himself and his nephew against all allegations, taking pains to be offended by every comment made to him, no matter how innocuous. This show of umbrage culminated in de Groot striding out of the hall in a temper, with his nephew trailing behind him like a naughty child, smiling with glee at the mischief he'd managed to cause.

Seeing an opportunity to speak to the boy, I caught up with Hans in the inner ward, gripping his shoulder and causing him to jump.

'What do you want?' he said, looking back at me with his strange, grey eyes. At this proximity, I could see that his fleshy lips were cracked and scaly from the cold.

'I have some questions for you, Hans,' I said.

'I don't know anything,' he protested, trying to wriggle away from my hold. 'You can't blame the murder on us,' he said, repeating his uncle's refrain.

'Just answer my questions,' I said.

He tensed. 'What questions?'

'I want to know why Edwin of Eden gave you a bag of coins.'

He looked at me blankly.

I pushed him against the nearby wall. 'You met Edwin of Eden in the stables today and he gave you a bag of coins.' I pressed my hand against the hard plate of his breastbone. 'You were seen, so don't waste my time with lies.'

'I don't know what you mean.'

'Yes you do,' I said. 'Either you tell me, or we can have this conversation in front of your uncle.'

This threat was enough to scare an answer from him. 'The coins were payment of a debt,' he said.

'What sort of debt?'

'Ask Edwin of Eden,' he said.

'No. I'm asking you.'

He thrust out his chin stubbornly, so I grasped his collar and pulled it tightly about his scrawny neck. 'Tell me why Edwin of Eden owed you that money?' I said.

Hans repeated his earlier words. 'I don't know anything.'

I tightened my grip on the cloth, feeling the bony outcrop of his Adam's apple. I didn't apply enough pressure to choke him, but he still made a show of coughing. 'What sort of debt?' I repeated.

'I won it,' he croaked.

I pushed his head back against the wall, hearing his skull knock against the stone. 'How?'

'We played at dice, and . . .' I loosened my grip a little to allow him to speak. He put a hand to his throat and let out a thin, pathetic moan. 'He lost every time we played. So he owed me that money.'

'Are you lying to me?'

'No,' he said. 'Ask . . .' He wriggled again, trying to get away from me. 'Ask Edwin of Eden.'

I released the boy from my grasp, and he scuttled away across the cobblestones with the speed of a cockroach. I then remained in the darkness for a few moments to consider his story. Edwin seemed the type to play at dice, and I knew, from my own bitter experience, that it's easy to accumulate large debts to a good player. I would have to ask Edwin for his version of the story tomorrow. But now I was tired and I wanted my bed.

Flakes of snow were fluttering to their death on the cold cobblestones of the yard as I headed back towards our apartment. I was hoping to get inside quickly because of the biting cold, but I found that Robert of Lyndham and Alice Cross were blocking my path. Mistress Cross held Lyndham's dog by its leash in one of her hands, as she waved the other into the knight's face.

Alice Cross turned to greet me, apparently pleased to see me for once. 'Ah, good evening, Lord Somershill,' she said, before nodding at Lyndham. 'Sir Robert here will not listen to me. But you might be able to make him see some sense?'

Lyndham inclined his handsome head to mine. 'This woman is trying to tie my dog to a post, de Lacy. She wants to leave poor Holdfast outside for the night. In this weather.'

'That's because I caught the filthy thing in my kitchen,' protested Alice Cross. 'Trying to steal one of the hams.'

'You can't leave a dog out here all night,' I said. 'It will die of cold.'

She folded her arms, disappointed that I had taken Lyndham's side. 'The dog is nothing but a menace, Lord Somershill. When it's not stealing food, it's lying in doorways, trying to trip people up. The amount of times I've nearly fallen over the mangy thing. I don't know why anybody would keep it as a companion. I've seen better looking beasts living in the shit brook.'

'How dare you,' said Lyndham. 'Holdfast is the purest-bred deerhound. He's worth a fortune in stud fees alone.'

'I don't care how much he's worth,' said Alice Cross. 'There's no room for useless animals in this castle. Particularly not the ones that steal our food. I've got to feed a lot of people, you know. For the whole winter.'

'I don't care what you say, Mistress Cross,' said Lyndham. 'I'm not going to let you tie Holdfast outside. I've already had to abandon a perfectly good horse to the nearest woods, so I am not about to lose an expensive dog.'

Realising that she was defeated, Alice Cross took a deep breath. 'Well, this dog is lucky,' she said. 'If the portcullis were still raised, then I'd open the gate and throw him out into the forest. To live with all those stray dogs we can hear baying at night.'

'I remind you, Mistress Cross,' said Lyndham, 'that you're a servant.' He yanked his dog back from her with a determined tug. 'And if I were your master, it is you who would be thrown out into the forest.'

Alice Cross lifted her voluminous skirts and turned on her heels. 'I might be a servant, Robert of Lyndham,' she said, as she stalked away across the cobblestones. 'But then again, so are you.'

Lyndham grasped his dog about the neck and then kissed the bemused creature on the head. Holdfast seemed neither to have noticed, nor to care that he was the subject of such a heated debate.

Lyndham stood up and turned to me. 'I'm sorry that you had to witness that, de Lacy. The woman is impossible.'

'Mistress Cross can be difficult,' I agreed. 'But then again, she has a difficult job. It won't be easy to run this castle all winter.'

Lyndham waved my excuse away. 'She's always been like this,' he said. 'Insolent with her superiors. Behaving as if she were mistress here.' He sighed. 'I don't know why the Eden family tolerate her. But there we are. She is their servant, not mine.' He bowed his head to me and wished me a good night.

By now the snow was falling in large flakes, so I made a second attempt to reach the door to our stairwell, when I met another person, looming through the silent, white curtain. It was the monk, Old Simon.

'Have you seen Corvina?' he asked me, his voice quavering. 'She's flown away, after that brute threw a stone at her.'

'She will have taken shelter somewhere,' I answered. 'It's a cold night and crows are very intelligent birds.'

'I'm worried about her, Lord Somershill,' he said, his face pale and strained. 'She always comes back to me at night.'

I opened the door to our stairwell. 'Don't stay out here in this cold, Father,' I said. 'Corvina is safe. I'm sure of it.'

Chapter Twelve

When I climbed into bed alongside Filomena, I discovered that we were alone for once, as Hugh was asleep in his own truckle bed in the corner of the room. But, if I had been harbouring any amorous ideas, they were soon thwarted when I discovered that my wife was still fully dressed beneath the sheets and blanket. She even wore her long cloak, with the hood raised over her head.

She turned over to speak to me once I had settled down, pulling her hood over our heads, so that we were hidden inside a fur-lined cocoon. 'Did you get any answers about the coins from that Dutch boy?' she asked, once she had kissed me lightly upon the lips.

'Hans says they were a repayment for a gambling debt.'

She paused. 'Do you believe him?' Even though it was dark, I could tell that she was frowning.

'It's hard to say,' I answered. 'Mind you, Edwin seems the type to play at dice, so it's quite possible that he lost a lot of money to Hans.'

'So you think Edwin is innocent?' she said with a disparaging sniff.

'I'm not saying that.' I leant forward and let my lips touch hers again briefly. 'But equally, I don't really have any evidence against him.'

She moved back sharply. 'Edwin has the most to gain by Godfrey's death, Oswald. You must suspect him, at least.'

'I don't know, Filomena. I still struggle to imagine him as the killer,' I said, before attempting to slip my hand under her cloak. 'My instincts tell me that he's innocent.'

'Could somebody else have entered the castle from outside?' she asked, foiling my move by pulling the edges of her cloak tightly about her body.

'I did wonder, at first, if there might be a secret tunnel or entrance,' I said. 'Especially as Godfrey said something about being able to slip in and out of the castle.'

'And?' she said, intrigued by this thought.

I hesitated. 'And . . . I don't think it exists, Filomena. The killer isn't somebody who crept into the castle. It's somebody who was already here.'

'So, what are you planning to do, Oswald?' she said. 'There is a murderer among us, and you haven't discovered anything yet.'

'Well, that's not quite true,' I blustered, a little hurt by this accusation.

'You think that Edwin is innocent because of your instincts. And you say that Hans is innocent because the coins were a gambling debt. So, if the murderer is not one of those two men, then who is it?'

'I don't know,' I admitted.

'If you ask me, you should take each person in this castle into a room, one by one. Question them until somebody confesses.'

'I don't think that would work,' I said. 'The killer would just deny everything.'

'Then make them afraid to lie to you,' she said. 'Use some force to scare them.'

'You want me to torture a confession?' I said.

'Yes. If needs be,' she said defiantly.

'I can't do that, Filomena. This isn't the Chamber of Torment in the doge's palace.'

She puffed out her lips. 'You English,' she muttered, as she turned her back on me.

We didn't speak for a while, but I hate to go to sleep on an argument – so I reached out my hand and gently touched her shoulder. 'I'm sorry, Filomena. I thought I'd made the right choice in coming here. I didn't foresee any of this.'

The apology worked. She twisted back to speak to me, her indignation gone. 'I know, Oswald,' she said softly. 'I know that you had good intentions. But I'm scared.' She paused, dropping her voice to the softest of whispers. 'Because there's something that I want to tell you.'

At first my heart sank, as I feared this might be another theory about Edwin, but she took me by surprise as she kissed my lips again. 'My bleeding is late, Oswald.'

I found her hand inside her cloak. 'Really? That's wonderful news,' I said, before I slowed my voice and made sure to curb my obvious delight. 'How late?'

Filomena sensed my trepidation, for she felt it just as acutely. We had suffered many disappointments in the last two years, and we knew that any premature celebration was certain to turn the Fates against us. 'Nearly four weeks.'

'Do you feel sick?' I asked, remembering Mary's pregnancy with Hugh.

'Not really.'

'Then perhaps it's too early to be sure?' I suggested.

She touched my face in the dark. 'You do want to have a child with me, don't you, Oswald?'

'Of course I do,' I insisted. 'I just think that it's wise to be cautious, that's all.'

'Cautious about what?'

How to answer this question, without causing her offence? 'It's just that we have had false news in the past,' I said. 'I don't want to celebrate. Not before we're certain.'

She gave a sigh. 'Yes, you're right. I wanted you to know, but we should not tell anybody else yet. Particularly not your mother.'

I knew why she was saying this. The last time that Filomena had suspected she was carrying a child, Mother had announced the news, without our permission, to the whole village at the Lammas Day feast. We had then spent the following months explaining the absence of her pregnancy to every tenant, reeve and passing lord.

Despite my concerns, I was excited. Even though we had suffered from disappointments before. And even though this child might be born into a world of plague and murder. I let myself enjoy a moment of happiness, burying my nose into Filomena's hair before falling asleep. But my dreams were not of the happy kind.

I was standing beside the burning plague house. Just as before, the flames were high as they danced about the timbers, engulfing the blackened bodies in the heat. But this time, rather than being lifeless corpses, these people were still alive. They called out to me repeatedly, though I could do nothing to help them – not until one voice rose sharply above the others. It was a voice I knew well. It belonged to my own son, Hugh. His face still pale and unblemished by the flames.

I fought my way inside the fire, desperate to save him, but every time that I caught hold of his hand, a burning timber fell in front of us, keeping us apart. The more that I failed, the faster he burnt. At first the flames crept about his face, only singeing his skin, but soon the fire consumed him, until there was nothing left of his body but a scorched and blackened shell.

I woke from this nightmare, sitting straight up in bed, until my heart stopped racing. I knew the meaning of this dream well enough. No wise woman was needed to interpret this tale.

I rose at first light, and tried not to wake Filomena as I crept over to my strongbox, but my stealth was in vain.

'What are you doing, Oswald?' she asked me as I turned the key in the lock.

'I couldn't stop thinking about the murder last night,' I said. 'You were right. I do need to make more progress. So it occurred to me to read Godfrey's letters again. There may be something that I missed last time.' I rummaged about in the valuable belongings kept inside this secure coffer. There was a leather purse of coins. A collection of belts. An astrolabe. And my mother's psalter. But no sign of the letters.

Filomena rose from bed, sensing my panic as I began to take each item out and stand it on the floor beside the box. 'What's the matter, Oswald?'

'The letters are not here,' I said.

'Maybe you put them somewhere else?' she suggested.

'No. I definitely locked them in here, Filomena. They're too precious to leave lying around.'

For a moment I felt angry with myself. Perhaps I had hidden Godfrey's letters in a different place and forgotten where. But another thought soon crossed my mind. I closed the lid of the strongbox to examine the lock.

Filomena guessed what I was thinking. 'Has somebody forced the box open?' she said.

'Not exactly,' I answered. 'I think they've managed to turn the lock without using a key.'

'How would they do that?'

'With a long pin, I expect,' I said, running my finger across the lock plate and feeling a few tiny scratches on the surface. These indentations felt new. There was even a little metallic dust on my fingers as I lifted them to my lips.

'But how could somebody creep in here and do that?' she said. 'This room is never empty.'

'What about at supper time,' I answered. 'When we're all in the Great Hall.'

'But so are all the other guests.'

I rested back on my haunches. 'But not last night. Remember. Hans arrived late. And he is a man with the tools for this job.' I got to my feet. 'I'm going to find him now.'

'He'll deny it, Oswald.'

'I don't care. I will not have that boy coming into our apartment and stealing from my strongbox,' I said, striding towards the door.

'Take Sandro with you,' she called to me. 'You shouldn't confront him on your own. Hans always has his uncle with him. And I don't like that pair.'

'I'll be fine, Filomena,' I said.

She caught up with me and pulled my hands to her chest. 'Do you have a knife with you?' I suddenly wanted to laugh, and didn't manage to fully hide this impulse. 'This is not funny,' she said. 'Hans could be the murderer we seek. I told you that before.'

I leant down and kissed her fingers. 'I have a knife, Filomena. I always do.' I then lifted back my cloak and showed her the dagger and sheath that hung from my belt.

She released my hands. 'Then be quick,' she said. 'And please, Oswald. Take care.' She patted her stomach. 'This child will need a father.'

Chapter Thirteen

Hans was scratching a short line into the surface of his wall as I swept into his dark chamber. The candlelight illuminated many more of these marks, all in groups of seven – recording the weeks that he had already spent in this castle. As I strode across the room, a chicken ran past my feet, heading desperately for the door. For some reason, the floor was littered with its curling, downy feathers.

The Dutchman turned to regard my entrance without any particular shock, before putting his knife to the floor and slowly rising to his feet – his grey eyes catching the thin light.

'You've stolen two letters from me,' I said, looking about the room, to see if Pieter de Groot was ready to leap to his defence. Thankfully there was no sign of the older Dutchman. 'I want the letters back,' I said.

Hans smiled at this request, but didn't answer.

'I know it was you,' I said. 'Don't deny it.'

He shrugged in response, and before I could think twice, I had drawn my dagger from its sheath and was holding the tip against the leather of his jerkin.

Hans lifted his hands in mock surrender. 'I haven't stolen anything from you,' he said, his voice steady and confident. 'You're wrong.'

I pressed my knife a little harder into his jerkin. 'Yes, you have. You crept into our apartment last night and opened the lock of my strongbox.' I twisted the knife, making an indentation in the leather. 'Now I want the letters back.'

It was at this moment that Pieter de Groot strolled in, holding a loaf of bread and whistling a tune, until he saw my face. 'What are you doing here?' he shouted at me as he dropped the bread to the floor. 'Get away from Hans.'

I kept my knife in its place. 'Your nephew has stolen two letters from me.'

'Stolen? Hans is not a thief,' he protested, but I saw the panic cross his face, and I guessed that this was not the first time Hans had been accused of such a crime.

'I just want the letters back,' I said.

De Groot threw up his hands. 'Letters? Why would Hans steal letters? He can't read.'

And then I realised my mistake. I turned to Hans. 'You stole them for Edwin of Eden, didn't you? That's why he gave you those coins yesterday. It had nothing to do with playing dice.'

'Answer the man,' said de Groot, as Hans remained steadfastly silent. 'I said, answer him!'

Hans threw his eyes to the floor and wouldn't meet his uncle's gaze. De Groot had the power to scare him, at least. 'Nobody paid me to steal letters,' he mumbled. 'I don't know anything.' But he was a surprisingly poor liar when confronted by his uncle, and his trembling voice betrayed him.

I stood back, replaced my dagger in its sheath, and then left the room – but as I closed the door behind me, I heard a violent argument erupt between the two men, ending in a screech of pain. I can only assume that de Groot was dishing out some discipline. With his fists.

Edwin of Eden was not in his bedchamber, so I headed straight for the kitchen, knowing this to be a favourite haunt of our new lord when he got out of bed. It was somewhere he would find food, warmth and the company of women.

Sure enough, I walked into the smoky chamber to find Edwin cornering one of the maids by a long trestle table. The girl was stirring a pot of foaming flour and water and doing her best to lean away from his attentions – so when I asked her to leave, she dropped the wooden spoon into the bowl and then eagerly scampered out, delighted to make her escape.

Edwin looked at me with watery, red-rimmed eyes, before flopping onto the bench beside the table. 'I was getting somewhere with that one, de Lacy,' he said as he waved towards the door. 'She's plain, I grant you. But what choice do I have? Locked up in this castle like a hermit.' He grabbed a slab of bread from a pewter plate and started to pull the crust from the crumb. 'What's so important? Have you found the killer?'

'I want Godfrey's letters back,' I said plainly.

Edwin placed the bread onto the plate, but didn't look up at me. 'What letters?' he said unconvincingly.

'The ones that Hans has stolen for you.'

He hesitated. 'I have no idea what you're talking about.'

'Yes you do, Edwin. You paid Hans to steal letters from my strongbox. The ones that Godfrey gave me for safekeeping.'

He patted the bench beside him. 'Come on, de Lacy. I think you're starting to imagine things. Come and sit down with me. Have a drink.'

I remained standing. 'I don't want to drink with you, Edwin. I just want the letters back.'

He inhaled a long breath of air. 'I've already told you, de Lacy. I don't know what you're talking about.'

'Yes you do. You paid Hans to steal those letters, Edwin. Particularly the letter about Godfrey's wife and child. The one that disinherits you.'

He turned his attentions back to the bread, starting to pull the crust apart in short, agitated tugs. 'I think you should leave, de

Lacy,' he said, his face now flushed. 'Go and get some more sleep.'

He was unnerved, at least. His hands were shaking, so I decided to change my approach. 'No,' I said, taking a seat next to him on the bench and making sure to sit uncomfortably close. 'I think I will join you after all.'

'Go away,' he said, as I shifted closer.

'You do realise that Godfrey will have written other letters, don't you?' I said, leaning over and taking some of his bread. 'The letter that you've stolen won't be the only proof that you're not the true Lord Eden.'

'Get away from me.'

I moved even closer, now able to smell the salty, pungent odour of his sweat. A vein in his neck was quivering. 'Godfrey was nothing, if not efficient,' I said. 'He will have recorded his son's birthright more than once.' I smiled sweetly. 'It seems to me that your thieving was in vain.'

Edwin growled. 'I told you to get away from me.'

I chewed on the bread and refused to move. 'It must be useful to have a man like Hans in the castle,' I said. 'Somebody who will do your bidding for money.'

'I haven't paid a farthing to Hans,' he protested. 'You're imagining it.'

'I'd like to believe you, Edwin,' I said, continuing to chew. 'But the evidence is building against you.'

'What evidence?' The vein in his neck was now raised and throbbing.

'You were seen passing a large purse of coins to Hans.'

'So?'

'Not long before that, your brother was murdered.' I wiped the crumbs slowly from my lips. 'It's very tempting to draw a conclusion from these two events.'

He pressed himself against the wall to get away from me. 'What are you trying to suggest, de Lacy?' he said – his voice now high-pitched and agitated. 'That I'm involved in the murder of my own brother? Is that what this nonsense is all about?'

'Are you?'

'Of course not!'

I paused for a while. 'But perhaps I'll mention this theory to the other guests, anyway. To see what they think. Particularly Lord Hesket, as he has asked me to keep him abreast of the investigation.'

Edwin was shaking now. His face wet with sweat. 'All right. All right,' he stammered. 'Look, I did give some coins to the Dutchman. But it was only for the letters. Nothing else. I certainly didn't pay him to kill Godfrey.'

'So you admit to theft, then?'

He froze for a moment. 'Well . . . yes,' he said, before quickly collecting himself. 'But was it really a crime, de Lacy?' He paused, before his lips curled into a sly smile. 'Now that I think about it, those letters were mine anyway. Godfrey was my brother after all.' He released his body from the wall and leant towards me. 'This is my castle now. I am Lord Eden.'

'Yes. But only until the spring, Edwin. Remember that.'

His smile disappeared and he retreated back to the wall.

I grabbed another crust of the bread. 'I feel disappointed in you, to be honest,' I said.

'What do you mean?'

'I've been your friend. Agreeing to help you with this investigation. Defending your innocence. Even when you're the most obvious person to blame for this murder.'

'No. That's not true. I'm not the killer.'

I puffed out my lips and sighed regretfully. 'But you were the last person to see Godfrey alive and you have so much to gain by his death.'

'I'm innocent, de Lacy,' he said, his face now knotted into a panic-stricken frown. 'I didn't kill Godfrey. You've got to believe me.'

'But you're making it so difficult for me, Edwin,' I said calmly. 'Especially when you behave so deceitfully. Paying somebody to break into my strongbox and steal letters. Letters that your dead brother entrusted to me.' I put down the bread and turned to look him in the eye. 'Give me one reason why I shouldn't throw you into the dungeon straight away.'

'Because you'd be arresting the wrong man, de Lacy,' he said defiantly. 'Lock me in the dungeon, and the killer is still free. Living in the same castle as your wife and child.'

'So give me back the letters,' I said. 'Prove to me that I can trust you again.'

He looked away. 'I can't.'

'Why not?

He bit his lip. 'I burnt them.'

This didn't really come as a surprise. Why else would he have stolen these letters, other than to destroy them? 'But it hasn't done you any good, Edwin,' I said. 'I told you that before. I can bear witness to the letter I was given by Godfrey. And he will have left others. You know what your brother was like. With his love for lists and records, he won't have left Simon's inheritance to chance.'

Edwin rubbed his hands over his face. 'Yes, you're right,' he said at length. 'I shouldn't have done it.' He paused and then turned his head to look me in the eye. 'But I'm not a killer. You must believe me.'

'That remains to be seen,' I said, standing up to leave.

'Oh, come on, de Lacy,' he said. 'I'm innocent. You and I can find the true killer together.'

'No,' I said emphatically. 'I'm investigating this murder on my own. I do not want your help, and I will not be reporting to you.'

I had reached the door when he scampered after me. 'Wait a moment, de Lacy. There's something I want to say.'

'Oh yes?'

'Something occurred to me when I read the letter that Godfrey wrote to that priest, John Cubit. I thought it might be relevant.'

'You're being helpful now, are you?'

'Please. Don't judge me so harshly,' he said. 'I want to find Godfrey's killer as much as you do.' He paused and then pulled at his ear. I couldn't help but see the pimples scattered amongst the hairs of his beard. 'Godfrey was acting very strangely in the months before he died,' he said. 'He locked himself up in that library for hours every night. He wouldn't even let Mistress Cross clean the room. Nobody was allowed to enter unless he was there. And, and . . .' He paused again. 'When I read that letter, I saw that Godfrey mentions some sort of secret project.'

'Do you know what it was?'

'I have no idea,' said Edwin. 'But Godfrey was up to something, that's for certain. Especially as he didn't want anybody else to know about it.'

'Were you reading Godfrey's private letters?' I asked.

He screwed up his face. 'What?'

'Godfrey suspected somebody was opening and then resealing his private correspondence. Was it you?'

'Absolutely not,' he protested. 'I'd never do anything like that. Why must you blame everything on me?'

'Because you're dishonest and deceitful, Edwin. That's why.'

'Yes. But that doesn't make me a killer, does it?'

We regarded each other for a moment, as I felt my eyes drawn again to those pimples taking cover beneath his unruly beard. Why does the eye seek out such blemishes, even when the mind tells it not to? I blinked and refocused. Was Edwin innocent of Godfrey's murder, as he so vigorously claimed? Or was I being fooled again? Did his treachery go beyond thieving?

I turned my back on him and walked away. I was still minded to give Edwin the benefit of the doubt. Which meant continuing to look elsewhere for the killer.

Chapter Fourteen

I returned to our apartment to find the usual chaos of the morning under way. Mother was dressing with Filomena's assistance, Hugh was crying because he had just woken up, and Sandro was trying to breathe some life back into the fire. I offered what help I could, and once we were finally able to leave the rooms and make our way to the inner ward, Filomena and I could speak privately at last.

'Did Hans steal the letters?' she asked me.

'Yes,' I said. 'Edwin paid him to do it. That's what those coins were for.'

She raised an eyebrow at this. 'Did Edwin give the letters back to you?'

'No. He burnt them.'

She gasped. 'Now will you believe me, Oswald? That man is evil. You must stop defending him.'

I rubbed my face with my hands. 'I know why you think that, Filomena. But I still don't believe he's the murderer.'

'So what do you believe then?' she said, folding her arms.

'I want to search Godfrey's library again.'

'Why?'

'I'd like to know what Godfrey was working on, before he died,' I said. 'Apparently he barely left his library in recent weeks. And then there was the mention of his "shared vision" in the letter to John Cubit. Something that he was hiding from "prying eyes". Do your remember?' She nodded in response. 'His secret work must be hidden in that room somewhere, Filomena,' I said, 'and I want to find it.'

'You think it's important?'

'Yes,' I said. 'I do.'

As Filomena and I climbed the many steps towards Godfrey's library, we could hear Alice Cross below in the inner ward, shouting at Sandro as he chased Hugh about the square. A kinder-hearted person would have been delighted to hear Hugh's squeals of laughter, but not Alice Cross. The joy of children only seemed to provoke her.

Once we had reached the second floor, I opened the heavy door to the library and then stepped inside to find this room was as dismal as ever. Without a daily fire, the chamber was rapidly surrendering to the damp of the marsh. A pervasive mouldy smell hit my nose and then lodged itself at the back of my throat.

Filomena was immediately drawn to Godfrey's new window, with its impressive view across the marsh. I joined her for a moment, seeing a pale sky meet a grey sea in a faint line across the horizon. The light was good today. The hills of the Kentish downs were visible to our left, covered in the snow from the previous night. In front of this line of raised land we could see the banks of the innings, where the local farmers were reclaiming the land from the sea in neat, square pockets.

'It's quite a sight, isn't it?' I said, as the clouds threw dancing shadows across the marsh — a vast panorama that was both earth and water.

She smiled sadly. 'It reminds me of Venice, Oswald.'

I tugged at her arm. 'Come on, then,' I said quickly, hoping to discourage a bout of homesickness. 'Let's see what we can find in here.'

She pulled her eyes away from the window with a sigh. 'Remind me what we're looking for, Oswald?'

'We need to find this "shared vision".' I said. 'Whatever it is.'

'You genuinely think it's here?'

I shrugged. 'I don't know, Filomena,' I said honestly. 'But this is where Godfrey was conducting his clandestine work. So, I can't imagine where else it would be.'

Filomena nodded her head. 'Very well,' she said. 'Where should I start?'

'We're looking for a secret hiding place,' I said, suddenly feeling a little foolish. 'There might be a hidden compartment in the walls or floor. Who can say?'

Filomena looked at me dubiously, before she went to work, lifting the damp tapestries from the wall and feeling along the wooden panelling. I turned my own attentions to the furniture. This room was plain, fitted out in Godfrey's favoured style of expensive simplicity – but there was still a good selection of chairs, side tables and coffers to inspect.

When our initial search revealed nothing, I then turned my attentions to the shelves of books along one wall of the room. I picked a book at random, finding it was a simple psalter. The inscription in the front of the book showed that it had been a gift from Godfrey's mother to his father in the year of 1325. I lifted the book to my nose and smelt its leathery binding. There was an odour of mildew, and some of the pages towards the middle of the psalter were sticking together and had to be gently prised apart. This damp chamber was not suitable for the storage of books. If left here for long enough they would only absorb the sea air like sponges.

I ran my finger along the other titles, when a thought occurred to me. Where was the manuscript that Godfrey had tried to lend me on the night he was killed? The book by John Wyclif. I returned my eyes to the shelf, checking that I had not missed this thin work, but *The Last Days of the Church* was definitely absent.

I then searched the room again – until another thought crossed my mind. I headed for the fireplace, and there, amongst the lumps of charcoaled wood and mounds of fine ash, were the flaked remains of something. Was this the missing book? It certainly had the look of a burnt manuscript.

I was poking my fingers around in this debris when somebody opened the door without knocking. I must have looked odd, with my hands in the grate, but thankfully Filomena was not feeling behind a tapestry at this point. Instead she had taken a break from her search and was once again staring out of the window at the marsh.

Our visitor was the monk, Old Simon, who shuffled into the chamber with one hand on his walking stick and the other raised to his chest. The steep ascent up this narrow, winding staircase had made him short of breath. 'Is that you, Lord Somershill?' he asked, straining to see my face through the poor light. 'I can't see you.'

I moved nearer the window. 'Yes,' I said. 'And my wife, Lady Somershill.'

The old monk creased his face into a smile. 'Ah,' he said. 'Mistress Cross told me that she'd seen you coming up here.' He placed his hand on my arm and leant against me. 'Could you help me to a chair, my Lord,' he asked. 'My legs are rather disobedient these days. And those stairs are very steep.'

Filomena hurried over from the window to assist me and we each took an arm, guiding the old man to one of the chairs near the fireplace.

'God bless you,' he said, as he sat down and then recovered his breath. 'You must think I'm very foolish to climb up all those steps.'

I was unable to lie. 'I'm surprised you've managed it,' I said. 'It's a steep ascent.'

'I'm still looking for Corvina,' he said. 'She's been missing since that brute threw a stone at her last night. I wanted to know if you've seen her? Sometimes she flies up onto these windowsills.'

'I haven't, I'm afraid,' I said. 'Have you?' I asked, turning to Filomena. My wife shook her head in response.

'Never mind,' said the old man with a regretful sigh. 'Perhaps she has left me at last, and gone to be with her own kind.' He lifted his hand to his eye to wipe away a tear.

'Would you like some help back down the stairs?' I asked.

'Thank you, Lord Somershill. That's very kind of you. But, if I might rest in this chair for a while longer, before I attempt my descent?'

We stared at each other for a moment, as I could hardly ask him to leave – but then again, Filomena and I could not resume our search with this man as our audience.

Old Simon didn't notice my reticence. Instead he looked about the room with sad eyes. 'Do you know that this library contains some of the most valuable books in England, Lord Somershill?' he said. 'They are treasures. Collected by my family over the centuries.' He cleared his throat with a cough. 'But they shouldn't be stored in this damp chamber. The air in this room is not kind to books.'

I nodded at this.

'Of course, Godfrey wouldn't hear of moving them, so I'll have to speak to Edwin on the matter.' He sighed. 'Though I'm afraid that our new Lord Eden doesn't care much for books or reading.' He then lifted a crooked hand to wipe another tear from his eye. 'It grieves me to come into this room, Lord Somershill. It was here that I taught Godfrey and Edwin to read as small boys. This place reminds me of those happier days.'

He struggled to hold back his tears, prompting Filomena to rush to his side. 'Please, Father,' she said, kneeling next to him. 'Don't be sad. Godfrey may be dead, but he's with the saints.'

Old Simon patted Filomena's hand. 'I pray for his soul, dear child. I pray for his salvation.'

'His salvation?' I asked, a little surprised at this choice of words.

'Yes,' he replied. 'My nephew's death was so sudden. I can't imagine that he had time to make his Last Confession. His time in Purgatory may be long.'

I raised an eyebrow at this, remembering Godfrey's own opinion of Purgatory. 'Godfrey seemed pious enough to me.'

'We are each of us sinners, Lord Somershill,' he said solemnly. 'Each of us must confess our sins before we can enter the Kingdom of God.'

Our eyes met for a moment, before I looked away, not able to let my gaze rest for too long upon his aged features. The lids that shrouded his eyes in folds of loose flesh. The blue tinge to his complexion that evoked the lavender shades of death. The veins that pulsed beneath the skin of his forehead like burrowing worms.

'Now that you're here,' I said, changing the subject. 'I wonder if you could help me with something?'

The old man folded his hands and released his back into the chair. 'Yes. Of course, Lord Somershill. What is it?'

I hesitated for a moment, exchanging a glance with Filomena. I sensed a note of caution in her eyes, but I proceeded nonetheless. These questions needed to be asked, sooner or later. 'Godfrey was working on something before he died,' I said. 'A collaboration with a priest called John Cubit.'

'John Cubit?' said Old Simon, screwing up his eyes, so that they disappeared completely beneath his heavy lids. 'I don't know a priest by that name. What sort of collaboration was it?'

'We're not sure,' I admitted. 'Godfrey described this work as their "shared vision".'

The old monk began to smile. 'And you're wondering if I know what it was?'

'Do you?'

'No,' he said with a regretful shake of his head. 'I cannot help you, I'm afraid.' He sank further into the chair. 'Godfrey and I have rarely spoken in recent years. Other than to argue about the condition of the books in this library, of course.' He grunted a laugh. 'I spend most of my time at the priory, you see. And I only arrived here at Castle Eden a day before you did,' he sighed.

'Sadly, Godfrey did not have the time to converse with me during his last days.'

'You've never discussed matters of faith with Godfrey?' I asked.

The old man scratched at his temple, causing a small flurry of dry skin to flutter down onto the black wool of his habit. 'No more than I've discussed faith with anybody else,' he said.

'Were you aware that Godfrey was unhappy with aspects of the church?'

He hesitated, before his frown was replaced with a smile again. 'Oh, I see what you mean,' he said. 'You're talking about his disdain for rosaries and relics, aren't you?' He then shook his head in mock exasperation. 'That was just talk, Lord Somershill. A foolish fancy.' He clutched his hands onto the arms of the chair and then leant forward to speak to me in a whisper. 'But I admired his conviction.'

'Why's that?'

'It is good to question, Lord Somershill. Especially when a man is young. When I was a novice at the abbey, we liked to debate amongst ourselves that the Papal seat should be located in Rome, not Avignon. Can you imagine such a thing?' He gave a distant smile. 'We thought ourselves so daring. Sitting in the cloisters and whispering, when we should have been praying in silent contemplation.'

'I think that Godfrey's work was more than a fancy,' I said. 'He and Cubit were followers of John Wyclif.'

The old monk furrowed his brow. 'Who?'

'John Wyclif. The master of Balliol College. He's a controversial figure within the church, I believe.'

The old man looked into the air, giving my question a lot of thought. 'I'm sorry, Lord Somershill. I've not heard of this man,' he said. 'Our abbey is very small and isolated, so we do not hear much news of the outside world. Are you sure that Godfrey was associated with this Wyclif?'

I went to say more, when we were taken completely by surprise as Alice Cross burst through the door, holding something to her breast, as if it were a child's doll. As she ran across the room towards Old Simon, I realised it was the limp body of a dead bird.

Old Simon recognised his crow immediately. 'Corvina?' he said, as he grasped the bird from Alice Cross's hands and let her lie on his lap. 'What's happened to her, Mistress Cross?' He attempted to shake the bird back to life. 'I don't understand.'

Alice Cross bowed her head to the old man — her voice soft and sympathetic for once. 'I'm so sorry, Father. I tried to stop him, but it was too late.'

'What do you mean?'

'It was that brute from the Low Countries. The young Dutchman.'

'He did this?' he asked, before letting out a long, rasping whimper. 'Are you sure, Mistress Cross?' He then pulled back the bird's wing to expose a breast denuded of feathers. The exposed, yellowish skin beneath was skewered with thin metal pins. 'Good God,' he said. 'What is this?'

'They are dress pins, Father,' she said. 'I caught him in the stable.' Her words were fast and her breathing was rapid. 'I tried to stop him, but he had already broken her neck.'

Old Simon pulled out one of the pins and then studied it for a moment, holding this thin strip of metal to the light, as if he still couldn't believe what he was seeing. He then set his face into a vicious scowl, clutched the bird to his chest with one hand and then pressed the other to the arm of the chair, rising unsteadily to his feet. 'The boy will pay for this atrocity,' he growled, before he made for the door, brushing away the walking stick when Filomena offered it.

'Wait for me, Father,' said Alice Cross as she scampered after him. 'You'll slip. You know how greasy those steps are.' When the monk didn't answer, she called again. 'Take care, Father. Please. You don't want to fall!'

The old monk did not heed her words. In fact, he lurched down the steps with hair-raising speed, before he threw open the door to the inner ward with the force of a much younger man. Filomena and I followed in his wake, emerging out into daylight to find a selection of the household gathered together at one end of the inner ward. Lord Hesket was strolling about with his wife on his arm, while his daughter, Lady Emma, was shyly watching Sandro and Hugh from a corner. Pieter de Groot and Hans were seated on a short bench, cleaning a selection of their tools with oiled rags.

Old Simon hobbled towards Hans, stopping in front of the young man and dangling the dead crow in his face. 'How could you do this? You devil. You know how much I loved this bird.' Hans reacted by peering at the creature, as if he were inspecting his work.

As usual, it was de Groot who spoke up on his nephew's behalf. 'What is this?' he said. 'Why are you showing us a dead bird?'

The old monk shook with rage. 'I raised Corvina from a chick. A poor, unwanted nestling. And now your nephew has killed her.' He lifted Corvina's broken wing and then released it to fall limply from his hand. 'Look what he's done. He's maimed her. For what reason? The boy is a devil.'

By now the other guests had wandered over, drawn to this scene by the shouting. Lady Emma took one look at the dead bird and began to groan, making that strange, unearthly sound in her throat. Sensing a tantrum was coming, Lord Hesket ushered his daughter away, commanding his uninterested wife to comfort the child. Lady Isobel grasped Emma's hand and dragged her to the other side of the inner ward, as Hesket returned his attentions to the confrontation over Corvina.

'What's going on here?' he asked.

Pieter de Groot was now on his feet, lifting one of his small hammers in the air. 'These people are making accusations against my nephew,' he answered. 'They say he killed a bird.'

It was Alice Cross who spoke next, still breathless from her ascent and subsequent descent from the library. 'I say that he did it,' she shouted. 'Because I saw him.'

De Groot regarded the woman for a moment and then unexpectedly turned to me. 'Did Lord Somershill tell you to say that?' he said, waving the hammer in my face. 'This man likes to blame everything on Hans.'

'No,' I answered. 'I didn't say a thing to her. Mistress Cross saw your nephew's cruelty with her own eyes.'

'I don't believe it,' said de Groot. 'This is just another of your lies. Hans has a good soul. He would never do the things you say.'

I glanced at Hans, not seeing the kind-hearted young man that de Groot had described. Instead I saw the face of a sly youth who was relishing the unpleasant drama of this skirmish. A devious smile had crossed his cracked lips.

'Your nephew has the blackest of hearts,' shouted Alice Cross. 'We should break his arms and stick pins into his chest. To see how much he likes it.'

De Groot turned on the woman. 'Who are you to say such things to me? You. A servant!' The Dutchman waved the hammer again, but this time it swung a little too close to my face.

'That's enough,' I said, grasping his wrist. 'Put the hammer down.'

De Groot tried to swing again, when Lord Hesket came to my assistance, pushing the Dutchman to the floor with surprising force. 'How dare you threaten a lord with a weapon,' he said, as he placed a boot onto de Groot's leg, preventing the man from returning to his feet.

'I was defending my nephew,' bleated de Groot. 'These people are always telling lies about him. He didn't hurt that bird. They just like to blame him for everything. Just because he's not English.'

'Oh come on,' said Hesket. 'The boy has a history of malevolence.'

De Groot struggled to answer. 'Well, what does it matter anyway?' He blustered. 'It was just a bird. Not a man.'

'She was not just a bird to me,' roared Old Simon, tears now flooding down the wrinkled furrows of his face. 'I loved Corvina.'

'We should have cooked it in a pie,' said de Groot. 'It's foolish to let a bird fly around a castle like that.'

Hesket depressed his foot again, causing the Dutchman to scowl. 'Be quiet, or I'll throw you and your nephew into the dungeon.' He pointed at Hans, who was now quietly retreating towards the nearest door. 'Do you understand me?' he said.

De Groot hesitated to answer, looking up at the faces bearing down on him – his own face flushed with a mixture of anger and humiliation. 'Yes, my Lord,' he said at length. 'I understand.'

Hesket released his foot from de Groot's leg. 'Then get back to your cellar and give us some peace from your unpleasant company.'

'But what about Corvina?' said Old Simon, still nursing the dead bird in his arms. 'The boy must be punished.'

Lord Hesket turned to the monk, ready to respond, when a thin wail rang through the air. It came from the other end of the inner ward, where Lady Emma was standing beside her stepmother and Robert of Lyndham. They looked on helplessly, as the girl threw herself to the ground and began to roar.

Hesket pushed past the onlookers to reach Emma, as the girl beat her fists against the ground. 'Hush now,' he said, as he knelt down to gently place a hand on her shoulder. But it was too late, for Emma's tantrum had set sail and would not be blown off course.

Hesket turned to his wife accusingly. 'You were supposed to be comforting her,' he said.

'I was trying to,' she protested.

'It didn't look that way to me.'

Lyndham stepped in at this point. 'This is my fault, Lord Hesket,' he said. 'I distracted your wife from Emma.'

'Oh yes?'

'I heard shouting and came out to ask Lady Isobel what was going on. I didn't mean to divert her from Lady Emma's care.'

Lord Hesket answered this with a peevish nod, before he turned his attentions back to Emma, attempting to haul his daughter to her feet. When he'd finally achieved this, refusing any help from either myself or Lyndham, he dragged the girl towards his apartment, leaving his wife to trail along resentfully in his wake.

The inner ward soon emptied after their departure, as Old Simon nursed his crow in his hands and wept as Alice Cross looked on awkwardly — as if she had no idea how to offer sympathy. I was tempted to leave myself, but it felt callous to walk away from this scene without making some effort to console the man. So I approached the monk and said something trite about Corvina having had a long and happy life, but my words were of no comfort. I could see he was heartbroken, for he shook with grief — a sorrow he had not shown at the death of his own nephew.

'I want to bury her beside the graveyard,' he told me.

'But that's not possible, Father Simon,' I said softly. 'It would mean raising the portcullis again.'

'What would you have me do, then?' he said. 'Throw her over the wall, as a meal for the foxes?'

I was momentarily lost for words. 'Could you not keep her body in a box for now,' I suggested. 'Bury her in the spring?'

He turned to me with bloodshot eyes. 'No I could not, Lord Somershill! I will not spend the whole winter smelling her body rotting away. Corvina will be buried in the graveyard,' he said firmly, balling his hand into a fist. 'And that's an end to it.'

I bowed my head and sighed. 'If that's your wish, Father Simon.'

'It is. You can come with me, or I will go alone.'

Chapter Fifteen

The light was fading as we emerged through the gate onto the bluff of land between the castle and the chapel. The sky was cold – violet blue and skirted by a line of small, downy clouds floating just above the horizon. The temperature was dropping with each moment, and yet here I was, accompanying an old fool on his mission to bury a bird in the hallowed ground of this graveyard. I asked Old Simon to be quick about his task. The less time we spent out here, the better. If I saw any movement in the nearby woodland, then we would retreat immediately to the castle, regardless of his desire to give the bird a Christian burial.

I kept my eyes on the trees, as the old monk knelt down to place Corvina's battered body into a very shallow grave. 'I shall never understand such cruelty, Lord Somershill,' he said, as he covered her body with handfuls of sticky soil. 'Why does a man kill another creature for no reason?'

'It's difficult to say,' I answered.

He wiped his hand across his eye, removing a tear. 'But, if I could comprehend the cause of this sin, Lord Somershill, then at least I could try to find forgiveness.'

I hesitated, unsure at first whether to share my own opinion about Hans. 'It seems to me that there are some people who gain pleasure by causing pain to others,' I said. 'They don't respect or even acknowledge the usual values of humanity.'

He looked up at me, his eyes glistening with tears. 'Have you met such people before?'

I wanted to tell him that yes, I had – most of whom had been at the monastery where I'd been educated. But now was not the time to launch an attack on his church. 'Not many,' I answered. 'I believe they are a rarity.'

Old Simon crossed himself at this. 'I will be praying for the Dutch boy,' he said, as he leant on his stick and rose shakily to his feet. 'Once I've found the strength to forgive him.'

I offered my arm to the old man, and we were heading back towards the castle when I became aware of movement behind the wall of the graveyard.

'Come on,' I said. 'There's somebody over there. We need to get back inside.'

'Who is it?' he asked me.

'I don't know,' I said. 'But let's not wait to find out.'

I steered Old Simon towards the castle gate, but he resisted me, looking back over his shoulder towards the wall. 'But look, Lord Somershill,' he said. 'It's just two little girls. They cannot hurt us.'

I turned around to see a pair of faces, peeping above the stone. The older girl looked at us earnestly and then gave a wave, but the younger girl tried to hide her face, pulling the edge of her shawl across her mouth. But she had not been swift enough, for I had seen what she was trying to hide. There was a fissure in her top lip – a gaping flap that revealed a pair of skewed teeth and the pink skin of her gums.

Old Simon called across to them, his words muffled by the wind. 'What do you want, my children?' he shouted.

They looked at one another, before the older girl called back. 'Our mother sent us here,' she said. 'To ask you to hear our brother's Last Confession.'

'What's wrong with your brother?' I called.

The girl hesitated, whispering something to her smaller sister before she answered. 'He has a fever,' she called back, but there was a note of uncertainty in her voice, and I knew immediately that she was lying.

'Are there others in your household with this sickness?' I asked.

The girl shook her head. 'No. Just my brother John,' she said, before she received a hefty shove in the ribs from the younger girl. This was clearly another lie.

Old Simon took my arm. 'I must go to them, Lord Somershill,' he said. 'I know this family. Particularly the boy they speak of. I baptised him.'

'But he's dying of plague, Father,' I whispered.

The old man frowned at this. 'Then I must hurry to him. Before it's too late.'

He went to move away from me, but I pulled him back. 'You can't go,' I said.

He looked at me in consternation. 'Why ever not? I am needed to hear the boy's Last Confession.'

'He is infected with plague,' I reiterated. 'You cannot risk going to their house.'

'I can do as I please,' he said indignantly.

'No, you cannot. We made a commitment to one another,' I said. 'We agreed to stay isolated from the rest of the island.'

'But—'

'You made the same promise as everybody else, Father Simon. Remember?'

'But I cannot abandon these people,' he said, trying to shake my hand from his cassock. 'The poor boy will die without Absolution.'

'I will not allow you to bring plague into the castle,' I said firmly. 'Not for the sake of this boy. Especially when there is nothing that you can do for him.'

'I can hear his Last Confession,' he snapped. 'He will have a good death, at least.'

'Then go to him,' I said, releasing my hand from the old man's arm. 'But do not hope to return. The castle gates will not be opened to you.'

'But—'

'I will not let you risk the lives of my wife and my son.'

He regarded me with rage for a moment, before the sense in my words filtered through. He then bowed his head and sighed. 'I understand, Lord Somershill,' he said. 'I see that you put yourself and your own family above all others. It is a common sin.'

'I only want to protect them,' I said firmly. 'I will not apologise for that. If you had children, then you would understand.'

The old monk looked at me for a moment, his expression unreadable. 'Very well,' he said. 'At least let me speak to these girls and explain myself.'

'No,' I said. 'Don't go any nearer to them, Father. They may be infected.'

'But—'

'The Pestilence spreads in miasmas. You know that.'

He sighed again, before he wiped his hands over his face and cleared his throat. 'I cannot come to your brother,' he called out. 'But do not fear. I will pray for his soul.'

'But our mother will be angry,' said the older girl. 'She said we must bring you to our house.'

'I cannot leave the castle,' he replied. 'But your mother may hear John's Last Confession. It is allowed for women to conduct this rite in such times as these. It will not impair your brother's passage to Heaven.'

The two girls looked at one another briefly – disappointment and apprehension written across their faces, before their heads disappeared again behind the wall. Moments later we saw them racing across the open grassland in the fading light, bounding forward like a pair of startled fawns.

Old Simon peered despairingly into the distance and then turned his head to look to me. 'I hope that satisfies you, Lord Somershill?' he said acidly.

'I'm only thinking of our safety,' I protested, but the old man had already turned his back on me and was now hobbling towards the castle, defiantly swinging his stick in front of each step in order to demonstrate that he would not accept my assistance – not under any circumstances.

At first I wanted to run after him and defend myself. I wanted to explain that I was not being callous, but pragmatic. In order to survive, we needed to hold to our promises. We needed to take decisions that would save our lives, even if those decisions themselves were difficult. But I knew he wouldn't have listened to me. He did not see the world as I did. He was old. He did not have a wife and he did not have a child.

And then my conscience got the better of me. There was something that I could do for these two children, so I turned back to follow them into the woodland, catching up with them on the path.

'Wait a moment,' I called out.

The younger girl quickly wrapped her shawl about her face again, while her sister looked over my shoulder expectantly. 'Is Father Simon with you?' she asked, as if the old man might have run along the path with me. 'Will he hear John's confession?'

'No,' I said, feeling guilty at disappointing the child again. 'He cannot leave the castle.'

The girl threw her eyes to the ground. 'Oh,' she said dejectedly. 'I see. I thought—'

'Listen to me,' I said, eager to quickly finish this conversation. 'I have some important advice for you both. Try to stay away from your brother, or any others in your family who are sick.'

They stared back at me in silence.

'The Pestilence moves through the air,' I continued. 'Especially if you get close enough for the sufferer to breathe on you.' I hoped they might ask some questions about this, but they continued to gaze back at me with bewildered expressions on their faces.

'If you have to go near to your brother,' I said, 'then wrap a stretch of linen about your mouth. If he has a high fever or his hands and feet are turning black, then leave him alone. There is nothing then that you can do to save his life.' This comment elicited a response at least. Their eyes widened in horror and they both drew back from me. The older girl then turned and ran away. My words had appalled her. But not so the girl with the gaping lip. She repeated the advice out loud and then thanked me – her gratitude only deepening my sense of shame.

Chapter Sixteen

That evening we filed despondently into the Great Hall for supper, to the accompaniment of a tune that The Fool was playing on his shawm – an instrument whose loud and piercing tones are better suited as entertainment for a tournament than a quiet meal. We took our places at the table and were served a stew of stringy boiled fowl – a dish that only seemed to remind Old Simon of his deceased crow. The old monk picked out a bone and sobbed as we tried to talk to one another, though this was not the only distraction to our conversation. Edwin of Eden was drinking at speed, guzzling down his wine and then calling immediately for his goblet to be refilled. We ignored his antics until he launched himself across the table and loudly demanded a kiss from one of the maids, at which point Hesket stood up and reprimanded our new lord in the most severe tones.

After this public belittling, Edwin retreated to his chair to glower at Hesket like a chastised child – but at least he was quiet. I watched him for a while, as the candlelight picked out the gleaming threads of his tunic – another fine garment from Godfrey's wardrobe, no doubt. This tunic would not stay in its pristine condition for long, however, as Edwin had already marked it with red wine and lumps of pottage.

Without Edwin's drunken performance to dominate proceedings, we could converse again – the topic soon turning to Corvina.

As Pieter de Groot and his nephew Hans were not in attendance at supper that night, the other guests felt able to speak freely about the pair.

My mother was first to find fault. 'Of course I've never trusted that Dutch boy,' she declared to the table. 'His eyes are too close together and his hair pokes up in tufts.'

'I'm not sure that we can infer anything about Hans's nature from his hair,' I pointed out.

She shook her head at my words. 'No, no, Oswald. Those tufts are an indication of perversion. I've always said so.'

I caught the eye of Robert of Lyndham, and we briefly exchanged a look of amusement. Lyndham then ran his fingers through his own hair. 'What would you say about my scalp, my Lady?' he asked, as he leant forward to let Mother examine the top of his head. 'Am I fair or foul?' I noticed that Lyndham's hair was thinning at the crown, and for some ignoble reason, it gave me a short frisson of pleasure to find some small flaw in his physical perfection.

Mother, unaware that Lyndham's question was a joke at her expense, peered closely at his head. 'Well,' she said after a few moments of solemn contemplation. 'I would say that you have an advantageous hair formation, Sir Robert.' Then she paused and circled her finger across the back of his head. 'Though I would take heed of this small whorl at your crown. It could be a sign of inconstancy.'

Lyndham raised his head. 'Thank you, my Lady,' he said with a mischievous grin, before he tapped the offending twist of hair. 'I will make certain to watch out for this defect. I did not know of its existence before.'

There was a titter of laughter at this comment, soon extinguished by Old Simon, as he coughed loudly and put his hands together. 'I would like us all to pray for the soul of the Dutchman,' he said. 'I fear his path is turning towards the Devil.'

Lord Hesket placed his goblet down upon the table, firmly enough to catch the attention of the other guests. 'It was a bird,

Father,' he said wearily, before patting his daughter on the head. 'Not a child.' Lady Emma plunged her eyes to her hands at this comment, embarrassed to be pointed out.

Old Simon bristled at Hesket's words. 'Cruelty must be censured, my Lord. No matter if the victim is man or beast.'

'I do not admire the actions of this Dutchman,' replied Hesket. 'But equally, we cannot damn the boy for killing a bird.'

It was Lady Isobel who answered this assertion – which came as something of a surprise, since she rarely contributed to the conversation at supper, other than to call for more wine, or occasionally to bid us good night. 'I cannot agree with you, husband,' she said. 'I don't feel safe with this Dutchman in the castle. I don't like him.'

Hesket turned to regard his wife, seemingly as shocked as the rest of us to hear her voice. 'Would you have us lock the boy in a dungeon, then? For killing a bird?' He pointed to her bowl. 'I would remind you that we are eating a chicken this evening. Should we arrest the cook as well?'

Lady Isobel took a deep and determined breath. 'There is a difference, husband,' she said calmly. 'The bird in question was a beloved companion. Not a farmyard animal.' She paused. 'And anyway. It is not the killing of the creature that has upset me. It is the manner of the bird's death.'

It was Edwin's turn now to contribute, breaking his petulant silence. 'Hans is just bored,' he said. 'Like me.' He then let forth a long belch that caused Lady Emma to cover her ears with her hands and groan.

Old Simon bent forward to fix Edwin in his line of sight. 'The Dutch boy may be bored, Nephew. But that is no excuse for entertaining himself with devilry. He should be punished for his sins.'

Edwin threw back his head in amusement. 'What sin is that, Uncle? Thou shalt not kill an old man's talking bird?'

'But he tortured Corvina,' replied the old priest, his voice lifting with agitation. 'Surely you do not condone that?'

'It was an ignorant animal,' said Edwin. 'A stupid crow.'

'No, no. Crows are very intelligent.' Old Simon was becoming flustered. 'I taught Corvina to speak, and sometimes she would dance for me, hopping from leg to leg and ruffling her feathers if I whistled a tune.'

Edwin looked at his uncle for a moment, before he roared with laughter. 'She was a crow, Uncle,' he said. 'Not a dancing whore!' He then nearly fell from his chair in amusement, prompting The Fool to take up his shawm again – as if a deafening tune might ease the awkwardness of this whole episode. At the very same moment, Lady Emma struck up a wail, causing her father to shout over the cacophony.

'That's enough, Eden,' he called. 'Stop this foolery. You're upsetting my daughter.'

'But it was just a bird, Hesket,' laughed Edwin. 'You said so yourself.' He then jumped to his feet, flapped his arms and strutted about like a chicken. 'A dancing bird.'

'That's enough,' repeated Hesket.

'No, it's not,' said Edwin, as he danced his way towards Lady Emma, standing behind the girl and flapping his wings in time to The Fool's tune. His antics caused Lady Emma to yell even louder, but this was not enough to stop Edwin, who only ceased his dancing when Hesket roughly pushed him to the floor.

'Get away from Emma,' he shouted, 'you drunken ape.'

The Fool dropped his shawm, and for a moment there was an uneasy hush to the hall. Hesket's shove had even silenced Emma.

'How dare you attack me?' said Edwin, as he struggled back to his feet and dusted himself down. 'This is my castle, and I will not tolerate it any longer.'

Hesket folded his arms. 'I'll treat you as I please,' he said, 'because you're an animal. A stupid, drunken animal.' He then pointed at our jester. 'I'd wager this man here has more sense than you. And he's the one we call The Fool.'

Edwin turned away from Hesket and peered along the table. 'Sir Robert,' he shouted. 'Where is Sir Robert?'

Lyndham puffed his lips and held up his right hand reluctantly. 'I'm here, Edwin. In front of you.'

Edwin squinted. 'Ah. Yes, I see you now. Hiding away over there. Well, get rid of this man,' he said, gesturing towards Hesket. 'He has offended me. Throw him and his family out of my castle at once.'

Lyndham flushed. 'And why should I do such a thing?'

'Because you are in my employ,' said Edwin. 'My brother paid you to protect my family. And now I want protecting.'

Lyndham's expression changed from one of awkwardness to anger. 'Godfrey offered me sanctuary from the Plague,' he said, 'in return for guarding this castle. He did not pay me anything. I am a knight, not your servant.'

'That's not true,' said Edwin. 'Godfrey told me so himself. Now I demand that you throw this man and his dimwitted daughter out of my castle.' He paused. 'Though his wife can stay. I might have some use for her.'

'Watch what you're saying,' said Hesket, his voice now low and menacing. 'I won't stand for this.'

'Or what?' said Edwin.

Hesket was bristling with rage – his beard no longer hiding the bright red face beneath. 'You will not speak that way in front of my wife and daughter.'

Edwin only laughed at this. 'Your daughter's mind is addled, Hesket,' he said. 'As addled as a rotten egg. The senseless girl doesn't understand a word that anyone says.'

Hesket thumped the table. 'I'm warning you.'

'You don't scare me,' said Edwin. 'I'm not Godfrey.' He then threw back his head with laughter again. 'Oh yes. You might have persuaded my brother to marry that imbecile,' he said, pointing at Lady Emma. 'But don't think I'm taking your defective offspring to my bed.'

Hesket launched his goblet at Edwin in response, spraying red wine across the table, before he then strode out of the hall to an audience of startled faces.

I followed the man, catching up with him at the far end of the inner ward, where the night was at its very darkest. We had both left the hall without our lanterns, and the moonlight did not reach into this shadowy corner.

When I placed a hand on Hesket's shoulder, he turned to punch me, but I drew back in time to avoid the blow. 'Is it true, Hesket?' I said, grasping his flailing arm. 'Did you plan to marry your daughter to Godfrey?'

He tried to shake me off, but I held firm. 'Get away from me, Somershill,' he hissed. 'This is none of your business.'

'Is it true?' I said again.

'Yes, it's true.'

I was hardly able to believe this disclosure. 'But Emma is only ten years old, Hesket. How could you make such an arrangement?'

'Emma is thirteen. And don't you dare to judge me. If you had a daughter with Emma's weaknesses, then you would understand.'

'No, I wouldn't,' I said, releasing his arm. 'I would never marry such a young girl to a man of over thirty.'

It was now Hesket's turn to grasp me, pulling at the cloth of my cloak and drawing me so close to his face, that the long hair of his beard tickled at my skin. 'You know nothing of our lives, Somershill. Nothing of our troubles.' He shook me. 'What do you think will happen to Emma when I die?' he said. 'I am fifty-five, and if the Plague does not kill me, then some other malady is sure to take my life in the next few years. I have to make arrangements for my daughter now, because there's nobody I can trust to protect her interests when I am dead. My wife will remarry immediately and the rest of my family are no better than grasping cockroaches.' He shook me for a second time, his voice becoming more urgent. 'Emma will need a husband to defend her. You must see that? A man who is kind and sympathetic. A man who can offer her a quiet home, away from the crowds of London.' He suddenly dropped his hands from my cloak and looked away. 'I chose Godfrey as her husband, because he seemed to possess all these qualities,' he said with a long sigh. 'And yet the man was a liar.'

The truth was emerging, taking shape before me. 'Godfrey told you he was already married on the night he was murdered, didn't he?' I said. 'That's why you were so angry when you left his library.'

Hesket looked up sharply. 'How did you know about Godfrey's marriage?'

'I only found out after his death,' I said. 'In a letter that Godfrey had given me.'

Hesket ran his fingers through his hair and composed himself. 'Well, Somershill. You're right,' he said. 'The liar did finally admit the truth to me that night.' He grunted a laugh. 'But how could he string me along any longer? Not when he was planning to bring his wife and child into this castle the very next day.' He took a deep breath. 'And yes, I was angry. Very angry. Both with him, and then with myself. For I shouldn't have been surprised at this final treachery, should I? Godfrey had already been deceiving me for many months.' He shook his head. 'All that money I lent him was intended to prepare this castle for Emma. So that she would have some comforts when she moved into this abysmal hole. So can you imagine how I felt when we arrived? To discover that Godfrey had spent all of my money on the most foolish whims.' He waved his hands in the air. 'Windows. Ventilation shafts. That damned clock! And then . . .' He balled his hands into fists. 'And then, as if that deceit were not bad enough, the liar then admits that he could not marry my daughter after all, because he already had a wife and a child!' He paused to catch his breath. 'So yes. I was angry.'

'Did you return to Godfrey's library later that night?' I asked.

He took a moment to answer. 'What do you mean?'

'Did you return to the library and kill Godfrey?'

Hesket hesitated. 'Be careful what you say. I've suffered enough insults for one night.'

'Well, did you?' I said. 'Godfrey's deception clearly infuriated you.'

'He lied to me, Lord Somershill. Worse than that, he betrayed my daughter.'

'I think the mazer just came to hand, didn't it?'

'What mazer?' he said scornfully. 'I don't know what you're talking about.'

I continued. 'You didn't mean to kill Godfrey, did you?'

'I didn't kill him.'

'But you lost your temper,' I continued. 'You swung the mazer at his head and before you knew what you were doing, you had killed him.' I paused. 'That's the truth, isn't it, Hesket? You're the killer in this castle.'

He stared at me for a moment, his dark eyes boring into mine. 'Is that what you really think?' he said with a scornful laugh. 'Oswald de Lacy. The great investigator?'

'Yes, it is.'

'Then you'll have to prove it, won't you?' he said, spinning on his heels and striding away into the darkness. Was this an admission of guilt, or merely a challenge? I could not say.

I turned to make my own way back towards the hall, allowing time for my beating heart to slow, when I saw a small face in the shadows. It was Lady Emma, her eyes bright and sharp as they looked back at me. Her expression was unreadable. At first I thought that I saw fear, but then I suspected animosity. Whichever was the case, I was certain that she had witnessed this whole conversation, for when I held out my hand to her, she backed away and fled.

*   *   *

I locked the door to our chamber that night, tucked Hugh into bed and then tried to sing the boy a lullaby. I felt tense, and my son picked up upon my apprehension, tearfully begging for Filomena instead. When I finally managed to find sleep, it was restless and disturbed, and did not prepare me for the horrors of the next day.

Chapter Seventeen

I was woken at first light by a thunderous bang at the door to our apartment. I rose quickly from bed, pulled on my cloak and opened the door, to be greeted by the ashen face of Alice Cross.

'What is it?' I said.

'You must come quickly, my Lord,' she replied. She was out of breath and could hardly speak. 'It's Lord Hesket. He's dead.' Before I could ask another question, she added, 'He's been murdered.'

For a moment I felt the blood rush from my head to my feet. 'Where is he?'

'In the stables.'

I stepped into the passageway and half closed the door behind me. 'Does anybody else know about this?' I asked her.

'Only one of the maids,' she answered. 'The girl went to feed the horses this morning and she came across his body.' She paused. 'It's a terrible sight, my Lord. Lord Hesket has been . . .' She took a deep breath and put out an arm to lean upon the door frame. 'His body has been sullied.'

'What do you mean?'

'I cannot describe it,' she replied. 'You must come and see for yourself.'

I told her to wait in the passageway while I quickly dressed, deflecting Filomena's stream of questions, as I pulled a thicker tunic over my head and then tightened my belt. 'Just lock the door behind me,' I told her. 'Don't open it to anybody.'

This advice did nothing to calm her. 'What's wrong, Oswald? I demand that you tell me the truth.'

'Very well then, Filomena,' I said. 'Hesket is dead.'

My wife raised her hands to her mouth and gasped. 'What?' she said in disbelief. 'Was he murdered?'

'Just make sure to keep this door locked,' I said. 'I'll be back shortly.'

I followed Alice Cross down the stairs, through the inner ward and then into the stables, but when our steward refused to go any further, I sidestepped the woman and entered the stall alone – peering past the horse that still occupied this stable, to see something propped up against the far wall. It was Hesket's body – his head drooping to his chest, and his arms and legs splayed, so that he looked like an abandoned doll. Once again, I had the impression that the body had been arranged into a pose.

I approached, kneeling down to look into Hesket's face. The sight that met my eyes was horrific. The killer had cut great swathes of skin from his scalp and scored his cheeks with the blade of a knife – though these injuries were only superficial and had not been the cause of his death. As I slipped my hand inside the loose neckline of his tunic to feel the temperature of his skin, I felt the wound that had really killed him. It was a slit across his throat – deep and cleanly cut. His death would have been instant and silent, for he would not have had the time to call out for help.

I was about to rise to my feet again, when I noticed that Hesket's chemise was torn. Pulling back the cloth to investigate further, I then made another grisly discovery – the skin of his stomach had been skewered with an array of metal pins, as if he were a tailor's pin-pillow.

I called out immediately to Alice Cross. 'Please fetch Robert of Lyndham. Tell him to come without delay. And to bring his sword.'

She did as I asked for once, without a word of argument, soon returning with the knight, whose hair was dishevelled and face darkened with stubble. 'Is it true?' he asked me, as he hung back momentarily from the body.

'Yes. Come and see,' I said. 'As long as you have a strong stomach.'

'I'm a soldier, de Lacy,' he reminded me – but even so, I think that the sight of Hesket's mutilated face shocked the knight, for he took a deep breath and rubbed his hand about his mouth. A sure sign that he was distracting a churning stomach. 'By the saints,' he whispered. 'Who would do such a thing?'

'Take a look at this,' I said, pulling back Hesket's chemise, so that Lyndham could see the pins that punctured the dead man's stomach.

Lyndham leant forward to view this new horror, before he turned his head back to mine, his handsome face now drained of colour. 'The Dutch boy?'

'Yes,' I said. 'This bears all the hallmarks of his butchery.' I stood up. 'So, come on. We need to find him.'

The castle was still silent, until we passed through the inner ward, scattering the brood of chickens that were gathering for their morning feed. They flew up in a noisy confusion, flapping their wings and cackling as if they were under attack. A pair of seagulls watched us from a windowsill – their screeches sounding like laughter at our expense. Perhaps they already knew what we would find when reaching the room where Pieter de Groot and his nephew slept. That Hans had fled.

De Groot could not explain his nephew's disappearance, but still attempted to defend the boy against our accusations – arguing that Hans was only hiding himself away somewhere, due to the constant persecution he received at my hands. I almost congratulated de Groot for shielding Hans in the face of such damning incrimination as the tailor's pins in Hesket's stomach, but when I looked at the clockmaker, I also saw fear in his face. He might have protested Hans's innocence, but I think he knew his nephew's faults well enough. It's why he always shouted so loudly in Hans's defence.

Lyndham and I split up to search the castle – I took the cellars, while Lyndham took the four towers, entering every unlocked room and knocking on every closed door. The castle was now in uproar, as news of Hesket's murder spread, which meant that everybody had joined us in the search – but after an hour of looking, we had found nothing. It seemed as if the Dutch boy had evaporated into thin air.

I was starting to think that Hans might no longer be inside the castle, so I climbed the stairs of the curtain wall to see if he had lowered himself from the parapet walk somehow. When I found no ropes attached to any of the crenellations, I thought again. Hans could not have descended from these heights without a rope, for the exterior masonry of the castle was deliberately smooth and slippery. Nevertheless, I walked the whole circuit of the parapet, looking down at the foot of the castle walls, to see if the Dutch boy had met his death in a failed escape. I saw nothing.

I met up with Lyndham again by the gatehouse. 'So what should we do now?' Lyndham asked me, as a note of deflation crept into his voice.

'Have you seen Edwin of Eden yet?' I asked, looking over at the other guests, who were now huddled together at the opposite end of the inner ward like a herd of wary sheep. Edwin was not among them.

'No. He wouldn't let me into his room,' said Lyndham, a little uneasily. 'I think he was still nursing a sore head, after all that drinking last night.'

'Or Hans is in there with him,' I said.

Lyndham was taken aback at this suggestion. 'Why would Eden be hiding Hans?'

'I have an idea,' I said.

His eyes widened. 'What is it?'

'Just come with me, Lyndham. We need to speak to Edwin.'

Lyndham thumped on the door to Edwin's bedchamber, until the man finally answered. We then rushed inside to look about for Hans, but the room was empty – Edwin's only companion being the pungent stink that always lingered about this chamber like an old friend. This morning Edwin's ratty scent was complemented by the bucket of piss and shit that was standing near to his bed.

Edwin grabbed me angrily. 'What the hell are you doing in here, de Lacy?' he said. 'Get out.'

'We're looking for Hans,' I said.

'Hans? Why? He's not in here.'

'Hesket is dead,' I told him. 'He's been murdered.'

'What?'

'I said Hesket has been murdered and Hans has disappeared.'

Edwin continued to squint at me, before my words finally appeared to make sense. He dropped his hands from my sleeve and then fell back onto his bed.

Wanting to speak privately to Edwin, I then asked Lyndham to leave the room – though my hope that Edwin would talk more freely to me if we were alone did not prove successful at first, since he only grunted the most incoherent answers in response to all of my initial questions.

'What exactly happened to Hesket?' he asked me, in the end.

'His throat was slit and his body was mutilated,' I said.

'Mutilated?'

'Yes. The murderer sliced the skin from his scalp and stuck pins into his stomach.'

Edwin recoiled at this description. 'What?'

'Does that remind you of anything?' I asked.

He gave a shrug in response. 'I don't know what you mean,' he said.

'Yes, you do. It's what Hans did to your uncle's crow.'

Edwin stiffened. 'Are you saying that the Dutchman killed Hesket?' he said. 'Why would he do that? They had no quarrel.'

'But you had a quarrel with Hesket, didn't you? And we both know that Hans will do your bidding for money.'

Edwin drew back. 'Now wait a moment, de Lacy,' he said, holding his hands aloft as if I were threatening him with a pike. 'Don't start that again. I've told you before. I would never pay Hans to kill somebody.'

'But you did argue with Hesket last night, didn't you?'

He was speechless for a moment. 'Yes,' he said, 'but that was just a silly falling out.'

'Oh, come on, Edwin,' I said. 'Hesket belittled you, Edwin. And then attacked you, in front of your own household.'

He paused, and let his hands drop. 'That didn't upset me,' he lied. 'You're wrong about that.'

'Where's Hans?' I said.

'How should I know?'

'He's not in the castle.'

'He must be.'

'There's another way out of here, isn't there?' I said. 'Godfrey knew about it, and so do you.'

'No there isn't,' he answered. 'That's nonsense.' But it was too late. I had seen the telltale twitch in the corner of his eye. I knew that he was lying to me.

I strode back to the door and pulled the large key from the lock.

'What are you doing?' asked Edwin, chasing me across the room with a panicked expression on his face.

'I'm making sure that you stay in here,' I said, as I opened the door.

'You can't do that!' he said. 'This is my castle.'

I hesitated. 'Tell me the truth about Hans, Edwin. And then I won't lock this door.'

'I don't know what you mean,' he bleated. 'I don't know anything about any of this. You've got to believe me.'

'But I don't believe you,' I said. 'That's the problem.'

He rushed forward to make his escape, but not before I had darted out into the passageway and pulled the door shut behind me.

Lyndham looked at me in surprise as I turned the key in the lock, whilst Edwin banged and kicked ferociously on the other side of the door. 'Let me out of here,' he shouted. 'Hesket's murder has nothing to do with me! Let me out, I tell you! This is my castle.'

Lyndham cocked his head. 'What are you doing, de Lacy?'

'I want to keep Edwin locked in this room for now,' I told him.

'Why?'

'He knows something about Hesket's murder,' I said.

The knight narrowed his eyes. 'Really?'

'Yes.'

'Have you got any evidence against him?' he asked.

'Not yet.'

He lowered his chin and looked at me from beneath his eyebrows. 'Then is it a good idea? This is his castle after all.'

'Edwin of Eden is involved in this murder somehow,' I said resolutely. 'So he can stay in this room until he decides to tell me the truth.'

Lyndham was not going to give up that easily, however. 'I would agree with you, de Lacy,' he said, now whispering even though we were completely alone. 'But—'

'But what?'

He puffed his lips. 'I'm not comfortable about locking him into this room.'

'Why?'

He hesitated and then cleared his throat. 'Edwin was right last night,' he said.

'Right about what?'

Lyndham wiped his forehead with uncharacteristic embarrassment. 'When he said that I was paid by Godfrey to guard this castle.' He paused. 'You see, my own affairs have been a little difficult in recent years, so I often carry out such work for noble families. I don't like asking for payment, of course. But I'm forced to.' He gave a strained smile. 'Because of my reduced circumstances.'

'We must all earn a living somehow,' I said blankly.

He frowned at my response. 'You're not understanding my point, de Lacy. Imagine how it will look for me if I've falsely imprisoned a nobleman? Especially as he's a member of the family who engaged me in the first place. Who will ever want to retain me again?'

I put my hand onto Lyndham's arm. 'Just leave Edwin in there for now,' I said. 'It's his bedchamber. Not a dungeon. I just want to give him some time to consider.'

'Consider what?'

'Telling me the truth.'

Lyndham heaved another long sigh. 'Very well,' he said. 'If that's your decision.'

'It is.'

'And what now?' asked Lyndham.

'I'm going to speak to Hesket's wife,' I said.

His face brightened at last. 'Would you like me to come along with you?'

'Thank you,' I said. 'But I should go alone. It's better if there's just one of us.' I could see that he was disappointed not to be included, so I quickly added, 'But, you can help in another way.'

'Oh yes?'

'Will you wrap Hesket's body in some linen and then lift him into a coffin? Before his daughter sees what's happened to his face.'

Lyndham took a deep breath. 'Very well,' he said with some hesitancy. 'But where am I to find a coffin?'

'There's a whole collection of them in one of the cellars,' I said. Lyndham looked surprised by this. 'Godfrey was very thorough in his preparations,' I told him. 'Ask Alice Cross to show you the room.'

Lyndham bowed his head and rested his hand upon my upper arm, clutching it tightly, as a child might grip his mother. For a moment I wondered what he was going to say, before he dropped his hand. 'Thank you, de Lacy,' he said quietly. 'These are dark days. I'm pleased you're here.'

Chapter Eighteen

I was informed by Alice Cross that Lady Isobel had requested privacy following her husband's murder, but I could not wait any longer to speak to the woman. Despite our steward's vocal objections, I knocked at the door to the Heskets' apartment and then entered without waiting to be called inside. Alice Cross followed me into the room, claiming that she needed to empty Lady Isobel's chamber pot – refusing to leave this chore until later in the day.

We found Lady Isobel sitting in a chair near to a roaring fire. She neither acknowledged my entrance, nor that of Alice Cross. As I walked across the carpet, I realised that Hesket's daughter, Lady Emma, was standing with her face to the wall, and did not turn to look at us – even when I placed my hand upon her tiny shoulder.

It was my interest in the girl that finally woke Lady Isobel from her reverie. 'It's no good trying to comfort Emma, Lord Somershill,' she told me. 'She won't move.'

'Does she understand what's happened to her father?' I asked.

'I think so.'

I moved away from the girl, realising that my touch was only making her more anxious. 'I would like to speak to you on your own, Lady Isobel,' I said, turning to Alice Cross, who was still lingering in the pretence of clearing away the chamber pot.

'Perhaps you would take Lady Emma to the inner ward, Mistress Cross,' I said, 'while I speak to Lady Isobel.'

Alice Cross bristled at this request. 'Me?'

'Yes.'

Lady Isobel looked up from the fire. 'Please do as Lord Somershill asks, Mistress Cross,' she said. 'It would be very helpful.' She then bestowed a rare but sorrowful smile upon our bad-tempered steward. 'And I would appreciate it.'

Alice Cross was cornered by a lord and a grieving widow — a difficult position from which to refuse a polite request. She puffed her lips and scowled. 'Very well then, my Lady,' she said brusquely, before she approached Emma and pulled at her arm. 'Right then, Emma,' she said. 'You've got to come with me.' When the girl didn't respond, she continued, 'Now don't be difficult. Your stepmother wants you to leave the room.' Still no response. Alice Cross looked at me in despair, before she huffed and then turned back to the child. 'Please come with me, Emma,' she said, coating her voice in a softer tone. 'There's a good girl. We can watch the flames in the bread oven.' She paused. 'You know how much you like to watch the fire.'

It was this suggestion that finally persuaded the child to turn her face from the wall, and place her tiny hand into Alice Cross's large palm. As she followed our steward across the carpet, she never once lifted her eyes to look at me or her stepmother.

Once I had closed the door on this pair, I joined Lady Isobel at the fireside, waiting for an invitation to take a seat. 'I'm so sorry about your husband,' I said, sitting down anyway, when the invitation didn't arrive. 'Lord Hesket was a good man.'

She nodded in response. 'Yes,' she said. 'You're right, Lord Somershill. He was a good man.' She poured herself a goblet of wine from a delicate rock crystal jug. 'I understand that you've seen my husband's body,' she said, before taking a long sip of the wine. 'I'm told that he was . . .' She paused for a moment. 'Damaged.'

'Lord Hesket's death was quick,' I said, clearing my throat. 'The . . . damage was caused after his death. He wouldn't have felt anything.'

'That is a consolation at least,' she muttered, before she took another sip. 'When can we bury him?'

'We should be able to do it later today.'

She let her gaze rest on the contents of the goblet, studying the wine as it swirled around in the bowl.

I let her continue this for a while before clearing my throat again to break the silence. 'I wondered if I might ask you some questions, Lady Isobel?'

She looked up at me, her eyes red and glistening with tears. 'Yes, of course,' she said. 'What would you like to know?'

'When did you last see your husband?'

'I went to bed after supper last night, but Lord Hesket didn't join me.' She smoothed the hair from her face, as this admittance seemed to make her uncomfortable. 'He was still very angry after the argument with Edwin of Eden. But my husband was not a good sleeper at the best of times,' she added quickly. 'He liked to read at night, or visit his horse. He found it restful to spend time with the creature.'

'So that's why he was in the stables?'

'Yes, I think so,' she said. 'Though he rarely explained where he was going or what he was doing to me.'

'Did anybody else know about these nocturnal visits?'

She lifted an eyebrow. 'Clearly the Dutch boy knew about them,' she snapped. 'I was right to say that we should be frightened of him, wasn't I? You heard my warning at supper last night.' She held back a sob. 'I know what that monster did to my husband's body, Lord Somershill. We might call it damage to be polite, but I know the truth.'

'Who told you?' I said, surprised that somebody had disclosed these details.

'It was Alice Cross.'

'I see. Does Lady Emma know as well?'

'Of course not. The girl has the strength of a mayfly. Emma could not bear such knowledge. Especially as the Dutch boy is still roaming the castle.'

'Lyndham and I will find Hans,' I said. 'You mustn't worry.'

'I wish I could be so confident,' she said. 'But who will be next? The boy has a history of malevolence and a taste for vengeance.'

'Vengeance? Why do you say that?' I asked.

'It's simple,' she said. 'The Dutch boy promised to take his revenge on my husband and Lord Eden. And now both men are dead.'

This was news to me. 'Why did Hans make such a promise?'

She arched an eyebrow. 'Did my husband not tell you this?'

'No.'

She crossed her arms about her chest and shivered, though this chamber was far warmer than any other room in the castle. 'There was a violent argument between the three of them, just after we first arrived here. My husband and Lord Eden . . .' She cleared her throat. 'I should say my husband and Godfrey, the deceased Lord Eden, were taking their morning ride together when they met the Dutch boy in the forest. At first they thought Hans was taking a walk, but then they realised that the boy had borrowed one of my husband's horses without permission. Worse than that. He was flogging the creature with a scourge.'

'Why?'

'Why does the Dutch boy commit any of these crimes?' she said. 'He is a devil. A monster. Of course, he tried to say that the horse deserved a beating because it had thrown him from the saddle. But my husband didn't believe a word of it.'

'Why not?'

'This was his most docile horse, you see. A chestnut mare that had been trained especially to carry Lady Emma.' She looked at me for a moment, and despite her sorrow, I caught some of the beauty in her sculptured, perfectly proportioned face. 'My husband was always very proud of his horses,' she said, 'so he was disgusted to see what the boy had done. The creature was beaten so badly that it was bleeding. Even about the face and eyes.' She hesitated again, holding back a tear. 'My husband was usually a gentle man, Lord Somershill, but he could be provoked. Especially when it came to his horses or his daughter.'

'What happened?'

She heaved a sigh. 'My husband took the scourge to the boy. To see how much he liked being beaten.' She paused, wringing her small hands. 'I think that Lord Eden had to intervene in the end.' She cleared her throat, as if embarrassed to say the next words. 'Or it might have gone too far.'

'You think your husband would have killed Hans?' I asked.

She looked up at me with eyes that were usually so diffident and discontent. Now they were intense and animated. 'Yes, I do, Lord Somershill. And now I wish that he'd succeeded. Because the Dutch boy swore to take revenge on my husband, and now he has carried out his threat.' She leant forward and took my hand. Her skin trembled against my own. 'I fear this man. I truly do.'

I pushed my way into de Groot's workroom without knocking, finding him sitting in a dark corner, wringing an oily rag in his hands. He was obviously upset about his nephew, but did his best to jump up at my entrance and hide his tears. 'Have you found Hans yet?' he asked me, before I had a chance to speak.

'No,' I replied.

'My nephew could also be dead. Have you thought about that? The murderer might have killed him as well.'

'Then where is his body, de Groot?'

He looked away from me, and began to rub at the frame of his clock, though I noticed that his hands were shaking. 'Hans has nothing to do with these murders, Lord Somershill,' he said, wiping the cloth over the crown of the bell. 'I told you that before.'

'Where is Hans?' I said.

'I don't know.'

'Of course you do.'

He whipped his rag against the bell, causing it to chime. 'I don't know,' he said in a sudden temper. 'It doesn't matter how many times you ask me the same question. I cannot answer you.'

If he had hoped to scare me off with his raised voice, then he was to be disappointed. I paused for a moment, and then wandered around the clock frame, letting my hand deliberately rest upon the rope that was wound about the central shaft.

De Groot watched me with nervous eyes. 'Please, take your hand away from there,' he said. 'You will damage the tension on the pulley.' I took my time to obey, causing him to snort with indignation before leaning down to dip his cloth into a bucket of dark brown liquid.

When he stood up again, I caught a familiar smell. 'What's in there?' I asked, pointing at the bucket.

'It's an oil,' he replied. 'We make it ourselves from birch bark. It helps to keep the frame free of rust.'

'That oil burns easily, doesn't it?'

De Groot looked at me strangely. 'Yes, it does,' he said. 'Why do you ask?'

I felt my stomach roll. 'Did Godfrey ever ask Hans to work for him?' I said.

'What do you mean?'

'You know what I mean, de Groot. Just answer my question. Did Godfrey ever pay Hans to do odd jobs? Outside of building this clock?'

De Groot hesitated. 'That was between Lord Eden and my nephew,' he said gruffly. 'I kept out of it.'

I thought back to the day we arrived at Castle Eden. To the masked figure, standing beside the burning cottage. The man who had mysteriously disappeared, when I called out to him.

'Did you know that Lord Eden paid Hans to set fire to a plague house?' I said.

De Groot took a sharp intake of breath, but returned to his polishing, now vigorously rubbing the cloth along the struts of the frame.

'But did you also know that Hans didn't follow Lord Eden's instructions,' I said. 'He was supposed to bury the dead, before he burnt down the cottage. Instead he left the bodies inside the flames, just so that he could watch them burn.'

De Groot stopped rubbing, but wouldn't meet my gaze. 'That's not true.'

'You know that it is,' I said, stepping towards him. 'You know your nephew's faults well enough, and yet you shout down any criticism of the boy. Even when he continues to fail you, time after time.'

'You're only blaming Hans because you can't find him,' he said. 'But I know that he's innocent.'

'Do you?'

He took a deep breath and looked up at me. 'Yes,' he said, 'I do.' However, it was trepidation and not conviction that I saw in his eyes.

I was about to say more, when we had an unexpected visitor. The door to the room slid open and the small figure of Lady Emma crept inside. Evidently she was already bored with the bread oven, and now wanted to see the clock.

'Not now, Emma,' said de Groot, obviously vexed to see her. 'Come back later.'

She regarded him for a while, obstinately refusing to move – before she threw me a look of hostility and then withdrew into the passageway.

'Does Lady Emma come here often?' I asked de Groot, when she had closed the door.

'Yes. She's no trouble,' he said. 'She likes to watch me working, so I don't object. And that poor little girl deserves some happiness,' he sighed, 'before she is sold into another barbaric marriage.'

'You knew about her marriage to Godfrey?' I said, with some surprise.

'Yes,' he replied. 'A tradesman often hears more than he should, Lord Somershill. Noblemen discuss many topics in front of us, as if we were not there.' He heaved another sigh, before he returned the cloth to the iron frame. 'But I fear for Lady Emma. The poor child has a bleak future. I feel sorry for her.'

I sat myself down on a nearby stool. 'And do you feel sorry for Hans?' I said. 'Is that why you tolerate his failings?' De Groot looked at me for a moment, and refused to answer. 'How long has Hans been your apprentice?' I asked.

De Groot huffed. He would respond to this question, at least. 'Since he was fourteen. Five years ago.'

'And is he your blood relation, or the nephew of your wife?'

'Hans is my sister's boy. When her husband died, she couldn't look after Hans any longer, so I offered to take him.'

'Why couldn't she look after him?' I asked.

He hesitated, annoyed with himself for letting this slip. 'Hans needed the influence of a man,' he said, now dipping the cloth back into the bucket of birch oil. 'That's all.'

'Why was that?'

'He was a little wild when he was younger. Nothing unusual. But I have tamed him with discipline and work.'

I raised an eyebrow. 'Have you?'

'Yes,' he snapped. 'Hans is a good boy. He would never do the things that you say.'

'So he didn't swear to take revenge on Lord Hesket?'

'What?'

'Lady Isobel tells me that her husband came across your nephew flaying one of his horses,' I said. 'Hesket gave Hans a beating for it.'

De Groot shook his head. 'That's not true,' he said blankly.

'It's not true that Hans received a beating? Or it's not true that he was cruel to a horse?'

De Groot looked at me with a strange expression, and then resumed his work, now running the rag over the teeth of the largest cog. 'Hans didn't like Hesket, that's all,' he said.

'And is there anybody else he doesn't like in this castle?'

'Well, Lord Somershill,' he said, letting a smile curl at the corner of his lips. 'I don't think he likes you very much.'

I stood up and leant over the man, making sure to put my hand onto the rope again. 'Should I be afraid of Hans, then?' I asked. 'Is that what you're saying?'

He turned his face from mine. 'Hans is innocent,' he mumbled. 'I know it.'

I pulled at the rope and deliberately loosened the tension in the pulley. 'You're so certain that Hans is innocent,' I said. 'And yet you don't have the slightest idea where he's gone?'

The clockmaker took a deep breath, his face flushed. 'That's right, my Lord,' he said adamantly. 'I have not seen Hans since last night.'

Chapter Nineteen

After leaving de Groot, I decided to return to the stable where Hesket had been killed – in the hope of finding some piece of evidence that I might have missed before. When I arrived there, I found that Lyndham had already removed Hesket's body from the straw and placed him into a coffin by the door, where his earthly remains were now attended by Old Simon. The elderly monk knelt beside the coffin, with his eyes shut and his rosary hanging from his hands. His crooked fingers worked diligently through the beads and his lips moved silently in prayer.

Old Simon looked up when he finally sensed that I was standing near him. 'There is devilry at work here,' he told me. 'Satan has been summoned to this castle.'

I gave a noncommittal nod in response, for I could not accuse the Devil of any involvement in this crime, since I did not believe in his existence. 'Can we bury Lord Hesket soon, Father?' I asked.

The old man sighed at this question. 'I believe that Sir Robert is planning to raise the portcullis later this afternoon.' He paused. 'We are fortunate that the soil has warmed, so poor Hesket should be easier to bury than Godfrey.' The monk then crossed himself and rose clumsily to his feet, using the side of the coffin as leverage. When I offered my hand in assistance, he waved me away. He still had not forgiven me for my behaviour towards the two small girls in the graveyard. Instead, he looked at me with a pained expression. 'I pray for you, Lord Somershill,' he said. 'I pray nightly for your soul.'

I ignored this comment, as I was not grateful for his prayers. 'You've known this castle for many years, haven't you, Father?' I said instead.

He scratched at his earlobe, confused at this swerve in our conversation. 'Yes. I was born here,' he answered.

'Do you know of a secret entrance?' I asked. 'Some way for a person to get in and out of the castle, without going through the gate?'

He rubbed his chin. 'I used to hear stories of such a tunnel, when I was a boy. After all, this castle was built during the reign of King Henry II, and an escape route was a common addition in those times, I believe. But, if it exists, I've never seen it.' He paused. 'Why do you ask?'

'The Dutchman is not inside the castle,' I said. 'So he must have escaped somehow.'

The old man paused again, now leaning forwards to study me in the diminishing light. Wrinkles cut across his forehead in deep, wavy lines, and his white eyebrows sprouted untidily above his eyes like overgrown hedges. 'It's as I told you,' he said. 'The Devil is at work here.'

I tarried a while longer in the stables, but there was nothing more to learn here. The bloodied straw had been swept up and burnt, and new straw had been laid down, as if Hesket's murder had never taken place. After this I strolled through the network of rooms that abutted the stables to see what else I could discover – descending some steps into the cellars, and then finding myself in the largest storeroom, with all the hams, cheeses, and sacks of dried peas and flour. The air smelt sweet and dry in here thanks to Godfrey's controversial ventilation shaft.

As I looked up this thin well and caught the grey light of the sky in the distance, I wondered, for a moment, if this could be Hans's mysterious escape route? I then dismissed this theory immediately, as it would have been impossible for any man to squeeze out of such a narrow chute. The Dutchman was thin, but he was not a maypole.

I left the storeroom and was returning towards the stables, when another door caught my attention. It was hidden in a corner at the bottom of the steps, and I had never seen it before. Could this be where Hans was hiding? I drew my dagger from its sheath and pushed at the door, but when I burst in, it was not the Dutchman whom I discovered in the near darkness. It was The Fool, asleep against the wall, with his jester's hat pulled down over his head.

Now that I had shed some light into this room, I could see that this space was no bigger than a large cupboard. The floor was littered with The Fool's instruments – the citole, shawm and two small drums, not to mention a heap of his comic costumes; the cape covered with feathers, a mock archbishop's mitre and a hobby-horse with a long, plaited mane. I have to say that these props looked even more dismal in this light than they did when employed as part of his act.

The man scrambled to his feet. 'Lord Somershill,' he said with a bow. 'I was just resting before Lord Hesket's burial.'

'Is this where you sleep?' I asked.

'Only at night,' he answered, forgetting that I had just caught him dozing in the middle of the day.

I looked about this hidey-hole, and had the distinct impression that this man spent a good deal of time here. There was a straw mattress rolled in one corner, a half-eaten loaf of bread and a selection of short-bladed knives, slotted into a leather belt.

'What are the knives for?' I asked, thinking immediately of the lacerated skin of Lord Hesket's face.

The Fool hesitated for a moment, and then grasped the belt. 'I'm training myself to throw knives at a wooden shield,' he said, presenting me with the line of blades. 'It's a very exciting trick, especially if somebody volunteers to stand in front of the shield.' He must have seen the look of horror on my face, since he then added, 'I've seen it performed many times at the Spring Fairs, my Lord. It's perfectly safe. Nobody is ever hurt.'

'I suppose that depends who's throwing the knives?' I pointed out. He smiled awkwardly in reply, taking the meaning of my words.

While the knives were under my nose, I took the opportunity to study them, on the off-chance that some blood might be lingering upon the blades. But there was nothing to note. They were rusting and blunt, and were unlikely to cut into anything, let alone any person stupid enough to stand in front of a wooden shield, whilst this man launched knives at them.

'Were you sleeping in this room last night?' I asked. 'When Lord Hesket was murdered?'

He answered cautiously. 'Yes. I suppose I was.'

'Yes or no?'

He hesitated. 'Yes.'

'You didn't hear anything?'

He looked at me with panicked eyes, as his mouth momentarily hung open. I felt he wanted to say something different to the words that finally came out. 'Er . . . no.'

'Are you sure?' I said. 'This room is very close to the stable where Lord Hesket was murdered.'

His mouth dropped further. 'I . . . I'm sorry, my Lord,' he stuttered. 'But I didn't hear anything.'

'Who knows that you sleep in here?' I asked.

He gave a cough. 'Well, nobody really,' he said. 'You see, I was told to sleep in the Great Hall with the other servants. But I find that room so cold.' He took off his hat, shook it and then replaced it upon his head. 'And I like to keep an eye on my belongings. These costumes cost me a lot of money, you see.'

'So the murderer might not have known you were nearby?'

'I hadn't thought about that,' he said with another gulp. 'No. I suppose not.' And then something seemed to catch his eye. For a moment he looked over my shoulder into the hallway behind me.

I turned around sharply, gazing into the empty passageway. 'What are you looking at?' I asked.

'Nothing,' he said. 'Nothing at all, my Lord.

'Was somebody there?' I asked.

'No, no,' he said, now screwing up his face. 'I just saw a rat running across the stones.'

I wandered out into the passageway to see if I could spot the scurrying rodent, but the creature had disappeared – assuming that it had existed in the first place. When I returned to the door-way of this enlarged cupboard, The Fool was jittery to say the least. He had retreated back into the shadows. 'Are you afraid of something?' I asked.

'No, no,' he said. 'Not at all.'

I hesitated. 'If you know something, then you should tell me.'

'I don't know anything at all,' he said. 'I was asleep all last night. I didn't see anything. I didn't hear anything.'

This sounded final, but I waited for a while longer, giving silence the chance to do its work. But this man was not going to cave in to such an obvious tactic.

'Very well,' I said at length. 'I will see you at Lord Hesket's burial.'

I quickly ascended the short flight of stairs to the stables and then hid behind a pillar, wanting to see if The Fool's mystery 'rat' would creep out from his hiding place, now that I had departed. I waited for a few minutes, hoping to catch them both out, but nobody appeared. All I could hear was a loud sobbing coming from The Fool's cupboard, followed by the unmistakable sound of hard objects hitting the wall.

I dashed back and flung open the door, to find that he was beating the walls with his hobby-horse. The creature's grinning head hung forlornly from its stick.

'What are you doing?' I shouted.

The Fool crumpled into a pile on the floor, throwing the hobby-horse to one side. 'I am frightened, Lord Somershill,' he sobbed. 'So frightened.'

'Why?'

He looked up at me as if I were mad. 'Why do you think?' he said, with sudden aggression. 'I didn't come to this castle to die.'

'Who says you'll die?'

He threw back his head, causing the ridiculous hat to fall from his head. 'We will all die, Lord Somershill. You know that, as well as I. Either the Plague will take us, or . . .'

'Or what?' I said, lunging forward and grasping him by the tunic. 'Or what?' For a moment he looked at me with confrontational eyes, and I thought he might retaliate with a punch or a kick, but then his courage faded. 'If you know something,' I said, tightening my grip, 'then you must tell me. For all our sakes.'

He shook his head feebly in response. 'I don't know anything,' he mumbled. 'Nothing at all.'

Chapter Twenty

It was late in the afternoon when we buried Hesket, and though we wanted to pay him every respect, we also wanted to get back inside the castle walls before the light disappeared. The day had been unusually clement, but, from our elevated position in the graveyard, we could see the storm approaching across the marsh. In the far distance, rain was sweeping across the sea in long, oscillating sheets, and a bitter wind was beginning to bite.

I had left my wife and son in our apartment, as Filomena had confided in me that she felt pains in her lower back – the same feeling that she'd experienced the last time we had lost a child. She assured me there was no bleeding yet, but I could see that she feared this conclusion.

Mother was not fooled by my story that Filomena was tired, however. She sidled up to me at the graveside, while Old Simon made his last incantations above Hesket's coffin. 'I do think that Filomena should have joined us,' she whispered. 'It's rather disrespectful, don't you think? Lord Hesket was a very important man.'

'I told you earlier,' I said. 'Filomena's not well.'

Mother altered her expression into one of exaggerated concern. 'Oh dear,' she exclaimed. 'She's not losing the child, is she?'

Was there any possibility of keeping a secret from this woman? 'She's just tired, Mother,' I said. 'There is no child.'

She gave one of her knowing smiles. 'Of course there is, Oswald,' she said. 'For the time being at least.'

I felt a flare of anger – so strong that I could have pushed her into the open grave. Thankfully the conversation ended as The Fool struck up a very mournful hymn on his citole, '*To Death, we stride*', as our cue to start filling the pit with soil.

I was helping Mother to negotiate the slope on our return to the castle, when a short scream rang out behind us. Turning around, I could see that Lady Isobel had fainted, and that Robert of Lyndham was kneeling beside her. Lady Emma stood to one side of this tableau, with both hands covering her eyes.

I rushed to Lyndham's side. 'What happened?'

'I'm not sure,' said Lyndham, with the back of his palm to Isobel's forehead. 'I heard Lady Isobel say that she saw somebody hiding in the trees over there.' He pointed towards the copse in the distance.

I dropped my voice to a whisper. 'Was it the Dutchman?' I asked.

'I don't know,' said Lyndham anxiously. 'I was standing behind them, and couldn't hear what she was saying exactly. She was speaking to the child.'

I looked at Lady Emma and tried to decide whether or not to attempt a conversation. The girl was still frozen to the spot with her hands over her eyes, and appeared even less disposed than ever to nodding or shaking her head in response to a list of questions. Instead, I asked Lyndham to join me and we quickly ran across the open field and then entered the nearby copse, hoping to catch Hans hiding behind a tree.

There was an eerie silence to the wood, without even the twittering of bird song, and I will admit that the place unnerved me at first. I was not alone in feeling this way, as I caught Lyndham turning constantly to check if there was somebody on his shoulder. We split up after a while, each going in separate directions, and it was then that I saw her. The young girl with the cleft lip. She was cowering against a tree, dressed in a very long cloak that must have belonged to her mother.

'What are you doing here?' I asked.

'They are all dead,' she said with a whimper. 'Everybody in my family.'

'Was it plague?' I asked.

She nodded. 'I don't know where to go,' she sobbed. 'Nobody will help me.'

I felt a great pity bear down upon me. A child with such a disfigurement would be shunned by the other villagers at the best of times. But now her situation was even more desperate. She had been living in a plague house and would never be given refuge. 'How old are you?' I asked.

'Eight,' she said.

I groaned inwardly, for I could not leave an eight-year-old girl in this forest – and yet I could not take her back to the castle with me. I was about to speak to her, but when I looked up, she was stumbling towards me, nearly tripping over the long cloak. 'Stay there!' I shouted instinctively. 'Don't come any closer.' She stopped still and began to cry. 'Listen to me,' I said, now trying to speak more gently. 'I can help you. But you must do as I say.'

She nodded between shudders.

'Do you have a cough?' I said.

She shook her head.

'What about a fever?'

'No,' she said. 'I stayed away from the sick. Just as you told me to.'

I rubbed my hands over my face, anxiously trying to think of a solution. 'I know. You can stay in the Eden family chapel,' I said. 'There is a stream in this forest for water, and I will drop some bread for you each day at dusk.'

'Where will you drop it?' she asked.

I thought quickly. 'From the parapet walk near to the north tower. To the island side of the gatehouse. Do you know where I mean?'

She nodded. 'Yes, my Lord.'

'But you must not approach the castle until it's dark, in case the others see you. And you cannot come inside. Not for at least six days,' I said. 'Do you understand that?'

She nodded again, though she continued to look at me with such a sorrowful, desperate expression on her face, that I felt thoroughly ashamed of myself.

'I have to be sure that you're not infected,' I explained. 'Once I'm certain of this, then I will allow you to join us.'

'I understand,' she whispered.

'Then wait until we have all gone back through the gatehouse, and hide in the chapel. I will drop the bread later.' I paused. 'And tell me your name?'

'It's Annora,' she said.

I paused again. 'Have you seen anybody else in this wood, Annora?' I said.

'No.'

'Were you watching the burial before?'

'No,' she said. 'I've been hiding by this tree all the time.'

'Are you sure about that?' She nodded firmly. 'Very well then,' I said, backing away. 'Follow my instructions, Annora. And I can help you.'

I did not mention the girl to Lyndham when we met again. Neither of us had discovered any sign of Hans, so we returned to the funeral party, finding that Lady Isobel had regained consciousness after her fainting fit and was now being comforted by Old Simon and Sandro. The old man limply held her hand, whilst my valet fanned her face with my mother's psalter.

'The woman is pretending to be ill, of course,' whispered Mother, as she sidled up to me. 'She's doing it for attention.'

'Is that so?' I said, resisting the urge to point out that this was one of her own areas of expertise.

Before Mother could reply, I knelt down beside Lady Isobel, making sure to keep my conversation private. 'We couldn't find the Dutchman, my Lady. Are you sure he was there?'

Her skin was ashen. 'I don't know,' she replied, before burying her face in a pair of trembling hands. 'I thought it was Hans, but I'm so disturbed today, Lord Somershill. I thought I could see him looking out at me through the trees.' She sobbed. 'But perhaps my mind is playing tricks on me? The devil killed my husband and now I fear that he will come for me.'

I felt a hand upon my shoulder. It was Old Simon. 'Speak to Lady Isobel later,' he said. 'This poor woman has just buried her husband. Give her some time to recover.' I went to respond, but he glared at me. 'It is cold out here,' he said. 'No place for one of your interrogations.'

'Let's get Lady Isobel inside the castle,' said Lyndham, as he offered his hand and helped her to stand. She rose to her feet, but her legs gave way again and she would have fallen, had Lyndham not caught her in his arms. It was a few moments before she regained consciousness and angrily instructed Lyndham to let her go.

It was an awkward moment, only heightened when The Fool started strumming on his citole, choosing this moment to play the song he had composed himself – the musical fabliau that had upset Lady Emma so badly on the night of our first supper together. At least The Fool had the sense not to accompany this tune with its coarse lyrics, but Lady Emma recognised the song well enough, and reacted by roaring like a caged baboon.

Amazingly this was not enough to persuade The Fool to stop playing – for it was only when he received a hefty shove in the back and loud reprimand from Lyndham, that he finally dropped the citole to his side and ran back towards the castle, as if he had been stung by a bee. By now Lady Emma was lying on the grass and thumping at the soil in a rage. When Alice Cross tried to calm the child, Emma fought back with a violence I had seldom seen in somebody so young. Our steward was a strong woman with a pair of hefty arms and a power-ful grip, but even so, she was no match for this girl. With a bite and a kick, Lady Emma freed herself from our steward's grasp and hurtled across the field towards the woodland.

It was Sandro who chased after Emma, catching up with the girl before she darted between the trees and disappeared for good. He held her tightly, while she continued to kick and punch, until eventually the force of her anger subsided and she calmed down, allowing Sandro to release her from his embrace. For a while, they stood together, as Sandro held her hand in his.

'What's happening?' said Lady Isobel, still dazed from her fainting fit. 'Where's Emma? Is she safe?'

It was Lyndham who answered. 'The child was upset, my Lady. She ran off towards the trees.'

'Has somebody caught her?'

'Yes,' said Lyndham. 'The Venetian boy.' The knight then strained his eyes to look into the distance. 'Emma is calm now, and they seem to be talking.'

'Talking?' said Lady Isobel, and I sensed a change of tone in her voice – the fragility replaced with indignation. 'Emma doesn't talk to anybody.'

I turned from Isobel and Lyndham to see Sandro leading Emma back across the field towards us. The girl had one hand in Sandro's and the other lifted to her mouth so that she could suck her thumb like an infant. She reminded me instantly of Hugh, though my son was more than eight years her junior.

As she and Sandro returned to the party, Lady Emma would not look up at our faces, and would not take her stepmother's hand when the woman offered it. Instead, she walked towards the gate-house in silence, only allowing Sandro to walk beside her.

'Emma seems fond of your valet,' observed Lady Isobel, her arm now linked with mine for support.

'Sandro has a way with children,' I said lightly. 'He's very good with Hugh. Always thinking of games and amusements to distract the boy.'

Lady Isobel looked at me blankly, and I wasn't certain that she realised whom I was talking about. Perhaps she had never even noticed that I had a son. 'Emma is very upset at her father's death,' she said instead. 'I feel it's best if she stays in seclusion for a while now.' I went to respond, but she removed her arm from mine. 'The child is easily agitated,' she said. 'You saw that your-self earlier. She suffers from uncontrollable rages.'

'But perhaps some distraction might help?' I suggested. 'A game or two with Hugh and Sandro might balance Emma's humours.'

She sniffed at this suggestion and was consequently forced to wipe her nose with her fingertips. This caused her some embar-rassment, so she did it quickly – almost hoping that I wouldn't notice. 'No games,' she said, turning away. 'Not yet, anyway. Let Emma settle for a few days. Solitude will assist her disposition.'

'Solitude seems rather harsh,' I argued. 'Especially as the girl has just lost her father.'

'Emma must learn to control her temper. Even in such terrible circumstances as these. She must not be indulged.'

'Well, she is your stepdaughter, Lady Isobel,' I said tersely, unable to disguise my opinion of her methods.

She turned on her heel to face me again. 'I consider Emma to be my actual daughter, Lord Somershill. So I trust you will respect my wishes.'

I regarded her for a while – not believing for one moment that she considered Emma to be her true daughter. Even so, I could not argue with the woman's wishes. She was the girl's guardian now, and would rule the unfortunate child's life.

We returned to our quarters to find that Hugh had been entertain-ing himself by making a tent from a bed sheet and draping it between two chairs. He rushed to greet us as the door opened, and then sped out of the room like a cow released onto grass in the spring. Filomena was lying in bed. Her face was pale and her hair was loose and untidy. A bucket beside the bed contained a few dribbles of bile. But vomit was better than blood, we both knew that.

When I had stoked up the fire and poured Filomena a mug of ale, I drew up a chair to her bedside and then described the events of the funeral. My tale of the hunt through the forest for Hans, followed by Lady Emma's tantrum, brought some colour to Filomena's cheeks at least, though I decided not to mention my meeting with Annora.

'What was Emma saying to Sandro?' she asked me.

I had already quizzed Sandro on this subject, but his answer had not been particularly illuminating. 'He said it was nonsense. Just a string of words that didn't make sense.'

'At least she spoke to him,' said Filomena. 'That's a good sign.' She then let out a yawn.

'Has Hugh worn you out?' I asked.

'Yes. A little. But he has so much energy, Oswald. He exhausts me. Particularly at the moment.' Instinctively she placed her hands upon her stomach.

I paused. 'No blood?'

'No.' She took my hand, and then spoke to me softly. 'Please don't worry.'

I lifted her fingers to my lips. 'I'm sorry, Filomena,' I said. 'I'm so sorry that I brought you and Hugh here.'

'Don't be gloomy, Oswald,' she said. 'We are safe now.'

'What do you mean?'

'Hans has fled the castle, of course. The murderer has gone.'

I tried to smile. 'Yes. I suppose you're right,' I said.

She clasped my hand. 'You know that I am.'

Should I have told her my fears? If the Dutchman could leave the castle without being detected, then it meant that he could also return.

*   *   *

I kept my promise to Annora. That night, I climbed the steps to the parapet walk, looked about to make sure that nobody was watching me, and then dropped a small loaf of bread and a lump of hard cheese in a length of sacking. I heard the package land in the long grass below with a light thump, as the shadowy figure of a young girl scurried across the grass and grabbed my meagre offering with the desperation of a starved animal. I didn't feel generous or noble, instead I felt as if I were throwing meat to a pack of foxhounds. My only consolation was the thought that the girl would be able to join us inside the castle when this period of isolation was over. After her six days in the chapel, I would consider her free of plague. It was one good deed at least.

I didn't rush back to our apartment after Annora had disappeared with her bread. Instead, I remained on the parapet for a while, enjoying some brief moments of freedom before I returned to our oppressive rooms. In this stillness I could hear the sounds of the island. The screech of the foxes and the hooting of the tawny owls, alongside the barking of the wild dogs that lived somewhere in the nearby woodland. Their howling seemed quieter and less frantic than usual, and I wondered if they were feeling as melancholy and detached from the real world as we did.

And then, for a moment, I fancied that I could smell something in the air – the scent of a fire. At first I imagined the happy scene of a family gathered about the hearth of a nearby farmhouse, before a different thought came to mind. Was this the smell of another plague house being assigned to the flames? I quickly made my way back down the steps, not wanting to give this notion any more thought. The castle no longer seemed confining and oppressive. Instead it was our sanctuary – somewhere that we could keep ourselves apart from this cruel world.

Chapter Twenty-one

At first light the next morning, I had wanted to organise another search of the castle – this time in the hope of finding the Dutchman's escape route. I had asked Lyndham to bring along his dog, thinking that the nose of a hound would be useful for this job, but when Lyndham failed to appear at our agreed meeting point by the gatehouse, I went looking for him. I found our handsome knight in the kitchen, arguing with his old adversary Alice Cross.

'I did no such thing,' said Mistress Cross indignantly, digging her hands into her hips.

'Well, where is Holdfast, then?' asked Lyndham.

'It's your dog, Sir Robert. How should I know?'

The pair were so involved in this argument that they didn't notice my approach at first. 'What's the matter?' I asked, after clearing my throat loudly to get their attention. 'Why are you arguing?'

As Alice Cross spun round to address me, I noticed that she was wearing a thick woollen kirtle on top of her tunic. She had tied a belt about her waist so that she now looked like a roped sack of grain. 'Sir Robert has lost his flea-ridden dog,' she said, 'and now he's trying to blame it on me.'

'It wouldn't be the first time you've tried to hurt him, would it?' said Lyndham. 'You've always hated that poor dog.'

'That's because the creature is always getting in my way, Sir Robert. He steals food from the kitchen. He sits in doorways and tries to trip me up.' She withdrew one hand from her hip and pointed a finger into Lyndham's face. 'Worse than that he shits everywhere.'

'You let him out, didn't you?' said Lyndham. 'When we left the castle for Hesket's burial yesterday.'

'I did not. How dare you accuse me of such a thing? If the dog escaped, then it's your fault. Not mine.'

I decided to intervene again, before this argument became a shouting match. 'Let's just get on with the search, shall we, Lyndham?' I suggested. 'We can look for your dog later.'

Lyndham answered this with a long groan. For once the expression upon his face was not pleasant. 'What's the point of looking any further, de Lacy? We've scoured this castle enough times already. We haven't found anything.'

'Hans has disappeared, Lyndham. So he's either hiding in this castle, or he has found a way of getting in and out without being seen. Either way, we need to know.'

The knight took a deep breath, and then ran his fingers through his hair. 'You're right. I'm sorry. It's just that it's so frustrating.' He threw back his shoulders. 'Where would you like me to look?'

'Try the cellars.'

'And where will you go?' he asked.

'I want to speak to Edwin again,' I said. 'To see if he's willing to talk yet.'

Lyndham raised an eyebrow, but wouldn't look me in the eye. 'I still think that you should let him out of his room, de Lacy,' he said.

'I know,' I answered. 'But he's not getting out until he tells me the truth.'

When I unlocked the door to Edwin's bedchamber, I found the man lying in bed with a blanket about his shoulders. He had only been imprisoned in this room for a day, but the place already reeked with the foul miasmas of the *Pozzi* in Venice – the dungeons in the flooded cellars of the doge's palace. I had once been locked in that prison, losing track of time in a putrid, hopeless hell, so I did not welcome any reminders of the experience. I held my nose and then removed Edwin's overflowing piss-pot into the passageway, hoping that this, at least, would alleviate the stink for a while.

'Are you the new scullion, de Lacy?' laughed Edwin, as he watched me removing the pot. 'You'd make a pretty maid.' He accompanied this insult by grabbing his crotch.

'Tell me how Hans got out of the castle,' I said, ignoring his insult.

He laughed again, before he turned his back to me and pulled the blanket over his head. 'You're mad, de Lacy. There are no secret entrances. You're imagining it.'

'There must be,' I said, 'and you will tell me. Sooner or later.'

'Just leave me alone!'

'Very well then,' I said. 'If that's what you want.'

I strode out, locked the door behind me, but then waited in the passageway for Edwin to have a change of heart and to call me back. When I heard no sound from within the room, I picked up the chamber pot again and unlocked the door.

'What are you doing?' he asked me, as he lifted his head over the blanket to watch my return.

'This is yours, I believe,' I said, carefully placing the piss-pot next to his bed.

Edwin sat up. 'Take it away,' he said. 'It's full.'

'No.'

'Tell Alice Cross that I need a clean one.'

'Sorry,' I said blithely. 'This is the only chamber pot we have.'

He leapt from his bed, running at me – but I was quicker, and had turned the key before he reached the door.

He thumped at the wood. 'Let me out of here, de Lacy. This is torture. I am the lord of this castle. I demand to be released!'

'You can come out when you've told me the truth,' I said.

'You'll regret this,' he seethed. 'When I get out of here, you'll be sorry. I'll summon the Royal Judge. I'll have you hung, drawn and quartered for this outrage.'

I walked away. 'We'll see,' I said.

I was crossing the cobblestones of the inner ward, heading towards the cellars to join Lyndham, when Alice Cross called out my name. She was standing with two of the maids beside the well, as the girls stared at something she was holding in her large hands. 'What's that?' I asked as I walked over to join them.

'Mary here has just pulled this up from the well,' said Alice Cross, releasing her fingers to reveal a long key. 'It's the one for Lord Eden's library. The key that's been missing.'

I took it from Alice Cross, before she had the chance to close her fingers again, and then held it up to the light. The key was cast from iron, with a large, kidney-shaped bow, and a complicated bit, notched with long, symmetrical indentations. It was probably the most sophisticated key I'd ever seen, and could only have belonged to our patron of innovation, Godfrey.

I turned to Mary, the girl who had pulled the key from the well. 'How did you find this?' I asked.

'I didn't know it was inside the bucket, until I emptied the water out,' she said nervously, as if I had accused her of a crime.

'Are you sure the bucket was empty when you lowered it?'

'Oh yes,' she said. 'This was the third bucket I've raised this morning, my Lord. The key came up with the last one.'

I thanked her and then studied the key again, trying to understand why Hans hadn't just left it with Godfrey's body. Why throw it down the well? This troubled me.

'Can I have the key back now, my Lord?' said Alice Cross, holding out her palm to me.

'No,' I said. 'I think I'll keep hold of it for now, Mistress Cross. It might be important for my investigation.'

She prickled with indignation. 'But I look after all the keys in this castle,' she argued. 'It makes sense for me to have it, my Lord.'

'Even so,' I said. 'I'll keep it for now, thank you.'

'As you like, my Lord,' she said, pursing her lips and glowering at me, before taking out her frustrations on the maids. 'Hurry up and get back to your chores,' she shouted. 'Stop wasting time standing about here.'

I made a quick exit, turning away to spot Filomena watching me from the window of our apartment. Our eyes met for a moment and I wondered what she was thinking. She stood so still, like a statue. Just staring down at me without making a single gesture of acknowledgment. She sometimes wore this unreadable expression, when she withdrew inside herself, and closed out the world.

Was I being closed out? I wondered, as I ventured a wave that was not returned. When she retreated from the window and disappeared into the shadows, I suddenly felt flooded by all of my old uncertainties about our marriage. Did Filomena truly love me, or had it suited her purposes to leave Venice as the wife of an English nobleman? That was certainly my mother's theory – that this beautiful Venetian had only agreed to become my wife when she had extinguished all of her other options. But there had to be more than expediency to our union – or so I had always told myself. Filomena claimed to love me, so I had chosen to disregard the story of the convenient marriage. But then again, my mother's words had a way of working themselves under the skin. Like stubborn splinters, they were difficult to remove.

I rubbed my face with my hands, telling myself to ignore this thought, when I saw Filomena again. She had returned to the window with Hugh. As she kissed the boy on the cheek and then waved down to me, I felt flooded again. This time with love. It came upon me so quickly that I felt a tear form in my eye. I waved back and blew a kiss to them both, but then my feelings of love turned quickly to those of guilt. More than anything, I wanted to keep them both safe, and yet I could not guarantee this safety. As I saw Lyndham striding across the inner ward to speak to me, I could tell, by the look on his face, that he had found no trace of Hans in the cellars. My investigation was stalling. We were no nearer to finding the killer that stalked this castle.

I acknowledged Lyndham and was about to question him, when there was a sudden explosion of noise. Shattered glass and a foul-smelling liquid rained down upon us, as an object fell to the cobblestones and smashed into pieces. We instinctively ran to the safety of the walls, before I looked up to see Edwin's face looking through a hole in the window of his bedchamber.

'Ha, de Lacy!' he shouted down. 'See how you like my chamber pot! Now for the love of Christ, let me out of here!'

I sped up the stairs to Edwin's room, followed by Robert of Lyndham, unlocking the door to find Edwin crawling across the floor towards us on his hands and knees, before he grasped at me, like a penitent falling at the feet of a bishop.

'For the love of Christ, de Lacy,' he said again. 'Let me out of this room. You have absolutely no reason to lock me in here.'

Lyndham glanced at me with disapproval, but said nothing.

'You haven't been honest with me, Edwin,' I said, ignoring Lyndham's silent opposition.

Edwin got up onto his knees, holding out his hands to me in supplication. I noticed that his beard had grown wilder. The spots redder. 'Please, de Lacy. Let me out. I don't know anything about these secret tunnels you've imagined. I don't know anything about Hans or these murders. You cannot lock a man in a room indefinitely without some evidence.' He then turned to Lyndham. 'Sir Robert. You know that's true. You know that I'm being tormented in here for no reason.' He threw himself at Lyndham's feet. 'Please, Sir Robert. You are a knight who has served the King. You must stop this crime against a fellow lord of England. My family engaged you to guard us. To offer us protection, not persecution. I beg you. Do not be party to this injustice.'

Lyndham looked at me again, evidently moved by Edwin's well-rehearsed appeal. 'He's right,' he said. 'We can't keep this man locked in here any longer.'

I hesitated for a moment.

Lyndham helped Edwin to his feet. 'I will vouch for him, de Lacy,' he said. 'But Eden must be allowed out of this room.'

What could I say? I had no tangible evidence against Edwin, other than my own suspicions. I walked away and left the key in the lock.

For the next three days we hardly left our family apartment, as it felt safer this way. There were no further signs of the young Dutchman, and no further clues came to light as to how he had escaped – but we still felt his oppressive presence anyway, making us watchful and suspicious. We avoided the Great Hall, taking a cold supper each night in front of our own fire, only venturing out as a group in order to take our daily exercise about the inner ward. Our universe had diminished to the few small steps between our apartment and a central courtyard, where we either looked up at the sky, or in at one another.

On the afternoon of the third day, we were trying, as usual, to keep warm beside the meagre fire in our apartment. Filomena and Sandro were amusing Hugh by teaching him to stitch, but Mother was bored and kept stretching out her legs and then releasing a particular sigh. It was a sound that I knew of old – long and tuneful. It was her way of letting me know that she had something to say.

Filomena recognised the noise instantly and gave me one of her resolute stares, warning me not to be provoked. I did my best to ignore Mother, but when the sigh came for the third time, I could not resist its call any longer. 'Is something the matter with you?' I asked.

She sat up, steadying herself by clutching onto the arms of the chair. 'I was just wondering how you felt, Oswald. Hiding away from this killer with a group of women, children and old people?' Filomena glared at me again, warning me not to rise to the bait – but Mother had already hooked me.

'What do you expect me to do?' I said. 'Rush around the island in search of Hans?'

'It's a thought,' she said mischievously.

'I have the best chance of catching Hans by staying here and lying in wait,' I said.

Mother huffed. 'I suppose so, Oswald. Though it doesn't seem very courageous to me.'

'Do you want your son to die?' said Filomena, suddenly breaking her own rules and joining the argument.

Mother was caught off-guard, as she was accustomed to my wife staying silent during these discussions. 'No. That's not what I said at all.'

'It sounds that way to me,' said Filomena, her face forged into a scowl. 'You're trying to make Oswald feel guilty about staying here to protect his family. Shame on you.'

Mother's jaw might have fallen open at Filomena's first statement, but now it quickly tightened again. 'I am simply pointing out the truth, Filomena. When this is all over, there will be those who think poorly of my son's conduct.'

'I think you need some rest,' said Filomena. 'Fatigue has affected your judgment.'

Mother turned to me, in search of some support, but found none. Following this, she rose to her feet and flounced out of the room, before slamming the connecting door.

'I'm sorry,' said Filomena. 'I shouldn't have said anything, but I hate it when she speaks to you in such a way.'

I was touched by Filomena's stirring defence, but also troubled by my mother's words – not least because she had hit a nerve. I suddenly felt the need to leave the apartment and get some fresh air, so I threw on my cloak, and opened the door, only to find Alice Cross waiting in the passageway outside, apparently about to knock.

'What is it?' I asked tersely.

She took a moment to answer. 'One of the scullions has noticed blowflies buzzing about the clockmaker's chest,' she said.

'And?'

She hesitated again. 'We think there's something dead in there, my Lord.'

'Have you looked inside the chest?'

'Of course we tried,' she answered, 'but it's locked.'

'What about Pieter de Groot? He has the key, I presume?'

She took a deep breath. 'No. He says his key is missing.' She paused again and heaved a long sigh. 'You should come down and see, my Lord. Master de Groot is very agitated.'

'Why?'

She wiped her lips. 'He thinks that it's Hans's body inside the box.'

'And what do you think?'

'There's definitely something dead in there, my Lord. Blowflies don't stir in the winter for nothing.'

I stepped back inside our bedchamber, called for Sandro and then grabbed my thickest cloak.

'What's wrong?' said Filomena, glancing up from her stitching.

'I'll be back soon.'

She looked at me darkly. 'Has there been another murder, Oswald?'

I paused. 'I don't know.'

Chapter Twenty-two

We ran into the cellar in question to find de Groot lying across his long wooden chest, as a handful of blowflies circled his head, clearly excited by something.

De Groot looked up as I approached. 'I told you that Hans was innocent, didn't I?' he said. 'I told you that's why we couldn't find him.' He wiped a tear from his face. 'He's been dead all along. Murdered like Lord Eden and Lord Hesket. And you did nothing but insult his name.'

'Where's the key to this chest?' I said, ignoring this gush of accusations.

'It was stolen from me,' he said.

'And you've only just noticed?'

'I'm not using this chest any more,' he argued, batting away a fly. 'I had no reason to notice.'

'Where do you keep the key?'

'I hang it on a hook inside my bedchamber.'

'That's not very safe, is it?' I said.

'I didn't think that a murderer would steal the key and lock the chest, did I?' he answered. 'With Hans's body inside.'

I let de Groot weep for a short time, until asking him to move away from the box so that I could examine it. Without his body lying across the chest, I could see that the lock had a sturdy plate and I doubted very much that we would be able to force it open.

By now, news of the blowflies had reached more ears than mine, and I turned around to see a group of the other guests crowded by the door.

'Is it true, Lord Somershill?' asked The Fool, as he edged forwards into the room. 'Is somebody locked inside there?' I hardly recognised the man in his plain woollen tunic and linen braies. He seemed much older without the mask of a brightly coloured hat and comic costume.

'We don't know,' I said quickly. 'But I think you should all go back to your rooms.'

'Why?' said Lady Isobel, pushing her way past the others. 'If there's been another murder, then we ought to know about it.'

Her words met with some approving nods and grunts from the others, particularly from my mother, who had made a surprisingly rapid descent from our apartment in order to witness this latest drama.

'Hans has been murdered,' shouted Pieter de Groot. 'And you are all to blame for his death. The poor boy was persecuted by every single person in this castle. Blamed for every crime, when he was innocent.'

I turned to de Groot. 'We don't know that it's Hans inside this box,' I said.

'Then what about all those flies?' said Mother. 'It can only be a corpse in there.'

I was about to argue when Lyndham joined us. 'What's happened, de Lacy?' he asked, sweeping past the others.

'We need to get this box open,' I said. 'There might be something dead inside.'

'Dead?' said Lyndham, taken aback by my words. 'Nobody else is missing, are they?'

'Hans is missing,' said de Groot. 'Everybody says he was the murderer, but he's not. He's locked inside this box.'

'He can't be,' said Lyndham. 'I checked inside this chest on the morning Hans disappeared. It was empty.'

De Groot pointed a finger and wailed. 'He's in there, I'm telling you. We must open the lid!'

Lyndham and I exchanged an uneasy glance, before he turned to de Groot. 'Do you have an iron crow?' he asked the clockmaker. The man nodded and then trudged from the room as if in a daze, returning shortly afterwards with the long metal tool that Lyndham had requested. Lyndham then jammed one end of the crow into the narrow slit between the lid and the box, before leaning on the other end for leverage. At first the lid would not give way, but the knight persevered, and soon there was a sharp crack as the lid began to lift.

'I think you should all stand away,' I said to the others, as the reek of death rushed out. But nobody moved. If anything, they gathered closer, to see what horrors the box contained.

'Is it Hans?' said de Groot, holding his hands over his eyes as Lyndham lifted the lid. 'Is it my poor nephew?'

I raised my lantern to look within, and it was certainly a repugnant sight that met my eyes. But one thing was obvious immediately – this was not the body of a man. There was something else dead inside this chest – its belly dissected with a long and deep incision, and the tangle of its guts removed and laid out upon its lacerated fur. Worse than this, its legs and head had been severed from its body. It was both a shocking and familiar sight. Just as had been the case with Corvina and then Lord Hesket, an array of pins punctured its coat. But there was a new addition to this barbarity. On the stump of its neck, where the creature's head should have been, sat a jester's hat.

Lyndham looked over my shoulder and then groaned, lifting his hands to his mouth. 'God's bones. It's Holdfast.'

'Are you sure?' I said, looking down at the slaughterous mess.

'Of course I am,' he said, before he turned to pull Alice Cross from the crowd. 'What have you done to my dog, you evil witch?'

'I haven't touched it,' she boomed, fighting him off. 'That's a disgusting accusation. I would never do something like this.'

The Fool was the next person to look inside the chest. 'It's wearing my hat,' he said in horror. 'Why is it wearing my hat?'

I went to close the lid as de Groot pushed his way forward. 'It's not a dog,' he said. 'You're lying. It's Hans in there, isn't it? Let me see. I don't believe you.' He stuck his head inside the chest, but it was only a moment before he let the lid drop with a loud bang.

I turned to the others as de Groot slipped down to the floor, faint with nausea and shock. 'You can all go now,' I said. 'This is a work of mischief, nothing more.'

It was Lady Isobel who answered my assertion. 'This is more than mischief, Lord Somershill. It's the work of the Dutchman. You know that.' I went to respond, but she did not allow me the opportunity to speak. 'He's found his way back into the castle,' she continued. 'And left this rotting animal here to torment us.' She screwed her hands into tight fists. 'I told you this before. He's more than a murderer. He's a devil. A madman. It's not enough that he's killed two men. Now he's taunting us.'

I held up my hands. 'Please. We mustn't give in to panic.'

'But the dog is wearing my hat,' said The Fool, as he backed away towards the door. 'Why is it wearing my hat?' He then turned on his heels and shot out of the room, once again fleeing the scene like a man who has been stung by a bee. I nodded to Sandro and quietly asked my valet to follow.

'What's the matter with The Fool?' asked Mother, as Sandro disappeared in his wake. 'The man is supposed to be keeping our spirits up.'

'He's frightened,' I said.

'We're all frightened,' announced Lady Isobel. 'But what are you doing about it, Lord Somershill? You told us that you were investigating the murders, but what good has come of that? This man has murdered my husband. And now he feels bold enough to creep back in here and terrorise us with this atrocity.' Her voice had become shrill. 'The Dutchman is laughing at us.

Laughing! It is no wonder that we're frightened.' The other women in the room, including my own mother, nodded in agreement with this sentiment.

'You should all return to your rooms straight away,' I said again. 'Lock the doors while Sir Robert and I search for the Dutchman.'

'So he wins again,' came Lady Isobel's reply. 'We scurry away like rabbits into our burrows, while this fox has the run of the castle. It's not acceptable, Lord Somershill.' With these words, she picked up her skirts and strode out of the cellar with determined affront. Others followed, and soon it was only Lyndham, de Groot and myself left in the chamber.

De Groot was now wringing his hands with an imaginary rag and muttering to himself softly in his own language. I leant down and put my hand on his shoulder. 'How is Hans getting in and out of this castle, de Groot?' I said. 'Now is the time to tell me.'

The clockmaker tensed. 'I don't know, Lord Somershill. I only ever saw my nephew leave or enter by the main gate.'

'Then where is he hiding?'

'I don't know that either,' he said.

'You must have an idea?'

He shook his head repeatedly, as tears streamed down his face. 'Please, my Lord. You have to believe me. I do not know.' I stood back, allowing him a moment to compose himself, before he wiped his face and rose to his feet. 'Now I must clean out my chest,' he announced. 'I must get rid of this dead animal. It will stain the wood.'

Lyndham heard this last comment and interjected. 'You will not touch Holdfast, de Groot. So keep away.' De Groot lifted his hands over his head, as if cowering from an assault. 'He was my dog,' Lyndham continued, 'and I will deal with his body. Not you.' Lyndham removed his cloak and wrapped the dog into a small bundle, before lifting the creature's ravaged body from the chest.

We were about to leave the room, processing out behind the knight and his dead dog, when Sandro hurtled back through the door and blocked our path. 'Come quickly, Master Oswald,' he said breathlessly.

'Why? What's the matter?'

'The Fool has locked himself into a storeroom. He's barricaded the doors with two trestle tables.'

'What?'

'Mistress Cross is shouting and screaming because the room is full of food,' he said. 'But The Fool says he won't come out.' He panted again. 'He says he's afraid for his life.'

Alice Cross was hammering her fists onto the heavy door of the storeroom as we arrived. 'You can't lock yourself in there forever, you stupid man,' she shouted. 'Now come out.' She turned to regard me with wearied eyes. 'As if I need a problem like this, my Lord,' she groaned. 'I've still got a castle to feed, despite all this killing. And now this idiot has locked himself up in here with all our best food!'

'Has he spoken to you?' I asked.

'No,' she said, folding her hefty arms. 'Other than to tell me to piss off,' she said.

Lyndham brushed past me and then bashed at the door himself. 'Come out!' he thundered. 'This is no time for one of your jokes.'

'I'm staying here,' came a muffled answer from somewhere behind the door. 'Go away.'

'How much of our food is in there?' I asked Alice Cross.

She raised her eyebrows and dropped her chin into her freckled neck. 'Enough,' she said. 'That room is full of hams, cheeses and pickles. Not to mention all the wine.' She gave a short huff. 'He chose the right storeroom, that's for sure. He's not locked himself up with a load of oats and peas.'

I turned to Lyndham. 'Can you break the door down?' I asked.

Lyndham frowned. 'I could try, I suppose,' he said, feeling about the frame of the door. 'But this is well-seasoned oak, and the posts are steady.' I then recalled Godfrey's boasts about making this doorway safe from raiders – though he had not foreseen this eventuality. That we would need to get somebody out, rather than stopping somebody from getting in.

Lyndham took me to one side, to be out of Mistress Cross's earshot. 'Listen, de Lacy. I know this man, a little.' He dropped his voice to a whisper. 'He is more than a fool in name. In fact, I have rarely met a more stupid fellow.'

'Didn't you recommend him to Godfrey?'

Lyndham poked his tongue around his cheek. 'Well, yes, I did, as it happens,' he said. 'Though I regret it now, of course. The man has been nothing but a disaster since he came here.'

'What's his real name?'

'It's William Shute.'

'And how did you meet him?'

'We've worked together in various houses and castles. I have to say that he used to be quite entertaining. But now he seems to have lost his head completely.'

'So what do you suggest we do?' I said. 'We can't leave him in there with all the best food.'

Lyndham took his time to answer. 'In my experience, Shute lacks determination. He won't stay in there for long, even if he does have months of food and drink. It's not like him to stick at anything.' He paused. 'Let's ignore him for a couple of days. Let him stew in his own company.'

I gave myself a few moments to think this through. 'I suppose he's safe in there, at least,' I said. 'If we can't get the door open, then neither can Hans.'

Lyndham drew back slightly at this. 'So, you really think the Dutchman is behind this?'

'Yes, I do,' I replied. 'And he's becoming bolder with each murder. First he puts Godfrey's body to bed in a chest. Then he displays Hesket like a slaughtered carcass. Now he's playing with us. Bragging that he feels bold enough to identify his next victim.'

'So he means to kill Shute? Is that what you're saying?'

I hesitated. 'Or you,' I said. 'After all. It was your dog inside that chest.'

Lyndham harrumphed. 'I'd like to see that scrawny Dutchman try to kill me, de Lacy. I'm a knight. And what's he? Nothing but a pasty bag-of-bones.'

'Even so. He's cunning. We need to be watchful.'

'I'm not frightened of him.'

'I understand that,' I said. 'But we still don't know how he's getting into the castle. So we need to set up a watch tonight. If he appears, then we can catch him.'

Lyndham bowed his head to this, and I caught sight again of the thinning patch of hair on the back of his head. For a moment I found myself wondering if he knew it was there.

Alice Cross's sharp voice cut through this daydream. 'So what are we to do about this fool in the storeroom?' she snapped.

'We'll come back tomorrow and see if he wants to come out,' I said.

'There'll be no Malmsey wine at supper,' she warned. 'It's all locked away in this room.'

I shrugged, as this was the very least of my worries. 'Then we'll just have to drink ale,' I said, 'won't we?'

Chapter Twenty-three

Our supper that night was a miserable affair, thanks to William Shute's siege of the storeroom. We were served stale bread and a broth, made from one of the egg-layers – a chicken that had been hastily killed that afternoon to make this meal. I had reserved half of my meagre ration of bread for Annora – though the girl did not appear that evening when I dropped my parcel of food from the parapet walk. I waited a while, looking down from my eyrie, high on the wall – but there was no sign of her. I even considered calling out her name, but this might have attracted attention from within the castle, as Lyndham had already begun the first stage of our night watch. It crossed my mind that Annora might be unwell, but I thrust this idea away, consoling myself instead with the thought that the girl had now spent five days in the chapel, and would be able to join us the following day. She would come and collect the bread later that night, when nobody was looking.

Lyndham had promised to wake me around the hour of Lauds to take my turn at the watch, so I retired to our apartment in the meantime, to spend a couple of hours with my family. Filomena was in a strange mood that evening, and did not want to look up from her embroidery. Whenever I enquired about her disposition, she would only shrug, which gave Mother the opportunity to inform me that my wife was in fear of another bleed. Filomena silently seethed at Mother's words, but said nothing – knowing that if anything were likely to provoke a bleed, it would be a needless confrontation with the old woman.

Sandro had taken the opportunity of The Fool's self-imposed imprisonment to borrow his citole and attempt to entertain us with the instrument. His playing was a little hesitant at first, but Sandro was a quick learner – soon able to pluck out a simple tune. In all honesty, we were grateful for some distraction, and nobody more so than Hugh, who kept jumping up and down and begging to have a turn on the instrument himself. I didn't think that this delicate citole would have survived the energetic attentions of a four-year-old's fingers, but Sandro did not deny Hugh the opportunity to join in. Instead of forbidding the boy to touch the instrument – which would have been my own approach – Sandro allowed Hugh to pluck out a single string at the end of each song. When we applauded this great musical achievement, Hugh nearly exploded with joy. Even Filomena broke away from her sulk to smile at the boy's happiness.

When Hugh was finally ready for bed, I asked Sandro to accompany me to the cellars, as I wanted to make another attempt to speak to The Fool, or William Shute, as I now knew was his true name. I was hoping that Shute might have been ready to open the door to us, having already suffered a few hours of solitude.

'What do you know about William Shute?' I asked Sandro, as we walked along the dark passageway towards his barricaded refuge.

'Who?'

'The Fool,' I said, holding the lantern up to look into Sandro's face. 'William Shute is his real name.' When my valet looked back at me with shocked eyes, I added, 'Goodness me, Sandro, The Fool wasn't christened with such a ridiculous name.'

Sandro gasped, as if this were a true revelation. 'Well, I think William Shute is the funniest jester that I've ever seen,' he told me.

'Really?' I answered, unable to hide my own astonishment this time.

'Oh yes,' said Sandro earnestly. 'When he gallops about the hall on his little wooden horse, it is so funny.' He giggled at the thought. 'And then, when he tries to tickle Lady Isobel, I want to cry with laughter.'

'He tries to tickle Lady Isobel?' I repeated, astonished for a second time. Her stiffness and lack of any sense of humour would surely deter any sensible person from attempting such an exploit. It was no wonder that the man was called The Fool. 'When have you seen this tickling?' I asked.

'When we first came here, Master Oswald. I was in the Great Hall with Lady Emma and Robert of Lyndham.'

'And did Lady Isobel like being tickled?'

'No, no,' said Sandro. 'But that's why it was so funny. She lost her temper and threw that water pot at his head. The aquamanile that looks like a lion.' He was laughing in earnest now. 'Luckily it didn't break. But then all the water ran out on the floor, so then . . .' At this point, he was nearly doubled up with hilarity, and could hardly speak. 'So then The Fool pretended to be a dog. He . . .' Tears were now streaming down his cheeks.

'He what?'

'He got onto his hands and knees, and then he lapped up the water with his tongue.'

I gave Sandro a stern look and we walked on in silence, until we reached the door to the fortified storeroom. On the other side, William Shute was already enjoying the endless supply of wine, as he was singing for all he was worth. The words might have been distorted, but the song was instantly recognisable. In his drunkenness he was not flinching from spewing out its crude lyrics at the loudest volume. From the corner of my eye, I could see that Sandro's shoulders were already starting to shudder with laughter.

> 'These castle walls are cold, 'tis true,
> They freeze with winter ice and snow,
> But a man can always warm his pole,
> Inside a tight and furry hole.'

I passed the lantern to Sandro and then rapped noisily on the door. 'William Shute,' I said. 'It's Lord Somershill.'

'Oh, piss off, Lord Somershill,' came the reply.

Sandro was now sucking in his cheeks in an attempt not to laugh out loud. My valet had never heard anybody speak to me so rudely, and, for a moment, I wanted to burst out laughing myself – for there was something so ludicrous about this whole scenario. We were attempting to have a conversation with a man who had locked himself inside a cellar, drunk a bottle of wine and was now bellowing out a vulgar song.

But this was not the time for comedy, so I cleared my throat. 'You would be safer out here,' I said. 'I can offer you protection.'

He gave a long groan. 'You don't know what you're talking about,' he slurred. 'If there's anywhere safe in this castle, then this is it. Nobody can reach me in here. The doors are indestructible.' He then took up his song again.

> 'If ever there was consolation,
> To this frozen isolation,
> It is found, in every guise,
> Between a woman's warming thighs.'

I went to bang on the door again, when Sandro nudged me and pointed to the shadows. There was somebody else listening intently to William Shute's song. As Sandro lifted the lantern we could see the small, elfin face of Lady Emma. I went to approach her, but Sandro put out his hand to stop me. 'Let her come to us, Master Oswald,' he whispered. 'Or she will run away.'

I watched the girl for a while as she stared into space and then, suddenly, she looked directly back at me with a pair of guarded, red-rimmed eyes. Her thin hair had been scraped back from her face and pulled untidily into a bunch at the back of her head. Her cheeks were streaked with tears. I felt the urge to embrace her, in some feeble attempt to offer comfort, but Sandro was right. Such a move would only have terrified the girl.

Instead, we stayed perfectly still, and sure enough, as William Shute continued to boom out his song, she slowly stepped towards us, her eyes now fixed upon Sandro. I had the impression that she wanted to speak, because her tiny mouth was moving with agitation, as if she was trying to force the words out. Sandro sensed this as well. He held out his hand to her, drawing her patiently towards us, as a man might tempt a robin to feed from his palm. Lady Emma was about to take his hand, when the moment was destroyed by Lady Isobel's appearance.

'Emma!' she shouted. 'There you are!' She strode forwards and grasped the child by the arm. Emma flinched at her touch and then froze, holding her arms taut against her body, as if she were protecting her limbs from a rabid dog. The Fool, unaware of this commotion, continued to chant out his song from the other side of the door.

> 'These castle walls are cold, 'tis true,
> They freeze with winter ice and snow . . .'

'What is Emma doing here?' Lady Isobel asked me, her face knotted into an angry frown.

'She just appeared,' I said. 'We didn't invite her to join us.'

> '. . . But a man can always warm his pole,
> Inside a tight and furry hole.'

Lady Isobel gasped at hearing these lyrics. 'And you allowed a child of her age to listen to this,' she said, waving at the door to the storeroom. 'This crudity.'

'As I said to you before, Lady Isobel. We didn't know Emma was here.' I paused. 'And anyway, I thought you were keeping her in seclusion?'

She took a deep breath, stung by the implied criticism. 'The girl escaped,' she said, grasping Emma roughly again by the hand. 'From now on I will lock the door to our apartment at every opportunity.' She tried to pull Emma away, but the girl resisted.

'I think Emma was trying to talk to us,' I said.

Lady Isobel flared her nostrils. 'What on earth do you mean by that?' she said. 'Emma cannot speak.'

'Are you sure about that?' I said. 'I'm told she used to speak to her lady's maid.'

'The girl is a simpleton, Lord Somershill,' said Lady Isobel, keeping a tight grip of Emma's small hand. 'Believe me. I've lived with her for the last three years. Even if this child could speak to you, then she would have absolutely nothing to say.'

As the girl was dragged away, Sandro turned to me, his face flushed with outrage. 'How can that woman be so cruel?' He pressed his hand to his chest. 'To that poor girl?'

'Lady Isobel is mourning her husband,' I said, feeling the need, for some unknown reason, to defend the woman. 'I don't think she's herself.'

Sandro looked at me with a sideways glance, disappointed at my reply, since we both knew that Lady Isobel's recent loss was a very poor excuse for her treatment of Emma. If anything, the widow's veil had revealed and not shrouded her true nature.

'Listen, Sandro,' I said. 'I'll visit Lady Emma tomorrow, and make sure that's she's not being mistreated. Does that satisfy you?'

He nodded cautiously in response – appeased for the time being, though I knew he would keep me to my word. 'I think that Lady Emma wants to tell me something,' he said.

'Really?'

He blew a curl from his eye, and now that I looked at him properly, I realised that he desperately needed to have his hair cut. In so many small ways, this castle was slowly turning us into barbarians. 'Yes, Master,' he said, in response to my question. 'I do.'

Chapter Twenty-four

It was the stench of smoke that first caused me to wake – its tendrils seeping under the door and poisoning the sweet air with fumes. Once I had opened my eyes, I could hear raised voices in the inner keep below our window.

'What's wrong?' asked Filomena, as I jumped from the bed and pulled on my boots.

'There's a fire,' I said.

She crossed herself. 'Mother Maria.'

'You should get dressed,' I told her. 'In case it spreads.'

She rubbed her eyes and pulled her gown about her shoulders. 'Where is the fire?'

'I don't know,' I said, running to the door. 'I'll come straight back. Just wake the others. Be ready to leave this apartment.'

I descended the winding staircase to hear Sandro's footsteps clattering down behind me. 'The smoke is coming from the cellars,' he shouted. 'From the storerooms, I think.'

I stopped and turned to look at the boy. We both knew what the other was thinking.

The smoke was billowing into the inner keep as we opened the door from our stairwell. It was white and cloud-like against the darkness of the winter's night, and I could see nothing at first, until the light of a lantern shone out through the murkiness. We ran towards it.

'Who's there?' said Alice Cross, as her face loomed from the smoke.

'It's me, Lord Somershill,' I said. She was standing over Lyndham as he held his head between his knees and coughed. 'What's happened here?' I said.

It was Alice Cross who answered. 'The Fool started a fire in the storeroom.'

'What?'

'He was drunk,' she said. 'Probably knocked over his lantern, and set fire to his clothes.'

I felt Sandro nudge me. He didn't believe this story any more than I did. 'The Fool didn't have a lantern in there,' I said.

Alice Cross frowned. 'How else did he start a fire then?'

'That's a very good question,' I said.

Lyndham raised his head from his knees. 'The flames went up so quickly, de Lacy. I couldn't do anything to help him.' He coughed. 'I tried to kick in the door, but it was too late.' He buried his face in his hands. 'It was terrible. Shute was trapped inside. He didn't have time to escape.'

Sandro crossed himself. 'The Fool is dead?'

Lyndham nodded. 'There was nothing I could do.'

I put a steadying hand on my valet's swaying shoulder. 'Has the fire spread?' I asked, turning back to Alice Cross.

She shook her head in response. 'No, no. It's contained within the storeroom,' she said. 'Those cellars are built of stone. It won't go any further.' She then threw up her hands. 'But think of all that food that's been burnt. What a waste.'

'What about the man who's dead?' I replied.

She puffed at my comment. 'The Fool brought it on himself, Lord Somershill. Nobody asked him to lock himself in there.'

Sandro tapped me on the arm and whispered, 'I don't understand, Master Oswald. Surely the poor man had time to get out before the fire spread?'

'I agree,' I whispered back. 'I don't think this was an accident.'
I nodded towards the door that led to the cellars. Smoke was still
issuing from this opening. 'Come on. Let's go and look.'

'Don't go in there, de Lacy,' shouted Lyndham, as we set off.
'The fumes will poison your lungs.'

'I need to see what's happened,' I said.

Lyndham struggled to his feet and followed us towards the
smoky passageway. 'God's bones, de Lacy,' he shouted. 'You've
got to listen to me. You cannot go in there. The smoke will kill
you.'

We stood at the door to the passageway, as the fumes continued to billow out, and I knew that Lyndham was telling the truth.
I could already feel the choking miasmas constricting the back of
my throat. 'What happened here, Lyndham?' I asked, turning to
the defeated-looking man. 'And please don't tell me that Shute
knocked over a lantern.'

Lyndham coughed again. 'All I know is that I was outside the
storeroom, when the fire started. It went up very quickly, and I
could do nothing to help.'

'You were outside the room?'

'Yes. I'd decided to guard the door, you see. After you said that
Hans was planning to kill Shute, I thought it would make sense
to wait there to catch him. If he wanted to get to Shute, then he
would have to get past me.' He coughed. 'But I must have fallen
asleep, because then I was woken by Shute's screams.' He
coughed again. 'I shouted at the man to pull down his barricade
and escape before the flames took him. But it was too late. Too
late.' His voice became flustered and shrill and he was struggling
to speak. 'The fire had taken hold so quickly, you see. Shute
didn't stand a chance.'

I ran my hands through my hair in frustration. 'Hans said he
would kill The Fool, and now he has,' I said.

'But I don't see how,' protested Lyndham. 'I was outside the
door all the time. Even if this devil is creeping into the castle

through some secret tunnel, there's no possibility that he passed me.'

'But you said you were asleep?'

He clasped my arm, and then squeezed his hand. 'Listen to me, de Lacy. Don't you think I would have noticed the door being bashed down? I don't sleep that deeply.' He paused. 'There is no possibility that Hans passed me.'

'So the door was never opened?'

'That's right.'

'So how did Hans get in then?' I asked. 'How did he start this fire without opening the door?'

Lyndham released his hand. 'I don't know,' he said, now shaking his head in frustration. 'Maybe the man truly is a devil. Able to walk through walls and slip under doors.'

'Or maybe he didn't come inside the castle at all,' I said.

'What do you mean?'

'Come on,' I said. 'It's nearly dawn. There's something I want to show you.'

The portcullis was raised at first light, the clank of the chains echoing about the castle. The door in the gate was unlocked and Lyndham, Sandro and I emerged into the thin morning light. As we looked out across the marsh, we could see the sun, peeking its head over the horizon – a ball of white heat at the foot of a cold grey sky. Flocks of birds were already darting in short bursts across the muddy waters, going about their daily fight for survival against the tyranny of winter.

The air was crisp and freezing, and caused Lyndham to start coughing as the cold hit the back of his throat. In other circumstances I might have suggested he went back inside, but he needed to see this.

I led them both about the perimeter of the castle walls, past the point where I usually dropped the bread for Annora, spotting that the loaf from the previous night was still lying in the long grass. The girl had not come to pick it up, so I kicked it out of sight before the others noticed. We then continued towards a section of wall that was smoking. There, at the foot of the wall was the ventilation shaft that Godfrey had so proudly added to the castle in his recent modifications.

'This shaft leads to the storeroom where Shute was hiding,' I said. Then I rubbed my hand about the stone facing to the hole and lifted my fingers to my nose. 'As I thought. Birch oil.'

'I don't understand,' said Lyndham.

'Hans and his uncle have buckets of this stuff,' I said. 'It's very flammable. The young Dutchman must have crept back inside the castle while you were guarding the storeroom door.'

'Oh God, de Lacy,' said Lyndham, coughing again. 'I thought I was doing the right thing by lying in wait there.'

'You weren't to know,' I said, in an attempt to comfort the man. 'You weren't to know that Hans would pour a bucket of oil into this cellar from outside the castle. It's easy to set this liquid on fire. That's why the room ignited so quickly.'

Lyndham held his hand in front of his mouth, trying to shield the cold air from the back of his throat. 'But I don't understand. How did he know that Shute was in the storeroom?'

'The Fool was singing loudly enough to wake the dead last night,' I said. 'This shaft must have broadcast his song to the whole headland.'

Sandro interrupted us. 'Look, Master Oswald,' he said. 'I've found something.'

We waved away the smoke to see Sandro holding a bucket aloft. It was a rotten-looking vessel, still stinking of the pungent liquid it had once contained. It was, indeed, the birch oil bucket from de Groot's workroom – so there could be no doubt now that my theory was correct.

'He's trying to kill us. One by one,' said Sandro, dropping the bucket in a dramatic flourish. 'Soon we will all be dead.'

'Stop it, Sandro,' I said. 'It doesn't help to panic.'

But then it was Lyndham's turn to give in to despondency. 'Your valet has a point, de Lacy,' he said, sinking to the ground. 'It seems impossible to protect ourselves from this man. If he's not sneaking into the castle and playing his tricks, then he's doing this. Killing us, one by one.'

'Which is why we need to find him,' I said.

'Find him? But how?' said Lyndham, with a note of scorn in his voice. 'We've had no success so far. The man is as fleeting as a ghost. He comes and goes into this castle as he pleases.'

'Which is why we have to leave the castle to look for him,' I said.

Lyndham raised an eyebrow at this.

'We should have done it before,' I said. 'Instead we've let ourselves become his hostages.'

The knight hesitated. 'But I thought we'd all agreed not to leave the castle,' he said, as another coughing fit followed, prompting me to pull him away from the wall to be clear of the fumes that were still belching out from the vent. I had always felt physically inferior to this tall and muscular man, and yet it seemed that something as ephemeral as a lungful of smoke had defeated him. He sat on a patch of rough grass and coughed again as we were overwhelmed by the smell of the fire. It was repellent – of tar, wood smoke and something else that I could identify from bitter experience. The smell of a burning man.

'Are you sure about this plan to leave the castle?' Lyndham asked me, once he had finally found his voice again.

'Yes, I am,' I said, 'it's the only way to stop Hans.'

'When shall we go then?'

I hesitated. 'I'm going to go alone,' I told him.

'Don't be so foolish, de Lacy. I'll come with you.'

'No. You can't,' I said.

He made a point of clearing his throat. 'Don't worry about this cough. It's just the smoke,' he said. 'It's nothing. I'll be back to myself within the hour.'

'It's nothing to do with the smoke,' I said. 'You can't leave the castle because of plague.'

He raised his eyebrow again. 'But you can?'

'Yes,' I said. 'I'll be safe.'

'But why should it be any different for you?' he asked, regarding me with a puzzled frown.

'Because I've suffered from this disease before,' I said. 'In the Great Plague of 1349. I've had it once, so I cannot catch it again.'

He looked at me with some scepticism. 'Are you sure about that?'

'Yes.'

'But how did you manage to survive?' he asked, continuing to frown. 'I thought everybody died when they caught the Plague.'

'A priest saved me,' I said, 'and not with his prayers.'

'What do you mean?'

I hesitated for a moment, for even talking about this experience was painful. 'The corruption of plague was killing me,' I said. 'The lumps in my armpits and my groin were so swollen and black that I didn't have long to live. So the priest took a knife to each boil. To release the poison from my body.' As I gave this description my scars prickled at the memory. In truth, I remembered little of the surgery itself, as I had been delirious with fever – but I recalled my recuperation in vivid, aching detail, not least because Brother Peter had regularly washed my wounds with vinegar.

'I have heard such stories before,' said Lyndham. 'But I also heard that this surgery never works.' He looked me over. 'You were lucky to survive.'

'It wasn't luck, Lyndham,' I said. 'This priest had once been a barber surgeon. He took great care that I should live.' Lyndham went to ask me more about this grim episode – so I quickly continued with my story. 'I've only told my mother and wife about this. I don't want the others to know.'

'Why's that?'

'Because it causes suspicion, Lyndham. Some people believe that the survivors still harbour the Plague. That its seeds lie within us.' Did Lyndham inch away at this? For a moment I thought that he had. 'Or there are others who believe that we were saved by unnatural forces. By the Devil or by witchcraft. You can see that my survival was both a blessing and a curse.' I paused. 'I also hope that you can see why I can leave this castle. And you cannot?'

'Very well,' he sighed. 'When will you go?'

'As soon as it's fully light.'

'And where will you look for this devil? He could be anywhere on the island.'

I rose to my feet and offered him my hand. 'There's somebody in this castle who knows where to find Hans. And this time I'm going to get answers.'

Chapter Twenty-five

I found de Groot hiding in his workroom, crouched down in one corner behind the large frame of the astronomical clock. I shone my lantern into his face, causing him to recoil his body into a ball – holding his hands over his head and sobbing. He'd heard the news. He knew what Hans had done to William Shute.

'Go away,' he said. 'Leave me alone.'

'Tell me how to find Hans,' I said. 'Then I'll go.'

'I don't know,' he mumbled.

'Yes you do,' I said, pushing one of his hands away from his face. 'No more lies, de Groot. I need to find your nephew before he kills again.'

His hands rebounded immediately and he wouldn't answer me.

'This is why your sister couldn't care for Hans, isn't it?' I said. 'The boy wasn't wild. He was cruel.'

'I thought I could cure him, Lord Somershill,' he whispered. 'I thought I could set Hans back onto the path of righteousness.'

'Cure him of what, de Groot? Taking pleasure from inflicting pain on others?'

De Groot dropped his hands and looked up at me with puffed and reddened eyes. At first he didn't seem able to speak – instead a line of spittle fell from his lips. 'He was a strange child,' he finally admitted. 'But I could not forsake him, Lord Somershill. You must understand that. He was my sister's boy.'

'Why do you say he was a strange child, de Groot?'

The clockmaker released the longest sigh, as if he had been holding onto these words forever, afraid to let them pass his lips. 'Hans could be cruel and heartless, my Lord. You were right about that.' He gave a sob. 'He did things that were . . . regrettable.'

'Such as?'

He hesitated. 'Once he poured boiling water onto a dog, though I forgave him because he told me it was an accident. And then he offered to kill the kittens that we couldn't keep. I let him do it . . . but I should not have. Those creatures did not die a gentle death.' He dropped his chin into his neck and panted, as if he was fighting the urge to faint. 'But you should know this, Lord Somershill. I do not blame Hans. This behaviour was the fault of his father. It was no wonder that my nephew had a disturbed mind. His father was vicious. A drunken tyrant. Always beating my sister, or locking the boy away for days in a cellar.' He wiped his brow and looked up at me again. 'When this man died, I promised my sister that I would care for Hans, as I had no son myself. I thought I could banish his morbid interests with hard work and discipline. I thought I could cure him.'

'Has Hans killed before?' I asked.

De Groot hesitated to answer this question. 'No,' he said, his voice trembling.

'You don't sound so sure about that?'

'It was just a story, invented by the villagers,' he insisted. 'The girl was killed by somebody else. They all tried to blame it on Hans . . . Because, because—' He was unable to finish this sentence.

I felt a wave of revulsion wash through me. 'Hans *is* a killer, isn't he? You've always known that.'

The man stumbled over his words. 'No, he's not,' he sobbed. 'I cured him.'

'But you didn't, did you? You only succeeded in protecting the boy so that he had the opportunity to kill again.'

'That's not true,' he said adamantly.

I leant down and grasped the man's tunic, pulling it tightly about his neck. He did not struggle against me. 'You can't protect Hans any longer, de Groot. You must tell me where he is.'

'I don't know.'

'Yes you do.'

De Groot trembled. 'I'm telling you the truth, my Lord. If I knew how to find Hans, then I would tell you without a moment of hesitation.' I tightened my grip. 'Please,' he begged. 'Please. Ask Edwin of Eden. He knows what's happened to Hans.'

'Why do you say that?'

De Groot was breathing rapidly – his face glowed and his brow was covered with sweat. 'Edwin of Eden came to our workroom. To see Hans on the night that Hesket was killed. He gave my nephew a bag of coins.'

'What for?'

'Hans wouldn't tell me,' he sobbed. 'My nephew disappeared, before I could get an answer from him.'

I stood up. 'You should have told me this before, de Groot.'

He looked up at me, his face stained with tears. 'I couldn't believe Hans was involved in these murders, Lord Somershill. I thought that I had cured him.'

I woke Edwin from his sleep, though the man was not in bed. Instead he was huddled into a ball on the floor, curled up like a cat around an empty goblet of wine. Edwin had moved into Godfrey's bedchamber since throwing a bucket through the window of his own room – but he had managed to transport the stink of that chamber into this one. Once again my nose was assaulted by the oily, musky scent of ferrets.

Edwin rubbed his eyes and stretched out his short arms. When he saw my face, he groaned. 'What do you want, de Lacy? I was asleep.'

'Get up. I need to speak to you.'

He rubbed his face again and yawned. 'What's that stench?' he said. 'It smells like a bone fire.'

'There's been another murder,' I told him. 'The Fool has been burnt to death.'

Edwin struggled to his feet and then grasped the blanket from the bed, wrapping it about his shoulders. 'What happened?'

There was no time to explain. 'Where's Hans?' I asked instead.

Edwin regarded me for a moment, puffed his lips in a show of exasperation and then wandered towards the window, affecting an interest in the view. 'Not this again, de Lacy,' he said, in a wearied tone. 'How many times do I have to say the same thing? I know nothing about Hans.'

'Yes you do,' I replied calmly. 'I've always suspected that you were involved in these murders. But now I have evidence.'

Edwin bristled, but continued to look out of the window. 'What evidence?' he said, feigning indifference.

'You gave Hans a purse of coins on the night that Hesket was murdered. De Groot saw you.'

He spun back to face me. 'I did not.'

'Stop lying to me, Edwin,' I said. 'It's twice that you've been seen giving a purse of coins to Hans. Twice that the Dutchman has committed murder.'

'You've got this completely wrong,' he said. 'I certainly did not pay Hans to kill Lord Hesket.'

'Then what were the coins for?'

He turned away from me. 'None of your business.'

I stepped closer to him. 'I think I'll lock you into the dungeon this time, Edwin. Rather than a warm bedchamber. A few days in a cold, damp cell should concentrate your mind.'

Edwin pulled the blanket about his shoulders. 'You wouldn't dare,' he said. 'Sir Robert wouldn't let you.'

'Don't fool yourself, Edwin,' I said. 'Lyndham would have no compunction in dragging you down to the dungeon. Not now that his friend William Shute has been burnt to death.'

'That's not true. Lyndham is on my side.'

'He wants to find Hans as much as I do,' I said. 'Lyndham would turn the key to the dungeon himself, if it meant getting to the truth.'

Edwin stared at me for a while, before he returned his eyes to the window. 'Very well, de Lacy,' he said, after a long silence. 'As it happens, I did give Hans a few coins that night.'

'Why?'

'I wanted him to do something for me.'

'What was it?'

He hesitated again, and then looked at me with a sideways glance. 'Before I tell you, I want you to know that this had nothing to do with these murders,' he said. 'You've got to understand that. I couldn't predict that the Dutchman would turn into this murderous lunatic, could I?'

'What did you ask him to do, Edwin?' I repeated.

He took a deep breath. 'All right. All right. Don't rush me,' he said. 'I asked Hans to leave the castle and find Godfrey's wife and child.'

'What?'

He smiled awkwardly. 'I wanted to offer them sanctuary inside this castle, you see. It's what Godfrey would have wanted. You said so yourself.'

I spent a moment stunned by the audaciousness of this lie, before a terrible realisation dawned upon me. 'God's bones, Edwin,' I said. 'You sent a murderer to the house of a defenceless woman and child.'

He pulled the blanket about his shoulders. 'As I said before, de Lacy. I had no idea of the Dutchman's bloodthirsty nature.'

'That's not true,' I said. 'You knew Hans's nature well enough. That's exactly why you sent him there.'

He backed away from me. 'I don't know what you mean,' he stuttered, heading for the door.

'You didn't send the Dutch boy there to offer Godfrey's wife and son sanctuary,' I said, making sure to follow him across the room. 'You sent Hans to kill them both, didn't you? Particularly the boy who would take your title.'

He made a bid for escape, but I caught up with him beside the bed, where I grasped hold of him by the back of his scrawny neck and pushed his face into a bolster. He struggled violently and squealed to be released, but I was determined to get the truth from him at last. As he struggled to breathe, I suddenly regretted not having listened to Filomena's advice all those days ago. I should have tortured an answer from this monster much, much earlier.

'How did Hans get out of this castle?' I asked, pulling his head back for a moment so that he could take a quick breath.

'I don't know,' he sobbed, blowing a feather from his mouth.

I pushed his face back against the bolster again. 'Of course you do, Edwin,' I said, speaking into his ear. 'Otherwise how could you ask Hans to leave?'

I pulled his head up again, giving him the opportunity to give me a better answer this time. 'All right, all right, de Lacy,' he groaned. 'Just let go of me. I can't tell you anything, if I can't breathe.' I was tempted to push his face back against the bolster until he couldn't take another breath, ever again, but I let this urge pass.

'There is a tunnel,' he said at length. 'You were right about that.'

'Where is it?'

He hesitated until I threatened to return his face to the bolster. 'Godfrey found it when he was cleaning out the well in the inner keep,' he said. 'The opening is halfway down the well. You can't see the entrance from above, as it's below a jutting sill.'

'Where does this tunnel lead?'

'It opens out onto a steep bank. One that slopes down to the marsh. The opening on that side is hidden by gorse.'

'Why did Godfrey tell you about it? Of all people?'

'He had to.'

I shook him. 'Why?'

'I'd been with a woman on the banks one afternoon last summer. I was having a sleep after she'd gone, and then Godfrey appeared from the undergrowth. He had no choice but to tell me what he was doing.'

'Did Godfrey tell anybody else about this tunnel?'

'Not that I know of,' he said. 'My brother thought it was a risk to the security of the castle. The fewer people who knew about it, the better.'

'Where does Abigail live?' I asked.

'I don't know.'

I caught hold of his neck and pushed his face back into the bolster. 'Of course you know, Edwin. You've just told me that you sent the Dutchman to find this woman. Remember? You must have told him where to go.'

I pulled his head back after a few moments, allowing him to gasp for breath. He was weakening now. His voice soft and quaking. 'Yes, yes. All right. You win, de Lacy,' he said. 'Godfrey had a small cottage in the woodland to the east of the island. He always told me it was a retreat for silent prayer and reflection, but I guessed this was where he was hiding his wife and child.'

'How do I find this cottage?'

Edwin coughed. 'You're not going out there, are you?'

'Of course I am. I need to find Hans.'

'All right, all right,' he said. 'Follow the path across the island until you come to the gallows at a crossroads,' he said. 'Turn right here and head for the large wooded glade. The cottage is hidden within the oaks.'

I threw him against the bed, stalked to the door and turned the key.

'Don't lock me up again, de Lacy,' he groaned behind me. 'Please. I can't stand it.'

'You'll get out soon enough,' I shouted back. 'If I find that Hans has murdered Abigail and her son, then I'll take you out into the forest myself. I'll hang you from the nearest tree.'

*　　　*　　　*

Filomena watched me prepare to leave the castle with silent, reproachful eyes. 'I don't understand why you're doing this, Oswald.'

I pulled the leather tunic over my head and wouldn't meet her gaze. 'I have to go,' I said. 'I have to stop him.'

'But I won't feel safe here without you here,' she said.

'Lyndham is staying in the castle,' I replied. 'And Sandro is a capable guard.'

She folded her arms and turned her back on me. 'The boy wants to go with you, of course.'

I dropped my dagger into its sheath. 'Well, he can't.'

She waited a few moments before making her next objection. 'You know that Godfrey's wife and son are probably dead already, don't you? You'll get to this secret cottage, only to find two corpses.'

'I have to try to save them from Hans at least.'

'But it's not safe to leave the castle on your own,' she said. 'You'll be at the Dutchman's mercy.'

'I don't fear him,' I said.

'But you should,' she replied. 'This man has already killed three people.'

'Which is exactly why I have to hunt him down.'

I continued to collect my things together into a large scrip, while she stared at me with disdain. I half expected her to refuse to say goodbye or wish me well, for Filomena sometimes had the most stubborn of natures. However, just as I had thrown my cloak over my shoulder she suddenly grasped me, taking my hands in her own.

'Please, Oswald,' she said. 'Stay here with your family. Now that we know how Hans is getting into the castle, we can block off this tunnel. Then we can lock ourselves away until spring. There's no need for you to leave. These murders are nothing to do with us.'

'I have to go,' I said again, pulling her towards me and kissing the top of her head. 'Mother was right. I cannot hide away in here any longer, waiting to be preyed upon.'

Filomena took a sharp intake of breath at the mention of my mother, before she leant back and looked me in the eye. 'But what about the Plague, Oswald? Think about that.' I went to speak, but she put a finger to my lips. 'You insist you're safe because you've suffered before. But how do you know if that is really true? This could be a different sickness.'

'It's the same disease, Filomena.'

'But what if you're wrong, Oswald? What happens if you catch Hans, only to catch this plague? Or worse than that, you are safe yourself, but you bring this infection back with you? You might save us from a murderer only to bring death here anyway.' She shook me again. 'And plague is the worst killer of them all. You said so yourself enough times.'

I pulled her back into my arms. 'I promise you, Filomena. With all my heart. I will return with a murderer and nothing else.'

She breathed in sharply, and then pushed me away. 'That's if you return at all.'

I descended the winding stairs to the inner keep, hoping to make a quick exit, but Sandro caught up with me as I reached the bottom step. The boy had dressed in his leather tunic and long woollen cloak, and clearly intended to join me on this mission, as there was a sword hanging from his belt.

'You can't come with me, Sandro,' I said, blocking his path with my arm. 'It's too dangerous.'

The boy shook his head at this. 'But you cannot go out there alone, Master Oswald. What if the Dutchman takes you by surprise?'

'I'll be able to defend myself,' I said. 'Hans is just a boy. Not the Queen's champion.'

'Yes, but he's cunning and sly,' said Sandro, his eyes widening at his next description. 'He may hide himself between the trees and then sneak up on you, like a snake.'

'I'm not scared of Hans,' I said. 'And I must go alone.' When he went to argue, I added, 'You're needed here to guard Monna Filomena.'

'Monna Filomena can defend herself,' he said indignantly. 'She's Venetian.'

'Very well then,' I replied. 'You must defend Hugh.' This elicited more of a grudging nod from my valet. 'And there is something that I need you to do while I'm gone.' When he sighed at this, I added, 'It's important, Sandro. You're the only person I trust.'

This compliment was designed to charm him, but he sniffed out its artifice immediately. He regarded me with cynicism, like a child who knows he's being placated with false praise. 'Yes, Master Oswald. What is it?'

'I'd like you to find this tunnel that Edwin of Eden described to me. Once you've located it, you must tell Sir Robert. It needs to be guarded at all times.'

'Where is it?' he asked.

'Climb down the well in the inner ward. Apparently the opening is below a jutting sill.' I paused. 'The tunnel travels under the castle wall and opens out onto a steep slope on the banks above the marsh.'

He wrinkled his nose, still not persuaded by the genuine importance of this commission, but at least he had accepted that he could not accompany me on my journey.

'When will you be back, Master Oswald?' he asked.

'By nightfall.'

'And if you're not?'

'I will be back by nightfall, Sandro,' I repeated. 'So don't come looking for me.'

Chapter Twenty-six

A low sun was crawling along the horizon as I left the castle and made my way towards the main path. The air was fresh, and stung at my skin as I walked purposefully across the grassland in front of the castle – knowing that Filomena and Sandro would be watching my departure from the parapet walk. When I reached the first patch of woodland, I hid behind a tree for a moment to look back. When I could be sure that Filomena and Sandro had deserted their post on the castle wall, I retraced my steps towards the chapel.

There was no answer when I knocked lightly at the old wooden doors and called out softly for Annora. I crept inside, and at first the chapel appeared to be empty, so I consoled myself with the thought that the girl had left this place to find another sanctuary – hopefully with a family who were prepared to offer her more care and compassion than I had shown. But then it hit me, wafting through the air in thick, concentrated streaks. I walked further inside the chapel, and it became stronger. Heavy, sweet and foul. The unmistakable scent of death. When I saw the small, lifeless body in the far corner, I went no further, for I knew without doubt that this was Annora's body. She had wrapped herself in her mother's long cloak, but her tiny hands were still visible above the cloth – swollen and blackened with plague.

I ran out, heading for the woodland without caring too much who might see me this time, before I leant against a tree to vomit. It was not only the sight of Annora's decaying body that sickened me, it was my own part in her tragic story. What had I done to help this girl, other than offer her a cold chapel and a daily crust of stale bread? But, then again, what more could I have done? Had I taken Annora into the castle, then she would have infected us. There was now no doubt about that.

I had made the right decision, and yet I did not feel vindicated. Instead I felt saddened and angry. Sad that her young life had ended in such a lonely and pitiful way. Angry that plague had turned me into this callous monster. I wiped the vomit from my lips, took a long sip of ale from my flask and then I set off again. There was no time for reproach. I could wallow in such feelings in the months to come – but now I needed to reach Godfrey's secret cottage. I needed to find Hans.

I tramped along the island path, always making sure to look ahead of me, in case I should see another traveller in the distance. It was my intention to avoid all contact with other people, but I need not have worried, since the track was empty. I met nobody – apart from a curious cat. I heard nothing – apart from the defeated barking of the wild dogs in the distance. It was strange to be outside again after two weeks within the high walls of the castle. The wide spaces were intimidating, if not overwhelming – and I was alone. For the first time in many days, I was completely without company.

After a while, I descended a path through a sheltered glade, finding myself out of the cold winds at last. As I entered a fold in the land, it seemed as if winter had been briefly held at bay. The ground was softer, even muddy in places, warmed by a quilt of fallen leaves. For a moment this cheered me, and then I recalled the last time I had walked along this track, on the night we had arrived at Castle Eden. The memories of that journey were fresh in my mind – the fog, the rain and the sense of foreboding that had borne down upon us – with good reason now it seemed. The castle had not turned out to be the refuge we had hoped for. Instead it had become a bear-garden, no better than those along the riverbanks in Southwark. Our pit had been the four walls of the castle. Our tormentor had baited us with murder.

It was this thought that urged me on, warning me not to linger in this valley. I found the gallows at the crossroads, where the same man still hung from the gibbet – his skeletal body now being picked free of flesh by the crows. I then turned right along a thinner path, soon heading into dense woodland. This path rose sharply to the brow of the hill and then dropped again into a valley on the other side – a glade of dense, untouched forest. If this island had been named after the Garden of Eden, then this valley was surely the inspiration – for, apart from this thin track, there was no sign of man here. No coppicing, no log heaps and no charcoal piles. My only company was the majestic oaks that held these slopes like an army of giants, supported by an infantry of holly and yew.

It seemed so unlikely that anybody lived here, that I began to wonder if Edwin had been telling me the truth about Godfrey's secret cottage. Suddenly I imagined him sitting in his bedchamber and laughing at his success in sending me out on this fool's errand. But, just as I was preparing to retrace my steps, I came upon a clearing in the forest, a circle of land surrounded by oaks – their branches reaching up toward the skies like the fan vaults of a cathedral. In the centre of this sylvan nave was a small cottage – newly built, with an oak frame and roofed with wooden shingles. It was plain and simple in its design, but this was not a peasant's hovel – it could only be Godfrey's retreat.

I watched the cottage for a while from the safety of the trees, but saw no obvious sign of life. There was no smoke rising from the hole in the roof, and no sounds coming from within. Even so, I didn't feel ready to approach the door yet, so I crept about the perimeter of the clearing, always keeping my eyes to the small cottage in the centre, hoping to catch some movement. But still I saw nothing, other than a pair of magpies that had landed on the roof ridge, and who were now watching my progress with interest.

It was when I reached the back of the cottage that something else caught my eye, however. It was a long mound of earth poking up through the carpet of leaves – freshly dug and large enough to be the grave of a woman and her child. This was enough to persuade me to now make my approach. I crept through the leaves and then crouched beneath one of the windows. The wooden shutters were closed, but there was a small gap between two of the slats and I was able to peep through at the room beyond. At first I could see little in the poor light, but then, as my eyes adjusted, I made out a pair of men's boots on the floor. They were brown and sturdy, and made in the Dutch style. They surely belonged to Hans.

I pulled my dagger from its sheath and slowly pushed at the unlocked door, opening it far enough to see that the main chamber of the cottage was empty. There was no fire in the hearth and no sign of Hans, other than his boots. I pushed the door a little wider and then stole inside, silently making my way across this room to poke my head through the dividing curtain into the chamber beyond. Here there was a single bed, inhabited by somebody with their back to me – but this was not Hans. It was a woman. When I looked more closely, I could see that she was still alive, her breathing shallow and erratic. In the corner I saw a cradle – as silent and cheerless as a sarcophagus.

I lifted my chemise over my mouth and edged forward, for I had guessed what was also lurking in this room.

'Abigail?' I said quietly. 'Is that you?'

The woman didn't respond.

'Abigail?' I repeated. 'My name is Oswald de Lacy. Lord Somershill. I was a friend of your husband's.'

At my second appeal, she turned over slowly. 'Lord Somershill. Is that you?' she whispered.

'Yes.'

'I prayed that you would come.'

This statement took me by surprise. 'You prayed this, Abigail? Why was that?'

She held out a hand to me, but I couldn't bring myself to touch her, as her fingertips were blackening. 'Godfrey trusted you, Lord Somershill,' she said. 'Above all his other friends and family. I knew that you would come for me, when Godfrey was murdered.'

'Who told you that Godfrey was killed?' I said.

'A man came here,' she said. 'He told me.' She coughed – a guttural, soggy churn that originated in her lungs and not her throat. 'It was a young Dutchman. One of the clockmakers that Godfrey brought here to build his clock.'

'Where is this man now?' I asked.

'He's dead,' she said. 'I buried him myself.'

I felt my heart beating faster. 'How did he die?'

'It was plague.' She coughed again. 'I should not have opened the door to him, Lord Somershill. But I thought Godfrey had sent him to me. To bring Simon and me back to the castle.' She closed her eyes, exhausted by the effort of speaking. 'But he brought more than the news of Godfrey's murder to this house. He also brought the sickness. The foolish man had visited a tavern on his way here. It was he who carried the seeds of plague to my house. It is he who has killed us.'

I found a stool beside the wall, and fell down upon it. Thoughts were flying wildly about my head. Thoughts that I needed to settle and then organise. 'When did the Dutchman die, Abigail?' I said at length.

Her breathing was laboured, and she struggled to say each word. 'Three days ago.'

This answer did not settle my mind, in fact it caused more agitation. 'And when did the Dutchman get here?' I asked. She was silent for a few moments, and I wondered if she had understood my question. 'Abigail.' I now spoke with urgency. 'I need to know when the Dutchman arrived at your house. It's very important.' Her response was a long and wearied groan. 'Please, Abigail,' I urged. 'Try to remember.'

There was another long pause, and for a moment I thought she had drifted into unconsciousness, when she surprised me by mumbling an answer. 'He was here two days before he died,' she said.

'Are you sure about this?' I said, as my heart continued to thump. 'I need to know for certain.'

She opened her eyes and suddenly focused. 'This man was already ill when he arrived, Lord Somershill. I let him in and I gave him a bed for two days. And then I buried him. It was my Christian duty, but I regret it.'

I put my head in my hands and pushed my fingers against my eyes. Hans was not the murderer I sought. How could he be? The man had been in this cottage for at least five days. I nearly shouted out in anger. Not only had I wasted my time in coming here, it now appeared that I had left my family back at the castle, at the mercy of the true killer. When I eventually looked up, I saw that Abigail had raised herself a little on the bolster and was now watching me intently.

'I prayed for you to come,' she said again. Her voice now had a strength and clarity. 'I prayed so often, Lord Somershill. I wanted you to save us.'

'I cannot take you back with me, Abigail,' I said. 'You're dying of plague.'

'I know that,' she said. 'My prayers were selfish to begin with. I understand that now. I only cared for my life and that of my son.'

At this, I stood up and edged over to the cradle in the corner, daring myself to look inside at the silent bundle of swaddling. I turned away, unable to gaze upon a second dead child in one day.

'When did Simon die?' I asked her, quickly returning to my stool.

'Poor Simon,' she whispered, her eyes closing. 'We named him after Godfrey's uncle, you know.' She gave a weak laugh. 'We hoped this would appease the old monk.'

'Appease him for what?' I asked. She didn't answer. 'Did you think Old Simon would be angry about your marriage to Godfrey?'

She opened her eyes again. 'God has brought you to me, Lord Somershill,' she exclaimed, 'I know that now for certain. He wants you to continue Godfrey's work.'

I couldn't help but stiffen at this suggestion. 'I don't know anything about Godfrey's work,' I said, 'your husband never confided in me.'

Her face had been pale and sweating earlier in our conversation, but now it was red with passion. It was a look I recognised – for I had seen Godfrey wear it enough times. 'You must do it,' she said. 'You must swear to it, Lord Somershill. It is God's wish for you.'

'Abigail,' I said softly. 'I cannot continue Godfrey's work, because I do not know what it was.'

'Then let me share this wondrous news,' she said, closing her eyes and letting her face dissolve into a blissful smile. 'My husband was working on the most important undertaking, Lord Somershill. The greatest step forward for Christianity in this land, since Augustine founded a church in Canterbury.'

'What was it, Abigail?' I asked, now uncertain that I wanted to know the answer.

'Godfrey was translating the New Testament into English,' she told me. 'It has taken him many years, but now it is near completion. Can you imagine the power of such a book? A bible that a person can read and understand for himself?' She opened her eyes and held out her hand to me for a second time, though once again I refused to take it. She carried on nonetheless, undeterred by my reticence. 'It was Godfrey's dream that each English man and woman might hear the Word of God in their own tongue. No matter who they were. The church cannot keep the scriptures to itself any longer. The age of Roman tyranny is nearly over.' She took a deep breath. 'You must find Godfrey's translation. You must take it to John Cubit in Oxford. Then you must help Father John to distribute Godfrey's bible to the four corners of our land.' She began to cough again, exhausted by this appeal. 'You must not fail, Lord Somershill. If you do, then Godfrey's life has been in vain.'

I was lost for words, for her plea was not a modest request. By making such a promise, I would be committing myself to a perilous venture. The church would not tolerate a bible in English, especially as it had been translated by Godfrey – a man with a reformer's eye. If I became involved in this mission, then I risked excommunication or worse.

And yet a dying woman's wish exerts a strong pull on a person's conscience. 'Where is this translation hidden?' I asked, deciding that I would deliver the document to John Cubit, and nothing more.

Abigail looked at me before slowly closing her eyes. She was only moments from death.

'Where is it hidden? I repeated.

She said something, but her words were barely audible.

'Where is it, Abigail?' I said for the final time, now lifting my chemise further over my mouth and creeping as close to her bed as I dared. 'I cannot help you, if you don't tell me.'

She took a deep breath, rallying her strength for this one last instruction. 'Look in the hood of the fireplace in Godfrey's library,' she said. 'There is a void behind one of the corbels.' She began to groan. A wearied, rasping sound.

'Are you sure about that, Abigail?'

But she did not hear me. From that moment onwards, her words were a jumble of muttered prayers and appeals to the

Almighty. Her chest rose and fell in shuddering spasms, before she suddenly became still. So still that I thought she had died, when she shocked me by opening her eyes for one last time. Her voice lucid and strong. 'I go to be with God,' she said. 'May He forgive my sins, and grant me everlasting life.' After this, she coughed, releasing a dribble of blood, before her head fell to one side and she was finally dead.

I said a prayer myself, and then stood up to leave, though a voice now whispered in my ear. It belonged to Old Simon. *A prayer is not enough, Lord Somershill. Give this woman and her child a good death. Give them the Christian burial that they deserve.* I shook him away, for I didn't have time for the chastisements of an old monk. I had wasted enough time already in coming here, and needed to return to my own family.

I closed the door to the cottage with a heavy heart, stepping out across the carpet of leaves, when I heard a sound. It was nothing louder than a faint mewling to begin with, not unlike the cry of a baby. And yet, I knew that it couldn't be Simon, because Abigail had told me that her son was dead. Moreover, I had looked inside the cradle myself and seen his silent, motionless body.

The sound stopped, followed by a peace that was only punctured by the caw of the magpies that were still watching me from the roof. Convincing myself that these birds had been the source of the mewling, I set off again – but as soon as I put one foot forward, the cry came once more. This time I knew that it could not be a magpie. This time the sound was louder and more insistent. It was definitely the cry of a baby.

I stood still for a while, wondering whether to return to the cottage or not. But what would be the point? I could not help this child. He would soon die of plague, just as his mother had done. I needed to be resolute and make my way back to Castle Eden, for the sake of Hugh and Filomena. But once again the voice of Old Simon came to me. *I see that you put yourself and your*

family above all others, Lord Somershill. It is a common sin. I banged
my ear to rid myself of his words, and yet they became louder
and louder at each step forward, not even drowned out by the
bleating calls of the child inside the cottage. *I pray for you, Lord
Somershill. I pray nightly for your soul.*

I finally reached the edge of the clearing and the safety of the
trees, but now the cries of the baby were so urgent that I held my
hands over my ears to blot them out. I could do nothing to help
this boy. He was not my responsibility. I was needed by my own
family. I stepped forward again with renewed determination,
and now that I was moving out of his range, Simon's calls softened
to a sob. The weak, heartbreaking tears of a child who knows
that nobody will ever answer his call. And then there was silence
– the cold and eerie silence of surrender – far worse than
anything that came before.

I tried to walk into the forest and leave him behind. I tried to
escape this turn of the Fates, but there would be no peace for me
if I left this place, no matter how many prayers Old Simon might
say for my soul. I knew that this silence would ring in my ears for
the rest of my life. I had left Annora to die on her own, but I
could not fail this child in the same way.

And so I retraced my steps to the cottage and opened the door.
I pulled my chemise over my mouth and crept over to the crib,
mustering the courage to look down properly this time. Would
his body be covered in the buboes of this cruel disease? Would his
fingers be swollen and blackened with plague? But no, as I pulled
back the swaddling, I saw only a small child with the pale white
skin and red hair of the Eden family. Simon looked up at me and
smiled, utterly delighted to see the face of another human being
– even one as craven as my own.

I lifted him from his cradle, finding that he smelt strongly of
his own filth, but he wasn't feverish. I removed the linen and
then returned him to the crib, so that he could kick his thin legs
about freely in the air. There were no obvious signs of illness, and

yet I knew better than to trust my eyes when it came to plague. It likes to lurk in the undergrowth, skulking like a wolf. The child might have looked healthy enough then, but I could not have simply wrapped him up and taken him back with me to Castle Eden. This might have appeased my own conscience, but the price of such recklessness could have been the deaths of others – in particular those of my wife and son.

So what was I to do? I could not leave Simon here to die, and yet I could not take him back with me. I stopped for a moment. I looked up and spoke a prayer to the rafters. An apology to Filomena and Hugh, and then I made my decision.

This cottage would be our home now. For at least the next six days. I would care for the boy until he either died, or proved himself clear of plague. My search for the killer would have to wait.

Chapter Twenty-seven

The soil was soft beneath the leaves, but I was so anxious to commit Abigail to the ground, that I dug only the shallowest of graves for her body. However, this was still the Christian burial of which Old Simon would have approved, as Abigail was laid down in the pit with her body facing to the East. At the Day of Judgment, she would be ready for resurrection, able to rise from her grave to face the return of Christ. Such beliefs mattered to her, so I would honour them.

With her burial complete, I took all of her bedding and clothes, and then built a fire in the clearing. Despite the cold, it wasn't difficult to light this pyre once I'd found Abigail's flint and iron striker, along with an assortment of her char-cloths. Once the fire was burning brightly, I closed the door on the outside world and looked about at my new home. My first thoughts were of the gloomiest kind. It seemed that I had swapped imprisonment within a castle, for imprisonment within this small cottage.

I built another fire. This time in the hearth. Then I boiled a couple of eggs that I'd discovered in a bowl. It was all that I could find to feed the child, apart from some stale bread that I chewed upon and then poked into his mouth with the end of my finger. I had seen the nursemaids feed Hugh in such a way, when he was being weaned. Typically my son had made a great fuss about this, spitting out the bread as if he were being poisoned, but this infant made no such protests. Simon had a strong and steadfast will to survive, that much was clear.

Over the next two days, I saw no evidence that Simon was suffering from anything other than hunger, and a vague sense of unease that his mother was missing. With nobody else to talk to, apart from this barely weaned infant, I found myself dwelling on the murderer I had left behind with my own family at Castle Eden.

I went over the facts, again and again, hoping to see what I had missed before – wishing that Filomena or Sandro were here with me, to listen to and argue with my theories. I even looked about the cottage, hoping to find some piece of parchment to write upon, but there was little in the way of writing materials, or even books in this home. Godfrey's love of manuscripts had not extended to furnishing his wife's cottage with anything more than the simplest of psalters. In the end I chose to commit each sequence of reasoning to memory – and these were my thoughts, such as they were.

The murderer had begun by killing Godfrey, although I still felt that this had been an unplanned act. The weapon had been a mazer – something that the killer had randomly picked up from Godfrey's desk in a rage. And so, for a while, I concentrated on what Godfrey might have done to anger somebody to the point of murder, knowing, full well, that my friend had a habit of causing offence.

Firstly there was his attitude towards his brother – continually belittling Edwin with menial tasks. Then there was Godfrey's disagreement with Pieter de Groot over the final payment for the clock, though this seemed like a poor reason for murder to me. And of course, Godfrey had infuriated Hesket regarding his secret marriage to Abigail – though I could easily discount Hesket as the murderer, for obvious reasons.

And then there was this new revelation – Godfrey's secret translation of the bible. Did anybody else know about this

dangerous project? Godfrey had suspected somebody was reading his private correspondence, so it was possible that he had
given the secret away in one of these letters. But then again, who
might have objected to this bible translation, other than the
priest Old Simon? And he had seemed relaxed about Godfrey's
attitudes towards the church when quizzed on the subject, even
admitting a little admiration for Godfrey's youthful dissent.
More than that, Old Simon could not have been intercepting
Godfrey's letters, since he had not been at Castle Eden until the
day before we arrived.

I put the cause of the attack on Godfrey to one side for a
while, to concentrate on the way in which the murderer had
disposed of his body. Why had the killer arranged Godfrey's
corpse into such a strange position inside a wooden chest? And
what had they hoped to achieve by leaving it in this place? They
must have known that a dead body could not have remained
undiscovered for long inside the castle walls. And lastly, why had
they thrown the key to Godfrey's library down the well? None of
this seemed to make sense.

Coming to no conclusions whatsoever about Godfrey's death,
I then moved on to the murder of Lord Hesket – a killing that
had definitely been planned. This time there had been no attempt
to hide the corpse – in fact his body had been left on display,
mutilated in a style that deliberately aped the cruel way in which
Hans had killed Old Simon's crow. It had been a clever and
successful ploy to divert our attention, since we had all been
fooled into believing that Hans was guilty. I felt stupid and angry
with myself for also making such a rudimentary mistake. I had
been naïve and foolish not to question this assumption.

I tried not to dwell on my error, and moved on to the murder
of The Fool, William Shute. It was my conviction that Shute had
witnessed something on the night of Hesket's murder. When the
killer had also realised this fact, they had tried to intimidate
Shute with a grisly warning – his hat placed upon the beheaded

carcass of Lyndham's dog. But, unlike the ploy to blame Hans for the murders, this plan had failed. Rather than silence Shute, this threat had only made The Fool more likely than ever to talk – especially once he had locked himself inside the storeroom with a never-ending supply of wine.

The murderer must have known that it would not be long before the wine loosened Shute's tongue and he sang out a name to the whole castle. If Shute could not be silenced with a warning, then he needed to be silenced by death. And so, not able to reach Shute through the door of the storeroom, the killer had then poured birch oil down the ventilation shaft that led into this cellar from outside the castle walls – setting the poor man alight and then burning him to death. But the murderer could only have carried out this plan by knowing how to secretly come and go from the castle – and who knew about the tunnel, apart from Edwin of Eden? The finger was beginning to point back in his direction, except that this man had been locked in his bedchamber when Lyndham's dog had first disappeared.

I moved on again, as each sequence of thought was breaking up almost as quickly as it formed – deciding to concentrate instead upon the identity of the three victims, searching for a link between them. I could discount the last name at least, for William Shute had merely been an unfortunate bystander – murdered for being a witness. Which left me wondering about Godfrey and Lord Hesket. What was the connection between these two men? Why had the murderer picked this pair out, and not others, as victims?

As yet, it was a riddle that I could not solve.

Chapter Twenty-eight

By the third day in the cottage, I could find little else to eat, other than a handful of oats and a scoop of barley. The child was now fading with hunger. His cries were less urgent and he seemed barely able to kick his legs or turn his head and call for food. For the most part he slept, sucking his thumb for comfort. I feared he would not live for much longer if I stayed here, and yet it was still too soon to leave. I dared not return to Castle Eden yet and risk being the agent of plague.

On the fourth day, our fates changed again for the worse. The child developed a fever, leading me to fear that he was now suffering from something worse than hunger. His skin was pale but sweaty – just like his mother's on her deathbed. Moreover, his body was limp and he would barely sip at a spoonful of water when I tried to make him drink.

Until this point, I had avoided having too much physical contact with him, always covering my mouth when I fed him and not letting him breathe on me. But we had shared this small cottage for four days now. Whatever was ailing him, would soon ail me. I had always maintained that I could not suffer again from plague, but in those dark hours I began to question that assumption. If the disease had changed since the last outbreak, then perhaps I was no longer resistant to its poison.

When I woke with a headache and stiff limbs the next day, I knew that it was time to write a last testament – a letter that I could leave for Filomena, so that she would know my fate if I died. Looking about the cottage for something to write upon again, I eventually found a letter that Abigail had hidden in the wall beside the bed. It was a sealed square of parchment, identical to the letters that Godfrey had given to me to deliver on that night in his library. I opened this letter without a second thought, since the contents no longer really mattered. Godfrey's wife was already dead, and it seemed as if his son would soon meet the same fate.

This letter was another addressed to the Archbishop of Canterbury, Simon Islip – so I had been right in one regard. Godfrey had written more than one letter to this man, in order to provide his son with every chance of inheriting his estate. I wrote on the back of the parchment, scratching out the words in ink that I'd made from soot, mixed with my own saliva. Given the shortcomings of this medium, the letter was short and to the point.

December 1361

To the finder of this letter,
If you are reading this, then I am dead. Taken by plague. If your nose does not lead you directly to my body, then look in the chamber beyond the curtain – for this is where I shall go to die. I would ask you to bury me, as this will give comfort to my family, but I shall not condemn you for taking the other option. These are wretched, savage times, and I know why the fires blaze and the bones burn.

If you have the heart to place my body in the soil, then wrap me in my cloak and bury me alongside the other graves in the ground behind this cottage. Elsewhere the soil is hard and icy, and will not yield to the spade.

If you are well yourself, then I beg you to take this letter to Castle Eden, as my wife must know my fate. She will not thank you for this news, but she will reward you for your service. You may look upon my decaying, corrupted body and see a poor man who has died in this lonely place, but you should know this. My name was once Oswald de Lacy, Lord of the Somershill estate.

I folded the letter and tied it with a piece of string – placing it on the table near to the door, in the hope that the person who found it could actually read. After this, I wrapped myself in my cloak and sat next to the infant's crib, patting his head with a damp rag as he convulsed with a fever. I felt sicker than ever myself. My own body alternated between shivering with cold and then burning up with a sweating heat. My back ached and my head throbbed, but I was determined that I would live long enough to bury this child alongside his mother.

That night it was bitterly cold, with a vicious wind howling about the house and lifting the wooden shingles from the roof. I barely had the energy to light a fire, and when I did, I found that the wood was so damp that it would not even heat a pan of watery soup. I had burnt the blankets from Abigail's bed on the day that I'd buried her body, so there was little more that I could wrap about the child to keep him warm. To compound the problem, his linen napkins were soiled, and the ones that I had washed were still wet.

I had never looked after an infant for long before, and was shocked by the mess Simon made with all his shitting and pissing. When my own son had filled his napkin, I had simply passed him to the nearest woman and let her deal with the problem – whereas now I was forced to manage it myself. I could not wrap Simon in damp clothes, so I stripped him of his bedclothes and then laid him in his cradle. I covered him with my cloak, but he continued to shiver and then look up at me with such clouded, lifeless eyes that I took him in my arms again. I had not touched him properly before, but I could not continue this discipline. He deserved the embrace of another human being before he died.

And so I held him to my chest, removing his clothes and letting his skin rest against my own. The boy felt both cold and feverish, so I clutched him tightly and blew warm air onto his head, hoping to comfort him. I had come to care for Simon in those strange, suffocating days. Almost as if he had been my own child. Our forced isolation had forged a bond between us, and I was determined that he would not die without the loving care of another human being.

I cannot say how long I paced about the meagre fire that night, only that I circled it many times. As I walked, I found myself singing psalms to the child — the hymns that I had learnt in my early years in the monastery. But these chants only brought back unfortunate and even unpleasant memories, so I changed my choice of song to something more cheerful. The nursery rhymes and tunes that I had sung as a child, sitting on my mother's knee. For a while, I even found myself repeating the song that The Fool had composed about Edwin of Eden. The lyrics might have been crude, but they could hardly offend the ears of a dying infant.

The slow repetition of my steps, and the thumping of the pain inside my head, induced a kind of trance. I had not been thinking about the murders for many hours, as the illness had taken over all of my thoughts. And yet, as I paced the room, ideas about my investigation began to slip in and out of my consciousness. I cannot say that they were intruding, merely that they were swimming in and out of my mind, and in doing so, they began to form patterns that I had not seen before.

Again and again, I found myself wondering about the link between the two victims — Godfrey and Lord Hesket. Why had the murderer chosen to kill these two men? Could this help me to predict the next victim, and if so, who would it be? My thoughts unravelled and reformed constantly, leading me down paths that I had previously ignored, drawing me to conclusions that I had not previously seen. The slow rhythm of my steps set the many cogs of my mind in motion, until they moved together in formation, as smoothly as a cascade of rotations in Pieter de Groot's clock.

During all this time, Simon slept in my arms. His cheek against my chest. His small, sweaty head of red hair against my skin. I expected to lose him that night, but then, remarkably, as a new day dawned he began to twitch and wriggle. When the light slowly crept into the cottage through the many cracks in the shutters, he opened his eyes and suddenly screamed for food. I nearly wept for joy at the sound, for these cries meant that he had survived the night and now he would live. And then, I realised that I, too, felt a little better. My fever had cooled. My aches had lessened. I still felt weak, but not defeated. Whatever had ailed us both, I knew, with all certainty, that it could not have been plague.

I placed Simon gently back in his cradle, as I looked about the cottage for something to eat – but there was not even a shrunken turnip or crust of stale bread. My first thoughts were that it was time to return to the castle. But even then, I held back. It was still my inclination to wait another day.

I was boiling some onion tops that I'd retrieved from the midden heap, when there was a thump at the door. 'Who's there?' I shouted, placing my hand upon the pommel of my dagger.

Before I could say another word, however, the door flew open and Sandro burst into the cottage. 'Master Oswald!' he cried. 'You're alive!'

He rushed forward to embrace me, and I was so overjoyed to see his face that I dropped the dagger onto the floor, lifted him in my arms and swung him in a circle. 'How did you find me?' I said.

'Monna Filomena told me how to get here. Turn right at the gallows and then follow the path to a small cottage.'

It was only when I had returned Sandro's feet to the floor, that I realised the rashness of my welcome. 'You shouldn't have come here,' I said. 'It's not safe.'

He looked crestfallen at my words. 'But we were so worried about you, Master Oswald. Monna Filomena cries all the time. And Hugh is so naughty. He won't eat his food or sleep in his own bed. Yesterday he even kicked your mother in the leg.'

'Why?'

'Because she told him to go to bed.'

I laughed out loud at this. It was so wonderful to hear their names again, even if I was listening to reports of Hugh's terrible behaviour. 'Are they safe, Sandro?'

He looked at me curiously. 'Of course they're safe.'

'No more murders in the castle?' I asked.

'No,' he said, cocking his head. 'We thought you had found the Dutchman. That's why the killing has stopped.'

'Hans is dead,' I said.

'Did you have to kill him?' said Sandro, his eyes widening at the thought.

'No,' I said. 'Hans was never the murderer. We were wrong about that.' I corrected myself. 'I was wrong about that.'

Sandro frowned. 'Are you sure?'

'It's not possible, Sandro,' I said. 'Hans was already dead when the last murder took place.'

'So, how did he die?'

'It was plague.'

'Mother Maria,' he said solemnly, crossing himself before he asked the next, inevitable question. 'But if Hans is not the killer, then who is it?'

I hesitated to answer this, embarrassed at this admission. 'I'm not sure,' I said at length.

Sandro narrowed his eyes, but knew better than to press me further. 'So, where is Godfrey's wife?' he asked instead. 'Did you save her?'

'No, Sandro,' I said. 'She died of plague as well.'

My valet stared at me for a while, his mouth hanging open, until we heard Simon crying. Sandro raised his jaw and looked towards the wooden crib. 'The infant is still alive then?'

When I nodded, Sandro marched over to the crib, bent down to examine the child and then lifted him out. Simon rewarded Sandro with the broadest of grins – far brighter than he had ever bestowed upon me in our five days together. But then again, Sandro always delighted babies – even those who had only just avoided the kiss of death.

My valet looked over his shoulder at me. 'This poor boy stinks,' he said accusingly. 'What have you been doing to him, Master Oswald?'

'There isn't any swaddling,' I said defensively. 'Nor any food.'

'Then it's good that I came to find you,' he replied, placing Simon back in the crib and then patting the large scrip that hung over his shoulder. 'I have some bread, cheese and ham.' He flashed a smile. 'And some dried figs. I know you like them, Master Oswald.'

The thought of the food was appealing, but I still felt uncomfortable about Sandro's presence here. 'You put yourself in danger coming to this cottage,' I said. 'For all you know, there could still be plague here.'

'But there isn't,' he said adamantly.

'You don't know that.'

He sucked in his cheeks. 'When did Godfrey's wife die?'

'As soon as I got here.' I paused. 'It was five days ago, I think. Though I've lost track of time.'

He clapped his hands together. 'There! You see. That's long enough. This house is safe.'

I wanted to be angry with Sandro for coming to find me, but it was so difficult. He had undoubtedly taken risks in leaving the castle, but he had also shown courage and loyalty, so this was no time for chastisements. Instead, I watched in gratitude, if not relief, as Sandro tended to Simon, making a far better job of the child's care than I had managed. Firstly he tore some linen from his own chemise and then made a temporary napkin for Simon. Once the child was comfortable, Sandro then washed his hands thoroughly in the basin of cold water before he dished up the food from his scrip onto two wooden plates.

I was so hungry that I shoved the bread into my mouth greedily, before taking a little more time to savour the cheese and figs. Sandro, by contrast, fed the baby with delicate precision, first chewing the cheese, dropping it onto his finger, before pushing the pulp into the infant's mouth. Simon was even hungrier than ever, and accepted this dinner without complaint, leaving his mouth hanging open between helpings, in eager anticipation of the next finger of food.

'I did as you asked,' Sandro told me, as Simon eventually began to tire. His tiny eyes closing. 'I climbed down the well and found the tunnel.'

'Does it lead outside the castle, as Edwin of Eden told me?'

Sandro nodded. 'Yes,' he said, 'though it's very narrow and dark.' He pulled a face. 'And foxes shit in there.'

'Foxes?' I asked with surprise. 'Are you sure about that?'

'Yes. I trod in some,' he said. 'It was disgusting. I couldn't get it off my boot.'

I changed the subject. 'How is everybody in the castle? Are they well?'

He looked up. 'Lady Emma spoke to me.'

'She did?' I said. 'That's wonderful news.'

He stiffened, realising that he had probably overplayed this story. 'Well. She sings to me, anyway.' His face relaxed into a smile. 'Sometimes she even holds my hand and lets me sing with her. But only if we sing the same song.' He paused and his face darkened. 'Until that terrible woman Lady Isobel appears, of course. And then I am chased away.'

'What do you sing with Emma?'

He paused, before looking down at his hands with an air of sadness. 'It is The Fool's song,' he said. 'That poor man.'

'I thought that Lady Emma hated that song,' I said. 'It always used to upset her.'

'I know,' he said. 'That's what's so strange, Master Oswald. She didn't like The Fool's song when he was alive, but now she likes to sing it. All the time. Over and over.'

The Fool's song. Here it was again – threaded through this story like a running stitch. I rose to my feet. 'We need to get back to the castle, Sandro,' I said.

'Now?'

'Yes. Immediately.'

He looked at me in surprise. 'Perhaps we should let this child rest first?' Simon was now sleeping in Sandro's arms, a thin bubble of spit on his tiny, contented lips.

'No,' I said. 'I need to get back. As soon as possible.'

Sandro bustled about the cottage before our departure, pulling a tapestry from the wall to make a shawl for the child and swaddling him tightly like a long sausage. While he did this, I picked up the letter that I'd written and placed on the table – my last testament, ready for the person whom I had imagined would find my dead body. When Sandro wasn't looking, I read through the words of this letter for one last time, before I scrubbed them from the parchment with a dampened cloth. I would not die here. I would not be buried in the frosted soil next to Abigail and Hans. Instead, I would return to my wife and son at Castle Eden and we would outlive the Plague.

As we closed the door to this cottage, I reflected on the last five days of my life. To begin with I had feared that I'd wasted my time in coming here to seek out Hans. I had left my wife and child at Castle Eden with a murderer, whilst I chased the wrong suspect to this lonely place. There had been rewards for this mistake, however – for if I had stayed at Castle Eden then Simon would have died in this remote cottage, since there was little chance that somebody else would have found him. Not only this, my investigation would have stalled, perhaps forever. I would never have discovered that Hans was innocent of the three murders, and I never would have learnt the true nature of Godfrey's secretive work.

But, I have to say, that these were not the revelations that finally shone a light into the dark heart of this mystery. Instead, it was the night I had spent with Simon, clutching his ailing body to mine, in the hope that we would both survive until the morning. As I endlessly paced about the cottage that night, I had been convinced that we were both succumbing to the same disease that had taken Simon's mother. My sights had been restricted, like a warhorse in an iron chamfron, for I had never considered that we might be suffering from a different affliction – a sweating sickness, or even marsh fever. In my ignorance, I had only seen one killer.

Chapter Twenty-nine

As we neared the walls of Castle Eden, I felt overwhelmed with the anticipation of seeing my wife and child again. Even though I felt weak after the last five days in the cottage, this excitement drove my feet forward with energy. I was even eager to see my mother again, though I suspected that this feeling would not last for long – not once we had spent some time in one another's company.

As Sandro and I approached the gates, ready to request readmittance to the castle, I put my hand on my valet's shoulder and asked him to listen to me carefully for one moment. 'I don't want to tell anybody else the truth about Hans,' I said. 'I want them to continue to believe that he was the killer.'

Sandro narrowed his eyes. 'Why's that, Master Oswald?'

'Just trust me, Sandro,' I said. 'I will explain my reasons later.'

'But what about Monna Filomena?' he asked, flicking the hair from his eyes. 'Should we tell her?'

'No,' I said. 'Nobody must know. Not even Filomena.'

He wrinkled his nose in disapproval, but bowed his head to me anyway. 'If that's what you want, Master Oswald,' he said warily.

'It is, Sandro. So please do as I say.'

After this short discussion, we shouted for attention at the gate, until we heard the clinking sound of the rolling chain as the portcullis was raised. Filomena was the first to emerge from the door in the gate, running to greet me, before showering my face with kisses – not seeming to notice the infant in my arms. The other guests and servants were less enthusiastic about my return, however, as they had bunched at the gate, and were watching us from a safe distance. I noticed immediately that my mother was among their number.

'Oswald,' said Filomena as she wrapped her arms about my chest. 'I thought you were dead.' She only stepped back when Simon began to mewl. 'Who's this?' she asked, with a look of astonishment on her face.

'He's Godfrey's son, Simon.' I pulled back the tapestry shawl so that Filomena could see him properly – suddenly feeling like a peddler presenting a basket of apples to a prospective buyer.

She drew back. 'Why do you have him?'

'His mother is dead,' I said.

She hesitated. 'Was Abigail murdered by Hans, then?'

'No,' I said. 'She died.'

Her face froze. 'Mother Maria. Was it the Plague?'

'Yes,' I admitted, with some hesitation of my own. 'But this child is free of sickness.'

She frowned at me and drew back. 'Are you certain about that, Oswald?'

I could understand her fear. Who couldn't? But she had to trust me. 'I am certain, Filomena,' I said. 'I wouldn't have brought this child back here otherwise. You must know that I wouldn't take any such chances. Not when it comes to you and Hugh.'

She regarded me for a moment, before she lifted Simon from my arms and held him to her own chest. There was something so touching about her act of acceptance, but the moment was spoilt when Edwin of Eden pushed himself to the front of the group who were still lingering by the gate.

'We can't allow you back in here, de Lacy,' he announced. 'You could be carrying plague.'

I turned to Filomena. 'Who let that man out of his bedchamber?' I said, in exasperation.

'It was Sir Robert,' she whispered. 'When you didn't return, he allowed Edwin to leave his room.'

I took a deep breath and then turned back to address Edwin and his entourage, who were now gathered about him like a troupe of watchful monkeys. 'I'm free of plague,' I said loudly. 'And so is the child.'

Edwin visibly winced. 'What child? What are you talking about?'

'This child,' I said, pointing at the baby in Filomena's arms. 'Godfrey's son, Simon.'

'Godfrey didn't have a son,' he said, remembering to puff out his chest and address the others about him. 'Everybody knows that.'

'Godfrey did have a wife and a son, Edwin. As you well know.'

'You can't just turn up here with such a story,' he blustered. 'Where's your evidence for this claim?'

'It is here,' I said, pulling Godfrey's letter from my scrip and waving it in the air. 'I will show it to anybody who cares to look.'

'What is that?' asked Old Simon, now having the courage to break free from the others. 'I can't see what you're holding, Lord Somershill.'

'This is written by Godfrey to the Archbishop of Canterbury, Father,' I told him. 'It confirms that Godfrey married a woman named Abigail Franklin, and that he was the father of this boy.' I paused and then pointed at Edwin. 'This man has already seen another of these letters. Godfrey wrote them to protect his son's interests, in the event of his death. When Edwin of Eden saw the first of these letters, he made sure to destroy it.'

'That's nonsense,' said Edwin, his face now ashen. 'Why would I do such a thing?'

I waved the folded parchment again. 'Because both letters prove that you have no claim to this estate.'

Old Simon turned to Edwin. 'Is this true, Nephew?' he asked. 'Do you know anything about these letters?'

'Of course not, Uncle,' he replied. 'It's a lie,' he said. 'You mustn't believe de Lacy's nonsense. That letter he's holding is nothing more than a piece of mischief. A forgery.'

'But perhaps I should have a look at it anyway,' said Old Simon, stepping towards me. 'Don't forget that I taught Godfrey to write, Edwin. So I'm familiar with your brother's handwriting. I could easily tell if it were genuine or not.'

Edwin put out an arm to block his path. 'But Uncle,' he said. 'Even if Godfrey wrote such a letter, we still have no evidence that this infant is his son. For all we know, de Lacy might have found this urchin in a plague house, and is now trying to pass him off as Godfrey's child.'

The old man regarded his nephew with a bewildered frown. 'I suppose that's possible, Edwin,' he said. 'But why would Lord Somershill do such a thing? What would he hope to gain by this deception?'

This argument silenced Edwin, but not for long. 'But what if de Lacy and this child carry the Plague? Think about that, Uncle.' Edwin then turned his attention back to the guests. 'Let's not forget that this man has been outside of the castle for many days. He has had every opportunity to catch the disease. I say that it's not safe to allow him back inside.' He paused for effect. 'I say that we keep him out,' he shouted rousingly. I couldn't help but notice that my mother nodded at this suggestion.

'We do not carry the Plague,' I shouted back.

'So you say,' said Edwin. 'But why should we believe you?'

'Be quiet, you stupid man,' hissed Filomena. 'Do you think my husband would return here, if he was suffering from the Pestilence? He knows the dangers of this sickness better than any of you. Shame on you for not welcoming him back.' As I scanned the faces of the other guests, I noticed that Mother wouldn't meet my gaze, finally ashamed that she had not taken my part in all this.

It was Lyndham's turn to speak up. 'Did you find the Dutchman, de Lacy?'

'Yes,' I said. 'I did.'

'And where is he now?'

'He's dead.'

Lyndham looked at me carefully. 'Dead? How did he die?'

It was now de Groot who addressed me. 'You killed him, didn't you, Lord Somershill? You executed Hans without a trial!'

'No,' I said firmly. 'He died of plague.'

'That's not possible,' answered de Groot, his face now agonised. 'I don't believe you.'

'It's true, de Groot. He caught the sickness in a tavern and then he infected Godfrey's wife.'

De Groot held his hand to his mouth, before he turned on his heels, pushed past the other guests and then ran back inside the castle, yowling like a cow that's been separated from her calf.

'You see,' shouted Edwin, hoping to exploit the alarm that had been created by de Groot's dramatic exit. 'De Lacy admits it. He has been in contact with the Plague. You all heard him say so himself.' Once again he turned around to address the other guests – now holding out his arms to them like a priest at mass. 'We cannot allow this man to come back inside the castle now. He could kill every one of us.'

The injustice of this inquisition was beginning to sting. I was tired, dirty and very, very hungry. 'Filomena is right,' I told them. 'I would not have returned to Castle Eden if I posed a risk to any of you. I have a child with me. He is Godfrey's son and the true Lord Eden, so I demand that you admit us back inside the castle.'

My plea was met with a cold, frosty silence, and I was contemplating having to return to Godfrey's cottage when Lyndham broke ranks, striding towards me with his hand held forward to take mine. 'Welcome back, Lord Somershill,' he said, as he then embraced me. 'I apologise for this disgraceful reception. You had the courage to hunt down Hans. And the courage to rescue this child. And I, for one, am very pleased to see your face again.'

'Get away from him, Lyndham,' shouted Edwin. 'De Lacy is infected with the Pestilence.' When Lyndham pointedly ignored this instruction, Edwin added, 'I'm warning you, Lyndham. If you don't get away from him, then you cannot come back inside my castle either.'

Lyndham turned back to face Edwin, and folded his arms. 'But it's not your castle, is it?'

'What do you mean by that?' said Edwin. 'Of course it is. I am Lord Eden.'

'I don't think so,' said Lyndham, as he arched an eyebrow. 'It seems that this child here owns that title. Not you.'

Edwin was now shaking with rage. 'De Lacy is tricking you all about this letter and this child,' he shouted. 'I am Lord Eden. The boy is an impostor.'

He turned again to his fellow guests for support, but this time he found that they had deserted his cause. Lyndham's gesture had turned the tide in my favour at last, and slowly they crept forward to welcome me – all thanks to this tall knight and his handsome face. I couldn't help but smile at this, for the fickleness of my fellow man never fails to surprise me. No longer a plague-stricken pariah, I was now a returning hero.

I was neither of these characters, however – as they would soon discover. I was not a hero or a pariah. I was a nemesis. The agent of the killer's downfall.

Chapter Thirty

We changed into clean clothes whilst still outside the castle walls, before wrapping Simon in a new blanket and then discarding our tunics, hose and surcoats beside the wall of the graveyard. I would burn these garments later in the spring – in case they were infected by the seeds of plague. As I did this, I looked over towards the chapel and thought of Annora and her small, forgotten body. And then, I'm ashamed to say that I deliberately turned my mind from her. After the last few days, I had no compassion left to give. When I burnt my clothes in the spring, I would also bury her within this graveyard.

Once we had returned to our apartment, Filomena sent Sandro to the kitchens to fetch some milk and cheese for the infant, and then we settled Simon into a wooden box, which we hoped would serve as a makeshift cradle.

When Simon finally slept, Filomena turned to me with solemn eyes. 'I don't think we can leave this child here when we go, Oswald,' she said. 'I don't trust Edwin of Eden.'

I held Hugh on my lap, trying to amuse the boy by blowing kisses into his hair, but my son was not interested in this game and kept wriggling, keen to get away from me. He was jealous of Filomena's previous attentions to the baby and wanted to sit with her, now that her lap was free.

'I agree,' I said, keeping hold of Hugh, despite his resistance. 'I think Simon should be our ward until he's older.' I paused for a moment. 'I don't think we have any other option.'

Mother spoke her first words to me, since a very sheepish welcome when I entered the castle. 'Another waif and stray to care for, Oswald?' she said, looking up from her corner. 'Somershill is not a home for foundlings, you know. The family apartments are already cramped.'

Filomena drew a loud breath at this. 'So you would leave this poor child at the mercy of his uncle? The man who sent out a murdering madman after him?'

Mother sat forward, pleased to have goaded Filomena into an argument. 'What about Old Simon?' she suggested. 'He is this child's great-uncle. Surely you would trust a man of God to care for an infant?'

'He's too old,' said Filomena. 'And he can barely see. He cannot be left in charge of a baby.'

'What about the castle steward, then?' said Mother. 'What's that woman's name?' She paused. 'Oh yes, Alice Cross. She could look after the child, couldn't she? Especially as she's part of their family.'

'What do you mean?' I asked. 'Alice Cross is not a member of the Eden family.'

Mother smiled at my question. 'Goodness me, Oswald. You call yourself an investigator? Surely you've guessed the truth about Alice Cross? Why else would the family put up with such a miserable and disobedient servant? The woman is clearly related to them. A bastard child, I would say.'

'Whose bastard child?'

Mother shrugged as if this didn't matter.

'Whose bastard child?' I repeated.

'The old Lord Eden's, I expect,' she said. 'Godfrey and Edwin's father. You can see it in their faces. She has the same shaped eyes, and pale complexion. The freckles in particular. I would wager that she had red hair as a young woman.'

Filomena folded her arms. 'Well, I don't care if Alice Cross is part of their family. She should never be trusted to care for a child.'

'It doesn't harm a child to have discipline in their upbringing, Filomena,' said Mother, pointing at Hugh, just as the boy was trying to bite my hand in order to effect an escape from my grip. 'Alice Cross would soon sort out this little monster.'

I intervened before the argument escalated. 'We are not leaving Simon at Castle Eden, Mother. That's the end of it. If we live to see the spring, then the child will return to Somershill with us.'

Mother poked her nose in the air at this. 'Well, at least it's a child for your wife, Oswald,' she said with a sigh. 'It doesn't seem that she will ever have another one of her own.'

'Be quiet,' seethed Filomena. 'This is not your business.'

Mother stood up from her chair and then breezed over to the window. 'I don't expect Filomena has said anything yet, Oswald. But she suffered her monthly bleeding while you were away from the castle. It seems she wasn't carrying a child after all.'

'Filomena's right,' I said. 'That isn't your business.'

'I just thought you should know,' said Mother. 'A wife should not hide such matters from her husband.'

I looked at Filomena and saw that her cheeks had lost their colour, so I dropped Hugh to the floor and then knelt down beside her, trying to whisper so that Mother could not hear us. 'I'm sorry, Filomena,' I said.

'Please don't be,' she answered. 'I was happy it happened. We are locked in this castle, in fear of plague. This is no time to be carrying a child.'

I touched her cheek. 'I'm sorry, nonetheless,' I whispered.

She grasped my hand for a moment and then pushed it lightly away. 'Hugh needs to have a sleep,' she said curtly. 'He's tired.'

As Filomena led Hugh through the door to the other chamber, he grasped at her skirts, begging to be lifted into her arms as baby Simon had been. When they were out of earshot, I turned to Mother. 'Why do you do it?' I asked.

'I don't know what you mean,' she said, flicking an imaginary mote of dust from her cheek.

'Why do you delight in being so cruel?'

I had expected her to repudiate this accusation, but instead she mustered a laugh. 'Why do you think I do it, Oswald?' she said, before she turned to look me in the eye. 'If I don't speak my mind in plain terms, then I am constantly ignored. I might as well be one of Hugh's wooden puppets. Sat in the corner and forgotten.'

'There are other ways of getting attention, Mother. You could try being kinder?'

'Why on earth should I do that, Oswald?' She continued before I could answer. 'Because that's what you expect of an old woman? Is that it?' She let out a loud laugh. 'What nonsense. I was not kind as a young woman. So, why on earth should I start being kind now?'

The argument might have escalated, but we were interrupted by a furtive knock at the door. I answered to find that our visitor was Old Simon, asking to look at Godfrey's letter. As the old monk shuffled into the room, I caught Edwin's profile in the passageway outside, waiting in the shadows for his uncle's verdict on the authenticity of this document. I made sure to shut the door on him, for this man would not gain admittance to our chambers.

Once I had also asked my mother to leave the room, I then retrieved the letter from my scrip and passed it over to the old man's gnarled and shaking hands. He studied the broken seal but did not unfold the parchment. 'You say that you found this letter in the home of Godfrey's wife?' he said.

I nodded. 'Yes. And Godfrey gave me an identical letter on the night that he was murdered.' I nodded towards the door, knowing that Edwin was still waiting on the other side. 'You should know that Godfrey was planning to leave the next day, so that he could bring his wife and son back into the safety of this castle. He gave me that letter for safekeeping, in case he died on this mission. He was afraid that his brother would not recognise his son's claim to Eden in the event of his death.' I paused. 'With every justification, I believe. Given that Edwin paid Hans to steal that letter from me, so that he could destroy it.'

The old monk smacked his lips at this, before he shuffled over to the window and unfolded the letter so that he could read it in the daylight. He scrutinised it for a while, muttering some words to himself, until he passed it back to me with a sigh. 'It does seem genuine,' he said, in a regretful tone. 'I recognise Godfrey's handwriting.'

'It is genuine,' I said, correcting him. 'And I expect you to confirm this to your nephew.' I cleared my throat. 'And then I expect you to acknowledge Godfrey's son as the new Lord Eden.'

'Yes, very well,' he said with a doleful bow of his head. 'But may I see the boy first?'

I led him into the adjoining room where Mother, Filomena and Sandro were gathered about the wooden box where Simon slept. Hugh was stroking Simon's hair with one of his small and pudgy fingers, in an attempt to look interested in his new rival. I asked them all to stand aside for a moment, so that Old Simon could look down upon the boy's face.

The monk crossed himself, said a few words of prayer and then leant his head over the sleeping child. The baby had red hair, just like his father's, but now that I also took the time to study his tiny features, I could see that there was also a look of his uncle Edwin, and his great-uncle Old Simon. There was even a look of Alice Cross about the child's face.

When Old Simon made no comment, I said, 'He is his father's likeness, don't you agree?'

The old monk sighed again. 'Yes,' he said. 'It seems that he is.' He then marked the sign of the cross upon the baby's forehead and hobbled out of this side room, heading back towards the door to the stairwell. He bowed his head in more prayer and then opened the door to find Edwin waiting anxiously for his verdict.

'Well?' said Edwin.

Old Simon gently put his hand upon Edwin's shoulder. 'The letter is genuine. The child is the rightful heir.'

Edwin pushed his uncle's hand away and then let out a growl that resounded about the stairwell. 'De Lacy is tricking you,' he screamed. 'Even if the letter is genuine. We have no proof that this child is Godfrey's son.'

'I have seen the boy myself,' said Old Simon. 'He bears the likeness of your brother.'

'This is nonsense!' Edwin shouted, before he let out another great howl, tearing down the stairs, as he voiced a string of curses.

Old Simon turned back to me, almost apologetically. 'I'm sorry, Lord Somershill,' he said. 'This is difficult for my nephew. But Edwin will come to accept the boy. You must understand. It's a shock for him.' He suddenly placed a hand against his chest. 'It is a shock for all of us.'

'I cannot leave Simon here,' I said. 'The child will return with us to Somershill in the spring.'

The old man frowned. 'I don't think that's necessary,' he said. 'Edwin would not harm the child.'

I wanted to laugh at his naivety. 'Let me keep him at Somershill,' I said. 'At least, until Edwin has become used to the idea.'

Another wearied look passed over his face. 'Very well,' he said. 'Perhaps that is the wisest path in the circumstances.' He turned his eyes to mine. They were the strangest shade of blue in this light. No longer opaque and watery, suddenly they seemed bright and focused. 'I see that there is some good in you at last, Lord Somershill. My prayers have been answered.'

The monk had barely left our apartment, when the first of our many other visitors arrived. It was almost as if they had formed a queue in the stairwell. It was Pieter de Groot, his eyes reddened and his face swollen with tears. I could offer him little consolation about Hans's death, though I soon realised that he hadn't come here looking for sympathy. Instead, he wanted to question me – keen to know if I had actually spoken to his nephew before he died. When I asked de Groot why this was so important to him, he maintained that he only wanted to know if Hans had admitted to the crimes with his own lips. When I revealed that I had not spoken to Hans myself, de Groot seemed strangely relieved. The sobbing ended, and he trotted out of the room with something akin to a smile upon his face.

Alice Cross was our next visitor. She arrived with the cook – a woman who was rarely seen outside of the kitchen. The pair pretended to be interested in what treats we would like to eat for supper, though how she was planning to meet any requests, I could not say. The best foods had been destroyed in the fire that also killed The Fool – and we were faced with eating dried peas and cabbage for the rest of the winter.

This pair couldn't keep the pretence up for long, as their gaping faces and lingering stares soon gave away their true purpose. In reality, they wanted to check that we were truly clear of plague, in case I had somehow hidden a bubo beneath my collar. What Alice Cross didn't realise, as she scrutinised me, was that I was returning the favour. Was this woman Edwin and Godfrey's illegitimate sister, as my mother had asserted? Now that this seed was sown, I couldn't help but see the Eden family in her face.

Once I had dismissed Alice Cross and the cook from our apartment, it was only moments before our next visitor arrived. This time it was Robert of Lyndham, who embraced me warmly for the second time that day, before revealing the true reason for his visit – wanting to know more details about Hans and the manner of his death. Like de Groot, Lyndham wanted to know if the Dutchman had confessed to the murders before he died. It felt uncomfortable to be lying about this again, but equally I was not yet ready to reveal the truth about Hans to Lyndham, nor anybody else in this castle for that matter. Instead, I told Lyndham that Hans had begged Abigail so desperately for forgiveness on his deathbed, that I was more than satisfied of his guilt. He was the killer we had been seeking, and now, thankfully, he was dead. My story mollified Lyndham for now, and he would learn the true story soon enough.

Our last visitors were Lady Isobel and her stepdaughter Lady Emma. Ostensibly Lady Isobel wanted to thank me for hunting down her husband's killer, but I think she was also keen to examine me for any signs of plague. During our short conversation we were constantly interrupted by the antics of Lady Emma, who kept peeping around her stepmother's skirts to spy upon Sandro. Each time their eyes met, the girl then coyly put her hands over her face, before squealing in a high-pitched giggle. It was pleasing to see Emma happy for once, but Lady Isobel seemed irritated rather than heartened by her mood. When she couldn't tolerate Emma's game any longer, she scowled at Sandro, grasped her stepdaughter by the hand and then dragged the girl from the room. As they descended the stairs, we heard Lady Isobel berate her stepdaughter for associating with servants, claiming that it belittled the standing of their family.

Now that we were finally alone, I turned to Sandro. 'Is that everybody?' I asked.

'Yes,' he answered. 'They have all come to see us. Each one of them.'

'Come on, then,' I said. 'It's time.'

Sandro's face brightened. 'Time for what, Master Oswald?'

'To catch a killer.'

Chapter Thirty-one

Alice Cross was never a difficult person to find within the confines of this castle. That afternoon, she was sweeping the cobblestones of the inner ward, taking advantage of the last rays of daylight, before dusk fell. The moon was already lurking above us, hanging awkwardly in the sky like a guest who's turned up too early for supper.

'Ah, Mistress Cross,' I said warmly, as I strode across the courtyard to greet her. 'I've been looking for you.'

She drew her broom close to her chest, alarmed at my geniality. 'Oh yes, my Lord?' she said suspiciously.

I nodded at Sandro, gesturing for him to leave us alone for a moment, before I stepped a little closer to the woman. 'I was hoping that you could help me with something.' I said, before turning to look over my shoulder.

She flushed. 'Oh yes?' she said, now bristling with suspicion.

'It's a delicate matter,' I whispered. 'To do with Godfrey's wife and something that she told me on her deathbed.' Alice Cross's cheeks reddened, but she did not answer this. 'Apparently there is a hidden compartment in Godfrey's library,' I continued. 'It's where he was hiding some very important work.'

This time she was shocked into making a response. 'I've never heard of anything like that before,' she said. 'I can't help you.'

I paused. 'Are you sure?'

'Of course I am.'

'That's a shame,' I said, making sure to add a sigh of disappointment. 'You see, I was hoping that you might be able to help me find this compartment. But never mind,' I said, 'I just thought I'd ask.'

Our eyes locked for a few moments before she looked away. 'I'm sorry, my Lord,' she said with uncharacteristic courtesy. 'I don't know anything about such matters. I was rarely allowed into Lord Eden's library.'

'Don't worry,' I said. 'We'll just have to go and look ourselves. Sandro and I should be able to work out where it is, from the description I was given.' I bowed my head to her. 'Perhaps you'd like to help us search?'

Her eyes flashed with panic. 'No, no, my Lord. I'm sorry, I can't do that. I promised the cook that I'd light the bread oven.' She then curtseyed to me, before scuttling away in the opposite direction across the inner ward – her dress bunched up in a bulge at her bottom, so that she looked like an escaping hedgehog.

Sandro turned to me with a smile. 'Has it worked, Master Oswald?'

'Yes,' I said. 'I think it has.'

The key to Godfrey's library was still in my possession, so this room had not been opened since I locked it, many days previously. I pushed at the heavy door to release the usual billow of cold and stale air into the passageway, before stepping inside a room that now smelt as damp as a cellar. I pulled back the shutters to let some light creep in, and then headed for the hearth, running my hands along the two stone corbels that supported the hood of this monumental fireplace. These stones fitted together so smoothly that it was hard to believe one of them could be depressed to reveal a secret cranny. But then again, I remembered that this compartment had been built to Godfrey's exacting standards. He was nothing, if not the champion of ingenuity.

Despite this, however, I was unable to move either of the corbels, prompting me to question Abigail's directions. After all, I doubted that she had ever been to this library herself, so she could only rely upon Godfrey's description as to the location of this hiding hole.

I cursed loudly until Sandro made a suggestion. 'Would you like me to try, Master Oswald?' he asked.

'The stones won't move,' I said, allowing a note of irritation to creep into my voice. 'I think Abigail was wrong about this.'

Sandro smiled. 'Please. Let me try.' He cleared his throat. 'If you remember, Master Oswald, I was very good at opening doors and locks in Venice.'

I stood back and bowed my head to my valet, acknowledging this truth – for Sandro had honed a full set of such larcenous skills in his first career as a thief. 'Very well then,' I said. 'But hurry up. They're coming.' I had already heard somebody lift the latch on the door at the bottom of the stairwell.

Sandro placed his fingers around each of the corbels and then lightly felt along the individual stones, until he concentrated on the corbel to the left of the hearth. 'It's this one,' he said, splaying his hands across the stone and cautiously pushing, as if he were pressing butter into a mould. 'I can feel some movement in it.'

At first nothing happened, but then the stone gave way, rotating slowly on a protruding tenon in the block below. When the corbel had revolved outwards, Sandro was able to reach inside the dark void that lay behind this masonry, and pull out a manuscript that was bound in leather.

'Is this what you were looking for?' he asked, passing the book to me.

'Yes,' I said, as the manuscript fell open. The words were written in the reddish-brown of gall ink, and the pages were unadorned with any decoration. The writing looked almost childish at first glance, until I recognised the words from the gospel of Matthew. I had never seen these verses written in English before, and I must admit that the effect was powerful.

The field is the world; but the good seed are the sons of God's kingdom, and the weeds are evil children. The enemy that sows the weeds is the Devil. The harvest is the ending of the world, and the reapers are angels. The weeds will be gathered and burnt. So shall it be at the ending of the world.

Sandro peered over my shoulder, clearly unimpressed with this small booklet. Perhaps he had expected to retrieve a grand piece of jewellery, or a large purse of coins.

'It's a translation of the New Testament. It was Godfrey's life's work.'

Sandro squinted at me, unable to muster any excitement at this revelation.

I was about to explain the importance of this small book to my valet, when our visitor finally arrived. The door swung open and he entered, obscured at first by the gloom of the passageway – but when he stepped forward, his loitering, lupine form dissolved into a familiar, benevolent shape. It was the monk, Old Simon.

He creased his face into a smile. 'Is that you, Lord Somershill?' he said. 'I heard noises in here.'

'Yes, Father. I'm here with my valet, Sandro.'

'I was passing by, and saw that the door was open.'

'You were passing by?' I said. 'Where were you going exactly?'

He paused, immediately aware of his mistake. 'Yes. I should say, I came here to look in on this room when Mistress Cross told me that you had opened the door again,' he said quickly. 'This library has been locked up for a number of days. And as I told you before, I am concerned about the damage that this damp is causing to the precious books.' He stepped towards me with his hand outstretched. 'Now, what's that you have there? Is it from this library?'

'This?' I said, lifting the manuscript out of his reach. 'I've just found it. It was something that Godfrey was working on. It seems that he had hidden it behind one of the corbels in the fireplace.'

His eyes lit up. 'You found it?' he said.

'*It?*' I repeated. 'So you know what this is, then?'

The old monk hesitated, again aware of having made a mistake. 'No, no,' he said. 'Of course not.'

'I don't believe you,' I said, nodding at Sandro to close the door.

Old Simon looked at my valet and then turned back to me. 'What's this all about, Lord Somershill?' he asked softly. 'I don't want any trouble.'

I placed the translation down upon Godfrey's desk. 'It's about this,' I said, pointing at the book. 'It's always been about this. Godfrey's translation of the New Testament.'

Old Simon crossed himself, but said nothing.

'You knew that Godfrey was working on this project with John Cubit, didn't you? You knew the true nature of their shared vision. Though you denied it, when I last asked you.'

He shook his head. 'No, no,' he stuttered. 'I don't know anything about such nonsense. Godfrey never told me anything.'

'Which is why you spied on his correspondence,' I said. 'Godfrey suspected that somebody was reading his letters in recent weeks, and I now know that it was you.'

'That's impossible,' he said. 'I only arrived at Castle Eden a couple of days before Godfrey's death. I couldn't possibly have been reading his letters.'

'You didn't open and read them yourself,' I said. 'You asked somebody to do it for you.'

'What?' he said, clearing his throat. 'Who do you mean?'

'It was Alice Cross. Your daughter.'

For a moment the old monk was speechless, before he eventually managed to summon a reply. 'What a contemptible accusation. I can see that you need more of my prayers,' he said, casting me a stern frown before hobbling back towards the door, only to find that Sandro had blocked his path. 'Tell this foolish boy to get out of my way.'

'No, Father Simon,' I replied. 'You cannot leave this library until you start telling me the truth.'

'I am honestly confounded by this attack, Lord Somershill,' he said, turning back to me with forlorn, pathetic eyes. 'I am just an old and infirm priest, coming here to look over my family's books.'

'Do you deny that you knew the true nature of Godfrey's association with the priest John Cubit?' I said, before adding, 'Remember that it is a sin to bear false witness.'

He hesitated for a moment and then looked away, unable to answer.

'So you did know that Godfrey was translating the bible, didn't you?' I said. 'And you looked for this work after his death, but were unable to find it.'

He took a deep breath, but once again refused to respond.

'I wondered why you've always appeared each time I've come into this room. You were hoping that I might have located the translation myself, and succeeded where you have failed.' I pointed to the table where Godfrey's manuscript was still lying. 'But now I have found it. And now I will make sure that this book reaches John Cubit in Oxford.'

The old man began to shake. 'No, no. You mustn't do that, Lord Somershill,' he said. 'I beg you. That travesty must not leave this room.'

'Why not?'

The old monk clenched his fists. 'Because it is a work of heresy, Lord Somershill. Godfrey was a fool. He should never have involved himself in this sacrilege.'

'So you did ask Alice Cross to open and read Godfrey's letters?'

'Yes,' he said with some irritation. 'I did. But that's only because my nephew wouldn't listen to sense, Lord Somershill,' he blurted. 'I told him, over and over again. Keep away from John Wyclif and his foolish acolytes in Oxford. They might enjoy the archbishop's protection for now, but there are plenty of us who oppose their views.'

'So you do know John Wyclif? Another lie.'

'Yes. Of course I know of him,' he spat. 'The man is a notorious heretic.'

'That's a strong word for the master of an Oxford college,' I said. 'Don't you think, Father?'

Old Simon waved this away. 'Some might call Wyclif a learned man, but he is a heretic to my mind. A fool who will not accept that the bible is written in Latin for a reason.'

'What reason is that?'

'So that it can be interpreted by educated minds, of course,' he said. 'Priests who properly appreciate the magnitude and the subtleties of its sacred messages. But this Wyclif . . .' Old Simon's face was now glowing red with anger and a bubble of spit was forming at the corners of his mouth. 'Wyclif wants to hand out the bible to the common man as if it were a loaf of Lammas bread. Can you imagine the ramifications of such stupidity? When the bible is read aloud to women and children about the fireside, as if it were a storybook? When every literate man thinks himself able to interpret the Word of God and invent his own foolish version of Christianity? There will no longer be faith in the one church, ordered and sacred. Instead we will descend into a wretched quagmire, whereby a man can attend the church he most fancies, like choosing a wife or a dog. Changing his mind, over and over again, until he doesn't know which way to turn . . . until he turns away from God himself.' He paused to regain his breath. 'This wicked translation will not only lead to the disintegration of my beloved church,' he said. 'It will be the end of faith itself. I have no doubt about that.'

'Were these your words to Godfrey?' I asked. 'When you confronted him on the night of his murder?'

The old priest met my gaze. 'I told Godfrey that I knew what he was doing,' he said. 'That he and Cubit were trying to twist the words of the bible into their own contemptible ideas.' Suddenly he threw up his arms in despair. 'Don't you see what had happened to Godfrey in Oxford, Lord Somershill? He had been seduced by the devilry of John Wyclif and his followers. Such as this man, John Cubit. Their beliefs had poisoned his mind, causing my nephew to question and then reject the most fundamental teachings of the church.' He counted these out on his fingers. 'Purgatory, monasticism, pilgrimages, praying to the saints.' The bubbles at the sides of his mouth had now proliferated into an ugly foam. 'Do you know that Wyclif even denies that the bread and wine become the true body and blood of Christ during communion? He says they are nothing more than a representation. A representation indeed!' His breathing was now laboured. 'This is wickedness beyond belief. These ideas are cankers that must be severed before they take hold.'

'Is that why you burnt John Wyclif's book in the hearth of this room?' I asked.

He froze.

'Is that why you killed your own nephew?'

'I am a monk,' he said, quickly regaining his composure. 'A Benedictine. I have dedicated my whole life to God's work. So when I discovered what Godfrey was working on, I had to oppose him. I was bound by my faith to do so.' His hands began to fidget. 'At first I asked Godfrey to stop this stupidity. I told him that he was shaming both his family and his faith. I had to make him see that he was risking his own eternal damnation.' He looked at me with tired, reddened eyes. 'I demanded that he end his association with Wyclif and Cubit.' He paused, pointing at the book on the table. 'And then I demanded that he destroy this abomination.'

'But Godfrey wouldn't listen to you, would he?' I said.

The old monk paused a moment and then shook his head. 'No,' he said wearily. 'I was too late. Godfrey's soul had been corrupted and I could not save him.'

'So, you took his life. For the sake of this translation?'

'You might dismiss it as a simple book, Lord Somershill. But this is the most dangerous work of devilry that I have ever encountered. And I would do anything in my power to stop it.'

At these words, he lunged forward and tried to grab Godfrey's bible from the desk, but I was quicker. 'Nobody will destroy this,' I said, once again holding the book out of his reach. 'When the Plague has retreated, I will take this translation to Oxford and hand it to John Cubit myself.'

The old monk started to shake. 'You must not do that,' he said, advancing towards me. 'You must destroy it, Lord Somershill. You were also trained as a Benedictine, I believe. So, you know that it's your Christian duty to stop this.'

'No,' I said. 'I promised Godfrey's wife that this manuscript would reach Cubit. And it will.'

Suddenly Old Simon was upon me. For all of his age and infirmity, he could fight with a wild passion. He clung onto me, grappling for this small and unremarkable-looking book with all the desperation of a man fighting for his life. It was the same fervour that must have fuelled his attack on Godfrey. My friend had not anticipated his violence, but I was prepared. Old Simon had religious conviction and zeal on his side, but I had youth and strength on mine. In the end there was no contest between us.

I pushed him away and he fell backwards towards the table, grabbing the weapon that had fallen into his hands at his last confrontation in this same library. It was the mazer. The large drinking cup that still rested on the table, next to Godfrey's quills and bottles of ink. In an instant, he grasped his hand about its wooden stem and then launched himself at me, waving the metal rim at my head, and only just missing my temple by the thinnest whisker. Sandro had remained out of the fight until now, but this latest attack prompted my young valet to jump to my defence, gripping the old monk about his waist and then throwing him to the floor with a terrible thud.

This did more than snuff out Old Simon's momentum. He was silent for a moment, before he grasped his chest and groaned in pain – his body shuddering and jolting in a series of short spasms. It was then that his daughter, Alice Cross, appeared at the door, before running across the room to take his hand. I couldn't say if she had been waiting outside, or whether she had just arrived at the top of the stairs, but now she flung herself down onto the floor beside her father, begging for him not to die.

The old man held her hand and gasped for air. 'They have the translation, Alice,' he groaned. 'Promise me. You must destroy it.' These were his last words, for then his body suffered one last, tumultuous seizure of his heart.

'Father?' she said, as she lifted his hand to her lips. 'Father?' she said again. 'Father. Wake up. Wake up!' When the old man did not respond, she shook him, over and over again – until she finally threw herself across his lifeless chest and wept.

I left her alone for a while, but when I stepped forward to offer my hand, she turned to me with ferocious eyes. 'You killed him,' she said, stumbling to her feet without my assistance. 'You killed Father Simon.' She launched a string of punches at my chest.

I caught hold of her wrists. 'I know that Old Simon was your real father, Mistress Cross.'

'What of it?' she said, pulling away from me, and then wiping a long line of spittle from her mouth. 'Plenty of priests have children. It's nothing unusual.'

'Really?' I said, as if this was news to me. 'But I wonder if many of these priests were as devoted to their children as Old Simon was to you?'

She sensed a trap. 'What do you mean by that?'

'Old Simon taught you to read, didn't he?'

'Yes,' she said tentatively. 'My father thought it was shameful that most women are illiterate.'

'But this was useful to him, wasn't it? It meant you were able to read Godfrey's private letters. It meant you could spy on your own master, and then report back to your father.'

Her reaction to this was to raise her chin proudly. 'I was happy to help him.' She screwed her hands into balls. 'Lord Eden's work was blasphemy,' she spat. 'It deserves to be destroyed.'

'But did Godfrey deserve to be murdered?'

She regarded me for a moment and turned away. 'That was a mistake. My father didn't mean for it to happen,' she said. 'He wasn't a murderer.'

'You saw the attack?'

'No,' she said. 'I knew nothing of it at all. Not until Father came to find me that night. This murder has nothing to do with me.'

'Except that you helped your father to move the body,' I said. She opened her mouth to object. 'I'm not stupid, Mistress Cross,' I said. 'Old Simon could not have moved Godfrey's body on his own.'

She took a deep breath. 'Father asked for my help,' she said. 'How could I deny him?'

'Did you help to arrange his body in the chest as well?'

She nodded guardedly in response.

'At first I thought that Godfrey had been displayed in a mocking pose, but now I realise my mistake. Laying him out with his arms crossed was supposed to be respectful, wasn't it? Almost as if it was an apology for his death.'

'Yes,' she said. 'My father was sorry.'

'But there was also another reason for trying to hide his body, wasn't there?'

She crossed her arms and gave a defiant shrug. 'I don't know what you mean.'

'You hoped it would give you some more time, didn't you?' I said.

She shook her head, but I knew that I'd touched a nerve, as she turned her face even further from mine.

I continued. 'The longer it took for other people in the castle to discover Godfrey's death, the more time your father had to continue his search for the translation in Godfrey's library. You knew it was hidden in here, didn't you? It's why you left the door unlocked and then threw the single key into the well. Your father wanted to make sure he could gain access to this library for as long as possible. You didn't want somebody else locking the door, so that you couldn't get in.'

She uncrossed her arms and took a deep breath. 'My father didn't mean to kill Lord Eden,' she said. 'I told you before. It was a mistake.'

'Then he should have confessed to this mistake immediately,' I said. 'Especially when Lord Hesket and The Fool were also murdered.'

She looked at me sharply. 'Those other killings had nothing to do with my father,' she said. 'He is innocent of those murders.'

'I know that now,' I said bitterly. 'But I wasted a lot of time chasing the wrong man, because of your father's lies. If he had confessed, then the other two men would still be alive.'

'That's not true,' she said.

'But it is, Mistress Cross. Hesket and William Shute are only dead because your father killed Godfrey. He might not have murdered them himself, but their deaths are on his conscience.' I paused. 'As they are on yours.'

She sank down into Godfrey's chair and crossed herself at this, her eyes now filling with tears. 'I only wanted to help my father,' she sobbed. 'I didn't know it would lead to this.'

'Then you must earn your penance,' I said.

She wiped a large, freckled hand across her face and then looked up at me. 'What do you mean?'

'If you truly repent of your involvement in Godfrey's murder, then you will agree to assist me.'

'What do you want me to do?' she asked, rubbing her eyes again.

'Help me to lay a trap.'

Chapter Thirty-two

The next morning we buried Old Simon, alongside the two other freshly dug graves beside the chapel. Alice Cross had played her part thus far, and told the others that Old Simon had died of a seizure after climbing the steps to Godfrey's library. It was not so far from the truth, after all.

As we stood about the grave that morning, the wind swept in off the sea and drove through us, penetrating even the thickest cloaks and the sturdiest boots. The women and children had remained inside the castle for this burial, for it was the grimmest and darkest of winter days. The tide was in and wrathful clouds advanced across the sky towards us like a fleet of invading ships. There was not even the weakest shard of sunlight to lift our mood.

Now that our resident priest had died, I was forced to perform the service of committal myself. Amongst our dwindling number, I was the only man with anything resembling a religious education. While I worked my way through the final words of petition, Sandro and Lyndham kept their eyes on the nearby forest. We had seen movement between the trees the previous night. People skulking on the outskirts of the castle. Fires burning and dogs howling. It seemed we were not the only souls to be seeking sanctuary from the Plague at this far end of the island. I don't know if these people had any desire to storm the castle, as

Godfrey had feared, but had they carried out any such plan, then they might have been surprised to find the dangers that still lay within these walls.

We retreated inside as soon as the coffin was covered with soil, before we lowered the portcullis and locked the gate. And then Sandro and I set to work, for there was no time to waste. Firstly I asked my valet to fetch the bucket of birch oil that we had found outside the castle walls, on the dawn after The Fool's murder. Since then, I had kept this bucket in the cellar, with the instructions that it was not to be touched. Sandro carried it to the castle dungeon, where he left it just inside the door to the unlocked cell.

The second part of my plan was a little trickier to carry out, because I needed Filomena's help for this, and I had not yet taken her into my confidence. I found my wife in the kitchen, holding baby Simon in one arm and stirring a cauldron of porridge with the other. Hugh was behind her, turning the bare roasting spit at speed and clearly causing the elderly cook a great deal of anxiety. I picked my son up in my arms and kissed his head. 'What are you doing there?' I asked him gently.

'Roasting a lion,' he said proudly.

'I'm sure it will be very tasty,' I said. 'But a lion needs to be turned very slowly.'

'Why's that?' asked Hugh.

I paused. 'Because he is very large and very fierce.'

'But he's dead,' said Hugh, looking at me as if I were stupid. I certainly didn't have Sandro's way with children.

'But how can you be sure?' I said. 'If you turn the lion too quickly, then he might wake up again.'

Hugh regarded me for a moment, before his face dissolved into an excited giggle and he struggled from my arms, returning to the spit, where he duly engaged the turning handle with more restraint. This still annoyed the cook, however, so I asked the woman to leave us alone.

Filomena eyed me with suspicion, rightly guessing that I had sought her out with an ulterior motive. 'What is it, Oswald?' she asked.

'I need you to distract Lady Isobel for a while.'

She continued to stir the porridge. 'Why?'

'I need Sandro to speak to Lady Emma on her own. But her stepmother watches her like a hawk.'

She stopped stirring. 'And what do you want with Lady Emma?'

'Can I tell you later?'

She looked up at me, and raised one of her eyebrows.

At this moment, Simon woke up and began to grizzle – which immediately prompted Hugh into making the same noise, only louder.

'I don't think that I have the time to help you,' said Filomena, brusquely. 'My hands are full with these two children.'

I picked Hugh up, though he squirmed like a piglet to reach Filomena. 'Please,' I said. 'Go to Lady Isobel now and ask for some help with the baby.'

Filomena laughed at this. 'Lady Isobel has no interest in children.'

'Then think of something else,' I said. 'I don't know. Tell her that you want to know about the latest fashions in London.'

Filomena laughed again – this time with even greater disdain. 'Is that all you think women want to talk about, Oswald?' she said. 'Children and fashion?'

'Please, Filomena. I really need your help with this.'

'I'm busy.'

'Very well then,' I said, putting Hugh to the floor and wandering back towards the door. 'I suppose that I could always ask my mother to help me.'

She put down the spoon and glared. 'No no. I will do it, Oswald,' she said. 'Just give me a moment to think of a story.'

*   *   *

Filomena was as good as her word. I don't know what excuse she dreamt up to get Lady Isobel out of her chamber, but it worked – for soon Sandro peeped around the door of their apartment to find Lady Emma alone. I hung back in case I scared the girl, but she seemed happy enough to take Sandro's hand and follow him out into the inner ward. Once there, Sandro encouraged her to start singing her favourite song, the pair of them skipping around in a circle like two mummers in a play. Their voices were soft to begin with, but as Sandro led her to the dungeon, Lady Emma's voice rang out at great volume.

> 'These castle walls are cold, 'tis true,
> They freeze with winter ice and snow,
> But a man can always warm his pole,
> Inside a tight and furry hole.
>
> I know I'm not the only man,
> Who longs for comfort from the cold,
> I've heard the creeping feet at night,
> Looking for a new delight.
> If ever there was consolation,
> To this frozen isolation,
> It is found, in every guise,
> Between a woman's warming thighs.'

I followed at a distance, before taking my place in a corner of this dark cell, as the words of The Fool's song resounded from the walls. Predictably, it was not long before Lady Isobel appeared at the door, her beautiful face contorted with rage.

'Stop that, Emma,' she shouted, marching into the room and grabbing the girl by the sleeve. She went to shake Emma violently, but froze when she saw my face in the lantern light. 'Lord Somershill?' she said. 'What on earth are you doing in here?' For a moment she seemed lost for words, until her stepdaughter began to sing again, and then Lady Isobel found her voice. She screamed, demanding that the girl be quiet, before she slapped Emma soundly across the face.

Sandro gasped at this and pushed Lady Isobel away from her stepdaughter.

Lady Isobel squealed in disgust at Sandro's touch, as if somebody had thrown the contents of a chamber pot at her. 'Get this filthy Venetian rat away from me!'

At this insult, Sandro turned to Lady Emma, and together they began the song again, even louder this time.

> *'I know I'm not the only man,*
> *Who longs for comfort from the cold . . .'*

Lady Isobel placed her hands over her ears. 'Stop singing that song. Stop it!' But the song resounded about the dungeon, achieving a new level of volume that must have reached the whole castle.

> *'. . . I've heard the creeping feet at night,*
> *Looking for a new delight.'*

She made another attempt to grasp the child, but Emma dodged her stepmother with ease, laughing wildly at her escape. Sandro and Emma then danced about her, until the woman screamed at the very top of her voice for them to stop.

> *'If ever there was consolation,*
> *To this frozen isolation,*
> *It is found, in every guise,*
> *Between a woman's warming thighs.'*

We were not alone for long. The bait had worked. The bird had sung and its mate had answered.

Chapter Thirty-three

Though the dungeon was dark, Lyndham strode in with all of his usual confidence, never imagining that he might be stepping into a snare. 'What's going on in here, Isobel?' he asked.

'Don't say anything,' she said quickly, nodding her head towards me. 'De Lacy is here.' Lyndham flinched for a moment, as he turned to look for me, finally seeing my face in the low lantern light.

He looked at me with confusion at first, before his expression changed to annoyance, especially when Sandro and Emma darted out of the door and locked it behind them. 'What's going on, de Lacy?' he asked me. 'I don't like being locked in a dungeon.'

'I want to talk about The Fool's song,' I answered.

He frowned in disbelief. 'What about it?'

'Those *creeping feet at night*,' I said. 'I always assumed that The Fool had written those lyrics about Edwin of Eden. But that was my mistake. The feet were yours, weren't they, Lyndham? As you crept about the castle to be with Lady Isobel.'

He laughed at this. 'It's just a stupid song,' he said. 'Pay it no heed.'

'But it's not, is it?' I said. 'William Shute spent long enough in your company to know the truth. And so has Hesket's daughter. It's no wonder that the song upset her so much, when she first heard it. She knew what those words meant well enough.'

'This really is nonsense, de Lacy,' he replied.

'Is it?'

The lantern light threw shadows across his smiling face, but I saw fear there as well. 'You mustn't read anything into Emma's behaviour,' he said, with a scornful raise of his hands. 'The girl is a halfwit. She cannot even speak.'

'Emma can speak, Lyndham,' I replied. 'As well you know. Which is why you killed the one woman in the world whom she would talk to,' I said.

He wrinkled his nose. 'What?'

'You pushed her lady's maid into the river, didn't you? In case Emma told the woman the truth about you and her stepmother. You even jumped into the river in a pretence of saving her, so you would never be blamed.'

'That is the wildest story I've ever heard,' he said. 'I think the marsh is seeping into your mind, de Lacy.' He managed to dredge up a laugh, but Lady Isobel was not finding this conversation amusing.

'Just let me out of here, Lord Somershill,' she said, her voice rising to one of her high-pitched commands.

'No,' I said. 'You're staying in this dungeon. Both of you.'

Lyndham pushed the hair back from his face. His skin was sweaty for once. 'Look, de Lacy. We've had enough of this. Just call your valet and get the boy to unlock the door.'

'Not until you admit that you are lovers,' I said.

They glanced at one another. 'All right,' he said at length. 'But you can't lock us up in here for such a trivial matter, can you? It was just a bit of merrymaking between the two of us. After all, Hesket was so much older than Isobel.'

'Be quiet, Robert,' hissed Isobel. 'He'll twist your words.'

'You're not locked in here for adultery,' I said. 'It's for murder.'

'What?' said Lyndham, frowning again.

'The murders of Lord Hesket and William Shute.'

Lyndham laughed. 'Now I know that you've gone mad, de Lacy. I've never heard such nonsense.'

'I told you not to speak to him, Robert,' hissed Lady Isobel. 'The man is trying to trick us.'

Lyndham strode towards the door, clenched his hands around the bars in the small window and shook them. 'Let me out of here,' he shouted. 'I'm locked in this cell with a lunatic.' When nothing happened, he kicked at the door, before he turned back to me. 'Come on, de Lacy. We're friends,' he said, straining to keep up the smile. 'Let us out of here and then we can talk properly.'

'You're not leaving this dungeon,' I said. 'Neither of you.'

'Listen to me,' he said calmly. 'Whatever it is that you've dreamt up about these murders is a lie. This investigation has exhausted you. Especially the recent episode in that cottage. So come on. Get your valet to open the door and then we can forget all about this.'

'No,' I said, holding the lantern up to my face. 'My mind is sound. I know exactly how you killed them both.'

The laugh came again. 'Oh yes?'

Lady Isobel grasped hold of Lyndham's arm. 'Please. Don't say another word to him, Robert,' she urged. 'I told you that before.'

Lyndham shook her away. 'No,' he said, as he prowled towards me, now with menace. 'I want to hear his great theory. After all, it's not often that a person is accused of murder by the famous Oswald de Lacy.' I could almost taste the bitter tang of his contempt.

I stood my ground, hoping that Lyndham couldn't sense my fear. 'You didn't come to Castle Eden with the plan to murder Hesket,' I answered. 'I'll say that much.'

'Is that so?'

I continued. 'The idea only occurred to you when Godfrey was killed, and then, suddenly, there was an obvious culprit in the castle. A strange boy from Delft with an unnatural interest in torturing and killing animals. Somebody who would quickly be blamed for the killings.'

'Still nonsense,' he answered.

'You saw Hans leaving through the tunnel on the night of Edwin's argument with Hesket. You realised that this was your opportunity.'

'A tunnel indeed?' he smirked, raising an eyebrow. 'How ingenious.'

'Yes. You've known about this escape route since Godfrey employed you to guard this castle. He told you about the tunnel himself.'

This mention of employment seemed to provoke him, more than the accusation of murder. 'Godfrey did not employ me, de Lacy. I was invited to protect Castle Eden.'

Behind us, Lady Isobel had sidled back over to the door. 'Let me out,' she whispered through the bars. 'Please, will somebody let me out? I'm trapped in here. Please. Help me!' The door remained shut, with no sound from the passageway beyond.

Lyndham leant his hand on the wall, pinning me against the stones. 'You're upsetting Isobel, de Lacy. And really, you don't want to do that. She's a rich and powerful woman.' He moved closer, his sweating face nearly touching mine. 'Known at court.'

I took a deep breath and continued, trying not to be intimidated. 'Isobel has no place at court. She is a murderer, Lyndham. A woman who killed her husband. With the help of her lover.'

'You'll have to prove that, won't you?'

'Once you'd seen that Hans had left the castle, you killed Hesket and tried to make it look like the Dutchman's work,' I said. 'You mutilated Hesket's body, in the same way that Hans had mutilated Old Simon's crow. Lady Isobel even concocted a story about Hans having a vendetta against her husband. Everything pointed at the Dutchman. Especially as he had disappeared.'

Lady Isobel pulled herself away from the door on hearing my accusations. 'I had nothing to do with this,' she called across the cell. 'You're wrong about my involvement, Lord Somershill.'

Lyndham turned to her sharply, with a slightly bewildered, even wounded look across his face. For a moment he was lost for words.

'You thought that you'd got away with it, didn't you?' I said, moving away from the wall and feeling a little braver, now that Lyndham had moved his arm. 'Until you realised that The Fool had seen something from his hidden chamber in the cellar. But you didn't want to kill the man, did you, Lyndham? You were old friends, working the circuit of palaces and grand houses of England together. Shute just needed to be warned. He needed to understand what you would do to him, if he talked. Which is why you put his hat onto a dead dog.'

Lyndham stepped away from me and broke out laughing. 'Are you suggesting that I did those things to my own hound, de Lacy? Now you really have lost your mind.'

'But it wasn't your dog, was it?'

'Of course it was,' he snapped.

'No, it wasn't. We only thought it was your dog because you told us so,' I said. 'I expect that the mutilated creature was from the pack of hounds that we can hear in the forest. No wonder they've not been barking so loudly in recent days. One of them is dead.'

'You're mad, de Lacy. If it wasn't Holdfast in that chest, then where is he?'

'You took him out of the castle first,' I said. 'I imagine that you're paying somebody on the island to look after him.' He laughed at this assertion, but not convincingly. 'I know the dog left through the tunnel Lyndham, as Sandro stepped in some of its mess.'

The handsome knight was becoming riled. 'I've had enough of this, de Lacy. I want you to shut up now.'

'A murderer doesn't like to be exposed, does he?' I answered. 'And you had to murder Shute in the end, didn't you? Because he couldn't be trusted. Especially not once he'd locked himself into that cellar with so many barrels of Sweet Malmsey. You knew that he would soon be singing out your names to anybody who was listening.' I pointed to the bucket that I'd asked Sandro to leave in a corner. 'Remember this, Lyndham?' I asked. 'It's full of birch oil. You stole it from de Groot's workshop and then poured the oil down the ventilation shaft. You burnt your friend William Shute to death.'

Lyndham looked at me, his face pale with shame, or fear – it was hard to say, but Lady Isobel's reaction was different. She bowed her head to me and held her hands together, as if in prayer. 'I want you to know, Lord Somershill,' she said earnestly, 'that these allegations have nothing to do with me. If Sir Robert has committed these crimes, then he acted alone.'

'Just wait a moment, Isobel,' said Lyndham, grabbing the woman by her arm. 'Don't you dare to blame all this on me,' he said. 'Most of it was your idea.'

'It was not,' she rasped.

'Don't worry, Lyndham,' I said. 'I'm perfectly aware of her involvement. Lady Isobel is every bit as guilty as you.'

'That's not true,' she exclaimed.

'You might not have carried out the murders yourself,' I said to the woman. 'But you won't be spared the same punishment.'

She regarded me momentarily with hatred, before a smile began to cross her lips. 'Very well then, Lord Somershill. Have it your own way. Yes. Robert and I are lovers. Yes. I did plot my husband's murder with Robert when the opportunity arose. And yes, it was my idea to kill Shute, though Robert spoke against it, since the two of them were friends.' She threw a smile at Lyndham. 'I'm sorry, Robert. I panicked when the door was locked. I should not have tried to blame you for these crimes, for we acted together.' She turned back to me, and gave a short, mocking curtsey. 'So, Lord Somershill. I hope that you're satisfied now? You have your confession.' She paused. 'Though I wonder what you are going to do with it?'

'I'm going to make sure that you're punished,' I said.

She smiled again. 'Yes. I can understand why that would be your intention. But then again, you'll have to get out of this dungeon first, won't you? And it seems to me that you are trapped inside this room with two people who don't really want to let you out. Not alive, anyway.' She strolled over to the bucket of birch oil. 'I think Lord Somershill might be interested in an experiment, Robert,' she said. 'A re-enactment of one of our crimes.'

'What do you mean?' said Lyndham, not fully placated by her apology.

'I think we should burn him, of course. Set fire to the man and let him see how The Fool died. After all, Lord Somershill has worked out how we did it last time, so let's celebrate his powers of deduction. And, of course, once there is a fire in here, I'm sure that somebody in this castle will come to our aid and let us out.'

Lyndham drew back, and for a moment I sensed indecision in his face. Part of him had liked me. Part of me had liked him. You might even say that we had become friends in the last few weeks, so I hoped he might resist Isobel's calls to end my life. That our friendship meant something to him. So, I didn't extinguish the lantern in my hand, instead I held it aloft, daring him to act. But, I should have guessed that he would take Isobel's part in the end. After all, he had already murdered two people in pursuit of this woman's affections. He looked to me with sad, almost apologetic eyes, but he still threw the bucket of oil over me. He still made the decision to kill.

I was soaked, but not in flames. My clothes were wet and the light of my lantern was extinguished.

'What's going on?' screamed Lady Isobel, now that we had been plunged into darkness. 'Why isn't de Lacy on fire?'

'It was water in the bucket,' I said.

'What?' said Lyndham.

'I wanted to see if you would attack me, Lyndham,' I replied. 'Now I have the answer.'

It took a moment for Lyndham to digest this information, before he found his voice again. It was a hostile growl, all remembrances of our fledgling friendship now obliterated. 'I underestimated you, didn't I, Oswald de Lacy?' he said. 'I can see that now. I thought you were just an observer, when we first met. Happy to untangle a mystery from the safety of the flanks. But I was wrong, wasn't I? Because it turns out that you do have courage as well as curiosity.' He grasped hold of my wet tunic and pulled my face to his. 'Do you know what makes me really sad about having to kill you? I think we could have been friends. I really do. But then you spoilt that friendship with all your annoying little investigations.' He shook me. 'So, tell me this, de Lacy. Why do you do it? Why not leave the dead to take care of themselves?'

I had been asked this before – by Lord Hesket – but this time I had an answer. 'You were right to call me an observer,' I told Lyndham. 'And yes, I do spend much of my life on the flanks. It's where I've learnt to watch other people.' I paused. 'And shall I tell you what I've observed about you, Robert of Lyndham?'

'What?' he said scornfully.

'We could never have been friends. You're wrong about that. Because there's an ugliness beneath your handsome face, that I could not fail to see.'

'Well, did you see this?' he asked.

Within a moment, his hands were about my neck, squeezing the breath from my throat. The pain was overwhelming at first. I fought back against him, but I was no match for such a skilled and practised killer. Soon I slipped into the dark nothingness of death – inert and unfeeling in a silent, empty oblivion.

It was the shouting that brought me back to life. For a moment, I was confused. The dark chamber about me was full of people

296 THE BONE FIRE

and movement. It was Sandro's face that I first registered. His bright eyes and halo of curls were a wonderful sight.

'Master Oswald,' he called as he patted my cheek repeatedly. 'Master Oswald. Wake up. Wake up!'

I rose onto my elbows, and then looked around to see that de Groot and Edwin were holding Robert of Lyndham against the wall. Filomena stood beside Alice Cross, as the sturdy steward of Castle Eden held a poker to Lady Isobel's chest. The woman was screaming that she was innocent, but to no avail.

'Did it work?' I asked Sandro.

'Yes,' he said. 'Mistress Cross gathered the guests outside the door as she promised. We heard their confession. Every word of it.' He clutched my arms. 'You did it, Master Oswald. You caught the killers.'

Epilogue

It was a spring day in the early April of 1362 when we felt it was finally safe to leave Castle Eden and return to Somershill. Sandro and I had already been out on a scouting mission in the days before our departure, making sure that plague had loosened its grip on the island. When we discovered that there had been no reported deaths for at least two weeks, we decided that it was time to leave the confines of this sanctuary.

My family might have survived all winter inside the walls of the castle, but we had still seen death in those months. My mother had suffered from a great sweating sickness, though she had recovered, whereas the same affliction had killed Lady Isobel – even after we had moved her to a drier, warmer cell in the coldest months of January and February. She and Lyndham could not be housed near to each other in the dungeons, as their bitter arguing had kept the castle awake at night. Each blamed the other for the murders. Each claimed the other had dreamt up the plans and then enacted some form of coercion to force the other to take part. There were no vestiges of love between the two of them now that their crimes had been uncovered. Lyndham only laughed when we told him of Isobel's death. He said that she deserved it.

His own death would be soon in coming, now that we could report the murders to the Royal Court. I left this task in Edwin's hands, hoping that he could be trusted to bring the murderer of Lord Hesket and William Shute to justice. But I could not trust Edwin with his nephew Simon. Edwin claimed repeatedly that he only had the child's best interests at heart, but I would never be convinced of this. Simon would become my ward until he was eighteen and could defend himself against his uncle. I would then release him from my care and he would take over the Eden estate.

Of course this plan depended upon two outcomes. Firstly that Simon's right to the estate was recognised. I still had Godfrey's letter to the Archbishop of Canterbury, but I could not be sure that this hand-written missive would be sufficient evidence to ensure the boy's future. I would deliver it to Islip myself, as Godfrey had requested – but as yet, I could not be certain that he had survived the Plague himself. A different archbishop might be less inclined to support Simon's hand-written claim to Eden.

The second assumption was this. That there would be an estate to inherit, after the Isle of Eden had been left in Edwin's hands for eighteen years. The man had not improved with familiarity. In fact, the longer I spent in Edwin of Eden's company, the more apparent his faults had become. Our winter together had only proved that Edwin was an ignorant, lazy churl with no aptitude for managing a large estate. Unfortunately it was quite possible that Edwin might have squandered Simon's birthright by the time the boy came of age.

We took a whole day to pack our belongings back onto the same cart that had brought us to Eden all those months ago. Sandro had rounded up the pony from the nearby woodland, whilst I buried poor Annora in the chapel graveyard, alongside the other victims of this cold and cruel winter. I hoped and prayed that we would not see plague again for many years, but I knew its cunning. I had hunted down three killers in this castle, but man could never wreak the same havoc as this disease.

Pieter de Groot was to leave Castle Eden the same day, heading back to the Low Countries with his large wooden chest full
of tools stowed away on the back of his own cart. He had offered
to stop at Somershill, to build me a small clock in thanks for
clearing his nephew's name. But I had refused his offer, on the
grounds, privately I should say, that I was still not convinced by
Hans's innocence. To my mind, it was quite possible that Hans
had travelled to Abigail's cottage with murder in mind. Of
course, I would never be able to prove this one way or the other,
as Abigail and Hans were dead, and Edwin still insisted the purse
of coins that he gave to the young Dutchman was simply in
payment for bringing Godfrey's wife and child back to the castle.
In truth, Hans had been the strangest of young men with an
unhealthy appetite for death and cruelty, but de Groot liked to
console himself with the idea that he had 'cured' the boy in the
end, and I felt no reason to disabuse him of this belief.

Lord Hesket's child, Lady Emma, was to accompany us to
Somershill, before I made arrangements for her to return to her
home in London. She had formed a bond with Sandro, and now
followed my valet everywhere like a small and loyal puppy, trying
to persuade him to play with the collection of wooden wheels
that de Groot had made for her. Sandro bore this devotion with
typical good humour, though I think the girl's affections were
sometimes a little too overwhelming, even for this warm-hearted
Venetian. I hated to think of the pain Lady Emma would feel
when separated from my valet, but I was not sure that I would be
able to keep her at Somershill. She was the heir to a great fortune
and I feared that she would soon be whisked away by her family
for a strategic marriage. I could only hope that her relatives
would choose a kind and understanding man as her husband.

It was the morning of our intended departure and I was checking
the contents of my strongbox, when I realised that something
was missing. I always kept this wooden box locked, for it

contained important documents, as well as Filomena's jewellery and two purses of coins. I had foolishly opened the chest earlier that morning to count out some pennies, and then forgotten to relock it before I wandered out of our apartment to check on the cart. In that brief time, she had crept in and retrieved it. I will say this for the woman. She had not wasted her one and only opportunity.

I rushed to the kitchens. 'Where is Alice Cross?' I asked the cook.

The woman told me that she had seen the steward leaving the castle earlier, so I bolted to the gatehouse. The portcullis had been raised at dawn and the door in the gate was unlocked. I then ran out onto the headland. The air smelt of salt and mud that morning. Gulls rose and fell above my head. Calling me to arms with their screeches. I couldn't see Mistress Cross anywhere ahead of me, but I could see a thin column of smoke rising into the air above the nearby woodland.

I ran towards the smoke, following the smell of burning wood. When I finally reached our steward, I knew immediately that I was too late – for she stood like a champion beside the flames. Victory was hers.

'Why did you do it?' I asked, as I watched the fire devour the last pages of Godfrey's bible translation.

Alice Cross looked back at me proudly, poking a long stick into the fire. 'I promised my father that I would destroy this heresy,' she said proudly. 'And I have. Look at it. Nothing but ashes and smoke.'

'Until somebody else makes another translation,' I replied.

She looked up at me sharply. 'Oh no, Lord Somershill,' she said with a triumphant smile. 'That will never happen.'

Glossary

Astrolabe
A circular instrument, typically about the size of a dinner plate – used in the Middle Ages to measure the altitude of stars, the height of buildings and also employed as a navigational aid.

Astronomical clock
The first mechanical clocks offering reliable timekeeping were built in the early fourteenth century. They also displayed astronomical information, such as the age of the moon and the position of the sun, hence the name.

Birch bark oil
A thin oil made from the bark of the silver birch tree. The bark is burnt to a charcoal within an airtight container, causing the oil to be sweated from the bark. It was used as a sealant, but is also highly flammable.

Bone fire
Going back to a pre-Christian tradition, the bones of oxen, sheep and pigs were burnt on large open-air fires to celebrate midsummer. 'Bone fire' is the origin of the modern word, 'bonfire'.

Braies

The medieval version of underpants for men. A loose undergarment – usually made from a length of linen that was wound about the legs and bottom and then tied at the waist with a belt.

Caparison

An ornamental covering for a horse, often decorated in the livery of the owner's family.

Chamfron

Sometimes spelt shaffron or chanfron. Metal armour designed to protect the face of a horse.

Citole

A stringed instrument, popular in the thirteenth and fourteenth centuries, and closely related to the medieval fiddle.

Dais

A raised platform at the end of the dining hall/great hall. Usually furnished with a long table and benches, it was reserved for people of high status within the household.

Fabliau, Fabliaux

A short story, sometimes told in verse, with crude and comic content.

The Falling Sickness

The medieval term for epilepsy.

Galingale

A rhizome from the ginger family, used as a popular flavouring.

Humours

Harking back to the teachings of Galen in antiquity, the human body was said to be ruled by four humours, or bodily fluids, which needed to be kept in balance. Yellow bile, phlegm, black bile, and blood. The balance of your humours ruled both your health and your disposition.

Indulgence

Usually taking the form of a letter or receipt, an indulgence was an award from the church for the remission of sin. It was earned by prayer and good deeds, but increasingly in the later Middle Ages through a money donation.

The King's Evil

Scrofula (the swellings in the lymph nodes of the neck caused by tuberculosis) was known as the King's Evil in the Middle Ages, because it was believed that this disease could be cured by the touch of the reigning monarch.

Lammas Day feast, Lammas bread

A feast, held during July or August to celebrate the first wheat harvest. The bread made from the first milled wheat was taken to church to be consecrated, before it was eaten as part of the festival.

Mazer

A highly decorated, ceremonial feasting cup.

Oblate

A child, often of noble birth, given to a monastic community by his parents, to be raised and educated as a monk.

Pottage

A soupy stew, usually made with vegetables, grains, meat bones and thickened with oats. It was a staple food of the Middle Ages, particularly amongst the poorer classes.

Psalter
A small, portable book of psalms and prayers.

Royal Judge
Royal judges, from the court of the king's bench, were responsible for justice with regards to serious criminal cases. Travelling to each county approximately twice a year, they tried those criminal cases that had been referred to them by the sheriff.

The Royal Touch
It was believed that the disease known as the King's Evil (see above) could be cured by the touch of the rightful monarch. This practice began during the reign of Edward the Confessor, and ended with Queen Anne.

Shawm
A popular medieval woodwind instrument, now replaced by the oboe.

Solar
A room that was set apart from the rest of the household for use of the lord's family. This room usually had a large window, giving rise to the idea that it was named after the sun. However, the word may have derived from the French word '*seul*', which means to be alone.

Spiced hypocras
An alcoholic drink, made from wine, sugar and spices.

Steward
A high-ranking servant, usually in charge of the domestic arrangements for the castle or manor house.

Sweet Malmsey
A sweet, fortified wine, made from the Malvasia grape and imported mainly from Greece.

Trencher
A large, flat serving plate.

Valet
A male servant assigned to a lord or knight, carrying out an equivalent role to a lady's maid.

Author's notes

I wanted to begin by saying a few words about the setting for this novel. The Isle of Eden is a place of my own invention, but is based loosely upon the Isle of Oxney in Walland Marsh, on the borders of Kent and East Sussex. In the fourteenth century, the Isle of Oxney could only be reached by ferry – from what was then a port, at Tenterden. Over the centuries, the salt marshes of Walland and adjacent Romney have been reclaimed for agriculture, and now Oxney is landlocked, being over eight kilometres from the sea. However, if you go to Oxney, it is still very clear that you are on an island rising from the vast, flat fields that were once below sea level. Even now much of this land is kept from flooding by the maintenance of sea defences at the coastline, and the constant dredging of ditches – or sewers, as they are known on the marsh.

I find it a very special and inspiring place. And though it is located in the populous south-east corner of England, it still retains an otherworldly, remote feel. In the fourteenth century, it must have been very isolated indeed – the perfect location for a family seeking refuge from the Plague.

In writing *The Bone Fire*, I have returned to the theme of plague, which cast such a dark shadow over the middle decades of this century. Whereas *Plague Land* and *The Butcher Bird* take place during the Black Death of 1348–51 (when roughly half the population of England were killed by this disease), *The Bone Fire* is set thirteen years later, when plague makes a very unwelcome return. People had only heard the rumours of the deadly pestilence spreading northwards through Europe before the Black Death arrived in 1348 – but in 1361 they knew exactly what was coming. This knowledge and the panic it must have created explain why my fictional family, the de Lacys, chose to seek sanctuary on the Isle of Eden. Oswald knew, from his own bitter experience during the first outbreak, that the only guaranteed way to stay safe from plague was to keep well out of its way.

Unlike the people of the fourteenth century, we now know that this infectious disease, often referred to as the Bubonic Plague, was caused by *Yersinia Pestis* – a bacterium that lives in the digestive tract of rodent fleas. It was transferred to the human population via flea bites, and caused death in one of three ways: via the lymph glands, causing the most well-known form of the disease, Bubonic Plague – but also via the lungs, causing Pneumonic Plague; or the bloodstream, causing Septicaemic plague. Once the sufferer was infected, plague could then be passed from person to person via the usual forms of contagion, i.e. touching or coughing.

When plague returned in 1361, it arrived with a new mutation – killing wealthy young men and boys in greater numbers than other parts of the population, causing it to become known as the Children's Pestilence. Modern day studies have suggested an interesting explanation for this – that many bacterial pathogens require a good supply of iron for growth. In those times, young, wealthy males were the most likely to have enjoyed a diet rich in meat and therefore high in iron – whereas the poorer in society and menstruating women were often prone to iron deficiency. Ironically, it seems that the healthier and wealthier you were, the more likely you were to die from plague.

In *The Bone Fire*, every character that you meet during the story is fictional, except for John Wyclif and Simon Islip, the

Archbishop of Canterbury. I wanted to say a little about John Wyclif in particular, since he had such an influence on one of my characters, Godfrey of Eden. For many years Wyclif was the master at Balliol college in Oxford, enjoying the protection and friendship of Simon Islip, and thus having a certain amount of freedom to speak his mind. Whilst at Oxford, Wyclif did much to promote the reading of the scriptures – something for which the church itself lacked enthusiasm. I must say that this really surprised me when researching this book, as the bible is so central today to the Christian faith – but in those times, as Oswald points out, many priests did not read the bible at all, preferring to study the works of the thirteenth-century religious philosophers, such as Thomas Aquinas and Duns Scotus.

Wyclif's calls for the scriptures to be at the heart of the church's teachings caused suspicion at first, and then alarm – particularly as Wyclif also courted controversy with many of his other ideas. He was opposed to many fundamental beliefs of the church, particularly the sale of indulgences and relics, and the doctrine of transubstantiation (the belief that the bread and wine of communion are transformed into the actual body and blood of Christ). Wyclif was greatly affected by the Black Death, claiming it was a punishment on the clergy for their many corruptions, and warning that the End of Days was coming if they did not repent. Wyclif attracted a group of followers at Oxford, men such as my character Godfrey of Eden – idealists who shared his apocalyptic view of the future. Men who were also impatient to start spreading the Word of God through the reading of the scriptures.

In *The Bone Fire*, my character Godfrey secretly makes a translation of the New Testament into English. This translation is entirely my own invention, but is based on the fact that Wyclif himself translated the bible into English in his latter years, before disseminating this work through a network of sympathetic priests. His bible proved to be immensely popular, as people were intrigued to hear the scriptures in their own tongue for the first time, but this popularity also alarmed the church – this time to the point of repression. In *The Bone Fire*, Oswald is reluctant to become involved with Godfrey and his work, fearing the retribution of the church. This fear was not unfounded, for the church did not willingly tolerate dissent, burning many of Wyclif's followers, a group known as the Lollards, at the stake for heresy. As for Wyclif himself, he died of natural causes in 1384, but was excommunicated after his death. His corpse was exhumed in 1415, his bones were burnt and then his ashes were thrown into a river.

Wyclif's works might have been banned and his followers might have been driven underground – but ultimately the church failed to suppress his ideas and his desire for a bible in English. Wyclif and the Lollards were the first vocal non-conformists in England, sharing many views with later reformers such as Luther, Calvin and Zwingli – thus paving the way for the Reformation and England's historic break with Rome.

Lastly, I wanted to say a few words about time-keeping in the fourteenth century. It is hard for us today to imagine a life without knowing the precise time, but this is how people lived before the advent of clocks – their lives defined by the rising and setting of the sun, or by the bells in the abbeys ringing out the canonical hours – time set aside for prayers such as Lauds or Vespers. Either way, time itself was an imprecise concept. The first mechanical clocks were developed in the early fourteenth century, but we don't see the grand astronomical clocks in the abbeys and palaces of England until the latter decades. By the end of the century there were such clocks all over Europe – changing the pattern of the working day forever, as clocks finally came to govern our lives.

Acknowledgements

My heartfelt thanks go out firstly to my editor Nick Sayers, and to my agent Gordon Wise. Your continued support, encouragement and words of guidance with this book are so greatly appreciated. My thanks also to my American publisher Claiborne Hancock and Jessica Case at Pegasus in New York, and agent Deborah Schneider at Gelfman Schneider. What a wonderful team behind my books! I would like to also thank my friends from the world of writing – the Prime Writers and the Historical Writers Association – and in particular, Martine Bailey, Nick Brown, Antonia Hodgson and Rebecca Mascull. My husband Paul continues to be a writer's dream partner – always keeping well out of my way when I'm obviously struggling with a knotty plot problem, and then turning up at just the right moment with a cup of tea, or glass of wine. And I must mention my children, Natalie and Adam, who are not only my trusted early readers, but also my most loyal cheerleaders – even books need some unconditional love. I want to save my biggest thanks, however, for my sister Kathy. We've had a difficult couple of years as a family, but she has been our tower of strength with her energy, love and sense of purpose.